THE CHRISTMAS OF A COUNTESS

LINDA RAE SANDE

Twisted Teacup
PUBLISHING

The Christmas of a Countess

V1.0

Cover photograph © PeriodImages.com

Cover art by KGee Designs.

All rights reserved - used with permission.

https://www.lindaraesande.com

ISBN: 978-1-946271-07-5

Library of Congress Control Number: 2017916817

Twisted Teacup Publishing, Cody, WY

PRINTED IN THE UNITED STATES OF AMERICA

To Jax, Michael, Sean, Nina, Yana, Alex, Samantha, Will, Angelica, Diana, Anastasia and all the other cover models who help make a book special

ALSO BY LINDA RAE SANDE

The Daughters of the Aristocracy
The Kiss of a Viscount
The Grace of a Duke
The Seduction of an Earl
The Sons of the Aristocracy
Tuesday Nights
The Widowed Countess
My Fair Groom
The Sisters of the Aristocracy
The Story of a Baron
The Passion of a Marquess
The Desire of a Lady
The Brothers of the Aristocracy
The Love of a Rake
The Caress of a Commander
The Epiphany of an Explorer
The Widows of the Aristocracy
The Gossip of an Earl
The Enigma of a Widow
The Secrets of a Viscount
The Widowers of the Aristocracy
The Dream of a Duchess
The Vision of a Viscountess
The Conundrum of a Clerk

The Charity of a Viscount

The Cousins of the Aristocracy

The Promise of a Gentleman

The Pride of a Gentleman

The Holidays of the Aristocracy

The Christmas of a Countess

The Heirs of the Aristocracy

The Angel of an Astronomer

The Puzzle of a Bastard

The Choice of a Cavalier

Stella of Akrotiri: Origins

Stella of Akrotiri: Deminon

Stella of Aktrotiri: Diana

Chapter 1

AN EARL PROPOSES A TRIP

*L*ate November, 1816, Worthington House in London
At precisely seven-fifty-seven in the evening, Milton Grandby, Earl of Torrington, entered the vestibule in Worthington House. A swirl of white followed him in, the large snowflakes quickly turning into tiny puddles on the marble floor. Those were joined by larger drips from the rivulets of melting snow that fell from his greatcoat.

The trip from White's in the town coach had taken longer than usual. Although he could have blamed it on heavier-than-normal traffic—shoppers clogged the streets in Jermyn Street and St. James Street—it was probably the cold, wet weather that had him returning from his men's club a few minutes later than usual. Dinner was served at eight o'clock, and he had no intention of being late for it.

He nodded to the Worthington House butler as Bernard gave him a bow. "I don't believe I've ever seen it snow so much in London," Milton remarked as he allowed the other man to take his greatcoat and umbrella.

"I do believe her ladyship said the very same thing last December, milord," Bernard commented, his brow arched in a manner suggesting he was in possession of information counter to the earl's claims. "When there was snow coupled with lightning," he added as a way to remind his fairly new master that he probably hadn't even been in the capital the December prior. Or in February, when a storm had delivered over a foot of snow to the city.

Milton blinked, wondering if the butler was teasing him. But he soon realized the rather dour servant was merely reminding him he wasn't usually in London during the month around Christmastide. He was usually at Torrington Park, his earldom's seat and old hunting lodge in Northumberland.

The reminder had him frowning.

He hadn't yet made plans to travel there for this year's Christmas, his first as a married man. The thought might have had other long-time bachelors wincing at the prospect of spending several weeks in the company of their wives—without the opportunity to escape to their favorite club—but Milton found he was looking forward to the holiday. Christmastide in Torrington Park was sometimes lonely, especially if other members of the Grandby family didn't accept his invitation to spend their holiday in Northumberland.

He hadn't issued any invitations this year. What with his recent wedding and days spent in Parliament, he simply hadn't given a thought to Christmas.

Now that he considered the possibility of spending the holiday with only his countess, doing what they had been doing last night just before he fell into a deep and rather satisfying sleep, he decided he wouldn't be issuing any invitations.

Except to his wife.

The thought had every one of his nerve endings firing in a thousand different directions. His manhood, suddenly reminded of the night before, followed suit as it attempted to escape the placket of his breeches.

Of all the places to experience an erection, the vestibule of Worthington House was probably one of the most inconvenient. He regarded the butler with a frown. "So glad I was in Kent at the time," he remarked in response to the butler's comment about the snow. "Huntington's house party," Milton added as he removed his top hat.

The fête in February had been the Duke of Huntington's gift, a bachelor party of sorts for an earl who had waited until well past the usual age of marriage to finally find and take a wife. Milton had thought to do the same for the widower when Huntington finally remarried, but the duke had quietly married an earl's daughter—one nearly half his age—the year before. Huntington didn't join the others who celebrated Milton's upcoming nuptials by taking advantage of the courtesans who joined the house party on the last night. Not even tempted by the painted ladies—he had already spent several months squiring his future wife to all the Society entertainments—Milton had instead challenged the duke to a game of billiards and managed to leave Huntinghurst with over a thousand pounds in his pockets.

Part of the winnings paid for a wedding ring as well as a necklace, matching earbobs, and a horse—all gifts for his bride.

"Dinner will be served shortly, milord," Bernard remarked as he took the earl's top hat.

"I was afraid I'd be late," Milton murmured as he hurried out of the vestibule and into the great hall, his attention immediately captured by the regal woman who was descending the stairs from the first floor. Dressed in a deep red silk gown and wearing a necklace made of tiny rubies, her blonde hair swept into a smooth chignon outlined by spiral tendrils, his countess held herself as if to the manor born.

Which she was. Her father had been the Marquess of Devonville, a title now held by her brother, William Slater.

"You look like a goddess," Milton said in awe as he gave a deep bow. "May I be your slave for the evening?"

Adele Slater Worthington Torrington angled her head as she resisted the urge to roll her eyes. She couldn't help but grin at her husband's antics. "And you look as if you might have had more than your usual brandy this evening," she countered with an arched brow. She leaned her head in the other direction so that he could buss her on the cheek, and when she was sure no one paid witness to his greeting, she allowed him a kiss on the lips.

Milton offered his arm as she took the last step down to the tiled marble floor. "Nonsense. I'm merely a victim of this awful weather." He gave a shudder to emphasize how chilled he had been on the way back from his club.

Pausing in mid-step, Adele glanced back toward the vestibule, realizing Bernard was still fussing with the earl's greatcoat. "I shouldn't think a few sprinkles would have you looking quite so... disheveled."

"Sprinkles?" he repeated, his eyes rounding. "It's been snowing since I left for the club." As for the comment about looking disheveled, he wondered what might be amiss. He wore his graying hair short to make it easier to don a periwig at Parliament, so he rather doubted any of it was out of place. Despite his boots having suffered a dusting of the white stuff, now melted into tiny droplets, they still displayed a bit of a shine. But a quick look in a hall mirror had him realizing his white cravat was crushed. He used a couple of fingers to lift it back into place, the motion causing the folds of fabric to reveal a sapphire-tipped cravat pin. Turning so Adele could reevaluate his appearance, he grinned when she said, "Much better."

Milton led his wife into the dining room and to her seat at the end of the mahogany table. The gong hadn't yet sounded, but given how close it must be to eight o'clock, he decided they could continue their conversation there just as easily as in the library where they usually met before dinner. "It was still snowing when I returned home," he said, realizing she probably hadn't noticed the snow given how dark it was beyond the window in her bedchamber.

Adele took the proffered chair, just then realizing she hadn't taken a look out her window whilst her maid had helped her dress for dinner. "I hadn't realized," she replied. "But given how awful the weather has been this fall, I suppose I am not surprised." With the incessant rains during July and colder than normal temperatures nearly every day since, London and most of England was suffering one of the worst years ever. Prices had risen several times as the effects of the weather took their toll. Some households were already rationing food, since the crop losses had been drastic. Others had let go of some household staff, unable to feed all their servants.

"I was hoping we had seen the last of the white stuff," Adele murmured in dismay. "I hear such awful news during tea. Except for Gisborn, it seems not a single farmer had a successful crop this year, and everyone is suffering as a result." The comment about the Earl of Gisborn was made with a hint of pride, for her niece, Hannah Slater, had married the farmer and inventor last spring and was now his countess. Henry Foster had built greenhouses and an irrigation system to irrigate as well as drain excess water from his farmlands in Oxfordshire. As a result, he had harvested a modest crop of wheat and beans and an impressive amount of hot house vegetables.

Rather surprised to hear that crops had been a topic of discussion during afternoon tea with her friends, Milton raised a brow. "I wasn't aware the ladies of the *ton* concerned themselves with such serious issues," he remarked as he took a seat in the carver at the other end of the table.

Adele's eyes widened. "But we must! Being the mistress of a household requires we do so." She paused a moment, suddenly uncomfortable with the topic of discussion. "Which reminds me that I must ask a rather delicate question of you."

Milton blinked. Given they had been married less than a year, they were still considered newlyweds, but he rather hoped Adele felt comfortable enough with him to put voice to her concerns without seeking permission to do so. "What is it, my sweeting?"

Adele blinked, her face pinking up as a footman entered from the butler's pantry at the exact moment her husband spoke the endearment. She waited until after the footman had filled their wine glasses and disappeared before asking, "Do you need to have Bernard let go of any of our servants?"

About to take a drink from his wine glass, Milton frowned. "No. Why ever do you ask?" He had a sudden thought that perhaps she suspected one of the servants of pilfering the silver. Or perhaps the randy footman assigned to the ground floor had finally tumbled the second floor maid and been caught in the act on the first floor.

Sighing, Adele leaned forward and said in a hoarse whisper, "Lady Pettigrew has had to let go of two of her footmen. She admitted there isn't enough food in the cellars to feed everyone who lives under Pettigrew's roof for the rest of the winter, and apparently Pettigrew is loath to spend a fortune on food and coal to heat their house."

Although he knew he should feel a bit alarmed at hearing her words, Milton Torrington could not, for he had heard similar comments from others whilst at White's. Murmurs in the Chamber of Lords merely reinforced the fact that England had suffered one of its worst years for agriculture, as had most of Europe. Famine plagued Ireland, and it would not be long before smaller villages throughout England suffered the same fate. As a result, food prices had soared. Only those with a good deal of money—and greenhouses— would survive the winter unscathed.

"Worthington House shall be keeping all of its staff," he announced just as the footman returned with the soup course. "And should you discover Worthington House is in need of any additional maids or footmen, please let me know, and I shall instruct the butler to see to their hire. I have it on good authority there are several qualified people available for hire." He had half a mind to have the head groom hire another stable boy, but given how much the man disliked children, he thought better of it.

Adele's eyes widened, and she was quite sure those of the

footman did as well. "Truly?" She couldn't help but notice the sudden spring in the step of the servant as he returned to the butler's pantry, no doubt to spread the word to the rest of the household staff that they wouldn't be suffering the same fate as so many servants in other houses in London.

"Truly." When Milton realized his wife didn't really believe him, he added, "Despite this past year's unfortunate weather, I am still rather rich, Adele. A result of careful investments made by my cousin, Gregory, on behalf of the earldom, and because the Torrington earldom does rather well, despite where it's located." Northumberland might seem a desolate wasteland by those who didn't know better, but the Torrington earldom was quite rich from its coal. He paused a moment. "And even if I wasn't rich, your inheritance would allow us a more than adequate living."

Reminded of her late husband's fortune—Samuel Worthington's involvement with the early steam ships had paid off handsomely—Adele finally relaxed a bit. Although the assets could have been claimed by Milton upon their marriage, he had instead insisted the money remain in her name. *You may keep it or spend it or divest it as you see fit,* he had told her on their wedding day. *I did not marry you for your fortune.*

Despite his words, she was quite sure he was glad when she didn't give it all to her favorite charity.

"I am relieved to hear it," Adele murmured, turning her attention to her soup.

Milton merely nodded, rather glad to assuage her concerns so easily. After swallowing a spoonful of soup, he decided to mention his plans for Christmastide. "I was thinking we could go to Torrington Park for the holiday. Just the two of us."

Adele's soup spoon clattered a bit before landing on the table, and the countess lifted her head to regard him warily. "Northumberland?" she repeated in alarm. "Without benefit of servants?"

Her husband blinked, and he blinked again before giving

his head a shake. "Oh, there will be servants. We will take my valet and your lady's maid, of course. Torrington Park always has a small household staff. And a butler," he explained, the last said as if there weren't usually any butlers in Northumberland. "I was just thinking I wouldn't invite anyone else to join us. So that we might... " He paused, realizing he was about to admit he wanted her all to himself for two or three weeks.

Wanted her undivided attention.

Most of all, he wanted her in his bed every night.

Truth be told, he wanted her in his bed all day as well.

Why the hell am I so randy these days?

"So that we might...?" Adele prompted, a shiver of excitement racing down her spine. Memories of what he had done to her the night before had her breasts swelling.

Milton allowed a shrug. "Spend more time in each other's company, I suppose," he said sheepishly.

Given his sudden temerity, Adele narrowed her eyes, intending to tease him. "Are you suggesting you wish to spend more time...?" She clamped her lips shut when the footman reappeared with the first meat course. The sudden silence between them had her giving her husband a beseeching look.

With the servant's attention on dishing up a serving on each of their plates, Milton took the opportunity to pantomime kissing, but he was forced to change what he was doing with his lips when the footman glanced up and asked if he wished to have more on his plate.

Stifling the urge to giggle, Adele simply waved a hand to indicate the amount on her plate was adequate when the footman looked her way. When he set down the plates and finally left the dining room, she allowed a smile of embarrassment. "Milton!" she admonished him. "You'll scandalize the servants."

Her husband wasn't about to inform her they were well past being scandalized.

"I cannot help myself," Milton replied, stabbing his fork

into his beef with a bit more force than was necessary. "There are times I want you so badly, I cannot think straight."

Adele's eyes widened, his words giving her a thrill she had never experienced with her first husband, and certainly not with the man's brother.

Whatever had she done to have Milton Torrington lusting for her so?

They were married. Had been for nearly seven months. She had feared that by now, his supposed thirst for her would have been slaked, his attention captured by some other woman.

Instead, he seemed more beholden to her than ever before.

He hadn't been this way with her at the beginning of their relationship. His initial overtures had been tentative, made during a rare event at Lord Huntington's townhouse. Adele knew of Milton's reputation, of course. He was famous for choosing a different widow every Season and squiring her about to the various entertainments the *ton* had to offer. If there wasn't a ball or a soirée, there was the theatre and *musicales*.

Then, at the end of the Season, when most aristocrats left the city to return to their homes in the country, he would bestow his latest paramour with a bauble from Stedman and Vardon, wish her well, and go about his life until the following Season when he would do it all over again with a different widow.

He never felt enough affection for any of the widows to propose marriage—that is, until he had spent just a month in Adele's company—before last year's spring events had even started, in fact. Indeed, the manner in which he had approached her after Lord Huntington's dinner party had her thinking he was merely being polite. A bit of small talk, a question as to how she was faring after the death of her husband, and the mention of her broken engagement with Weston seemed to have set the stage for him to make his move.

Except he didn't.

He did ask if he might pay a call on her the following day. *Join me for luncheon*, she had suggested, sure her sudden blush was apparent to the earl.

I thought you would never ask, he responded before lifting her hand to his lips to kiss the back of it. He didn't stop there, though. He also kissed her on the corner of her mouth, as if he was completely oblivious to the others who milled about in the vestibule until Huntington's footmen had their coats and mantles draped over their shoulders. Then he escorted her to her town coach, helped her inside, and followed her in.

Although she had half a mind to put voice to a protest, Adele knew it would come off as false. She wanted the earl's company as much as he seemed to want hers.

Once at Worthington House, she noted how he ignored the disapproving frown Bernard bestowed on him as he assisted her with her mantle. Then, when it appeared as if he would be taking his leave of the house—as if he had only ridden with her in the coach to ensure she arrived safely at Worthington House—she placed a staying hand on his arm and invited him to stay for a drink. *I have a bottle of my younger brother's very best scotch*, she said with an elegantly arched brow.

Of course Milton would be familiar with Donald Slater's scotch. The Devonville marquessate benefitted from the sales of the golden fluid, her older brother, William, having funded the enterprise back when he first inherited. Before that, their father hadn't considered the distillery a means to earn an income.

I would be honored, Milton had replied, placing a hand over hers and leading her to the library. How he had known where to go, she had no idea. As far as she knew, the earl had never been in Worthington House.

Once inside the library, he had shut the door, saw to it she was settled on the small divan near the fireplace, made his way to the silver salver on which stood a bottle and several crystal tumblers, and poured them both a finger's worth.

Although she rarely drank the Devonville scotch, Adele did on this occasion. There was something about the earl that had her feeling nervous and excited and ever so vulnerable just then. Despite knowing him nearly her entire life, she had never known him like this. Never thought she might be the focus of his attentions.

The focus of his intentions.

Emboldened by the fiery liquid, she leaned against the back of the divan and watched him drain his scotch in a single gulp.

I've a proposition for you, he had said then, setting his tumbler on a library shelf before joining her on the divan, one of his thighs suddenly pressed against hers.

Oh? she had replied, amazed at the thrill that shot through her body just then.

Do an old man a favor by allowing me to escort you to this Season's events.

Do an old widow a favor and help me host my musicale, she countered, rather shocked at how bold she sounded with her rejoinder. But it would be the true test of how serious his intentions might be, Adele figured.

I would be honored.

Adele had blinked. Her surprise at hearing his response must have showed, for Milton gave a slight shrug before kissing her on the cheek. When she turned her head toward him, he kissed her on the lips. The slow, sweet kiss had her lifting a hand to his head so that she might spear her fingers through his graying hair. The move, interpreted as an invitation to continue, had him pulling her body atop his lap, one hand slipping beneath her skirts to push them up along her stockinged calves, along her bare thighs—

• • •

"*I* do hope whatever you're imagining includes me," Milton commented from the other end of the table, his wine glass held aloft as he gazed at his wife. "You look as if you're in ecstasy."

Adele gave her head a quick shake, as if to clear it of the memory of the first time Milton had ever made love to her. "I almost was," she murmured, managing to keep a mewl of disappointment from sounding. "Forgive me. I was... remembering the night you put voice to your proposition."

Intrigued, the earl set down his wine glass and regarded his wife. "Fondly, it would seem," he ventured.

"Indeed." She allowed a teasing grin and may have colored up a bit at having been discovered reminiscing.

Milton suddenly rose from his chair, toppling it in his haste to get to her end of the table. He jerked her chair from beneath the table and scooped her up from the seat.

Momentarily stunned—she actually felt a bit of fear as his arms lifted her bottom onto the table—Adele couldn't help the rush of excitement that passed through her body as one of his hands pushed her gown up one leg, couldn't help but assist by gripping the other side of the red silk to pull it up her other leg. When the fabric was nearly to her hips, Milton was suddenly between her knees, the placket of his breeches already unbuttoned. She couldn't help the thrill she experienced at hearing his growl of satisfaction as he impaled her. Or the secret delight she experienced when she heard his sigh of contentment as his face pressed onto the mounds of her breasts above the edge of her bodice. And, finally, she couldn't help her own cry of pleasure as one of his thumbs pressed at exactly the right place to set off the orgasm she had almost imagined in her memory of their first night together. His own release followed, leaving him nearly unable to remain upright.

"I probably should apologize," he started to say as he finally lifted his head from her breast.

"Oh, don't you dare," Adele countered just before kissing his forehead. "But if you must, you may do so when we share a bed this evening."

He allowed a murmur of agreement. "Given how cold it is every night, I should think we shall be sharing a bed for the remainder of winter," he murmured. "And at Torrington Park?" he added, his voice tinged with hope.

Adele gave a nod. "And at Torrington Park," she finally agreed.

It seemed a trip was in her future.

Chapter 2

PONDERING A TRIP

*L*ater, in Adele's bedchamber

Wondering what might have happened should the footman have reentered the dining room during her husband's sudden fit of passion, Adele had to suppress a giggle. Ever the gentleman, Milton had seen to putting her gown to rights before reseating her at the table. Then she had watched as he made his way back to his carver, buttoning his breeches as he did so.

The rest of dinner would have been boring except for his enthusiastic words about what they might do when up at Torrington Park. By the time the dessert course was served, Adele found she was looking forward to the trip to Northumberland.

Remembering his comment about how it had been snowing, she moved to the bedchamber's only window and pulled aside the drapes. At first only able to see her reflection in the wavy glass, she leaned forward and gave a start as something white flitted past. She cupped her face with her hands so she could better see what was beyond the cold glass.

There it was again. A snowflake, twirling about in the slight breeze as it made its way down from the dark gray gloom above. Angling her head in an attempt to make out the gardens below, Adele allowed a gasp.

There were no gardens. The entire area she could see behind Worthington House was covered with snow!

Adele angled her head the other way, wondering if she was merely seeing a reflection of something else. But, no, everywhere below appeared white. Or light gray. It was hard to be sure, since the sun had never made an appearance on this or for several days prior. The eclipse on the eighteenth had completely blacked out what little sun there was, blanketing London in a twilight that seemed to last far longer than two minutes.

This entire day had been gray, the city of London shrouded in a kind of perpetual gloom. Snow had begun to fall just before dinner, the flakes starting out as large, wet globs of crystals that dropped from the sky. When the temperature suddenly dropped, the flakes were smaller, more likely to get caught in the air currents between buildings so they danced about before finally making their way to the ground.

Adele tried to remember a time when snow had blanketed the city and could only recall this past February as well as a few days in her youth. Back then, the white snow had quickly turned dark gray, soot having covered it shortly after it fell. At the Devonville country estate in Wiltshire, the snow would stay white for the entire time it was on the ground, making it possible to create delightful ices and snow ice cream.

Adele rather doubted the Worthington House cook would be doing anything with this snow, though. By morning, it, too, would be as gray as the clouds and fog.

She grinned at the thought of snow ice cream, wondering if her brother, William Slater, Marquess of Devonville, was thinking about snow ice cream over at Devonville House.

Probably not. He was probably in bed with his younger wife, Cherise, thinking more carnal thoughts. The woman, a widow, had been on her brother's mind since well before her husband's death over a year-and-a-half ago. Why, the marquess had made sure he was the first to court Cherise the very day after she was out of mourning!

It was no surprise they were married only a couple of weeks later.

Adele couldn't help but grin in remembering that her brother had at least waited to marry until *after* marrying off his only daughter, Hannah, to Henry Foster, Earl of Gisborn.

She suddenly wondered if they were experiencing this same sort of snow up in Oxfordshire.

Despite the huge crop losses across England, Milton had assured her he could afford the bauble he had purchased for her birthday. Adele fingered the bracelet on her left wrist, wondering how much the earl had spent. *Stedman and Vardon will have a very happy Christmas*, she thought with a wry smile. They had no doubt had a happy spring given the diamond and sapphire ring Milton had bestowed on her the day they wed. And later that night, when he wrapped her neck in a matching necklace as well as the following day when he wrapped her wrist in diamonds and sapphires.

Your man of business must be rolling his eyes, she remembered saying in a scolding tone.

Perhaps. But he knows I have good taste and the funds to back the purchase, he had replied proudly.

Good taste, indeed. Although Adele wasn't the first to be bestowed with jewels from the Earl of Torrington, she would be the last. The man had proposed at the end of February, claiming to have fallen in love with her.

Having been left a widow when her first husband, Samuel Worthington, died, and having learned her next likely husband, William Weston, merely wanted her for her fortune to pay off gambling debts, Adele accepted the Earl of Torrington's suit.

No one had ever claimed to *love* her before.

Despite having developed a rather hardened heart from her experience with Weston, she wasn't positive Milton's words were heartfelt. Not back then.

She knew better now, though.

Months of having been worshipped in either his bed or hers had quickly changed her mind.

The thought had a shiver racing up her spine. And it wasn't from the cold that permeated the glass pane in front of her.

Adele glanced about her bedchamber, wondering if she would be spending the night here or in the master suite.

She rather hoped it was the master suite. This room was rather chilly and growing colder by the moment. Daring a glance in the direction of the fireplace, she realized why.

A fire hadn't yet been lit. There weren't even any lumps of coal in the bucket next to the fireplace.

Adele allowed a sigh of disappointment.

Simpkins obviously hadn't paid a visit to the mistress suite during dinner. Nearly cursing her lady's maid's oversight, Adele moved from the window and made her way to the vanity.

Although Simpkins would be joining her shortly to help her undress, she had half a mind to send the slightly older woman away. Simpkins had been her maid for nearly twenty years, so time had allowed the servant to put voice to her opinions more freely than would be allowed in most households. Adele found those opinions more and more annoying these days, and once Simpkins learned what she and Milton had discussed during dinner, Adele was sure the maid would complain.

Bitterly.

Milton Grandby, Earl of Torrington, had proposed a trip.

The idea hadn't surprised Adele. Indeed, despite the weather, she'd been expecting he would be announcing some kind of travel. They hadn't been away from the capital except to attend the Duke of Chichester's wedding in Sussex followed by their wedding trip, a short excursion to a Torrington estate in Kent. An especially chilly early spring was followed by a Season full of entertainments, including her annual *musicale*. She and Milton attended any number of balls and soirées, and they simply hadn't had a chance to get away from the city during the summer.

Milton's plan certainly assured her they would be leaving the capital for a time. Perhaps for a month or more.

Northumberland? she repeated at hearing his rather cavalier suggestion.

Indeed. The Torrington earldom is there, and I usually go there for Christmas. Now that we're married, I figure it's time I bring my bride.

Although she recalled blinking at the suggestion, she thought it a good one. She was the Countess of Torrington, after all. The least she could do was meet those who worked for her husband.

Adele moved to her vanity and took a seat. The light from the candle lamp bathed her face in a golden glow, a rather flattering color given her pale complexion and blonde hair. Although gray hair could be found amongst the blonde strands, they hadn't yet taken over her coiffure. With any luck, they wouldn't be evident for a few more years.

Hopefully after the children were born.

Despite her husband's frequent visits and attentive nature, she wasn't yet pregnant. She wondered if she was too old, or if Milton was too old. She shook the thought from her head. The queen was still having children, and she was far older than Adele!

Adele settled onto the small cushioned chair and gave a sigh. She rather liked having a few minutes alone every night. A few moments to reflect on the day's events and wonder how those to whom she was related were faring—her nephew, Will Slater, a commander in the British Navy; her niece, Hannah, now the Countess of Gisborn; her brother, William, no doubt in bed with his marchioness; her other brother, Donald, up in the northernmost regions of the country making scotch and probably bedding every willing tavern maid in the county.

A knock on the bedchamber door had her giving a start. "Come," she called out.

Simpkins entered, her labored breaths a testament to her having hurried to reach her mistress' bedchamber. "I apologize, milady. Bernard insisted I help with the dinner service below stairs. Don't know how that man keeps his position," she complained as she rushed to the fireplace and worked at lighting several lumps of coal.

"It's only fair you take your turn at the servants' table," Adele replied as she regarded her reflection in the vanity mirror. "Besides, I don't have need of your services this evening," she added with a wan smile.

At Simpkins' look of disbelief—the older woman looked as if she might have a coronary at any moment—Adele gave her a shrug. "Go to bed, Simpkins. Get some sleep, and I'll see you no earlier than ten in the morning."

Simpkins' eyes widened at hearing her mistress' words, but she quickly curtsied and hurried from the bedchamber, the only words loud enough to be overheard having to do with the horny earl who had wormed his way into Worthington House.

Rolling her eyes, Adele found she couldn't agree more.

But Milton Grandby, Earl of Torrington, was her horny husband, and she could think of no one else she would welcome into her bed.

Or her house.

As for Simpkins, there might just be one servant who would be dismissed. And it wouldn't be because of the weather.

Chapter 3

A VALET AND HIS MASTER
DISCUSS A CERTAIN
SOMEONE AND A SITUATION

The following morning
Milton regarded his reflection in the cheval mirror, rather impressed his valet had been able to repair the tear in his favorite breeches. He'd been a bit too hasty in how he unbuttoned the placket—he had actually torn it open— during dinner the night before. Even if he'd had to replace the breeches, the brief tumble with his wife at the dining table had been worth it.

What other woman of the *ton* welcomed such attentions before the meat course?

Well, he could think of at least a couple of others. But other than Adeline Carlington, Countess of Morganfield, and perhaps her daughter, Elizabeth Bennett-Jones, Viscountess Bostwick, he rather doubted there were any in London. He was sure he would have heard about them at White's.

"You've once again impressed me with your sewing skills, Banks," he said as he turned to regard his valet. Although the man was about his age, Banks had held his position as a valet to the Earl of Torrington longer than Milton had been the earl. Although he could have chosen to keep the valet who served him during his years at university, he had instead elected to keep his late father's last valet, Alonyius Banks.

There was much to be said for experience.

He knew his former valet would have failed at fixing the breeches. The man was all thumbs when it came to a needle and thread.

In the case of Banks, Milton now knew why the man was so good at his position. Although he hadn't worked in service from the time he was old enough to walk, Banks had grown up as the son of a textile manufacturer in Yorkshire. Not particularly wealthy, the valet's father, Marcus Banks, had carefully modernized his business over the years, making sure to retain the best employees to do what the machines could not. Expanding the mill to include lacemaking meant employing other, less-educated workers. As result, the Luddites hadn't yet targeted Banks Textiles.

Marcus Banks hadn't been able to keep his youngest son in Yorkshire, however. Although Alonyius Banks understood how the machines worked and could read and write and even keep the business ledgers—he was meant to inherit the business along with his older brother, Thelonius—he had absolutely no interest in the concern.

His mother, a former lady's maid, had instilled in him the value of working in service, however, teaching him skills he would need should the servants suddenly leave their employ. For some reason, she had never trusted her husband's business acumen enough to embrace the life of middle-class wealth and leisure. Or perhaps the spectre of Luddites had her thinking the mill would be burned to the ground, immediately ending their source of income.

In any event, when the opportunity to serve as a valet in a London household presented itself, Alonyius packed a valise, accepted his mother's gift of one-hundred pounds, and left Darlington in a stagecoach.

That had been three-and-twenty years ago.

In the meantime, Marcus Banks had died. Although Alonyius' older brother, Thelonius, was running the firm, word had come by way of Milton's cousin, Gregory, that the man's health was failing. *I invested in Banks Textiles years ago,*

Gregory had explained at White's the night before, just after Milton arrived for his pre-dinner drink. *The oldest heir has been running things with the help of his aged mother*, his cousin had explained. *He doesn't have an heir, and I rather doubt he'll make it to Christmas.*

At first, Milton wondered why Gregory Grandby saw fit to tell him about Banks Textiles, and when he finally asked, Gregory gave him a quelling glance and shook his head, as if he thought the earl was a candidate for Bedlam. *Because your valet will inherit the concern, of course,* he had responded with a roll of his eyes.

He remembered blinking a few times. And then two thoughts had Milton reacting with a bit of shock.

No, make that three.

Alonyius Banks hadn't been involved in his family's business for over twenty years. How could he be expected to simply step in and pick up the reins?

It was rather doubtful Banks Textiles could be run from London. A textile mill required oversight. An involved owner. A manager of some skill and experience. Which meant Alonyius Banks would have to relocate to Darlington and either relearn the business or hire a manager.

And the last thought was the most selfish.

I'll lose my valet.

Well, he supposed valets were replaceable. He had just never thought he would lose his, especially because the man was the only heir to a textile manufacturer!

Milton's reverie was interrupted when he realized his valet was regarding him with an expectant look. "Good work," he stated with a nod, wondering how he might bring up the situation of Banks Textiles. He had to hope the valet was already aware of his brother's situation.

"Thank you, milord," Banks replied with a nod. "Did you wish to wear those again today? Or change into the doeskins?" He waved toward the bed, where a pair of doeskin breeches were spread out.

Milton bobbed his head from side to side. "Oh, the

doeskins, I suppose. I doubt it will snow today, so they shouldn't get wet," he reasoned. Although the doeskin breeches were a good fit, and he had the body to display them properly, they were nearly impossible to get off when they were damp from rain or snow. The earl likened them to peeling a banana when attempting to remove them.

The banana being his body.

"Very good, milord." The valet assisted his master in removing the wool breeches and pulling on the doeskins, his deft fingers employing a tool to fasten the closures.

Milton watched in fascination as the man completed his task, and then considered the other duties his valet had had to perform over the one-and-twenty years he had been his servant. Although there had been nights when he was too deep in his cups to undress, Banks had seen to it his boots were removed and his cravat pin unplucked from the folds of his neck cloth and safely stowed in the jewelry box. There had also been nights when he arrived home so late, it was nearly morning, yet his valet was there to see to undressing him.

Banks never complained. Never seemed disappointed or distraught or angry or... Milton shook his head, realizing his valet had never given him a reason to wonder if he had made a mistake in keeping him on. "Do you like your position?" he asked suddenly.

Having completed his task, Banks stepped back and regarded the earl with a raised eyebrow. "I certainly don't dislike it, my lord," he said with a shake of his head.

"You've never put voice to a complaint," Milton accused.

His head jerking back as if he'd been punched in the face, Banks blinked. "There's been nothing about which to complain, milord," he replied. When he realized his master was expecting him to say more, he added, "The food is good, the company of the other servants is congenial. The butler is one of the best in London. And my master is generous and of good character." This last was said with an arched eyebrow, as if he dared the earl to counter his claim.

He countered his claim.

"Good character, huh?" Milton repeated with a teasing grin. He could remember a time many years ago when he might have been accused of being a rather bad character, especially when it came to bedding women. Time and the experiences of others had taught him that widows were generally safe lovers and to stay away from married women and debutantes too young to know better. "I admit, I am better these days. Marriage does that to a man."

Banks didn't offer a reply but instead held open a waistcoat.

Milton slipped his arms into it and turned so the valet could button it. "Have you ever been married?"

Banks shook his head. "No, my lord."

"Are you courting anyone?"

"I am not," Banks replied as he completed buttoning up the waistcoat.

"If you don't mind me saying, you're getting a bit long in the tooth. Should you ever want bairns, you need to be thinking of taking a wife," Milton suggested, his words sounding rather gentle.

Straightening, the valet regarded his master with a look of shock. The two of them had never discussed his love life. Or rather, lack of one. Although he had at one time carried on an *affaire* with a lady's maid in a nearby household, he'd had to end it when she insisted they marry and move to the country.

Alonyius Banks had no intention of living in the country.

"I cannot say as how I have ever considered *bairns*, my lord," he replied.

"Then you must at least have a lover," the earl reasoned, just before his eyes widened, as if another possibility came to mind.

Was his valet a molly?

Banks cleared his throat and gave his master a quelling glance. "I have enjoyed the pleasures that can be found in a marriage bed many times, I assure you, my lord. I just haven't…" He paused, realizing he hadn't done anything about finding a woman with whom he could spend an occasional night since ending his last liaison. Lea Hopkins had been a delight for a time, but she had been after a husband.

And a life in the country.

What would he do in the country? He had always been and would always be a valet. A valet for the Earl of Torrington. As for what he might have to do instead, he hadn't yet given the matter enough thought. His mother's most recent letter had ended with a plea for him to come home.

"Haven't?" Milton prompted, apparently determined to learn about his valet's love life. Or lack thereof.

"My last lady required marriage and a life in the country."

Milton recoiled, as if he'd been struck in the face. "Och, that wouldn't suit you," he agreed with a shake of his head. "Anyone else strike your fancy?"

Frowning, Banks had half a mind to tell the earl his question was inappropriate, but the man did have a point. He hadn't found another woman with whom to share his bed.

Or hers.

"Not yet," he hedged. "I had my eye on a maid from the Norwick household, but I discovered only last week that she is married to a footman from Chamberlain House."

The earl shook his head again. "I suppose all the good ones are spoken for." He slipped into the navy top coat Banks held for him. "Tell me, how do you find the servants in this household?"

Relieved at the change in subject, Banks angled his head to one side. "I admit to a level of surprise at just how well Mr. Bernard runs the house," he stated. "Lady Worthington's late husband apparently hired him when it was under construction. He's been here ever since."

"A bit on the dour side, but I suppose that's to be expected," Milton said as he allowed the valet to button the top coat. Weren't all butlers dour? Or stoic? Or proud? "What about the others?"

Banks stepped back to regard his master's appearance, frowning when he realized the mail coach knot in the cravat lacked a pin. He moved to the jewelry box and extracted a diamond-tipped pin. "Word has spread that you won't be firing any servants, so the pall that has settled over most Park Lane households is not present here," he stated as he threaded the pin into the cravat.

Secretly pleased his news had reached his valet—the footman must have told everyone in the household—Milton allowed a grin. "So, everyone's happy now?" he asked with a bit of hope. The last thing he wanted was a dissatisfied staff. Other aristocrats might not realize it, but the great houses were great because of their staff. A happy staff meant a happy household.

A great house.

Banks seemed to give the earl's query some thought. When he hesitated too long, he took note of the man's expectant look and allowed a sigh. "Not everyone," he admitted.

Milton blinked, stunned by the words. "Who is left unhappy?"

The valet shook his head. "I do not believe she ever thought it possible she would be fired, so Lady Torrington's maid seems to suffer from some other malady, my lord."

Milton blinked. And blinked again as he considered his valet's words. Adele hadn't mentioned her lady's maid being unhappy. Did she not know?

"Do you know *why* she's not happy?" he asked, hoping Banks could share some insight. The longer he kept the man engaged, the easier it would be to bring up that other matter. The matter of him not being his valet any longer.

"I do not," Banks replied with a shake of his head. "I overheard the cook claim she used to be rather content. Her dissatisfaction seems to have developed over the past several months."

Milton considered the timeline. He had moved into Worthington House seven months ago, just after he and Adele had married. Did his presence have something to do with her lady's maid's discontent? He was about to put voice to the question when Banks sighed again.

"Perhaps she has simply grown older and has no one in her life, my lord," he suggested. "No family. It's rather common among those of us who have reached a certain age."

Milton furrowed his bushy eyebrows. Although his valet's words held merit, he knew they didn't apply to him. The man had an ailing brother. An aging mother. He wasn't sure they applied to his wife's lady's maid, either. Alice Simpkins had been without family for far longer than the time he had been married to Adele. There had to be another reason for her unhappiness.

And when that reason seemed to hit him upside the head, the thought was so powerful he actually jerked his head back. "Good God, Banks! She just needs a good lay," he claimed suddenly.

It was Banks' turn to blink. "Pardon, sir?" he whispered in shock, unable to believe what his master had just said.

"She probably hasn't been laid in..." Milton paused, not quite sure how long it might have been since Simpkins had participated in a tumble. "Probably since I moved into Worthington House," he ventured, his attention on something not in the room. "She's been my wife's maid... for the entire time Adele was married to that other man," he claimed, determined not to mention Samuel Worthington by name. The very thought of that man was never pleasant.

"She has an impeccable record, my lord," Banks agreed. He moved to the bed and picked up the short top hat. He offered it to his master.

Milton absently took the hat, his attention suddenly on Banks. "We're going to Torrington Park for the holiday," he stated. "I expect we'll stay at the usual inns. Can you see to making the arrangements in advance?"

Banks gave a nod before putting voice to the inns he had in mind. "The *Black Bull, Angel Inn, Crown Hotel,* and *The George?*" They were the coaching inns the earl's party usually stayed in when they made the trip to Torrington Park. Evenly spaced along the Great North Road, the towns of Alconbury, Grantham, Boroughbridge, and Darlington made for the best locations at which to spend the nights. Other coaching inns along the way, such as the *Bell Inn* in Stilton and the *Red Lion* in Epworth, offered a change of horses and a suitable parlor in which to take a luncheon or have tea.

"Indeed. The countess will wish to buy some cheese in Stilton, so we'll have to stop at the *Bell*," Milton murmured. "Let's be sure not to mention the *Angel* might be haunted. I'd hate to have the women in a twitter," he added as he regarded his reflection in the mirror.

Frowning, Banks was about to ask for more information about the *Angel Inn*, but thought better of it.

"You may find yourself providing protection for a lady's maid if she thinks there's a ghost in her room," the earl went on with a grin. "Oh, and I'm considering a change in how we celebrate Twelfth Night at Torrington Park," he suddenly stated. "Depending on the weather, we may not stay until Epiphany, but I want the servants to enjoy a ball and the gifts I normally give out for Boxing Day. If you could see to it, procure six dozen Dutch biscuits and a good number of shortbread biscuits, and be sure they're packed in tins. Oh, and have Cook make some Christmas cakes to take along as well."

His brows furrowing with the instructions—just how did the earl expect to change the traditional servants' ball?—Banks gave a nod. "Yes, milord."

The earl regarded his valet for a moment. "If you'd like, you can plan an extra overnight stay or two in Darlington for yourself and the servants' coach. In fact, you should."

The valet stared at the earl a moment, his breath held as if he were waiting for the man to say something else. "Pardon?" he finally responded.

Sighing, Milton wondered how to admit he knew about the valet's brother. About the textile mill. "My cousin, Gregory, is an investor in Banks Textiles. He told me last night about your brother," he said in a soft voice. "I am very sorry. I know, too, you have a decision to make. That is, if you haven't already."

Banks finally gave a nod. "I haven't had a chance to give the matter much thought, actually. I just received a letter from my mother yesterday with the news."

The earl nodded. "I am a selfish bastard, so I'll tell you right now I don't wish to lose your services," he stated. "That being said, you may be about to inherit your family's textile mill, along with a fortune, no doubt."

"I have made no decision, milord," Banks replied with a shake of his head, hoping the earl wasn't already making arrangements for a replacement. "My brother might yet recover from his latest malady and go on to live another forty years."

He rather hoped Thelonius would recover. The very last thing he wanted to do was leave London and have to take over the family business. Especially at a time when the weather was making living so expensive in all of England.

"I'm sure my cousin would like to believe that," Milton replied.

Deciding the comment didn't require a response, Banks said, "If that's all, I'll see to sending out some letters. On what date would you like to leave London?"

Realizing there would be no further talk about Banks Textiles, the earl sighed. "Let's plan on the seventeenth and hope the weather cooperates," Milton replied. "I'll tell the countess the date during dinner this evening. If you happen to see her lady's maid, you might make a mention of it. Poor woman will probably have to start packing yesterday." He suddenly sobered again as he turned to regard his valet. "Speaking of Mrs. Simpkins. Is there any chance you might be the least bit *interested* in her?" he wondered. He didn't wait for a response from Banks, whose eyebrows shot up with the odd query. "I can't help but think she just needs the attentions of a good man. Perhaps a tumble or two whilst we're on the road? Or maybe at the hunting lodge?"

His eyes widening in shock, Banks wondered if his

master was deep in his cups. But that wasn't possible. It was nine o'clock in the morning! He dared a glance at his pocket watch, just to ensure it was nine o'clock.

In the morning.

It was.

"Are you quite sure that's a good idea?" Banks finally asked, suddenly a bit unsteady on his feet. At no time in the past had Milton Grandby, Earl of Torrington, ever suggested he bed a woman.

Happy or not.

The earl gave his question a moment of thought and then shook his head. "Probably not. Forget I mentioned it," he said with a wave of his hand.

Banks exhaled, as if he'd been holding his breath, the idea of bedding the lady's maid almost abhorrent. "Thank you, my lord. I'll see to writing those letters now."

Alonyius Banks gave a bow and took his leave of the master suite, his thoughts going back to the earl's words and his quick dismissal of them. Why, the man had probably already forgotten he had said them.

Thank the gods.

The problem with having heard such a suggestion, however, was that Alonyius Banks couldn't put it out of his mind, no matter how hard he tried.

At least it gave him something to think about besides his family's textile business.

Chapter 4

A LONG TRIP REQUIRES
TRUNKS

Tuesday, December 17, 1816
Standing in the middle of three open Louis Vuitton trunks, Simpkins let out a sigh of satisfaction. She had managed to pack every winter gown and every carriage gown Adele Torrington owned as well as two riding habits, ten dinner gowns, and all the accoutrements to go with them. The matching slippers and boots accounted for half of one of the trunks, each pair carefully wrapped in Dutch cloths. A separate valise held two cases of jewelry below a layer of corsets, stockings, and two night rails.

Not that her ladyship would ever wear the night rails. But it could happen. Why, it might be so cold in Northumberland, the countess could elect to wear both of them.

At the same time.

Simpkins grinned. For the first time in a long time, she felt a hint of happiness. Although she didn't look forward to six days in a coach (five, if one believed the boasts of Haversham, the groom scheduled to drive the servants' coach), she did look forward to a change of scenery. London in winter was proving rather bleak this year.

"Oh, my goodness. Are all those for *my* clothes?" Adele asked a moment after she entered the mistress suite.

"They are, milady," Simpkins replied as she dropped a

curtsy. "There are a few redingotes and a mantle we should probably include as well, so I sent a footman to the attic for another trunk. He'll take these out when he gets back."

Adele sighed. "I suppose it's a good thing these will be riding with you. Torrington has an old Besant he says makes an excellent coach for hauling trunks. Bernard says it's already pulled up to the curb out front. It might be old, but according to my late husband, Besant made the very best coaches for traveling long distances."

Simpkins frowned. "But which coach will you and his lordship be traveling in, my lady?"

Adele allowed a smile. "Why, my own Besant, of course. The driver said it's just about ready." She dared another glance around the bedchamber, noting how her vanity was nearly clear of its usual bottles and hair accessories. "About the jewelry..."

"In the case at the bottom of the valise," Simpkins said as she pointed to it.

Adele gave a look of worry. "The real ones?"

Simpkins nodded. "Above the case of real jewels is the fake bottom his lordship's valet delivered last night, and above that is the case with the jewels made of paste," she explained.

Intrigued, Adele gave her maid a look of appreciation. "A fake bottom?" she repeated.

"It was his lordship's idea, my lady. Said we might be set upon by highwaymen, seeing as how his coach has his crest painted on the door," she said in a lowered voice.

The countess gave a wave of her hand. "I cannot imagine a highwayman laying in wait for us given the weather is so frightfully cold," she replied with a shake of her head. "Now explain this contraption Torrington has devised."

Adele lifted the valise onto the bed and opened it. "The fake bottom looks just like the real bottom of the valise. Fits like a glove, too. Mr. Banks borrowed the valise yesterday and made the piece himself out of an old valise he cut apart." She paused a moment as she pulled out the garments. "It's a tight fit for good reason, of course, but he showed me the trick of how to get it out." She slid a thumb down into one corner and gave it a slight jerk as Adele watched. "Now I'll just have to be sure to keep the real jewels in the proper case," she added as she returned the garments to the valise and closed it.

Adele furrowed her brows. "Which is which?"

"The black box has the real jewels. The wood one has the paste."

Nodding her understanding, Adele allowed a sigh. "And the books? Where are they?" She had spent a good deal of time at Hatchard's the day before, selecting a number of novels she could read whilst riding in the coach.

Simpkins pointed to another valise. "It's rather heavy, but they're all in there. I'll have the footman load these into your coach, my lady," she said as she indicated the two valises.

"Very good. And you? Are you all packed?"

Simpkins gave a tentative nod. "I am. At least, I think so. I wasn't sure of the livery required for Torrington Park."

Adele gave a wave. "What you're wearing will do. But you needn't wear it in the coach. Torrington said we may be on the road for as much as ten hours a day, so be sure to wear your warmest coat and plenty of warm stockings."

Simpkins swallowed, suddenly not so excited about the thought of traveling to Northumberland. "Yes, milady," she managed.

When the footmen appeared for the trunks, Adele took her leave of the mistress suite and went next door. Finding the door to her husband's bedchamber wide open, she peeked in. Milton and his valet were finishing a discussion that had to be similar to the one she had just had with her maid. "Almost ready?" she asked. Her gaze went to the bed, where a stack of brightly wrapped boxes in a variety of sizes were festooned with ribbons and bows. She was about to ask about them when the valet turned and bowed. Milton hurried to give his wife a peck on her cheek. "Ready as we'll ever be. And you?"

"The footmen are loading my trunks now," she replied, her head nodding in the direction of the packages. "What, pray tell, are those?"

Milton grinned. "Gifts, my sweeting. For Christmas and for Boxing Day. I've been looking forward to this trip for a month."

Adele blinked. She had shopped for him, of course, but not with the same fervor he had apparently employed when he shopped for her. A book about geology, his current interest, and an emerald cravat pin were the only gifts she had for him. Although they were wrapped in festive paper, neither package featured bows or ribbons. "Milton!" she scolded. "There won't be room in the coach for us," she claimed.

"Och, Banks is seeing to a trunk for those," the earl replied with a dismissive wave of his hand.

As if on cue, Banks gave a bow and said, "Pardon me, sir." He took his leave of the bedchamber, apparently to see to another trunk for the gifts.

"They're not all for you," he said in an apologetic tone as he gave her another peck, this time on the lips.

"I should hope not," she murmured, returning the kiss with one of her own.

Milton purred, his arms moving to embrace his wife. "There's my valet to consider, and your lady's maid, and the Torrington House housekeeper, and the butler, and the cook," he listed, separating each with a kiss. "Liquor for the drivers and footmen, and fruits and cakes and ribbons for the maids."

Adele gave him a quelling glance at the mention of liquor but brightened at the mention of cakes. "You're a good employer," she said with a grin.

"I am, aren't I?" he teased. He suddenly sobered, afraid the temperatures might have dropped considerably overnight. "Now let's hope I still have a couple of coach drivers and grooms in my employ when we get to Torrington Park," he added. "Or we may be stuck there."

Chapter 5

ON THE NORTH ROAD

An hour-and-a-half later

The problem with travel in London, especially in the winter, was simply getting *out* of the city. Between having to dodge costermongers and stop for cross-traffic, there was the wait for drayage carts, and horses and their riders, to clear off the skinny streets to allow the coaches to proceed.

Although only an hour or so had passed when snow-covered pastureland replaced the soot-soiled snow of London, Alice Simpkins felt as if it had taken an entire day! She spent most of the time gazing out the coach window to her right, taking in the sights of the world's largest city as it prepared for a holiday. Shops featured the colors of the season, their elaborate window displays made more real by the snowflakes that clung to the glass panes. Although it was too early for members of the *ton* to be out shopping, the rest of London seemed to be on a quest to ensure the streets were clogged and the shops full.

The last time Alice had been in a coach on its way out of London was when her ladyship had traveled to Brighton for a summer with her brother's family. Still in mourning, Adele had spent her days wearing widow's weeds while pretending to mourn a husband she had come to realize had only wanted her for her connections to the *ton*. They had made the trip in just a day, the road to the popular holiday town having been improved. Despite a dozen invitations to various entertainments having arrived at the Devonfield townhouse before they did, her ladyship hadn't accepted a single one. She preferred instead to spend her days on the beach under a rather large-brimmed hat and her nights ensconced in her brother's small library reading Gothic novels. *They're ridiculous, really*, Lady Worthington had said of the books at one point. *But I enjoy them.* Her brother, a widower, and her niece, Hannah, took in the sights and visited the palace upon invitation of Prinny himself.

Her ladyship had acted as if she didn't care one whit.

Alice realized she probably didn't. Lady Worthington had inherited a fortune, making it possible for her to do whatever she pleased when it came to Society.

Including allowing Milton to escort her to that fall's events, despite knowing full well he chose a different widow every Season to squire about London. Had Lady Worthington known then the earl had marriage in mind? That he had always intended to marry the younger sister of one of his best friends?

Well, Alice only knew he intended to marry her because she had overhead his lordship speak of it with his valet one evening. She hadn't intended to overhear the conversation—she was merely passing the master suite at the time, its door wide open—but his claim was said in a clear voice that suggested he hadn't drunk too much at White's that night.

I married her because I always intended to marry her. I just had to wait my turn, is all.

Alice rather wished the earl had arranged for Samuel Worthington to die a year or two earlier than he had. The pompous man had become almost impossible to live with once his fortune was secure and he had the attentions of the aristocracy.

Blinking away the odd thoughts of her mistress' first husband, Alice was startled to discover the landscape out the coach window had changed dramatically. The snow barely covered the ground here. She almost put voice to a question as to where they might be—she hadn't said more than a polite greeting to the valet since she had joined him in the coach—but a signpost appeared ahead on the road.

Highgate. Although she had never ventured this far north of London, she recognized the name as a staging post and wondered if they would stop to change horses. She was about to ask Banks if he knew, but the telltale signs of the slowing horses gave her the answer.

She was tempted to slide across the short bench to the other side of the coach and look out that window, but her knees would have grazed those belonging to Alonyius Banks.

When he first stepped foot into the coach that morning, the valet had settled into the squabs on the bench facing the rear of the coach, which allowed Alice to ride in the direction of travel. Alice thought it rather chivalrous of him to take that particular seat since he was the first to get into the coach. Perhaps she would offer to trade places with him after this first stop.

"I rather imagine the earl and his countess will wish to stretch their legs and perhaps have a cup of tea whilst the horses are changed," Banks said from his side of the coach, the news sheet he'd been reading set aside on the bench next to him. Alice could read well enough to know it was an issue of *The Times* from earlier in the week. "I can escort you inside if you'd like."

Stunned at the invitation, Alice blinked. "That's very kind of you, Mr. Banks," she replied. "I believe I will join you." Hopefully the public room in the inn would be warmer than the coach. Alice could barely feel her toes.

When the coaches halted in the yard, a flurry of activity accompanied the flurry of snow that surrounded them as they stepped out of the coach. Alice watched as the Torringtons made their way to the tearoom, suppressing the urge to cry out in alarm when she paid witness to the earl picking up his countess and carrying her—apparently against her will—until they were well clear of the mud in the yard.

Banks pretended not to notice, although Alice knew he dared a glance in her direction. "He is an unusual earl, to be sure," she said with a shake of her head. "But is he a good employer?" she wondered aloud, giving her companion a sideways glance. When he didn't look in her direction, Alice thought perhaps he was ignoring her. But then Banks finally spoke.

"I am blessed to have worked for his father and now for him," he stated, cold clouds of white surrounding him as he spoke. "Even if he is a bit... unconventional. I find it difficult to refer to him as 'Grandby', however, which he prefers, when he is and always shall be 'Torrington'." He held out an arm when they reached the wooden walkway that led to the front door of the coaching inn.

Alice dared a glance up at him before she rested her gloved hand on his arm. She hadn't touched a man in over a year, and rather liked how solid his arm felt beneath the wool of his cape coat. "Her ladyship is most taken with him. Far fonder of him than of her first husband," she remarked.

Not one to gossip, Banks merely nodded his understanding. "Have you been in her employ long?" he asked as he opened the door.

"Nearly twenty years," she replied, letting go her hold on him so she could step over the threshold and into the smoky public room. Her first thought was how warm it was compared to outside. Of how the chill of the coach seemed to leave her body to be replaced by the comfort of a woolen blanket. But the odor of unwashed bodies and the smoke from cheroots nearly had her turning around and heading for the fresh, snowy air outside.

The valet followed her into the establishment, his face impassive as he considered her length of employment. She was obviously adequate in her duties or she wouldn't have stayed in the countess' employ all those years. As for her demeanor, he found it very different from the one he had come to expect every night at the dinner table. Indeed, this woman seemed a much lighter, more content version of the Simpkins he had come to avoid in Worthington House.

His gaze immediately going to his lordship, he realized the earl had already been recognized by a short, rotund gentleman seated at a trestle, a pint of ale in front of him and a tavern maid mounted on his stubby knee. *Lord Brougham?* he wondered. *No doubt here for a tumble*, he thought with a bit of disdain. The man was a rake in every sense of the word.

When a tavern maid approached, he stepped into her path and whispered, "Tea and biscuits for the Earl of Torrington and his countess and two servants. In the parlor." He pressed a coin into her palm.

The tavern maid straightened and gave a quick curtsy. "I'll see to it right away," she replied, her gaze darting to Alice and then back to him. "My lord."

Banks was about to correct her when the earl turned in his direction, giving a wave that indicated his impatience. They had only twenty minutes before the coaches would be ready to depart. Banks nodded and led Alice through the throng of travelers and opportunists who frequented the coaching inn. "Stay close," he warned as he increased his steps and his speed. "Pickpockets and thieves thrive on this place." He didn't add that he expected he would have to pay more than the posted rates for the tea and biscuits.

Alice struggled to stay abreast of the valet, annoyed when several unsavory types reached out in her direction, as if they wanted to grab her. When one managed to hook her arm with one of his own, she glared at him, thinking he would let go. But it was Banks who reached over and jerked the offending hand off of hers. "She is a lady of quality," he hissed to the ruffian.

Surprised at how quickly the valet had rid her of the offending man, and rather stunned at his words, Alice stared at Banks. "Thank you," she murmured as the valet continued on through the public room as if nothing untoward had happened.

"You're welcome, Mrs. Simpkins. I would apologize for

those of my sex who are idiots, but it would do no good, I fear."

The comment had Alice smiling despite the tone in which the words were delivered. "You needn't, really," she replied, finding it hard to hold her breath against the foul odors and speak at the same time.

A moment later, they were in a well-appointed parlor, the noise of the public room suddenly reduced to a faint hum. She took a deep breath and turned to the valet. "Thank you for your escort."

Banks nodded and turned to the earl. "Tea and biscuits have been ordered, my lord, my lady," he said as he gave a deep bow.

"I don't know why Haversham favors this staging stop," Grandby complained as he moved to stand in front of the fire. "This has to be one of the worst in London."

Banks straightened, tempted to tell his master that Haversham enjoyed a certain ladybird at this particular inn, and was probably doing so at this very moment. "I couldn't agree more, my lord, but it is said they have the best horse-flesh," he claimed with a nod.

Alice frowned, wondering at the valet's odd reply. Certainly they had stopped at Highgate for the storied prosti-tutes who occupied the third-story rooms. Although she might not have traveled this far north of London, she had heard the gossip. Why, she was sure the two coach drivers and their grooms were enjoying a tumble this very instant. And Lord Brougham was probably just waiting his turn in the public room!

Since her ladyship had taken a seat at a table in front of the fireplace, Alice moved to one not far away. Banks joined her, taking a seat when he was sure his master didn't require his company.

"You've obviously been here before," Alice whispered as Banks joined her.

The valet leaned back in his seat and finally nodded. "Many times. His lordship has made this trip every year I have been in his employ," he said quietly. "It seems he wishes to continue the tradition now that he is married. The weather was only this disagreeable in eighteen-thirteen, though."

Alice nodded her understanding, relieved when an older woman appeared at the parlor door. She carried a huge tea tray laden with far more than the usual tea service. A young girl followed with a smaller tray and hurried to place it in front of Alice.

"I'll do the honors," Adele said to the woman, giving her a nod as the large tray was set onto the table.

"Very good, milady. May I say, it's an honor to have you pay a visit on such a cold day? And I must apologize for all the mud. It's not usually this bad," the woman claimed with a shake of her head. "Now should I just add this to the bill for changing out the horses?"

Alice stiffened when she heard the question, but Banks suddenly stood up and quickly moved to stand next to the woman. "Pardon me," he said as he gave the server a nod. "Could you join me at the door?" he whispered, his hand moving to her elbow to guide her away from the earl and countess.

The apple-cheeked woman—Alice just then realized she was probably the owner's wife—gave the earl and countess a quick curtsy and a worried glance before following the valet to the door.

Watching out of the corner of her eye, Alice realized Banks was settling the bill. Having produced a velvet pouch from his waistcoat pocket, he was counting out coins into her pudgy hands as she looked on. Her grin widened until it was apparent she was missing some teeth. A moment of whispering ensued before she gave Banks a curtsy and quickly exited the parlor.

When Banks returned to their table, Alice poured him a cup of tea and set it on a saucer in front of him. "If I remember correctly, you don't take it with milk or sugar," she said in a lowered voice. "Is that still the case?"

A bit surprised she would know such a detail—the two

had never taken tea together before—the valet arched an eyebrow. "That is correct, Mrs. Simpkins." He watched as she added milk to hers, noticing her small hands and slender fingers as she held the pot with one hand and stirred the tea with the other. He continued to watch as she brought the cup to her lips, her eyes closing a moment as she took a delicate sip. Seemingly pleased, she sat up and afforded him a grin.

"Surprisingly good," she murmured.

Something about how her face lit up with her grin and her compliment had Banks regarding her in a new light. He dared a taste of the tea before taking a larger swallow and had to agree with her assessment. It was better than what was served in the kitchens at Worthington House. "Indeed. I wonder from which tea shop the inn buys it."

Alice lifted the plate of biscuits from the tray, holding it out so he could help himself to a Dutch biscuit before placing the dish between them. She took a lemon biscuit and nibbled on the edge, realizing it had come from the oven within the last hour. "The biscuits are even fresh," she added.

Biting into his, Banks widened his eyes as he considered the flavor. Once he had swallowed, he leaned forward. "It's still warm," he whispered, his eyebrow arching up, almost as if he were sharing a secret.

The grin on Alice's face widened into a smile. "Why do you suppose we expected anything less?" she wondered as she angled her head.

Inhaling as if he were about to answer, Banks simply shook his head. "Unfortunate, isn't it?" he murmured as he took in the furnishings in the parlor. Nothing looked too terribly worn. There were no scorch marks on the ceiling or around the fireplace. The tables were covered in clean linens. And although the settings were sparse—just spoons for each of them and a knife next to a bowl of jam—the spoons did appear to be of fine silver.

"I do believe they have served their very best." Given the condition of the coaching inn's public room, Alice had underestimated the proprietor when it came to accommodating the earl and countess.

"Are you warm enough?" Banks asked suddenly. He had shed his cape coat upon entering the parlor, quickly seeing to the earl's coat before doing so. The earl had already helped the countess out of her coat and handed it to Banks even before they were seated. Meanwhile, Alice kept her redingote in place.

The maid nodded. "I am now." She seemed ready to say something else, but thought better of it.

"What is it?" the valet asked, curious as to what kind of complaint she might make.

Alice gave a shrug. "I was hoping we might add a lump or two of coal to the foot warmer in the coach. I'm afraid I am not in possession of suitable boots for this weather," she added, her face taking on a pinkish cast.

Banks frowned, realizing they hadn't lit the few lumps already provided in the older coach. He had made sure the lumps of coal in the foot warmer in the earl's coach were lit and giving off enough heat to keep the countess' feet warm before they left Worthington House, but he had neglected to do the same for their coach. "I'll see to it before we take our leave," he replied with a nod. "You only needed to let me know you were cold. I could have seen to it earlier." He didn't mean to chide her with his words, but the sound of a scold couldn't be helped.

"I didn't wish to complain," she countered with a shake of her head. Concerned she may have offended the man, she wondered if he might like more tea. She held up the pot. "May I warm up your tea?"

Banks blinked and regarded his half-empty cup before placing it back in the saucer. "Yes, thank you," he said. He was still mulling over her comment about not wanting to complain—*since when?* he had almost asked in response—when Haversham suddenly appeared at the parlor door. Banks gave Alice a nod before hurrying to the driver.

While the two servants talked in quiet tones, Alice

concentrated on her employer. Apparently enjoying her tea as well as the conversation she was having with the earl, her ladyship seemed in good spirits. She certainly looked younger than she had when she was first widowed. *Younger and happier,* Alice thought.

Could a marriage of affection truly be the reason? Or was it merely the nighttime attentions her husband showered on her? Why, the countess seemed to welcome the earl into her bed nearly every night! Of course, given how cold the winter had been—and almost the entire year before it—Alice couldn't blame the woman. The thought of sharing a bed with a warm body had her wishing she could do the same, although there wasn't a servant at Worthington House she thought might feel the same way.

At least, not with her.

She was fairly sure the randy footman from the second floor had his eyes on a maid who worked on the ground floor. He was probably young enough to be her son, though.

A quick glance in the direction of the parlor door had Alice wondering about the driver. The man was huge! Tall and broad and only educated in the subject of horses and equipage, Mr. Haversham wouldn't be her first choice to warm her bed. Probably not her second or third, either. As for Mr. Banks...

She didn't have an opportunity to consider the valet, for he had suddenly turned and directed his attention on her. Alice rose from the table, realizing she was being summoned with his pointed glance. Hurrying to join him at the door, she asked, "What is it?"

"Mr. Haversham says he can light the coals in the foot warmer, but we'll both have to sit on the same side of the coach if he does so. Apparently there isn't enough room between us to have it lit without one or both of us being inconvenienced," Banks explained.

A shiver of something skittered down Alice's spine just then. "I do not mind if you do not," she managed without sounding too breathy. She might never share a bed with a man again in her life, but the thought of sharing the coach bench with the valet had her feeling entirely too warm all over.

"You'll have to ride in the direction of travel," Haversham said in a low voice. "Weight's all wrong no matter what, so Mr. Davids is goin' ta take one of her ladyship's trunks in his basket," he explained, referring to the driver of the coach in which the earl and countess were riding. "He needs the ballast at the back given the snowy roads."

Banks turned to Alice. "Is there a particular trunk that should go ahead with the countess?"

Alice frowned, wondering if Haversham expected there to be trouble getting through to the next inn. She thought of what was in each trunk. The valises in the coach contained whatever Adele might require for her toilette and for sleeping, as well as her jewels, but the largest trunk contained her carriage gowns and redingotes. "The largest trunk, Mr. Haversham. If anything untoward happens, she can do without the others until we reach Torrington Park."

The driver nodded. "Save some biscuits for me," he whispered before he disappeared into the smoke-filled public room.

"Anything amiss?"

Milton Grandby's low voice, only inches away, had both Banks and Simpkins jumping in surprise.

"No, my lord. Just a discussion about the need to redistribute some of the luggage," Banks said in a whisper.

The earl dared a glance back at his countess. "Wife's trunks too heavy?" he asked with a hint of humor.

"Something like that, my lord," Simpkins replied with a curtsy.

"Well, we'll be ready to leave in a few minutes," he claimed. "Be sure to bring all the biscuits, won't you?" he added as he pulled on his coat with Banks' help.

Alice blinked before giving the earl a nod, glad to know he shared their assessment of the inn's baked goods. "Of course, my lord." She grabbed Adele's coat from the hook near the door and hurried back to where the countess was regarding them with a frown.

"What's happening?"

"The biscuits have been deemed too good to leave behind, so I'm to bring whatever I can," Alice said as she held the redingote open for her mistress, deciding not to mention the problem with the luggage.

"Agreed," the countess whispered. "Take them all. I'm sure Grandby had to pay dearly for them."

Alice moved to the table at which she and Banks had been sitting. She produced a hanky from the pocket of her redingote. The remaining biscuits from that table, as well as the one on the earl's table, made it impossible to tie up the small cloth into any kind of pouch, but she stuffed the bundle into her pocket and hurried to join Banks before he headed back through the public room.

She wanted her arm on his as they made their way back to the coaches.

Chapter 6

ARISTOCRATS ON PARADE

The following day, Wednesday, December 18, 1816, at the Red Lion

"One would think the proprietors had never hosted a peer before," Adele commented as her husband helped her into the coach. "I cannot decide if the woman who brought our tea was pleased to host us or not."

Milton settled into the squabs and yawned. "Just not used to waiting on aristocrats is my guess," he murmured, thinking he would take a nap in preparation for that night's stay at the *Angel Inn* in Grantham.

If tonight's inn was anything like the *Black Bull* in Alconbury, then he intended to have his way with Adele again. Besides, he wanted to keep her occupied lest she become convinced the *Angel Inn* was haunted. He supposed the rumors of ghosts couldn't be helped since it was one of the oldest inns in all of England. "Some just don't know how to act around peers," he continued. "I've had some treat me as if I were the king and others act as if I was the poorest pauper."

On that thought, he remembered he needed to give his valet some more blunt. Banks had informed him in an urgent whisper that this latest inn had charged double for the tea and biscuits, and a porter insisted on being paid despite the fact that no trunks were added or removed from either traveling coach when the horses were changed out. "We, sir, are being fleeced," the valet had said between clenched teeth, his anger evident.

And Banks was never angry. He was usually a very calm man. Content. Professional. Milton knew the man had made arrangements in advance for all the stops they were making —Banks was fastidious when it came to travel arrangements.

So, what was different this year?

Milton realized just then his wife had a point.

Although he had stopped at or stayed in every coaching inn they were using on this trip, the service they were receiving was different from past visits. They were being charged more and encouraged to leave sooner.

He wondered if it was the time of year. None of the stagecoaches operated in the winter time, so the coaching inns didn't serve as many customers nor change out the number of horses they did during the summer months. But if the weather wasn't bad, aristocrats were likely to make their way to their country homes for the holiday—to the seats of their dukedoms or marquessates or earldoms. The tracks in the snow—the ones their driver, Mr. Davids, was following —were indications others were using the same route despite the weather. The Great North Road was a Royal Mail Coach route as well as a delivery route for Wellingham Imports. His cousin Gregory's brother-in-law, Thomas Wellingham, owned his own coaches and horses to deliver goods for his import business. Even in the winter, his coaches made the trek north, sometimes all the way to Edinburgh.

This winter was certainly different from others, though. There hadn't been a summer. Just rain and even snow when there should have been sunny skies and warm temperatures for the farmers. It was definitely colder. The earl had encouraged the drivers to take turns riding in the coach for a time while the grooms saw to driving the coaches between stops. Although the grooms were along to provide protection for the coach, who would dare rob a coach when it was snowing and cold? Only the most intrepid highwayman would attempt such a feat, and Milton thought it rather unlikely such a thief would appear on this route.

So, why exactly had they received such odd service at the past few inns?

Milton's eyes widened as he realized just what was different from his past visits.

"You," he said out loud, his attention on his countess. Adele was riding in the direction of travel, a book held up in her gloved hands.

"Me?" she repeated, her brows furrowing in confusion as she regarded her husband .

"I've never had a lady in my company whilst I've made the trek to Torrington Park before," he stated with a shake of his head.

Adele dropped the book in her lap and angled her head to one side. "Are you saying we're being treated differently because of *me?*" she asked in alarm.

Milton was about to agree, but realized he shouldn't agree. Otherwise, he might not enjoy the benefit of her wakefulness at midnight. "Not exactly," he replied with a shake of his head. "It's just that, when I've made this trip before, it's always just been my valet and me," he explained. "I suppose they're not used to me having a wife on my arm."

Angling her head to one side, Adele asked, "Are you sure they know I'm your wife? And not some... courtesan?" she asked in annoyance.

Milton furrowed his bushy eyebrows, realizing he needed to be very careful in how he answered. "Banks is very clear when he announces our arrival," he stated with a nod.

Perhaps he hadn't been so clear when he sent out the letters of arrangement, though. Milton hadn't bothered to read the missives, merely signing his name to the notices of his intent to patronize their establishments. He trusted his valet to represent him appropriately.

Adele merely sighed, still rather bothered by the cut direct she suffered in the parlor at the last inn. She had never traveled this far north before, and now she was wondering if it might be her last to this part of England.

Was she being too sensitive?

"Do you think I'm overreacting?" she asked, deciding to put her husband on the spot just a bit. The inns they had visited were his choices, after all.

Milton knew when he was being baited. "Not at all. I shall see to it you are treated as the countess you are," he replied, his head lifting in a manner that suggested he might even lift a fist or two in her defense. "At every stop from here to Torrington Park," he added.

Adele grinned, and not because she agreed with his claims. She just liked seeing him act like an earl on occasion.

"I look forward to it," she said with a teasing grin. "And in the future, we shall never again stop at that particular coaching inn."

Her husband nodded. "Agreed," he replied, making a mental note to tell Banks.

At least things would go better at their next stop. *The Bell Inn* sold Stilton cheese, and Stilton cheese was his wife's favorite.

Chapter 7

A SERVANT SEEKS WARMTH

ecember 21, 1816 at The George in Piercebridge Despite the gray gloom and the snow flurries that danced about her face, Alice gave Mr. Haversham a tentative smile as he assisted her into the traveling coach. "How much longer, do you suppose?" she wondered as she took a seat in the direction of travel. The trip had already taken far longer than any she had been on before, and the farther north they went, the colder it seemed to get.

"At least today, maybe tomorrow," the driver replied. "Got you a hot brick in the brazier, though. That should help until the coals get hot." He had positioned the foot warmer so it didn't interfere with where the two servants were seated, but allowed them both to benefit from its warmth.

Alice gave him a nod. "It's much appreciated." Although the heat from the brick, and later the lumps of coal just beginning to turn gray at the edges, wouldn't last long, they would keep the coach warm until the driver stopped for a change of horses and luncheon. If they stopped for luncheon.

She regarded her traveling partner with a curt nod. "Good morning, Mr. Banks." As usual, the earl's valet was impeccably dressed. His gray wool traveling suit had been pressed, and his black cape coat brushed. Given the man's aristocratic bearing and proper speech, the clerk at the coaching inn, *The Crown*, in Boroughbridge, where they had stayed Thursday night, originally thought Mr. Banks was the earl rather than the jovial man who followed them into the inn a few minutes later.

Then, yesterday, the Torrington coach had allowed the servants' coach to pass at some point so that Mr. Banks could see to confirming his arrangement of the rooms at *The George* prior to the arrival of the earl and countess. The proprietor of *The George* apologized profusely to the valet, informing him that although they could accommodate 'his party' for just the one night, they would be closing for Christmas and would be unable to provide rooms for the following night.

When Banks had informed them he only required rooms for the one night, the owner seemed rather surprised and then said something about how difficult it would be to travel north given the drifts that had formed over the road.

But The Black Swan *in Darlington is open*, the man said.

Standing behind and to the right of Mr. Banks, Alice had wondered at the mention of snowdrifts covering the road. She was thinking of it now as Alonyius Banks tipped his hat and gave her a nod. "Mrs. Simpkins. Rather sporting of you to be ready to depart so early. You probably had far more to do than I did."

Alice had half a mind to put voice to a complaint about just how early it was—the earl had insisted her ladyship be ready to leave the coaching inn just after dawn—but she thought better of it.

Lately, it seemed as if she had been complaining about everything. And she had done so to other members of the household staff as well as to her mistress. She might not have noticed but for having overheard one of the kitchen maids complaining about her complaint of that night's meal. And then there had been her complaint to the housekeeper about the earl's tendency to barge into the mistress suite before Alice had managed to comb out and braid Lady Torrington's hair, let alone get the woman into a night rail.

She sincerely hoped the earl helped in that regard, for

otherwise her ladyship was forced to sleep wearing nothing at all!

Alice shuddered at the thought. The nights were entirely too cold to sleep in the nude. Besides, no self-respecting countess would sleep in the nude.

Would she?

The kitchen maid's overheard comment had occurred the night before they departed London. What was she saying about Alice now? What were the other servants saying about her? They were probably glad she was gone. Relieved they were no longer subjected to her bouts of bitterness. Her words of complaint. Her scowling face.

What is wrong with me?

She used to find joy in her position as a lady's maid, her skills with Lady Torrington's hair garnering well-received compliments, her ability to mend and press gowns unmatched by the other maids in Park Lane. She socialized with the servants next door and managed a walk in the park across the street when her mistress was out shopping or attending a charity event and didn't require her presence.

From the smallest of tasks to the largest responsibilities of everyday life as a lady's maid, she found nothing in which to take satisfaction these days. Something was missing, and yet she couldn't determine just what it might be.

One thing she knew for certain. Her melancholy had started about the same time her mistress had married Lord Torrington. Although he was a far better match for Adele Slater Worthington than Samuel Worthington had been—the late husband was all about showing off his wealth and good fortune—Alice couldn't help but wonder if he was a better man. Time would tell, of course, but she expected the earl to take a mistress, or develop a sudden gambling habit, or say something to earn him the wrath of others in Parliament.

She didn't know quite why she expected such an uncharacteristic event. Milton Grandby, Earl of Torrington, had done nothing in his past to suggest he might do something stupid now that he was married. And yet...

Alice blinked. Perhaps her unease with the new order at Worthington House had nothing at all to do with the earl, but rather his servants. He had brought a few with him upon his move into the townhouse, including the rather handsome man who sat across from her. There was also a young footman who seemed competent, even if he was almost mute. The poor man never said a word during the servants' dinner, so intent on eating he was. Despite his height—he was nearly six feet tall!—he could certainly bow better than most. Otherwise, he was barely noticeable among the staff. Then there was a kitchen maid. She had replaced the young girl who had succumbed to the ague the year before and had a rather pleasant demeanor despite her rank among the servants.

"Did you sleep well?"

Alice blinked, the question pulling her out of her reverie. She regarded Banks for a moment before realizing he had been the one to ask the simple question. No one had ever asked if she had slept well.

"I did. The bed was very comfortable," she replied with a nod. After a moment, she realized she really should keep up her end of the conversation. "And you? Did you sleep well?"

Banks angled his head to one side and then the other. "I found the accommodations more than adequate for a coaching inn so far from the city. I do believe they would have served an excellent luncheon had we been allowed to stay a bit later."

Nodding her agreement, Alice brightened. "Oh, yes. Last night's dinner was most unexpected. Why, they must have had a prolific garden this past summer, despite the rain and cold," she offered in reply. Before she had even finished the comment, Alice realized it was the first time in months she had spoken at such length without putting voice to a complaint.

There was another reason the inn had served them so

well, though. *The George* would not be accepting any more guests until after the holiday, so they had probably cleaned out their stores in preparation for closing.

"Indeed. Those were my thoughts exactly," Banks said with a nod. He took a breath as if he was about to say something more and then thought better of it.

Alice noticed.

"And?" she prompted, allowing a teasing grin to appear. It felt so good to grin again!

"Do you think your husband would share your good opinion of *The George?*"

Blinking in alarm, Alice shook her head. Why ever would the valet think she was married? And then she remembered how he had addressed her. *Mrs. Simpkins*. Most just called her 'Simpkins'. Few in the household even knew her forename. "Oh, I don't have a husband, Mr. Banks."

The comment seemed to surprise the valet until he suddenly angled his head again. "I apologize. I didn't realize you were a widow."

Alice shook her head, realizing why Banks was confused. "I've actually never been married," she explained quietly.

His brows furrowing into a frown, Banks seemed to think on this bit of information for a moment. "Then why is it that some of the servants refer to you as '*Mrs.* Simpkins'?" he countered, emphasizing the 'Mrs.' as he did so. It was true that housekeepers were always addressed as 'Mrs.'—even if they weren't married. But lady's maids?

He had little in the way of experience with the creatures whilst in service—he had been valet to a bachelor for so many years.

Managing to lift one shoulder in a shrug, Alice allowed an audible sigh. "Some servants simply think I have a husband, or that I am a widow, and I've never let them know otherwise," she replied, realizing just then how lame her excuse sounded.

She never left the house in the late evenings as a few other servants did. Those who were married to servants from other households tended to pay conjugal visits to their spouses on occasion.

"But you're being courted by someone, certainly," Banks stated, as if Alice would be a catch for any man.

Alice blinked again, stunned by the man's assumption. "Why, not at all," she replied with a shake of her head. *Never, in fact*, but she decided not to put voice to that particular thought.

The comment seemed to bother the valet. His eyes suddenly widened. "You minx. You have a secret lover," he accused in a hoarse whisper, his body leaning forward as a teasing smile displayed his perfect white teeth.

Alice gave a thought to fainting just then. No one had ever accused her of being a *minx*. Not even the footman who had flirted with her back when Samuel Worthington still ruled Worthington House. The first floor footman who had since taken a shine to the second floor maid and was seeing to her carnal happiness at least two times a week on the third floor.

Probably because I never flirted in return, Alice realized just then. *Faith!* Had she missed out on an opportunity for love—or at least a bit of affection—because she hadn't returned the man's attentions?

"Actually, I truly do not have a lover," Alice finally replied. "Although I suppose I would be amenable to such an arrangement should one present itself."

The words were out of her mouth before she realized just how scandalous they sounded.

What is wrong with me?

Or what was it about Banks that had her...?

Flirting!

There could be no other word to describe what she was doing with the earl's valet.

"Indeed?" Banks whispered, apparently as shocked as she was by her words. "Should the opportunity present itself from someone such as... me," he replied in a quiet voice. "Do you suppose you would be... amenable?"

Alice inhaled sharply, stunned by how his words had her insides taking a tumble at the thought of a tumble.

It had been a year since her last encounter with a randy under butler. Both tipsy from having imbibed too much wine during the Christmas dinner, they had fallen into his bed and made love several times during a night of revels and revelation. The night she had decided she couldn't abide a marriage to an overbearing under butler. His proposal the following morning, although probably heartfelt, had been met with a polite, "Thank you, but not if you were the last man on the planet," kind of response.

She might have ended up with his pension, though. The man died the following spring whilst in the kitchen maid's bed.

Probably died of the same ague that took the kitchen maid, she realized just then.

"I haven't entertained a man in my bed for some time, Mr. Banks," she stated boldly, rather shocked she could put voice to the claim. Suddenly embarrassed, she sighed and whispered, "I'm left wondering if I would remember how."

The valet's eyes narrowed just then, the pupils dilating so their black seemed to swallow up the blue of the irises. "I'm quite sure I could... remind you," he whispered.

Her breasts suddenly swelling at the thought of Mr. Banks bedding her, Alice inhaled sharply. She might have scolded him. Probably should have scolded him. But a scold would only sound like a complaint, and she was quite finished complaining about everything in her life. "I'm fairly sure you could," she agreed with a slight nod. She dared a glance about the coach, just then aware they had suddenly come to a stop.

They couldn't have already arrived at their next stop.

Could they?

Why, it seemed as if they had left the coaching inn only moments ago.

The traveling coach jerked a bit to one side as the driver stepped down. Alice glanced in the direction of the door, aware it would open at any moment. She also kept a bit of attention on Banks, waiting for his reaction to her comment. Although he continued to regard her with his dark eyes even after the coach stopped, he suddenly turned his attention to the door, his countenance once again that of an earl's valet.

A swirl of snow and a blast of cold air preceded the appearance of Mr. Haversham. His dark woolen scarf, wrapped tightly about his neck, was encased in icicles and tiny balls of snow. "We have to turn around," he said before cupping his leather-clad hands in front of his face and blowing into them. A cloud of white billowed around his head. "The snowdrifts are too deep, and this coach is too heavy for the horses."

A bit of panic set in as Alice considered the driver's words. What about her mistress? Had the Torrington coach been forced to turn around, too? Or were they able to make it though the deepening snow? "What of the other coach?" she wondered.

Haversham shook his head. "I can see their tracks up ahead. Been trying to use them, in fact. They had quite a head start on us, though, and they aren't so heavy, so I have to believe they can make it to Torrington Park 'afore nightfall."

Banks gave the driver a nod. "The trunks weigh us down," he agreed, his impassive expression not giving away his thoughts on being left behind by his master. "By all means, return us to Darlington. *The George* was to close for the holiday, but I made alternative arrangements at *The Black Swan*. Take us there, and I shall see to rooms for us until we can try again."

The driver nodded. "May take me a few minutes to get the team turned around. There's a bit of a clearing here I can use. I think it's the road to Bishop Auckland, but damn if I can make out the signs. They're all covered with snow."

A bit surprised at the thought the driver could read, Banks realized Haversham could probably at least make out the names of towns on the directional signs posted at intersections such as this one. "Do you require assistance?" Banks asked, leaning forward as if he intended to get out of the coach.

"Shouldn't, as long as the horses don't protest too much. You sit tight and keep warm," Haversham replied. He closed the coach door, another flurry of snow entering the coach in his wake.

"Oh, dear," Alice murmured, her first thought as to how her mistress would manage without her services.

Without her clothes.

Well, at least one of her trunks was on her coach, although it was the one containing her carriage gowns and coats. Her shoes, dinner, and day gowns were on the trunks loaded on this coach!

Well aware their brief moment of flirtation was over, Banks took the opportunity to console Alice. "Lady Torrington will be fine. The earl is quite experienced in..." He paused, realizing he was about to say something that would leave her with a poor opinion of his master. No need for her to know that Lord Torrington enjoyed undressing his wife. "In conditions such as these. Her ladyship has nothing to fear."

Alice nodded, wondering what he might have been about to say. Something different about the earl, no doubt. Probably something he thought unfit for her ears. Well, if he was about to say something of Torrington's penchant for undressing his wife, then she already knew about that. There had been far too many nights of her being dismissed before she had finished helping her ladyship into a night rail, if indeed she had even finished helping her out of her dinner gown.

"Thank you. I had forgotten he has been a frequent visitor to this part of England," she managed, a chill suddenly evident in how her body shivered. The coals were nearly ash, their glow having dimmed to a deep red, although two lumps remained in the foot warmer.

The two lumps that were to have kept them warm until they reached Torrington Park.

The valet's hand landed on her knee, as if to steady her. Although she wore several layers of clothing, Alice felt as if his bare hand had touch her bare knee. The thought had another shiver passing through her, although it wasn't a shiver of cold. Indeed, she felt a bit warm just then. Almost too warm.

"Might I join you on that side again?" Banks asked. "I can't help but think it would help the weight distribution to have us both on that seat." Not to mention sharing the warmth. He wondered how Haversham and the groom were managing the cold and figured they probably had a bottle of spirits tucked into their coats.

Remembering the first day of travel, right after they had taken their leave of the Highgate coaching inn, Alice allowed a nod and was quick to slide over to one side. "Of course, Mr. Banks."

Rather surprised at how accommodating the maid was behaving—they had ridden together on the same side the afternoon of their first day of travel despite her apparent discomfort in such close quarters—Banks quickly reseated himself on the bench and settled into the squabs. The part of the bench on which she had been sitting was noticeably warmer than the part nearest the wall of the coach. "It's kind of you to have warmed the seat for me," he said in a hoarse whisper. He swallowed, realizing just then that he was actually thinking about kissing the maid.

Alice shivered again, the sound of his whisper made more intimate in the cramped coach. "It was my pleasure," she whispered in reply. Her breath caught when she realized how her words must have sounded to the man. Why, Mr. Banks must have thought her fast! And yet, he looked as if he was the one who was going to kiss her!

Would she allow such a bold move? They were in a traveling coach, unseen by anyone. Who would know if she allowed it? If she returned the kiss?

The thought had her holding her breath, hoping he would make the move.

The coach suddenly lurched forward and then turned sharply to one side, which had her gripping the front of the bench closest to the wall. Her other hand couldn't take purchase on the other side of her thighs given the position of Mr. Banks' thighs, though, and she was nearly dislodged from her seat.

One of the valet's arms was around her waist in an instant, pulling her hard against the side of his body. "Are you hurt, my lady?" he asked as he looked over to be sure she was still seated.

Alice inhaled sharply, quite sure she was about to end up atop the foot warmer. She turned her head to regard the valet, not about to chide him for holding her so. Not when his arm provided so much warmth. Not when she inhaled the pleasant scent of Bay Rum and wool. Not when just a moment before she was thinking of kissing the man. "I am quite fine, thanks to you," she murmured. She might have continued to gaze at Banks, but the coach rocked again and then moved backward a bit before coming to a sudden halt.

Banks glanced out the window nearest him. "Although, Mr. Haversham has managed to get the team turning, it seems at least one of the horses is giving him some trouble."

Following his line of sight, Alice understood the valet's meaning. The lead horse on the left stomped in protest, his head tossing. A whinny accompanied another series of head tosses before Banks inhaled sharply. "I beg your pardon," he said as he let go his hold on her and suddenly left the coach.

The blast of cold air and loss of the valet's warmth had Alice wrapping her redingote more tightly around her body. She watched through clouds of white breath as Banks joined the driver and groom in helping to calm the lead horses. The other two horses had grown restless as well, their heads nodding about, their nostrils flaring at their lack of movement.

Within moments of his departure from the coach, Banks

seemed to have the lead horse settled, one gloved hand stroking the horse's neck as he spoke softly. Meanwhile, Higgins, the groom, had hold of the other. Haversham repositioned himself and then led the team forward and at an angle while the groom returned to his seat to take the reins. The coach swayed, but Alice was ready, her gloved hands clinging to the bench and to the strap above the door. In only a few minutes, the team was turned and ready to head south. She heard a few shouts—*and was that laughter?*—before the coached pitched a bit as the driver climbed up to his seat. Banks opened the coach door and poked his head in. "I fear I am covered in snow. I dare not..."

"Oh, do come in from the cold, Mr. Banks. I've a linen in my bag. We'll have you free of your snow coat in only a moment," Alice insisted, rather startled at just how covered in snow the man was given the short amount of time he was outside.

Her words coming as a surprise to the valet, he removed his top hat and tapped it against the outside of the coach. A flurry of snow from the thin brim quickly dissipated. "Well, if you insist, my lady." He made his way back into the coach, but took the seat opposite after giving his cape coat a quick swipe with a gloved hand.

Meanwhile, Alice fished the linen from her bag and began brushing off his cape coat, the flakes of snow sizzling as they hit hot coals in the foot warmer. "I didn't realize it was snowing so much," she remarked, daring a glance out the window to her right.

"Oh, it's not," Banks replied with a shake of his head. Snow from his short hair scattered about the interior, quickly melting into tiny puddles. "However, Mr. Haversham is a dead shot with a snowball," he added, a grin splitting his face.

Alice inhaled, shocked the driver would have indulged in play at a time like this. "The cur!"

"Oh, I returned the favor, I assure you," Banks replied quickly, his grin turning into a mischievous smile.

A jolt of something quite pleasant had Alice inhaling sharply. She had always thought Alonyius Banks a rather handsome man, but when he smiled, as he was doing this very instant, he was quite possibly the most handsome man in all of England.

But what did she know of all the men in England? She had lived in London her entire life and had only visited a few of the larger towns, like Bath and Brighton, when her mistress traveled on holidays. Still, she couldn't imagine there existed another man whose sky blue eyes lit up with such mirth, whose delight was so well displayed in the lines that radiated from the corners of his eyes and from around his mouth. A slight dimple even appeared in one cheek.

And if she didn't stop staring at him and close her mouth immediately, she was quite sure he would think her a candidate for Bedlam.

Resuming the task of brushing the snow from his coat, she pretended to look for more snow when he gave her a nod. "Much obliged. I should have known you would come prepared." He pulled the gloves from his hands and reached for the poker. "But I fear we'll both be inconvenienced by that bit of fun."

Why he had felt compelled to engage in a snowball fight with the driver, Banks had no idea. It had been years since he had last thrown a snowball. That had been in Darlington during one of the rare years in which there was enough snow to make snowballs. He and his brother, Thelonius, had played until they were both soaking wet, their mother admonishing them for their behavior before seeing to it they were both served a steaming cup of chocolate and wrapped in wool blankets.

Blankets that had been made at the family's textile mill.

The memory struck him so suddenly, he gave a start and then wondered how long he had been daydreaming. He dared a glance at Alice, noticing how her attention seemed directed to the wet linen as she folded it once and then seemed at a loss as to what to do with it. If he wasn't careful, Simpkins would think him a candidate for Bedlam.

"Allow me," he said as he reached for the linen and then draped it over the bench next to him. He opened the foot warmer and stirred the coals, a few of the lumps glowing bright red for a moment. The coach began to move, its pace increasing until they were once again moving at a decent clip. "I seemed to have let all the warm air out of the coach."

About to deny his claim—Alice felt far warmer than she had all morning—she merely shook her head. "It's already as warm in here as it was before you took your leave," she murmured.

His manner more sober, Banks regarded Alice for a moment. "Remind me again of how long you have you been in service to Lady Torrington."

Blinking at the statement—for a moment he had seemed lost in thought, although he still displayed an expression that suggested his thoughts were at least pleasant—Alice allowed a shrug. "Nineteen... nearly twenty years, I suppose. And you?"

Banks frowned before allowing a 'humph'. "One-and-twenty years," he replied. "I served as a valet for his lordship's father for two years before that."

Alice considered this bit of information for a moment. "Do you... enjoy working in service?"

Inhaling slowly, Banks gave the question a good deal of thought before finally allowing a shrug. "'Enjoy' may not be the appropriate word. I am honored to serve an earl. I am thankful my master is a man of means and not the least bit proud. He is fair and obliging should I require time off. So, let us say I am glad of the employment." He paused a moment before angling his head to one side. "Your question compels me to ask it of you. Do you enjoy working in service?" He had already decided she would be lying if she claimed she did. Everyone who worked at Worthington House had heard her complaining about one thing or another. No one who put voice to complaints as she did could possibly be enjoying their time in service.

Alice sighed. She should have expected the question, although it was still a surprise to hear it asked out loud. "I used to. Very much," she replied with a nod.

Banks furrowed his brows. "But now...?"

"I do not," she admitted, her eyes brightening with tears. She seemed to have trouble catching her breath before she settled herself. "I don't know why, though," she whispered, staring at one of the glowing embers in the foot warmer. "The smallest annoyances seem far larger than they should. I find I am impatient when I used to be a paragon of patience. Lady Torrington is a very good mistress. She is never cross with me. I don't... I don't understand why I find reasons to complain when there are none." She raised her eyes to find Banks regarding her with a look suggesting he was truly concerned.

And suddenly convinced his master had guessed right. Alice Simpkins needed a man in her life. *A good lay,* he remembered Lord Torrington saying that morning when they discussed this trip. Back when he believed the maid to be married based on how the woman was addressed during the servants' evening meal.

The two weren't exactly the same thing, but he supposed the earl had the gist of it.

"Perhaps you are simply in need of a diversion," Banks finally replied. "An evening out at Vauxhall Gardens or the theatre," he suggested. He wasn't about to suggest the earl's suggestion. Why, the poor woman would probably be so offended, she would take her leave of the traveling coach and freeze to death in an effort to get as far away from him as possible.

Or would she?

He was about to suggest she take a lover when Alice suddenly brightened. "I haven't been to the theatre in an age! And I do so love to visit the museum. To see the marbles."

Banks blinked, stunned by how beautiful she appeared when she smiled. Her green eyes—how long had it taken him to determine their color?—were suddenly filled with mischief, the crinkles on either side of their corners a testament to her maturity. Color suffused her cheeks while a dimple dented the left one, youthening her oval face.

How had he not noticed before?

"Perhaps I can escort you on your next day off," he suggested. "I've been just the one time, but I never tire of looking at beautiful things."

Alice managed to stifle the urge to inhale sharply at his words. At how he had said them. As if he found her beautiful. "I would like that very much, Mr. Banks."

The valet nodded and dared a glance out the window. The trip to *The Black Swan* wouldn't take quite as long as their attempt to leave *The George*.

Lost in thought for some time—he was thinking of the exhibits at the museum in between thoughts of the lady's maid's radiant face—he was about to suggest they get some rest when he realized Simpkins had already dozed off. A slight grin had her looking almost angelic as her head rested in the squabs. Deciding he, too, would get some sleep, Banks closed his eyes and imagined what he might do to the woman should she ever agree to warm his bed.

Chapter 8

A MAN'S HUNTING LODGE IS
HIS CASTLE

*D*ecember 21, 1816, rather late in the afternoon
"I thought you said Torrington Park looked like a castle," Adele murmured as the top of a building came into view. The slate tiles making up the roof didn't give it the appearance of a crenelated castle. And as the coach climbed the slight incline a bit more and the building beneath the roof was revealed, it was even more evident it wasn't a castle.

"Och, that's not Torrington Park," Milton replied with a shake of his head. "That's the stables and carriage house." He leaned over to the other curtained window and glanced out, wincing when he realized it had started snowing again. He rather hoped the weather would improve as they made their way north, and although there was less of it, snow blanketed the area around this end of Hadrian's Wall. He raised a finger and pointed in the opposite direction. "That's Torrington Park."

Adele slid over to the other side of the coach and peered out the window, her eyes widening as she did so. "It's a *castle*," she murmured in awe.

"A money pit, is more like it," her husband replied with a sigh. "My six-times-over great-grandfather was sure there was treasure buried there, but by the time he'd employed every able-bodied man in Northumbria to dig for it, he had spent a fortune and had a huge hole to show for it."

"I take it that's how the moat came to be?" Adele guessed.

"Indeed. But it's been a hunting lodge to the earls since the fifteen-hundreds. Notice the lack of crenelations."

Furrowing her brows, she studied the tops of the turrets and the walls. The rectangular cut-outs that would have allowed archers to defend the structure were missing. "Why isn't it crenelated?"

Milton shrugged at first, but then allowed a sigh before he whispered, "The Torrington who built it never got permission from the Crown. Can't build a crenelated castle unless you have the king's permission," he reminded her.

The countess was about to ask if the Torringtons had been part of the uprising against Queen Elizabeth I—she was fairly sure the lodge had been built before that time—but realized the question might be a sore point. Instead she turned her attention back to her husband and angled her head. "So who is the mistress of such an interesting example of a hunting lodge?" She glanced back toward the structure and silently counted the number of turrets and wondered if the moat was wet or dry.

Milton grinned. "Why, *you* are, of course," he replied. At her look of surprise, he gave a shrug. "My cousin might stay there on occasion, but his wife doesn't want anything to do with the place. And Mum's been gone..." He paused, realizing his mother had been dead for ten years.

Where did the time go?

"I'll do my best to make you proud," Adele murmured as she leaned over to take one of his hands in hers. "But if there are animal heads mounted on every wall inside, I may have to ask you to find a different mistress for it," she teased.

Swallowing hard, Milton figured it probably wasn't the best time to admit that, indeed, there were a number of animal heads. It was a hunting lodge, after all. But at least the trophies were only found on the walls of the great hall.

His mother had seen to that bit of redecorating. Now

that he had just learned exactly how Adele felt about animal heads, he wondered if she would be seeing to another round of changes at the lodge.

"I'll introduce you to the servants, and then we can get settled in our rooms up on the first floor," he said as the coach turned onto the cobblestone drive that led to the gate. There was no arched opening nor the courtyard typical of most castles. Just a set of double doors with the barest hint of a portico to prevent snow from collecting in front of them.

On either side of the drive, the ground sloped away into a dry moat, but a thin strip of land remained around the base of the castle on which a number of evergreen trees were planted at even intervals. Adele wondered if flowers encircled the estate and was about to ask when Milton said, "In the spring, the yellow tulips bloom all the way around the base. There's a few red ones, too, so from far away, it looks like the lodge is sitting in a ring of fire."

Adele's eyes widened at the image his words created. "What about in the summer?"

Milton's face took on an expression of disgust. "My mother planted rhododendrons. Pink ones. All the way around the other three walls, too."

Grinning at the thought of a hunting lodge surrounded with green foliage festooned with pink blooms, Adele couldn't help the giggle that escaped. "Surely by hunting season the flowers would be done."

"Och, no. That's when all the *mums* are in bloom," he countered. At least they were orange. "Haven't been here in the autumn for several years, so I'm not sure what colors the castle gardens feature. But the moat in the back attracts the geese."

"The moat is filled then?"

Milton frowned before he dared a glance out the coach window. They were already outside the main entrance. "The one in the front is usually dry, but the one in the back stays filled," he explained.

"Two moats?" Adele replied, not familiar with a castle that could claim both kinds.

"There's a wall of earth that separates the two on either side," he explained. "It's rare, true, but it means we can swim in the summer and go sledding in the winter."

Adele frowned. "However do you get back up after you've ridden a sled down into the moat?" From her vantage, the sides of the dry moat seemed almost vertical.

"The ends of the dry moat aren't so steep, and a footman would tie a rope around a post so we'd have something to hang onto as we made our way up," her husband explained. "You've not lived until you've tried sledding in the moat." He suddenly sobered, a memory causing him to blink. "Do you remember the first time your brother and I took you sledding in Kent?"

Adele furrowed a brow, but the memory of the sunny winter afternoon she had tagged along behind William as he and Milton had made their way to the top of a hill came back to her in a flash. The two had brought along wooden sleds on which metal runners had been attached. Riding the sleds on their fronts, heads lifted up, the two boys had sailed down the snow-slick hill and laughed as they came to a halt.

Trudging back up to the top of the hill, they found Adele wearing an expression of fear—she couldn't have been more than six or seven at the time—and yet she bravely sat down on William's sled. The boys gave her a good push to her back, which had her screaming at the top of her lungs as she descended the steep incline. Once the sled came to a rest, she didn't get up from the sled, but from the way her shoulders shook, it must have looked as if she were crying. A moment later, Milton hurried down the hill on his sled to join her.

"I was sure you were crying. I don't think I've ever sledded so fast to get down that hill," Milton murmured. "I felt terribly guilty. And then I reached you, I heard you giggling."

Adele allowed a grin. "I remember I was frightened, but it was a thrilling ride. I think I was giggling because I had gone farther than either one of you," she recalled in a quiet voice.

"I loved the sound of your giggle." Milton sighed. "I might have fallen in love with you then."

Her eyes widening in disbelief, Adele nearly snorted. "What were you then? Twelve?"

Milton swallowed, the reminder of their age difference a sobering thought. "More like fourteen," he replied. He suddenly brightened. "I think I would be up for a slide down the moat. Just have to find a sled. There must be one around here somewhere."

Wondering if the earl was daring her to do such a thing, Adele merely shook her head. "I do believe I shall find my excitement between the pages of a book," she murmured. "But I do appreciate the reminder that I once did such a thing."

And giggled about it. Could he really have had feelings for me back then?

The coach came to a halt on the cobbles outside the front doors, the shadows long as the driver opened the door and stepped aside. Adele allowed him to assist her down as she struggled to regain the use of her legs. Right behind her, Milton gave the lodge a quick glance. A bit stunned that no one appeared to greet them, the earl allowed a sigh of relief when one of the large front doors opened and a butler appeared and bowed.

"Ah, Trasker. I feared there might be a problem," Milton said as he hurried to join the servant.

The butler straightened at the suggestion he might not be on duty. "Welcome, Lord Torrington. Your rooms have been readied. A footman will be seeing to your trunks right away." He dared a glance beyond the coach, suddenly frowning.

"The servants' coach should arrive the day after tomorrow," Milton said *sotto voce*, one eyebrow rising in an attempt to make the butler understand he wasn't to say anything more about it. Adele was only a few feet away, and he didn't want her knowing about the planned delay until he had to tell her.

Probably when he would be forced to help her dress for dinner.

Trasker nodded his understanding. "Very good, my lord. Cook has dinner in hand for this evening. Does eight o'clock still suit?"

"Indeed. Anything I need to know before I introduce my countess to the staff?"

Angling his head to one side, the butler finally shook it. "Mr. Banks was quite clear on the matter in his last letter. They are ready for review."

Milton allowed a sigh of relief. He should have known that in lining up the accommodations for their trip, Banks would contact Trasker to let him know about their impending visit.

A flurry of activity seemed to occur just beyond the large doors before the butler raised his head a fraction.

Milton placed one of Adele's hands on his arm and gave her a wink. "Prepare to meet the staff of Torrington Park," he said with a good deal of pride. "This is Trasker. He's been the butler here for at least twenty years."

Trasker afforded the countess a deep bow before he opened the door. "Good afternoon, my lady." Once inside, he stepped aside to reveal a line of eight servants, all facing the same direction and apparently dressed in livery. Apparently, because not all of their clothing matched. In fact, only three maids wore the same black gowns with white aprons. The two footmen, one very tall and the other quite short, both wore dark breeches and black waistcoats over shirts, but neither seemed to match. The housekeeper wore a simple day gown of blue muslin, and the last servant, apparently the cook, wore a clean apron over a brown muslin gown.

Milton thought perhaps a few were missing from the line-up. Like several more kitchen maids, a few footmen, and a groom or two.

"Lady Torrington, may I introduce you to your staff?"

Adele glanced over at Trasker and back at the line of servants. "Is this all of them?" she asked in a quiet voice, her query meant only for the butler.

Trasker dipped his head a bit. "There are others, but the grooms are seeing to the horses and coach, two footmen are seeing to your trunks, and the kitchen maids are... preparing dinner, I believe."

Adele allowed a sigh of relief. "Then proceed, Mr. Trasker."

Over the next few minutes, Adele stepped before each servant and learned their name and responsibility. Each one afforded her a bow or a curtsy and seemed ever so nervous as they did so. Goodness! *What had Banks written in his letter?* Milton wondered when they finally finished the introductions.

A maid stepped forward and gave another curtsy. When Adele acknowledged her—she remembered her as the first floor housemaid—she said, "I can see you to the mistress suite, milady."

"I was hoping for a tour of Torrington Park," Adele replied, giving her husband a beseeching look.

Milton blinked, realizing he had misjudged what might happen when they arrived. He was sure Adele would want to see her bedchamber. "I'll show the countess around and then escort her to her room," he said as he gave the maid a nod. He almost felt sorry for how the maid's face fell, as if she had been practicing what to do and thought she had lost her chance to win over the countess.

"Of course, my lord," the maid replied with a curtsy. She stepped back into line.

"You'll find I'm not one to order servants about," Adele stated suddenly. "You all know your responsibilities, and my presence here shouldn't change how you go about your duties." She turned to Milton and gave him a nod.

The earl felt as if he were being dismissed, even though he knew he still had to give her a tour of the lodge. "You're excused," he said to the line-up of servants. They all gave bows and curtsies and hurried off through the same door at the back of the great hall.

Given it was her first opportunity to study the large hall in which she stood, Adele suddenly gave a start as she glanced up. Animal heads were mounted above and around the entire circumference of the plank-floored room. A rather large stone fireplace opposite the door held a fire, but its size dwarfed the bit of flame that hissed and crackled in its opening. An ancient trestle flanked by benches was the only furnishing, although it looked as if at least sixteen people could be comfortably seated there.

"Please tell me—"

"It's the only room like it in the entire lodge," Milton stated, patting the hand that was still resting on his arm.

Adele let out a quick breath. "Thank the gods." She deliberately avoided looking at any of the heads she was sure were staring at her as Milton quickly led her to an arched opening opposite from where the servants had disappeared. Next to it was a set of wide stairs.

"This is the east hall," he said as they made their way down the long hall adjacent to the stairs. Only a few doors interrupted the stone hallway. "I expect you'll be spending a good deal of time in here," he said as he opened the arched wooden door into the library. Although the fire wasn't lit in this room, it was surprisingly warm. Several upholstered chairs were arranged around the single fireplace, and a low table was positioned in front of a settee. "My mum used to like to take tea in here," he added, a pang in his chest suddenly taking his breath away.

"It's rather cozy," Adele said as she admired the wall of books and the room's only window. It looked out on what appeared to be a courtyard.

"In the summer, there's a garden out there," Milton said in a quiet voice. "But I haven't seen it in years."

Adele wondered at the remark. "When was the last time you were at Torrington Park in the summer?"

Milton blinked. Had it truly been before his mother had died? "Ten years, at least," he murmured.

Stunned at this bit of news, Adele sighed. "We shall have to pay a visit when it isn't snowing," she whispered.

Turning toward her, a look of surprise on his face, her husband said, "You would be willing to make this trip again?"

Frowning at the implication she hadn't enjoyed the trip in the snow, Adele leaned in and kissed her husband on his cheek. "Why ever not?" she replied with an arched eyebrow.

Milton allowed a sigh of relief. Would she feel the same when she discovered the upper servants wouldn't be joining them for another two days? He almost regretted ordering the driver to see to it they were stranded in Darlington for two days.

Almost.

He had to hope Banks was keeping Simpkins occupied.

In more ways than one.

"Because it's a long way, and although the staff will see to our comfort, it's not London," he replied with a shake of his head.

Adele allowed a smile. "Which is exactly why I agreed to make the trip."

Her husband closed his eyes and said a prayer of thanks. "I've a mind to make love to you this very minute," he said in a hoarse whisper.

Glancing about the library, Adele wondered just where they might do such a thing.

"I wasn't thinking in here," Milton added with a shake of his head. "The bed in the master bedchamber is rather large," he offered.

"Then why did you bring me here?" she countered, a grin defying her words.

Milton blinked. "You minx," he accused. He had her out of the library and climbing the nearest stone stairs before she could form a reply. But just as they reached the door to his bedchamber on the first floor, the rather tall footman appeared with a trunk and asked where it should go.

Adele's eyes widened when she realized she had no other clothes but the carriage gowns that could be found in the trunk the footman carried. All her other trunks were on the servant's coach. "The mistress suite," she replied. "The valises from inside the coach can be taken there as well," she added. She was about to ask her husband if he had dinner clothes in the event the servants' coach didn't arrive there in time to change for dinner, but he was already leading her into the giant master suite.

A moment later, clothes were forgotten as the earl had his countess stripped and giggling on his bed.

He loved the sound of her giggle.

Chapter 9

A BATH AT THE INN

*M*eanwhile, back in Darlington

Pulling back the counterpane and bed linens, Alice felt a bit of relief in noting how the linens had been changed since the last occupants had taken their leave. There wasn't any sign of vermin, either, which meant Mr. Banks had done some research prior to this trip. Tonight's stay at this particular inn was entirely unexpected, and yet he had known where to have Haversham take them for accommodations.

Perhaps he had intended they stay at *The Black Swan* if rooms weren't available at *The George*. Given how clean the other four coaching inns had been, Banks was proving as fastidious in his arrangements for this trip as he did when he performed his duties at Worthington House.

Daring a glance at the dying fire, Alice wondered if she should wear a mob cap and then thought better of it. Her hair, well past shoulder-length, was nearly dry, and although she had given some thought to braiding it, she instead left it loose. Except for one stubborn lock in the very front, her hair seemed to curl under at the end of each strand. If she cut the front the way she'd seen it done in one of her mistress' issues of *La Belle Assemblie*, she would look positively modern.

What I am thinking? she chastised herself. The only

reason she thought to leave her hair unbraided was so that she could appear younger. More attractive.

Never in here life had she considered such a thing. She'd never worn cosmetics, or used henna to redden her dark tresses, or styled her hair in anything other than a severe bun atop her head.

Well, it was time for a change, she decided. Spending entire days in Alonyius Banks' company was obviously having an effect on her, but she hadn't yet decided if it was a good effect.

Especially since she had agreed to share her room with him.

He had gone down to the taproom, apparently to allow her time to get ready for bed and into it. She supposed she should be glad he wasn't in the room when she had to doff the bath linens and pull on her night rail. It was bad enough he had seen so much of her whilst she took a bath!

The memory of how his hands had held her head, of how he had taken such care in washing and rinsing her hair, prompted a frisson that seemed to pass through her entire body.

How had that even happened? she wondered, quite sure she hadn't lingered too long in the bath. But with the copper tub—a copper tub!—set so close to the fire, it actually rested on the hot bricks. As a result, the water had stayed warm. Was probably still warm, she considered, daring a glance at the tub. At least there had been a few bubbles floating atop the water, although she couldn't remember if there was enough to hide most of her from the valet's intent gaze.

How long had he been standing next to the tub before she opened her eyes? Before she sensed she was no longer alone? With the usual sounds of a coaching inn muffled due to the snow outside and the large rug on the room's wooden floor, she hadn't heard him come in. He would have had to use his key to gain entry. Had she slept that soundly?

Apparently.

But then, to slowly awaken and find Mr. Banks regarding

her with an arched brow—and was that appreciation?—well, at least she hadn't screamed. She hadn't even let out a sound of protest, or reacted in a manner that would have flooded the room with bath water, or sent a cascade of water onto his breeches in one particular location.

She had simply returned his gaze, mentally assuring herself that even if her bent knees were on full display, her rather flat breasts were below the edge of the water.

"I'll be done in a moment if you'd like to use the tub," she said, her voice surprisingly calm. "I was just about to wash my hair."

Banks crossed his arms and angled his head to one side. "I rather imagine the water has cooled a bit too much for my liking," he countered, almost as if he were scolding her. He probably thought she had been sound asleep.

Perhaps I was.

Alice dropped her head back and gave it a quick shake. "Not at all," she whispered. "The bricks beneath are rather warm."

She hadn't intended her words to come out so breathy, or for her mention of washing her hair to be some kind of invitation for him to make his way behind her, pull the room's only chair from the small writing desk, and actually wash her hair.

But he had.

Crossing her arms over her chest, Alice straightened in the tub and turned a bit. "What do you think you're doing?"

The mischief in his sky blue eyes was unmistakeable as he dipped a finger into the water, just behind her back. With just the slight movement of his finger in the water, Alice thought the temperature had suddenly risen to match that of the waters in Bath.

Rather surprised at the warmth of the water, Banks gave an expression of satisfaction. "I'm going to wash your hair. With any luck, the water will still be warm enough for me to take a bath." He had an odd thought that he should simply climb into the tub with her, but he rather doubted there would be room enough for the both of them, and he didn't want her to flood the floor should she react as he expected she might.

"Have you done it before?"

Banks blinked as he regarded the maid. "Washed hair? Of course," he replied with a shrug, glancing about for what she might use to wash her hair. What appeared to be a rather special ball of soap was perched on the bottom of one of the overturned water pails. He reached for it and hefted it in his palm, a slight citrus scent wafting in his direction as he did so. He brought it to his nose and took a sniff, nearly grinning when he realized Alice was watching his every move.

Was she scandalized by his claim he had washed hair before? He hadn't actually washed a woman's hair before, but he had certainly washed the earl's hair. Nearly every week for the entire time he had been in the man's service.

Or was she merely intrigued by the claim?

"Dip your head back as far as you can," he said, his tone no different from one he would use to order about a lowly servant.

Alice slowly turned away from him before scrunching her body tighter against her bent knees. Moving forward a bit so there was enough space behind her to drop her hair below the water, Alice realized almost immediately she wouldn't be able to keep her arms crossed over her chest. She would have to hang onto the tub's sides or risk falling completely into the water.

Well, given most of the bubbles were gone, he had probably already seen most of her through the mostly clear water. She gripped the tub's edges and slowly lowered her head, arching her neck back until only her face remained above the water's edge. For that moment when her head was nearly submerged, she was well aware of two things.

Make that three.

Both of her breasts were entirely out of the water, and Alonyius Banks glanced in their direction. Not just glanced at them, though. He stared at them. Ogled them, as if he had never seen a pair of naked breasts before in his entire life.

Alice supposed she could have feigned a bit of annoyance. Or put voice to a request that he look away, or at least pretend he wasn't leering at her.

But she found she couldn't.

She wasn't exactly a well-endowed woman, after all. While most women of her age could boast of breasts the size of small apples or peaches, she could not. It took an extra tug of her corset just to gain a hint of a décolletage, and that at the expense of being able to breathe.

Another thought struck her just then.

Perhaps the valet had never seen breasts as flat or as small as hers. Perhaps he was appalled at her lack of the feminine charms so many seemed to covet. Perhaps he...

Thoughts of what Banks might be thinking flew from her head when one of his hands reached beneath her head and lifted it from the water. He didn't let go, though, as he used the other to draw the ball of soap over her hair.

"You can relax. I've got you," he murmured, his voice sounding a bit strangled.

Her eyes widened as she watched the upside down version of him from her vantage. His attention was completely on her hair as his free hand worked the soap into her hair, his fingers gently massaging the bit of lather into her scalp.

Two things were suddenly evident.

Make that three.

Up close, Alonyius Banks was a very handsome man. Even upside down.

Sky blue eyes were rather dark by the light of a fire. Sapphire, almost.

Having one's hair washed by the hands of a man was an entirely new experience. A rather erotic experience.

Could he be compelled to do it every week? she wondered. *How much might he charge for the service?* A rather naughty thought as to how she might compensate him had her suddenly blushing.

Suppressing the urge to gasp at what she had just imagined, Alice was about to make an attempt at conversation when the hand holding her head suddenly dropped back into the water. She managed to close her eyes and inhale sharply, thinking he would dunk her entire head beneath the water. But the level of water never reached beyond the sides of her face as his fingers speared her hair and worked their way through the soapy strands. After a moment, he switched hands, using the fingers of the other to separate and slide through her suds-slick hair until the soap had mostly dissipated.

"Close your eyes," he murmured, just before he hefted one of the water pitchers and poured the last of the warm water over her hair.

Alice would have sighed her contentment, but for the water that sluiced from her hair and down the front of her face. When she finished wiping the water away from her eyes, she opened them to find Banks holding a bath linen while another was draped over one arm.

"I suppose this is your way of suggesting I remove myself from this tub," Alice murmured, a bit of a pout forcing her lower lip beyond the upper.

"Actually, it's far more than a suggestion, my lady. If you take a look at the ends of your fingers, you will find them..."

Alice let out a cry of shock. The pads of every finger displayed wrinkles! Never before had her fingers taken on the look of a piece of dried fruit! Her ladyship's had, on occasion, but only when she insisted on staying in the bath in order to finish reading a chapter in one of her books.

Alice took the linen from the valet, careful to keep it out of the water as one of her wrinkled fingers twirled in the air. "Do be a gentleman and turn around," she insisted when Banks made no move to do so. She couldn't help but notice that the other bath linen was suddenly in front of his body, still hanging from his arm.

Almost as if he were hiding something.

Alice stilled her movements when she realized just what the valet was hiding.

At least he was entirely clothed.

She was sure her entire body had turned a pinkish red, and it wasn't because of the hot water from the bath.

About to put voice to a protest—hadn't he already seen just about all of Alice Simpkins?—the valet did her bidding and turned so he faced the bed.

The only bed in the room.

"I need to take my leave of you for a time," Alonyius said suddenly, holding out the linen behind him so Alice could reach for it. Having wrapped her body in the first one, she went about securing her hair in the second one.

"But, why?" she asked, afraid she might have offended the man.

"I wish to give you some time for your evening toilette. I shan't be long. Just enough time for a pint of ale with the proprietor," he said, his attention still directed towards the bed. "To settle the bill and be sure we may keep the rooms should we be unable to leave on the morrow. Lock the door behind me, and do not open it for anyone but me. Do you understand?"

Confused by the change in the valet's manner, Alice finally said, "I understand. I shan't take long, though, I promise." She noted his quick nod and the manner in which he left the room.

And what he left behind.

The man's topcoat was draped over the back of the chair. Of course, he had taken it off to wash her hair. He had even rolled up his shirt sleeves—and left the room with them rolled up! Had she ever seen the valet without his top coat? She couldn't remember ever having done so.

A bit dismayed by his sudden change in behavior, Alice quickly toweled off the remaining water droplets from her skin. Shivering from the sudden chill in the room, she quickly pulled on her night rail before trying to dry her hair with the linen.

The thought of how attractive—or not—she was to Alonyius Banks prompted her next move.

Pulling her valise from beneath the bedstead, she located a comb and found the small pair of embroidery scissors in her sewing kit. Moving to the shaving mirror above the room's only pitcher and bowl, she took a deep breath and went to work. Long strands of dark hair drifted into the shaving bowl. Soon, shorter ones joined the longer strands as she evened out the long bangs left in front. When she was satisfied, she stepped back to regard her image in the looking glass, a grin forming when she decided she liked what she saw.

Returning the utensils to her valise, she dared a glance toward the door. The memory of Banks entering while she was still in the copper tub had a shiver racing through her body. Although she had felt embarrassment from the top of her head to the tips of her toes, she was quite sure she saw his eyes darken as he stared down at her. He didn't even turn around, or beg forgiveness, or behave as if his presence was the least bit scandalous. He merely balanced the linens he carried in one hand as he stood watching her.

And so she hadn't reacted. Oh, she had made sure her breasts were beneath the top of the water but her bare knees had breached the water's surface. She straightened her legs enough so they settled just below the surface.

I rather imagine the water has cooled a bit too much for my liking, he had stated as he regarded her. The fact that the tub was also near the fire had her thinking the water was suddenly boiling hot.

Not at all. The bricks beneath are rather warm, she had replied with a nod. She had almost—almost—asked if he wished to join her, but she knew there really wasn't enough room in the tub for the both of them. Even if they sat at the same end, her body in front of his, she rather doubted there would be enough room.

Now, she would never know for sure.

The thought that the weather wouldn't clear and that they might be stuck at *The Black Swan* another night had her breasts swelling, the space between her thighs throbbing in anticipation. Banks wouldn't have to say a word. She would probably be the one to propose they use the time to frolic on the entirely-too-small bed.

Alice rolled her eyes, almost unable to believe what she was imagining for her and the valet. She felt positively wanton.

She had no idea if the valet's arrangements for the room were truly as he described, but she had agreed because... well, what else could she do? She supposed if she had put voice to a protest, Banks might have moved to the inn's parlor or practiced a bit of chivalry and attempted to share the other, smaller room with Haversham and Higgins. *He could have put me in that room,* she thought, a bit of a thrill passing through her when she remembered what he had said.

It's hardly appropriate for a woman, Miss Simpkins, he had said, as if it was the room used for tumbles with the tavern maids.

Perhaps it was.

Besides, I would fear for your safety. You may take the bed, and I shall sleep in the chair.

You'll do no such thing, she had replied in a hoarse whisper. That was before she had seen the size of the bed.

Or rather, its lack of size.

The two of them would barely fit side-by-side! And the thought of that arrangement had her entire body feeling far warmer than it should given how chilly the room was getting now that the fire was dying. At least there were some lumps of coal in a bin. She added a few to the fire, wiped off the coal dust from her hands, and folded the used linens.

Settling into the bed, Alice dared a glance at the door and wondered how long it would be before the valet joined her.

Chapter 10

THE SERVANTS ARE MISSING

*L*ater that evening

"Where do you suppose they are?" Adele wondered for at least the tenth time since she and the earl had arrived at Torrington Park. Although Davids, their driver, admitted to a bit of trouble in negotiating the snow-covered road, he had the coach-and-four arriving in the late afternoon. The servants' coach—the coach that held their valet and maid as well as their trunks—was to leave a bit later, if only because one of Adele's trunks still hadn't been loaded by the porter when they departed *The George.*

Glancing out the same window Adele stood in front of, Milton allowed a sigh. "I told Haversham to get to the nearest coaching inn if he had the least bit of trouble. His coach is far heavier than the one we rode in," he reminded her.

"And if they got stuck?" Adele's voice was filled with worry.

"Now, now. There's no need to fash yourself. They won't get stuck, and even if they do... " The earl paused, not having given that possibility a thought. There was that fairly deep snow drift just outside of Darlington. "My valet is a clever man, and Haversham has been a driver for me for years. He knows the way, as does Higgins, for that matter. Banks knows all the coaching inns. Higgins is a crack shot, so I rather doubt a highwayman will give them trouble. They're fine, my sweeting."

He hoped his voice sounded more sure than he was. Truth be told, he was a bit more worried than he had been before Adele put voice to her concern. Perhaps he shouldn't have ordered Haversham to see to it they spent an extra day or two in Darlington. But just to make sure the valet had the time to visit his family, he had given Haversham a sovereign and told him to be sure they stayed in the town at least two nights.

Besides, the extra days would allow a few more horses and lighter coaches to pack down the snow. The mail coach from Edinburgh would also help establish a track they could follow. Until then, it would be nearly impossible to get a heavier coach through.

In the meantime, he and Adele would manage without the servants. He knew he could.

He merely had to convince his countess she could, too.

Chapter 11

A VISIT TO THE TAPROOM

eanwhile, back at The Black Swan
Alonyius Banks closed the door to his and
Simpkins' room and leaned against it, taking a deep breath
and then wishing he hadn't as the odor of stale cheroot
smoke and ale filled his nostrils. He couldn't go back into the
room, though. Not yet. Not when his cock was still throbbing, and the hot blood of arousal coursed through his veins.

Although he had thought to simply share the room with
Simpkins and maybe enjoy a tumble or two, he hadn't
expected to *like* the woman so much. Her character was so
different from how she behaved back at Worthington House!
She was nothing like the lady's maid everyone complained
about because she complained too much. Why, even his
interrupting her bath hadn't brought out a peep of protest
from the woman!

But that wasn't the worst of it. She wasn't at all what he
expected beneath her livery. She was a lithe creature with
beautiful knees and silken hair and breasts he'd give anything
to suckle. Just the thought of her budded nipples as they
surfaced from beneath the bath water had his manhood
straining against the placket of his breeches.

Banks rolled his eyes, realizing he was only making the
situation worse by replaying the events of the past half-hour

in his mind's eye. Better he go downstairs to the public room. Or better yet, to the taproom. Spend time with the other bawdy men trapped in Darlington by the snowy conditions. Down a pint or two and see if he couldn't forget what he had seen. See if his cock could forget what he had seen.

Pushing away from the door, he made his way down the short hall to the stairs, the din from below increasing in volume as he negotiated the tight stairwell. When he reached the bottom, he found the public room almost empty, but the taproom was filled to bursting with local laborers and intrepid travelers.

A half-filled pint in one beefy hand, Haversham waved him over to where he sat at a trestle. Two bored tavern maids flanked him, although their expressions brightened at the sight of the valet. "Kicked you out, did she?" the driver asked before taking a swig of the bitter ale.

Frowning at the odd comment, Banks took a moment to realize the driver was referring to Simpkins. "Is that what happened to you?" he countered, remembering the groom's comment about finding a whore to help warm his bed. There was no sign of Higgins in the taproom. From the way one of the tavern maids had hooked an arm into Haversham's, Alonyius thought she might be joining the driver in his room once Higgins was done with what was probably going to be a quick tumble.

Haversham angled his head. "Merely waiting my turn. Cold nights mean there's not enough tail to go 'round, if you catch my meaning."

The two tavern maids both gave expressions of disbelief and then broke out into a fit of giggles.

Not having thought about engaging a lady of the evening —he hadn't been in the company of a prostitute since before he was employed as a valet—Banks was once again reminded of why he had left his room. He wondered how many prostitutes might ply their trade at the coaching inn, and then, upon studying the collection of unwashed bodies in the crowded taproom, he quickly dismissed the idea of hiring a lady of the evening for a quick tumble.

Acquiring a venereal disease was the very last thing he planned to do on this trip.

Besides, there was a rather delectable creature up in his room this very moment. And she was newly bathed and smelled of citrus. His cock certainly remembered even if he was trying to forget. "Are all these men waiting for a bit of tail?" Banks asked in a lowered voice, his query directed to the driver alone.

Haversham shrugged, his nearly empty glass about to spill what little was left in it. "Dunno. Think they was just tired of being cooped up in their cottages, what with this snow and all," he replied. "One of 'em claims we won't get out until day after 'morrow. Which works perfect seein' as how the guv'nor told me to spend a night or two here," he added, an arched brow suggesting he knew something Banks didn't.

Or that he was sure Banks knew the plan, too.

Banks straightened. He knew perfectly well what the earl had in mind, even if he hadn't agreed with the idea. Apparently he had ensured the servants' coach would be stuck in Darlington by paying the driver to see to the delay.

Damn him.

"I believe he simply wishes to spend some time with his countess. Without many servants about," Alonyius suggested with a shrug, wondering what the driver knew.

Haversham gave a nod. "In the meantime, they got a crew working to clear that big drift that stopped us so as to make way for the next mail coach that comes down from Edinburgh. We'll probably head out the day after 'morrow."

The day after tomorrow?

Well, this didn't sound good. Even in good weather, they were still several hours from Torrington Park.

Alonyius Banks frowned as he realized two things.

Make that three.

He didn't have enough reading material to keep him

occupied for another whole day, so spending time in the inn's parlor wasn't the least bit appealing.

The snow and cold meant venturing outside, perhaps to visit some shops or take a meal at a public house, wasn't very appealing either. There was that other place he really should visit, though. Apparently he would have an entire day to so.

There was a rather delectable creature up in his room. A woman that would be there all day tomorrow unless she chose to venture out in the cold and snow. A woman he might prevail upon to stay in bed with him if only so they could keep each other warm in more ways than one.

Banks was still considering the third option when Haversham gave him a pointed glance. "You're not thinking of killing her, are you?"

The valet blinked, wondering at first how the driver might have come to that conclusion. Why, he was just imagining how he might tumble her three ways to Thursday! Not put her in an early grave. "Not yet," he replied with a shake of his head, allowing a slight grin. "I am merely allowing the woman some time to settle in is all."

Haversham nodded. "'Taint fair you've had to spend so much time in the coach with her. She's why I haven't come in from the cold, if you catch my meaning."

His eyes widening with the driver's claim, Banks was about to admonish the man for choosing to nearly freeze to death instead of sitting in the warmth of the coach when the groom took the reins, but he thought better of it. He supposed he should be glad they hadn't been subjected to his odoriferous state. "I don't suppose you would believe me if I told you she's nothing like she is back in London."

His comment was met with a quelling glance. "Nope, probably wouldn't," Haversham answered, apparently unaware the question was supposed to have changed his poor opinion of the lady's maid.

"Well, then, I believe I have given Simpkins enough time. What time shall we be ready to leave the day after tomorrow?"

Haversham considered the question. "We'll leave at dawn. Prob'ly get there by one o'clock."

Nodding his understanding, Banks moved toward the tap and ordered a pint of ale. He thought of staying in the public room to drink it, but instead made his way back to the room. Having acquired the odor of stale ale and cheroot smoke, he wanted a bath now more than ever.

Chapter 12

OF PRINCES AND PALACES

eanwhile, at Torrington Park

"I do hope Mr. Banks hasn't killed her," Adele said as she pushed herself away from the south-facing window of the master suite.

Milton frowned at the comment, not having given another thought to the servants' coach still out there somewhere.

Probably in Darlington.

In Darlington, he amended to himself. At *The Black Swan*, if Banks had followed his instructions. "My valet is not a man of violence, I assure you," he countered, just then remembering what else he had encouraged the man to do whilst on this trip—attempt to lift Alice Simpkins' spirits by lifting her skirts. He knew what method he would employ only because making love to his wife seemed to do the trick every time. "Besides, your maid probably just needed a change of scenery. When was the last time she was away from Worthington House?"

Adele gave the question some thought. Although she had made the trip to Wisborough Oaks with the earl for the Duke of Chichester's wedding earlier that year, she hadn't taken her lady's maid. They had been to Brighton just the summer...

The summer before Milton made his bid to escort her to all the events of the Little Season. That had been a year-and-a-half ago. "We went to Brighton for the summer of eighteen-fourteen," she finally replied. "It was Devonfield's idea," she added, referring to her brother. She gave her husband a pointed glance. "He thought I should be away from London. I was still in mourning at the time."

"Nothing wrong with Brighton," Milton replied as he undid the buttons of his topcoat. He had almost decided against wearing one whilst at Torrington Park. Other than the servants and his wife, who would see him? "I do hope you were invited to the palace."

Giving a slight shrug, Adele nodded. "I was. Prinny held a few soirées during that summer. His mistress was there, of course," she added with a hint of disgust.

The earl ignored the comment about the mistress. The Prince Regent's taste in women was as varied as the size of his waistline, so his mistresses seemed to change with the seasons. With every different mistress came a different bauble to appease the last one, a practice that had most in Parliament wincing as the Crown's coffers were further drained. Milton had followed that precedent, bestowing a jewel on each widow to whom he bid adieu at the end of each Season. *But I could afford it.* "What did you think of the palace?"

The question had Adele considering her first impression of the rather odd structure, what with its colorful bulbous protrusions topped with spires. Reminiscent of buildings in India—she had only seen drawings of those in books—the palace's exterior was nothing like the others in England. The grounds were impressive—the gardens had been in full bloom at the time—and although the interior boasted some amazing furnishings and beautiful artwork, she found it bordered on excess. Prinny had even included a room dressed in Chinese chinoiserie. "He has rather exotic tastes," she replied, deciding not to answer as truthfully as she would if asked her opinion by one of her best friends.

The palace had been built at the expense of the English

people, their taxes funding a venture meant as a way of allowing the prince to escape his father's censure. *Escape his mad father*, she now knew. But still. Despite being the daughter of a marquess, she wasn't so sheltered by privilege that she was ignorant of what was happening in the rest of England. Of who was really paying the bills.

"I found the Chinese room quite interesting," Milton remarked as he unbuttoned his waistcoat. He had hoped Adele would notice he was preparing for bed and take a turn at undressing him.

Adele stiffened. "I have no plans of redecorating Worthington House," she responded, hoping he wasn't suggesting she redo one of the rooms in black and red and gold.

Unless it was his study. In which case, she really didn't care. She rarely, if ever, stepped foot in the study.

Milton frowned. "I wasn't," he replied with a shake of his head. He pulled off the waistcoat and plucked his cravat pin from the elaborate knot at his neck. Adele was suddenly in front of him, her deft fingers undoing the knot. "Truly?" she countered with an arched brow.

Carefully considering her query, Milton realized it would only be safe to repeat his initial response. "I wasn't. I merely thought the decor interesting," he replied, rather hesitant. "But the dining room was tasteful, don't you think?" Goodness, if he wasn't careful, he would find himself strung up by his cravat and sleeping in the master suite—alone. He thought it best to return the conversation to its beginning. "Your lady's maid will be right as rain after this trip," he commented as Adele unwound the silk from around his neck.

"If she hasn't frozen to death," Adele replied with a hint of annoyance, tempted to use the cravat for a nefarious purpose. Why, if Milton thought for one minute she would be amenable to redecorating even one room of Worthington House in the manner of a Chinese brothel, then she would be using his cravat to tie him up to one of the giant carved bedposts that seemed to dominate the master suite.

And then leave him there for the entire night.

Before she could give the matter another thought, Milton took the length of silk from her and wrapped it around her back, pulling the ends so she was suddenly pressed against his front.

Apparently she didn't share his good opinion of the dining room at Brighton Palace, either, he considered.

"She'll be fine, Adele. I promise. They will have turned around and gone back to Darlington, if they even left—"

"But *The George* was closing for the holiday—"

"—To stay at *The Black Swan*," he continued, his voice quieting in an attempt to quell her worry. "Mr. Banks had it set up as an alternative in the event *The George* couldn't accommodate us," he explained softly. "As soon as the next mail coach comes down from Edinburgh, the roads will be clear enough for them to get through. They'll be here in a day or two."

When he finally relaxed his hold on the cravat to give her a quick kiss, Adele allowed a sigh. "If you're sure," she murmured.

Milton blinked. Well, he wasn't completely sure. But he was fairly sure. And he was quite sure he would never again put voice to his opinion of the rooms in Prinny's palace.

Now was not the time to find himself sleeping alone.

Chapter 13

A VALET RETURNS

eanwhile, back at The Black Swan
Alice didn't have to wait long for the valet's
return to their room. The sound of the key in the lock had
her sitting up in the bed, a look of relief settling over her
features when Banks appeared and stepped into the room.
His sleeves still rolled up to nearly his elbows, he carried
what appeared to be a nearly-full glass of liquid. His expression suddenly changed and he started to back out, his
murmur of, "Pardon me, madam," barely audible.

Frowning, Alice sat up straighter. "Mr. Banks?" she called
out, wondering what had him taking his leave almost as
quickly as he was about to enter the room.

Alonyius Banks paused in the doorway and angled his
head. He stepped back into the room and shut the door
behind him, although he stayed where he was. He held the
pint of ale at his side, apparently forgetting he carried it.
"Miss Simpkins?" he whispered hoarsely, as if he didn't recognize her.

"Yes?" she countered, wondering what had him so addled
just then. The room wasn't that dark. The coal she had added
to the fire before climbing into bed had the room lit in a
golden glow. "How many pints have you drunk?" she asked

in a hoarse whisper. She couldn't decide if she was amused or annoyed by his odd behavior.

Somewhat offended, the valet straightened. "Not even one". He seemed to remember he carried a pint and took a quick swig of it. Grimacing, he placed it on the nearby desk. "The taproom is packed with villagers, Higgins is... in his room," he said, deciding he really shouldn't tell her what the man was *doing* in his room. "And Haversham appears to have made a number of friends at this establishment." Not the least of which were the two tavern maids who were vying for the driver's affections—and probably his purse. Once they saw the size of his room—and his purse—Alonyius rather doubted they would continue their ruse to curry his favor.

That is, unless the earl had given him some blunt to see to it they remained in Darlington.

Damn him.

Alice resisted the urge to smirk at the valet's remarks. She was quite sure she understood exactly what the groom was doing in his room, and Haversham's friends were no doubt lightskirts out to make some blunt from a quick tumble. "The water is still warm. In case you wish to bathe," Alice remarked, her gaze going to the copper tub. Despite its weight, she had managed to move the tub even closer to the fire, its metal base still resting on the warm hearth.

Banks frowned. "Is there something you wish to tell me, Miss Simpkins?" he asked with an arched brow.

Alice blinked, not meaning for her comment to suggest the valet needed a bath. Indeed, the man smelled quite clean, the scent of his cologne as enticing as the citrus and lemon used to launder his clothes. "The sooner you join me in this bed, the warmer it will be," she replied in a huff.

She hadn't meant to sound impatient. Or fast, certainly. But the expression on Alonyius Banks' face had her realizing her comment was wholly inappropriate. "I apologize, but it's going to get cold in here," she said with a sigh.

The valet allowed a grin. "I am torn. As much as I want a bath, I also find I want to join you in that bed," he responded as his hands went to his hips. When Alice didn't put voice to a reply, he glanced over at the tub. In two steps, he was close enough to dip a hand into the water. "Perhaps I could do both."

It took all of Alice's resolve not to make a sound, for she knew right then he would be doing both. And he would probably strip his clothes from his body and settle into the tub without benefit of a dressing gown or bath linens to hide his nakedness.

She dared a glance at the chair next to the tub, aware of the two bath linens she had deliberately left for him. She was glad he had managed to secure four of them—there were none in the room when they arrived. Having already used two of them, Alice would have liked to use yet another to help dry her hair, but thought it best not to be selfish. Banks was larger, after all. Taller.

And broader of shoulder.

As if he could read her thoughts, Banks went about undoing the buttons down the front of his waistcoat, carefully folding and setting aside the garment on the back of the chair before undoing the knot of his cravat. Unwinding the length of white silk from around his neck, he dared a glance in the maid's direction and gave her an arched brow when he realized she was watching his every move. He waved a finger in the air—in a circle, as if to tell her to turn around—and pulled his shirt from his body.

The sound of Alice's gasp reached his ears, and he allowed a grin. "I did try to warn you," he murmured before he turned toward the fire. He pulled his boots from his feet and his stockings after that before he went to work on the fastenings of his breeches.

"I have seen a naked man before," Alice replied, not about to hide beneath the covers. She had never watched a man undress like this. The show he was providing was fascinating.

Banks gave her a quelling glance, as if her having been in the company of a naked man annoyed him. "Hopefully not one of the Worthington House servants," he stated, as if he dared her to counter his assessment.

Giving her very best look of offense, Alice frowned. "Of course not." She paused a moment, realizing he wasn't going to shed his breeches until she admitted just whom she had seen in the nude. "Her ladyship took me with her to the British Museum once," she finally admitted, a bit sheepish in her response. She dared not tell him she had at one time had a lover. A servant in another household. A younger man than her, in fact. Why, she was quite sure the valet's apparent jealousy might lead to fisticuffs if she should mention he had been an under butler at another house in Park Lane.

Had been because he was no longer alive.

Banks seemed to relax, a slight grin touching the corners of his lips. "One of the statues in the Towneley collection, perhaps?" he queried. "Or—?"

"The marbles from the Parthenon," she blurted. Well, she had studied the ones in the Towneley collection, too, but he didn't need to know that. Especially given how his eyes seemed to darken again.

As if he could see through the fabric of her night rail.

Perhaps he could. She had never considered if the fine lawn was completely opaque.

"Ah, the Greeks, of course," he murmured as he returned his attention to shedding his Nankeen breeches. "Never ones to cover their subjects in clothing."

Although he wore smalls beneath the breeches, Alice couldn't help the strangled sound that erupted from her throat, nor the way her breasts swelled or how color suffused her entire body. "Not like the Romans," she agreed with a shake of her head.

Stupid Romans.

Somehow, she had missed him removing his smalls, or else he had simply stepped into the tub and sat down still wearing them, for when her attention returned to him, she found Alonyius completely in the tub. "Is the water warm enough?" she asked, concern evident in her voice.

"Why, it's positively hot in here, Miss Simpkins."

"Alice," she said in a breathy voice. "Please, call me 'Alice'." At his sudden glance in her direction, she sighed. "I hardly think it appropriate for you to call me 'Miss Simpkins' if we're to share a bed," she murmured.

"Alonyius," he replied, rather surprised to learn he was expected in the bed. It only made sense, of course. In sharing the bed, they would be sharing their warmth. When the little bit of coal in the fireplace went to ash, the room would get cold. "It's very good to meet you. Finally," he added as he smoothed the cake of soap over his arm. "We were never properly introduced," he added when he noted her look of confusion.

"Weren't you with the earl the day his lordship introduced himself? And his staff?" she asked.

That day had been most unexpected. The Earl of Torrington had come to the servants' wing and had seen to introducing himself to every servant in Worthington House as well as introducing them to the few he had brought with him from his bachelor quarters. The entire episode had been such a surprise. The staff hadn't been warned the earl was due to visit that day. Alice couldn't remember if Alonyius Banks had been there or not. Certainly she would have remembered if he had.

"I was not," Alonyius replied as he continued washing. The cake of soap was now sliding over his chest and through the blondish-gray curls that covered it.

Alice tried her best to keep her voice steady. "Where were you?" she countered. Although she really would have preferred to stay in the comfort and warmth of the bed, she pushed aside the quilt and bed linens and made her way to the side of the tub. She knelt down, holding onto the side of the tub as she did so.

Alonyius regarded her a moment, realizing just then why he hadn't recognized her. Her hair was down—not even braided—and soft bangs gave her face the appearance of one many years younger. "Making arrangements with the butler on what was to be moved from his lordship's townhouse to Worthington House," he replied, determined to keep his voice as impassive as possible. No need to let the lady think she had him a bit discombobulated. "And then I paid a visit to his tailor's shop to pick up his wedding clothes."

Nodding her understanding, Alice rolled up the sleeves of her night rail. She held out a hand, palm up. "Would you like me to wash your hair?"

His eyes darkening with her query, Alonyius shook his head. "Perhaps another time," he murmured. At seeing her sudden look of disappointment—did she really want to wash his hair? Or was she offering merely to return the favor?—he leaned toward her and allowed a teasing grin. "But you can wash my back if you wish."

A frisson shot through Alice, and she returned the grin. Alonyius placed the ball of soap into her waiting hand and leaned forward. Moving to the end of the tub, Alice regarded the valet's bare back and wondered where to start. *At the base of his neck?* Where the gray-blond hair formed a slight V that curved off to the right? *Or at the top of his shoulders, still straight despite his age?* She considered his shoulder blades, the bones evident in soft relief as his arms rested on the sides of the tub. Then there were the bumps of his spine, barely visible but evident should her hand travel from his neck to the base of his spine.

She wet her hands and rolled the soap between them, generating a bit of lather before finally settling her palms onto the tops of his shoulders. His body jerked a bit at the touch, but he didn't recoil from her. In fact, it felt as if he pressed into her hands, as if he wanted her to push harder. Moving her palms around to the sides of his arms and then to the middle of his back, she took delight in the patterns in the soap left behind by her ministrations. A few more swipes and she had his entire back—or rather what was showing above the water's edge—covered in soap. She was so intent on her work, she barely noticed how Alonyius had turned his head and was resting his chin on one soapy shoulder.

"Are you... enjoying this?" he asked in a husky whisper.

Stopping her movements, Alice wondered how to respond. Should she admit she was enjoying this... this wholly inappropriate whatever-it-was she was doing? Is this what she had heard referred to as *foreplay* in overheard whispers? Or was she merely engaging in an exercise that would cement her as *fast* in his opinion?

"I am, actually," she replied in a quiet voice. "Are you?" She had begun to move her hands again, this time dipping them below the water, sliding them to his sides and up again.

"It is rather pleasant," he replied, trying hard not to purr.

Although there was just a hint of the fat pads so many men sported above their hips, he was a lean man. "I've never done this before," Alice said suddenly, smoothing her hands so her soapy thumbs traveled along his spine and up to the nape of his neck. "I do hope I'm... doing it right," she added, wondering how he might respond.

"Since I have never had my back washed in such a manner, I'm sure I wouldn't know," Alonyius said as he straightened his head and then allowed it to drop down so his chin rested on his chest.

Slowing her hands, Alice frowned. "Do you... like it? Truly?"

His body vibrated in response, just before a chuckle erupted. "'*Like*' isn't exactly the word I would use," he whispered.

Alice pulled her hands away, rather dismayed by his response. She was about to rinse off the soap from her hands when Alonyius suddenly tipped his head back, forcing his back beneath the water as he gazed at her upside down. "I was trying to come up with a word that would describe a rather pleasant situation I should like to have oft repeated. '*Like*' simply doesn't do your ministrations justice, my lady."

Heartened by his response, Alice allowed a wan smile. Regarding him for a moment, she realized it was now or never. If she wanted this man to share the only bed in the room, and do so with more than mutual warmth in mind, then she needed to make her intentions clear.

So she leaned over and placed her lips over his.

Although it might have seemed a bit awkward at first—his lips were upside down to hers—she found it every bit as intimate as the only kiss she had ever experienced before. Back when a footman had placed his hands on either side of her face and taken her lips in a scorching kiss he meant only as a demonstration of what could be should she agree to accompany him to Vauxhall Gardens. Alice had refused the invitation, but only because it wasn't her day off. She had to wait for Lady Torrington to return from the theatre so that she could prepare her for bed.

Moving a hand to rest against the side of his face, more to steady herself than to keep him in place, Alice continued the kiss when Alonyius made no move to end it.

At some point, she had to give up her hold on him, though, for his wet hands moved to the sides of her face as he deepened the kiss. When he finally let go, he didn't pull away as much as simply settle his head against the edge of the tub. "I do believe it's time we move to the bed," he whispered. And then he allowed his entire torso and head to dip into the water before he finally emerged and slowly sat up.

Alice couldn't help the shiver of anticipation that passed through her, the way her body seemed to thrum at the thought of his entire body pressed against hers. The way her own throbbed at the thought of what he might do. She imagined all manner of debauchery, wondering what the valet might expect her to do once they were beneath the bed linens.

What he might do to her.

When Alonyius slowly straightened to a sitting position, the water sloshing just a bit as he did so, Alice was jolted from her reverie. She pulled a bath linen from the chair and unfurled the fabric, holding it out for him as he rose from the tub. Alice couldn't help but watch as the water sluiced from his body, as he used the linen to scrub at his wet hair and face. She quickly grabbed the other linen, ever so glad she hadn't been selfish and used it herself. When she shook it out and offered it to him, he was regarding her with what could only be desire.

"Thank you, my lady," he murmured.

Alice could only nod, her gaze taking in his entire body as he stepped up and out of the tub. She slowly stood up and took the linen from him. Ignoring his frown, she rubbed it over his damp skin, from his shoulders down to his hips and both sides of his body until she reached his manhood.

His fully erect manhood.

She dared a glance up, wondering if he would still her movements or allow her to proceed. But she found his eyes closed, and his breathing seemed labored as she finally saw to drying him there.

His breath hitched. She felt how his body stiffened. She wondered if she should continue, but when he said nothing, she knelt and dried his legs and his feet.

She had never seen a man's bare feet before. Marveling at the bones that showed in slight relief beneath the skin, she reached out to trace one of them. But her touch had him jerking his foot away before she had completed the track of a single bone. And then he was suddenly bent over, his hands beneath her arms, pulling her up and hard against the front of his body before his lips took purchase on hers.

The kiss was searing in the heat it seemed to generate. Alice was sure her lips burned and swelled under the sweet, intense assault. When he pulled away, he left his forehead pressed against hers.

"First, I shall taste you. I will not stop until you beg me to do so," he warned in a voice filled with what sounded like menace.

Alice nodded. What else could she do? She didn't know quite what he meant, but her thighs throbbed in anticipation. If she refused, her body would never forgive her.

"Then, I am going to rid you of this," he hissed, referring to her night rail.

She nodded, rather wishing he would do so that very moment.

"And then I'm going to fill you with this." One of his hands took one of hers and moved it to his manhood. She wrapped her fingers around it even before his hand could force them to do so. Her thumb brushed over the end of it so he suddenly squeezed his eyes shut and let out a groan of surprise.

The silk-satin-covered rod was heavy in her hand, alive and throbbing in its own anticipation of a release it hadn't experienced in a very long time. "Over and over again until I can stand it no more," he whispered hoarsely. "Do you understand?"

Alice nodded against his forehead. "I do." She kissed him again for good measure, for she rather doubted they would be doing any kissing for the rest of the night. The simple act of intimacy would be replaced by the more coarse version, if intercourse could even be considered intimate.

His hands moved over the fine lawn of her night rail until they came to rest on her breasts. He broke the kiss to take a deep breath and then recaptured her lips at the same time he pressed his palms over his captives.

It was Alice's turn to break the kiss, her inhalation of breath loud in the quiet room before the steel bands of his arms were suddenly around her waist.

"And finally, when I fall asleep, I expect to be holding you against me for the rest of the night."

Alice pulled away to regard him with a quizzical expression. Although she had always expected they would share the bed for carnal activities, she was gratified to learn he intended to sleep with her, too. "I think I shall like that. Although *like* is such an inadequate word..." She allowed the sentence to trail off because she had to. Alonyius suddenly had her in his arms, carrying her to the bed and settling her onto it before she could put voice to a protest. Even before he had her positioned in the middle, his body was atop hers, his lips taking purchase on one of her hardened nipples through the fabric of her night rail.

Despite the chill in the room, an inferno seemed to erupt between them as her night rail was suddenly rucked up well beyond her hips. His hands were possessive as he splayed them and ran them down the sides of her body, over and under her thighs. When he lifted one—forcing her to bend her knee—and then lowered his face to kiss the inside of it, Alice suddenly realized exactly what he meant with his first warning.

She inhaled at the sensation his lips created on the tender flesh of her thigh. No one had ever kissed her there. Instead of waiting for him to move it, she bent her other leg and allowed it to drop to the other side. Feeling ever so wanton, she speared his short hair with her fingers and scraped his scalp with her nails, hoping to guide his head so he could repeat the exquisite torture on the other thigh. She didn't even mind that the man's whiskers abraded her skin as he saw to thoroughly kissing it.

But he merely slowed his movements before lifting his head. Despite her whimper of protest, or maybe because of it, he whispered, "Patience, my lady."

Alice sighed in protest, realizing she had to slow her breathing or she would faint. Even now, her entire body seemed to buzz in anticipation. She was about to put voice to a plea for surcease when a dart of pleasure came out of nowhere. Not exactly what she expected to experience just then, she held her breath in wonder and was stunned when it happened again, although whatever had set it off was harder, more intense. The darts of pleasure were soon replaced with wonderful waves that rolled through her entire body.

It was then she wondered what had her entire body reacting so, what had her experiencing a spasm of pure pleasure unlike anything she had felt before. Lifting her head slightly, she confirmed her suspicion, shocked to find the valet's head between her thighs, his tongue obviously the culprit as he laved her engorged womanhood. If she hadn't just bathed the hour before, she would be appalled. Now, she could only hope he would continue whatever it was that...

She inhaled sharply, her chest rising from the bed as the intensity of the sensations increased. Whimpering and verging on the edge of begging him to stop, Alice cried out. The dart of intense pleasure subsided, and she relaxed a bit. Satiated and warm, she relaxed a bit more and allowed a sigh of contentment.

So she was entirely unprepared as Alonyius delivered a final swipe of his tongue, covered her womanhood with his lips, and then began suckling it. The intensity of the resulting pleasure had her mewling in between screams of 'yes' before she finally put voice to a plea for him to stop.

"If you don't stop, I'll faint," she whimpered.

A bit reluctant to heed her warning, Alonyius finally pulled his lips away from Alice's delectable body. His hands remained splayed on her thighs, his fingers covering the bruises he'd left behind by holding her down as she writhed about. He still tasted her ambrosia on his tongue, its aroma engulfing his senses.

Never before had he been in the company of a woman who opened herself so completely for him. Never before had a woman allowed him such liberties—at least without first putting forth a string of protests. And never before had he been as ready to plunge himself into a woman. If he wasn't careful, his release would come before he was even halfway into her.

The memory of his earlier words reminded him to remove her night rail. He wanted to see her breasts again, to hold them, and to take her engorged nipples between his teeth and do to them what he had done to her womanhood.

He crawled up the front of her body, one hand pushing the offending fabric up as he went. Her hands joined in the effort to remove the night rail, and soon she was naked before him, her dark hair splayed out on the pillow beneath her head. One hand had moved to his shoulder, as if she needed something to hold onto, while her other arm attempted to cover her breasts.

Alonyius frowned. "What is it?" He couldn't have her turning modest now. Not when his need was so great.

"I've not been blessed with much in the way of breasts," she whispered in despair.

"Then you should know that more than a mouthful is a waste, my lady," he countered. He lifted her arm from her chest and reveled in the sight before him. With breasts too flat to fall to the sides of her chest, her nipples were erect and perfectly positioned for his tongue and lips. Perfectly sized so that he might encompass one with his mouth. He did so, although slowly and carefully—he didn't wish to bruise her or cause her pain. Besides, they had all night. Probably all day tomorrow and tomorrow night as well.

Grateful for the bit of reprieve Alonyius provided her, Alice forced her breaths to even out. She watched as he regarded her, surprised when he seemed pleased with her poor excuses for breasts. And then he dropped his face onto one, and another round of exquisite pleasure took her breath away.

She was quite sure his tongue was responsible for the shivers that raced down her torso, for the skitters of pleasure that radiated from her breast. When his worship moved to her other breast, she wondered if they might ever do this again. And before she could give that thought its due, Alonyius moved his member into alignment with her body and allowed her fingers to help it find its new home.

Although his first thrust was a bit tentative, Alice was still forced to inhale sharply. However did he expect to bury himself in her when he was obviously far too large? But his slow movements, careful and controlled, soon had him inside her wet sheath as far as he could go. When she lifted her knees a bit more to grip his thighs, he was suddenly deeper, and a growl sounded from his throat.

When her chest arched up in response, Alonyius took the

opportunity to once again kiss her nipples. His body demanded surcease, though, so he quickened his thrusts.

He delighted in how her body responded by rising to meet his, countering his every thrust and making it impossible to hold off the spasm of pleasure that finally had him releasing his seed into her.

Groaning, his face contorted in what looked like pain, Alonyius struggled to catch his breath as his body seized in ecstasy. Overwhelmed and unable to speak or even move, he fell atop Alice's body and passed out.

Her body suddenly covered with the length of his body, his cock still firmly inside her, Alice slowly lowered her legs and moved a quilt into place over them both. Allowing a sigh of contentment, she wondered how she would ever stop smiling.

Chapter 14

REMEMBERING A PRIOR LIFE

*M*eanwhile, back at Torrington Park

"I never asked you about your first husband," Milton murmured after a moment of quiet. The hand that held hers beneath the covers squeezed slightly as he made the comment, as if he already regretted putting voice to his thoughts.

Adele furrowed her brows, wondering why he would mention Samuel Worthington at a time like this. The earl had barely recovered from their latest tumble, his labored breaths just now returning to normal.

She turned her head to regard him, but in the darkness, she couldn't make out his face. "What would you like to know?" Rolling onto her side so her entire body faced him, she nearly let out a yelp when his arms gathered and pulled her against the side of his chest.

"I'm not sure I wish to know anything, but I cannot but wonder why you never speak of him," he replied before kissing her hair. His words were almost a whisper, but they still sounded loud in her ears. "Do you miss him? Did you feel affection for him? Did you wish to have children with him? Was he kind to you, or did he hurt you? Did you spend the nights in bed with him? Did he snore?" The questions came tumbling out, as if he had banked them for just this moment.

Considering how to respond—or not—Adele allowed a sigh. "My brother introduced us at a ball. Apparently Worthington asked Devonville if he might be allowed to dance with me. I was nineteen at the time and quite certain I didn't want to wed." She paused a moment, not the least bit surprised when she heard a hint of a guffaw erupt from her husband's chest.

"I remember. You were a feisty chit," Milton said as he tightened his hold on her, the tips of his fingers drawing circles on her arm.

Adele couldn't help the grin that came to her face just then. She remembered Milton, of course. Remembered that the night she had first danced with Worthington was the same night the earl had agreed to be a godfather to yet another daughter of the *ton*. "You had just announced your ninth or tenth goddaughter," she replied, lifting her head from his shoulder. "And you were quite foxed."

He allowed a chuckle. "I was quite sober, I assure you," he countered. "I take my duties as a godfather very seriously." There was a long pause before he added, "I didn't get foxed until after I saw you dancing with Worthington."

Adele gave a start and turned over to hold herself up on one elbow. "What are you implying?" she asked, surprise evident in her voice.

Milton took the opportunity to pull her onto his chest. "I was a fool. I was four-and-twenty. I'd already been in Parliament over seven years. I was supposed to marry and start a nursery, and I wouldn't have any of it. My cousin, Gregory, had already proven himself a much better manager of money and had a woman in mind to be his wife. I figured eventually he or his son could inherit. He would make a better earl..."

"Nonsense," Adele interrupted. Gregory Grandby would make an excellent earl, but the younger cousin wanted nothing to do with Parliament. He was all about making money for his coffers and those of his clients and the companies in which he had a vested interest.

"Devonville told me Worthington had already asked permission to court you…" He paused when he felt Adele's sudden gasp. "He had all that blunt from those steamships he helped create. And since I wasn't about to be leg-shackled, I had no grounds upon which to challenge the man for your hand."

Adele stared at her husband in the dark, shocked by his words. "You wanted to marry me back then?" Beneath her, she felt the rumble of laughter even before she heard it.

"Me and every younger buck in the ballroom," he claimed. "Christ, woman. You were the most beautiful woman in London. Still are, actually," he added, hoping he hadn't allowed too much time to pass between the comments. "But Devonville was looking for a man like Worthington to marry you. Someone with a fortune. Someone who wasn't looking to gamble away your dowry. Someone who—"

"Someone who claimed to love me," Adele put in softly, remembering how Samuel Worthington had gazed at her during the waltz they shared. And how he continued to do so when he escorted her to the gardens. He had actually asked her if he might be allowed to kiss her, seeing as how he had every intention of marrying her.

How could she respond? Especially when she had already decided she found his overtures endearing? His intentions honorable? For some reason she couldn't quite sort, the idea of marriage was suddenly not so daunting. Perhaps the prospect of marrying a man who wasn't an aristocrat made all the difference. Or perhaps it was the prospect of marrying a man who wasn't after her dowry.

The man was rich.

They were married two months later. In those two months, Worthington had purchased the mansion in Park Lane and had it decorated according to her wishes, bought her a town coach and a quartet of Cleveland Bays to pull it, and was the high-bidder on an Irish Walker on which she could ride during the fashionable hour—even though she already owned a Welsh pony for the same purpose. He bestowed her with a diamond and sapphire ring. More jewels followed even after they were married.

Despite knowing he felt some affection for her, though, Adele always wondered if she was merely another acquisition Worthington could show off during their frequent attendance at balls and soirées, the theatre, and on trips to port cities where he saw to his burgeoning empire.

"I was quite flattered by his attentions," she murmured softly. "Although I couldn't help but feel I was merely an ornament on his arm."

"Tsk," Milton replied, his arm tightening a bit. "He had to have thought of you as more than that, given how faithful he was to you."

Adele lifted her head from his chest, shocked at his words. "How would you know such a thing?" One of her brows furrowed. "How did you even know him?"

Milton gave a shrug, the movement barely noticeable in the dark. "Tattersall's, White's, horse races, and the like. I warned him if he should ever embarrass you or hurt you, there would be hell to pay." He didn't add that he had been deep in his cups at the time. He had been feeling a bit lonely, thoughts of what he had missed out on by not laying claim to Adele when he had the chance making him a bit surlier than usual.

It was at that point he realized he had to find a woman to call his own, at least for the Season's entertainments. A mistress wouldn't do—he needed someone he could escort in public. Who better than a widow of the *ton?* Most weren't looking to remarry, and he simply avoided those that were.

"You didn't," Adele breathed, suddenly wondering if it had been Milton's comments that had Samuel behaving in a more loving manner after their wedding.

"I did. It was that or challenge him to a duel, but I didn't think you would consider my suit if I had shot and killed your husband," he added with an arched eyebrow.

The merriment in his voice had Adele rolling her eyes. "I had no idea you were the least bit interested in me," she murmured.

They had known each other for years, although only as acquaintances—probably since before Adele was out of leading strings. Her brother had inherited the Devonville marquessate before her come-out.

Then she remembered his tale of the day they had gone sledding, and she felt a pang in her chest. He claimed he wanted to marry her even back then.

"And if you had known?" Milton pressed, his voice suddenly hoarse.

Adele took a breath, rather wishing she had known of Milton's interest. Would she have waited for him to realize he needed a wife? An heir?

Probably not. The sudden desire to run her own household had her accepting Worthington's suit far more than any thoughts of affection. She might have saved herself a great deal of heartache after his passing, however. "I might have sent you a note after Samuel's death," she whispered.

Milton felt a tightening in his chest. "Oh?" He paused a moment. "Missed his snoring, did you?"

Ignoring his comment about the snoring, Adele wondered if she should tell him about Stephen Worthington. Their conversation about Samuel had gone rather well, although the memories of him—both good and bad—had her on the verge of tears. "I found the nights too lonely to mourn as I should have," she whispered hoarsely. Her eyes brightened, tears collecting in their corners.

"Did you take a lover?" he wondered, jealousy apparent in how he suddenly straightened on the pillows.

Adele shrugged and gave a quick glance toward the window. Darkness engulfed the room despite the faint glow from the fireplace.

"Worthington's brother," she replied finally, ignoring the

hissing sound Milton made at the comment. "I discovered very quickly that Samuel's younger brother was more skilled in bed, but then, rakes usually are," she added with a sweep of a finger over one of his nipples, a bit relieved when she felt his quick intake of breath. "I was so flattered—Stephen is at least five years younger than I am—so I was led to believe he was taken with me. That is, until he admitted he had promised Samuel he would look after me if something should happen."

Adele waited a moment, wondering if her husband might say something, and then, when he didn't, she added, "I was never sure if he bedded me because of his promise to Samuel or because he found me desirable."

Milton gave a grunt as he covered her hand with one of his own. "Of course, he found you desirable! Christ, I would have shot him if I'd known anything about the two of you," he claimed, his manner far more serious.

Adele gave a start. "Milton!" she cried out. She gave a long sigh when he merely responded by cocking an eyebrow, the expression evident in the dim light from the fireplace. "I've told no one but you about Stephen," she whispered. "And I'm rather glad no one discovered our arrangement."

Milton frowned again. "Because of the potential scandal?"

Adele nodded. "Of course. It would have been as much of an embarrassment for him as for me," she commented lightly. "I was essentially his mistress for those seven or eight months." Her eyes lifted to Milton's. "I was so relieved to hear Weston wanted to court me, and I was so certain I wanted to marry again, I accepted his offer without even knowing enough about him," she went on, her eyes clearing. "And then, one day during tea, Lady Ellsworth informed me she'd overheard her husband say something about Weston's gambling debts—"

"Because I was the one who told him," Milton interrupted. "I hoped someone might pass along what I had discovered. Remind me to give Lady Ellsworth a compliment when we're next in her company," he murmured.

"Milton!" Adele admonished him before considering what had gone unsaid. "Was it true? The part about Weston being a gambler? And being in debt?"

The earl blinked. "Oh, aye. He had markers spread all over Cheapside. Frank O'Laughlin, the owner of the *Jack of Spades*, claimed Weston had run up a debt of over ten-thousand pounds just on faro."

Adele couldn't help the hiss that escaped her lips just then. "I never heard any particulars, but just hearing he was a gambler had me so stunned, I thought I *would* die of embarrassment. I ended the engagement that very night. Gave the ring back to Weston. It was probably paste," she murmured in disgust.

It was probably won over a game of cards, Milton almost said in reply, but thought better of it. "There's no need to feel as if you had been bamboozled. It happens to far more women of the *ton* than they would like to admit," he whispered.

"But my wedding was so close, I had already set a date!" Adele countered. "It was at the Harvey ball when you told Michael Cunningham you were looking for a widow for the Season. Olivia Cunningham informed you I was available, bless her heart."

A small grin lifted Milton's lips. "I remember," he murmured before placing a kiss on the top of her hair. "Olivia is one of my oldest goddaughters. Has a good head on her shoulders, that one. Her husband is a bit of a numbskull—"

"Milton!" Adele admonished him.

"Well, he is. Especially in the matter of marriage. The man is like my cousin when it comes to making money—he's an excellent businessman—but he can't keep track of time to save his life." He paused a moment before squeezing her hand again. "How was it Olivia knew you were no longer betrothed to Weston? She couldn't have been in London more than a week before the Harvey ball."

Adele grinned at the memory. "She knew because the modiste sold her my gown. Madame Suzanne had just finished my wedding gown when I found out about Weston. Thank the gods it suited Olivia. She wore it to the Harvey ball—her first as a married woman."

"You didn't want it?" he countered, thinking she would have looked rather lovely wearing the gown his goddaughter had worn that night at the Harvey ball.

Giving him a grimace, Adele shook her head. "I didn't want any reminders of Weston. I was sure just breaking the betrothal as I did would cause a scandal. I told Devonville first, of course, and when I chided him for not having warned me about Weston, he claimed he would have put voice to a protest during the reading of the banns." She allowed a sound of disbelief. "There are times I wonder about my older brother."

The earl couldn't help the bark of laughter that erupted just then. "Figures Devonville would want to wait until the last possible moment to offer his opinion on the matter." He didn't add that William Slater had known of Milton's interest in Adele and would have acted on his behalf had it become necessary.

"I rather wish he had told me what he knew, though. Before I accepted Weston's suit," Adele argued. Despite having her own, her brother had offered his coach-and-four should she have wished to escape London. Adele couldn't help but think the man felt guilty about not having informed her of what he knew about the rake. *If I had, would you have believed me?* she remembered him asking after she had given back the ring.

The question had stunned her. Of course, she would have believed her older brother. He had learned his lessons about marriage far too late, but he *had* learned them.

William had been married to his marchioness for nearly two-and-twenty years before she died of a sudden fever.

During the early years of their marriage, Devonville had spent far too much time in the company of a mistress, sure his wife eschewed his company. Even fathered a bastard son. Once he realized they truly loved one another, they had only a few years in which to live as husband and wife. Given her brother's experiences—and a lesson learned far too late—Adele had no reason to doubt his views on the subject of affection and marriage.

"I rather wish he had as well," Milton murmured with a sigh. "We could have been sharing a bed an entire Season earlier than we did," he added in a voice tinged with humor.

Adele was tempted to refute his claim, but sighed instead. "Is bedding a woman all you can think about?" she asked suddenly.

Her husband feigned offense. "I'll have you know that I only think of bedding *you*, and although it may seem as if I'm doing so all the time, I do occasionally have other thoughts."

At first thrilled at hearing her husband's claim, Adele lifted her head and regarded him in surprise. "Other thoughts?" she repeated. "Do tell."

About to claim he was famished and wished to raid the kitchen for a midnight snack, Milton allowed an impish grin when his stomach growled rather loudly. "I wonder what we might be having for breakfast. Or if it's going to rain whilst I'm at White's. Why, just last week, I wondered if I should take you to Newcastle for the horse race next year."

"The horse race?" she repeated, rather surprised by the possibility. She didn't know many who owned race horses, nor had she been to any races besides the Ascot, but she supposed it could be an entertaining diversion. "On which horse would you place a bet?"

"Which ever one you tell me to," he replied with a guffaw.

Adele giggled and rolled off of his body, taking the bed linens with her as she stepped out of the bed. "Since I don't have a maid to do my hair, I'll meet you in the breakfast parlor in half an hour," she murmured as she wrapped the linen around her body. At his sound of protest, she added, "If I had my maid, it would take an hour."

Adele hurried off to the door that connected their two suites and had nearly disappeared behind it when Milton cleared his throat.

"Where do you think you're going?" he called out, doing his best to gather up a blanket to cover his suddenly exposed body. With the fire having gone out and his wife out of the bed, the room was rather chilly.

Adele stopped and slowly turned to regard her husband. Given the expression on his face, she realized Milton had no intention of taking his leave of the bed. She gave a sigh. "At least help me with my corset and buttons," she suggested as she opened the only trunk that had made it to Torrington Park.

"I have a better idea," Milton countered. "Come back to bed until it's time for breakfast. Sweeting, it's the middle of the night. When it's morning, we'll have breakfast brought up, and you can wear what you have on."

About to put voice to a protest—*was it really only two in the morning?*—Adele considered his words and realized just why he made the suggestion. "You want a tumble after breakfast, don't you?" she accused.

Despite his failed attempt at maintaining a look of feigned shock at hearing her accusation, he finally shrugged. "You know me too well, my sweeting."

Sighing, Adele climbed back into bed. "You're incorrigible," she accused.

Chapter 15

IN THE MIDDLE OF THE NIGHT

A few hours earlier, in Darlington

The pleasant sensations of warmth and comfort, tingling skin, and the clean scents of lemon and orange were slowly replaced with a waft of cold air as Alice slowly awoke. Every morning for the past year, she woke up at four o'clock so she could dress and make her way to the kitchens. She was completely awake before she remembered she didn't have to go to the Worthington House kitchens on this day. Not this day or any other for the next few weeks.

She was in... *Where am I?*

She closed her eyes, trying to recapture the dream that had been playing in her mind's eye. Tried to recapture that sensation of extreme pleasure and subsequent satiation. The sensations of warmth and comfort a man's body provided whilst sleeping.

Except that it hadn't been a dream, she remembered suddenly. She had been lying with a man, her entire body pressed against the length of his, one leg resting betwixt his legs because he insisted she cover half his body and place her head in the small of his shoulder.

Expecting it to be awkward—she had never been held atop a man's body before—she instead found it rather comforting. Safe. Warm.

Halfway through the night, Alonyius had coaxed her to move to his other side, and rather than have her leave the bed to walk around it to reposition herself on the other side, he had simply moved her with strong arms and carefully positioned hands, kissing the top of her head when she was finally resettled on the other side. She couldn't remember what she murmured just then, or his whispered response, but she was soon back to sleep in the most satisfying slumber she had experienced, probably in her entire life.

Darlington. *The Black Swan*, she suddenly remembered. But her head was no longer in the small of a warm shoulder, and she was no longer sprawled over the body of a warm man. Moving her hand about and finding only cold linens, she realized Alonyius had taken his leave of the bed, and with it, his warmth and comfort.

Sitting up, Alice glanced about the chilled room, her eyes slowly adjusting to take in the golden glow from the fireplace. They darted to the window, where the silhouette of Alonyius stood in stark relief as he stared out the room's only window. *He must be freezing*, she thought, quite sure he was still naked.

Crawling out of the bed, Alice wrapped one of the quilts about her body, surprised to find the hem of her night rail falling to her knees. *When did I manage to pull it back onto my body?* she wondered.

Joining him at the window, she opened up the quilt and hung it over his shoulders. Even before she could ensure he was covered, one of his arms pulled her hard against the side of his body. "What is it?" she asked in a worried whisper.

"Nothing, really. I just woke up and..." He allowed the sentence to trail off as he stared into the darkness. "The fire was nearly out. I found some cut wood." He would have to venture downstairs at some point. The split log he had added a few minutes ago was the last of what had been provided in the way of fuel for the fire.

Alice considered his words, finally relaxing into his hold

even though she didn't believe his reason. "You're cold. Come back to bed," she whispered.

Her hand was suddenly captured in his, lifted to his lips before he pressed a kiss onto her knuckles and then into her palm. "I wish to, believe me, but I fear my body has deceived me," he murmured.

Alice frowned. "Whatever do you mean?" she wondered as she moved to press the front of her body against the front of his. His arousal was suddenly evident as it nudged her belly through the fabric of her night rail.

"I am an old man, and—"

"Nonsense," Alice replied with a shake of her head.

"—Once in a fortnight is usually quite enough for me." He didn't add that it had been far longer than a fortnight since he had last bedded a woman. "And yet, despite having had my way with you, I find I am desperate to do it again."

Had he been able to make out her eyes in the dark, he would have seen them darken with desire. "Then do so," she replied, her voice filled with far more than an invitation.

It was Alonyius' turn to frown. "Truly?" he replied, his surprise evident.

"Of course," Alice replied before lifting herself on her toes and kissing the corner of his mouth.

His lips took hers then, his kiss urgent and hungry, his tongue invading her mouth to touch her teeth and tangle with her tongue. One of his arms released her so that his hand could move to cover a breast, to knead it in his palm until the nipple hardened and was trapped between two fingers. She broke the kiss to inhale sharply, the darts of plea-sure already sending her body into readiness for his assault. Far too warm, she backed into the cold wall and raised one lithe leg to wrap about his hip.

Understanding her need, Alonyius used his hands to push her night rail up past her hips and then cupped the globes of her bottom. Lifting her up so she was leveraged against the wall, he pushed his manhood into her. A groan accompanied his movements as he squeezed his eyes shut against the impending release. For that moment of bliss, he merely wished to stay close, to have her arms wrap around his shoulders and hang onto him. He might have allowed his own pleasure just then—he'd been hard for far too long—but he wasn't about to leave her wanting. Not when she was so willing.

Alice inhaled. The cold against her back and the searing heat on her front had her body in turmoil, the space between her thighs throbbing and yet completely filled with his manhood. Although she feared there might be pain, she instead felt a need so great, she couldn't help her plea of, "hurry," from escaping her lips.

Hurry?

With her desperate word filling his ear, Alonyius stilled his breathing before thrusting his hips as hard as he dared. He reveled in how her entire body reacted, in how her chest arched out toward him, in how her head was thrown back against the wall. The night rail, an impediment against what he wanted to be doing to her breasts, had to go. One hand let go of her to push it up farther, and understanding his wishes, Alice let go her hold on him to pull the offending garment from her body so she could toss it aside. Her arms once again gripped the back of his shoulders as he pumped himself into her, over and over as his mouth covered a breast to stifle his groans. Despite knowing she was about to come, he was still a bit surprised when she arched suddenly and then hugged him hard as she cried out.

The maelstrom of pleasure and stars and blinding light and darkness had him stilling his movements lest he crush her into the wall anymore than she already was. A moment later, he felt her teeth grip the lobe of one of his ears, and he jerked awake. Sliding his hands from her bottom so she could lower her legs, he heard her sigh—*was that disappointment?*—as his manhood left her body.

She kissed him then, a sweet kiss accompanied by another sigh. "Come to bed," she whispered. "Before you fall down, old man," she added in voice filled with what sounded like amusement.

Alonyius had no idea how he managed to make it to the bed, although it was only a few steps away from the window. He ended up on his side, his knees bent in an effort to retain the warmth of their coupling. Never before had he taken a woman whilst standing up, and he rather doubted he would again.

Whatever had he been thinking to attempt such a feat?

I wasn't thinking, he reminded himself. *Just reacting.* What else could he have done in response to her blatant invitation?

Or had that been a dare in response to his claim of being an old man?

He suddenly found he didn't care.

Bed linens and quilts quickly covered him against the chill before a naked body pressed against his back, warm thighs rested against the back of his, and a soft arm wrapped about his middle. Sleep took him, but not before he managed a murmured, "Thank you."

Such an inadequate thing to say, but what else was there?

Closing her eyes and taking a deep breath, the scents of citrus and musk filling her nostrils, Alice grinned and managed to murmur, "You're welcome," before allowing sleep to take her once again.

Chapter 16

A WIDOW IN HIS PAST

he next morning, Sunday, December 22, 1816
The bright sunshine pouring into the mistress suite had Adele blinking awake far later than usual. She dared a glance in the direction of the bedchamber's only window and squinted. Her husband, bare naked, was almost entirely silhouetted in the light.

"Come away from there, or you'll freeze to death," Adele admonished him as she rolled over.

The earl gave her a glance, his grin turning to a huge smile. "The sun has decided to make an appearance, my sweeting," he replied, his happiness apparent in his voice. "First time in..." He paused, realizing he didn't know how long it had been since the yellow ball had been visible.

Several weeks?

"The entire year?" Adele offered from where she lay regarding him. Despite his age, her husband was still rather fit. There wasn't a hint of a belly so many of his peers displayed, nor the humpback of a spine about to give out. His hair was graying, of course, but the man was in his early forties! He had already outlived some of his contemporaries.

"Two months, at least," Milton agreed as he returned to the bed. "Which means we could go outside today."

Adele's involuntary shiver was apparent to the earl, and

he gave her a chiding grin. "Now, now. I was thinking about hitching up the sleigh. I'm sure there's a horse or two that would like some exercise, and the fresh air will do us both some good."

The idea sounded rather fun, although going out in the chill didn't hold any appeal. "Are there rugs we can ride under?" she wondered. "I rather doubt my redingote will be warm enough."

Milton's eyes widened. "Och, we have something better than coats," he claimed happily. "Furs! Several blankets of them, and I rather imagine we can find you a warmer muff," he replied with enthusiasm. "Why, the furs are so warm, we could go in our birthday suits."

Adele blinked and then regarded her husband with suspicion. "You're not joking, are you?"

Suppressing the urge to laugh, Milton shook his head. "I was, actually... but I suppose I could be talked into it if you'd like to try," he offered with a bit too much enthusiasm. He climbed back into bed, careful not to touch his wife given how cold his skin was just then.

Shaking her head in her pillow, Adele groaned. "As long as it took you to get me to sleep without wearing a night rail, do you really think I would agree to such an arrangement out of the bedchamber? Out of doors?" she countered lightly.

"It was worth a try," Milton reasoned. He pulled the covers back over his body and snaked an arm behind Adele's shoulders. "Did you sleep well?"

His wife nearly snorted. Was the man joking about that, too? Although she never believed she would be able to spend an entire night in bed with a man and actually sleep while doing so, she found she slept rather soundly with Milton—once she was able to drift off. "Once I stopped wondering what you meant about *sharing* me," she whispered.

Milton inhaled sharply and turned his head to regard her. "I believe I said I don't wish to share you." He lifted his head from the pillow in alarm. "Are you considering taking a—?"

"No, of course not," Adele interrupted with a shake of her head. "But what did you mean, exactly?"

The earl settled his head back into his pillow and sighed. "I meant in general, I suppose," he muttered. "You're a rather busy woman, what with all your callers and your charities and the *musicale* you host every year. I just thought it rather advantageous that I could have you all to myself for a time."

Adele allowed a wan smile. "Are you jealous when we're in town?" she asked in a teasing whisper.

Frowning, Milton considered the question. "On occasion, I suppose," he admitted.

"There's no need to be," she assured him. "Should you ever think I'm too busy, you need only say something, and I'll be sure to arrange a replacement."

A guffaw answered her comment. "You, my dear, are irreplaceable," he murmured. "One of the reasons I made you my wife."

It was Adele's turn to make a sound of disbelief. "If I hadn't agreed to marry you, who do you suppose you would have pursued as your wife?"

Milton should have realized that no matter how he answered the seemingly innocent question, he had fallen into a trap from which there was no easy way out.

And maybe no hard way, either.

"Maybe Lady Pendleton," he replied, not giving the question much thought.

Adele stilled herself, realizing he referred to Edith Harrington, the widow of the Earl of Pendleton. The red-headed, green-eyed woman had been his choice of widow to escort to *ton* events the third Season he had decided to squire widows about town. Adele couldn't remember having seen them much in public, though. "Edith?" she whispered in disbelief. She suddenly sat up, the covers falling from her front as she did so. She quickly gathered them to cover her bosom as she stared down at her husband. "Do tell me you're joking."

Now, *this* was the moment Milton could have given her

one of his devil-may-care expressions and agreed, that yes, he was joking.

But he wasn't. And he didn't.

And he hadn't yet figured out his comment would have the Green Monster of Jealousy unleashed inside his wife.

"Not at all. We suited well, for a time. She's rather gorgeous, although not as pretty as you, and she was already a countess, so she wasn't after a title, if you take my meaning."

Adele could only stare at him for a moment before she furiously gathered up more of the covers and moved to leave the bed, the bed linens hastily wrapped about her naked body.

Suddenly left completely uncovered, Milton sat up and grabbed the end of one of the bed linens, pulling on it with a jerk so that Adele's exit was impeded. "Let. Go," she demanded, her eyes dark with warning.

Her husband released the linen sheet and frowned. "What is it?" he asked, his manner one of innocence.

"Edith Harrington?" Adele repeated with a huff. She shook her head. "She's a... a... *seductress!* An opportunist. A *trollop.* Why, she'll sleep with anyone who gives her half a glance!"

His eyes widening with her rant, Milton realized just then he shouldn't have answered her question. He should have dodged it, or claimed he hadn't given a thought to a second choice. Or at least come up with a different widow's name. But, dammit, her question had him considering one, and he had answered without much thought. He hadn't had to give it much thought. He rather liked his time with Lady Pendleton—at least at first—and thought the two would suit. Edith would have had to give up her other lovers, of course, but she had been able to do so during part of their Season together. "I apologize, Adele. You asked, and I just said the first name that came to mind."

Adele's expression turned to one of anguish. "Do you still... *see her?*" she asked in a hoarse whisper. Reason told her he didn't, merely because he was home every night, and usually in her bed. But that didn't mean he wasn't spending an afternoon now and again in the company of the trollop.

Milton gave a shrug. "Well, on occasion—"

"Oh!" The cry of anguish increased in volume, and Adele hurried to the door that led to the dressing room.

"—Because we do attend some of the same events," he soldiered on, realizing he had dug a rather deep hole for himself, and he didn't even have a shovel!

"Out!" Adele yelled, her finger pointed toward the bedchamber door. "Out of my bed!"

Blinking, Milton realized he had never before seen Adele Slater Worthington Torrington so agitated. So annoyed.

So *angry*.

Not even on the occasion when Lady Pettigrew deigned to hold a soirée on the very same night as Adele's annual *musicale*. "Sweeting," he started to say, hoping to assuage her anger.

"Do not *ever* again use that endearment with me, you two-timing... cheating... *bastard*," she hissed. "Now get out!"

Recoiling as if he'd been slapped across the face, Milton swallowed hard. He watched as she reached for a vase from the room's only dresser. She was attempting to hoist it over her head when Milton realized she was going to throw it at him.

"I'm out!" he shouted as he struggled to get out of the bed. Despite his nakedness, he left the bedchamber by way of the room's door to the hallway—his exit by way of the dressing room door was blocked, after all, the priceless vase having come to a rather high point above Adele's head. The door slammed behind him, and he was forced to cover his manhood with his hands as he rushed down the hall in an attempt to make it to the master bedchamber without being seen by a chambermaid or footman.

He almost made it.

And he would have made it if the door to the master suite hadn't been locked from the inside.

"Jesus, Mary, and Joseph," he cursed, which had the housekeeper peeking around the corner from an adjacent hallway to discover him banging his head against the door.

Without a word, Mrs. Miller approached and held out the key from her chatelaine. "Let me get that door for you, my lord," she offered in her most dispassionate voice.

Milton blinked, rather stunned the housekeeper had just been around the corner and even more stunned by her efficient manner. "Most appreciated, Mrs. Miller. I seemed to have locked myself out this morning," he commented in a matching voice. "The view of the sun from the hall window is most unexpected. Why, it was so bright, I was nearly blinded."

Mrs. Miller unlocked the door and stepped back. "Yes, it is, my lord. Why, it would be a perfect day for a sleigh ride. Have a good day." She gave a quick curtsy, arched an eyebrow, and disappeared around the corner.

Although he was about to bow to her curtsy, Milton thought better of it and simply rushed into this bedchamber. He managed to kick the door shut behind him before he let out a curse that might have been heard by the nearest neighbors had they not lived nearly four miles away.

What the hell had just happened?

His wife had asked him a simple question, and he had answered. Somewhat truthfully. Somewhat stupidly.

A mistake, he realized now.

He rolled his eyes and hung his head, wondering if it would be safe to attempt a reconciliation before breakfast. But what could he say? The damage had already been done. Adele was convinced...

Well, he wasn't exactly sure what she was convinced about, but he had to do something to assure her his time with Lady Pendleton had been over for more than ten years.

Moving to the door to the dressing room, he pressed an ear against it and listened intently. Although he heard a bit of banging about—were those shoes being tossed against the wall? Or his Hobys?—he was more surprised to hear whimpering.

Was Adele crying?

Or had the stable dog been allowed upstairs?

Milton gave a shake of his head. He had a thought to simply climb into his bed and go back to sleep, but he knew he wouldn't be able to do so. Not without Adele at his side.

When had his need for her become so intense? His dependence so acute? Although he had bedded a number of widows over the years, he had only ever enjoyed serial relationships. He knew from his philandering friends that having more than one woman in his life at a time would lead to consequences.

Consequences much like he was experiencing at this very moment.

How the hell did this happen? he asked himself for the fourth or fifth time.

I told the truth.

Well, that wasn't exactly all of it, he had to admit. But he'd had no idea Adele had such a poor opinion of Lady Pendleton.

Were other ladies of the *ton* of the same opinion about Edith Harrington? Did she suffer the cut direct because others of her sex believed her to be a *trollop?*

At the precise moment he almost felt sorry for the woman, he also realized there was some truth to his wife's opinion, for Edith could play him—and did—with little effort, he suddenly remembered.

The seductress had him spending most of their nights together in her bed in her townhouse in Westminster, assuring him they could miss important *ton* events in favor of creating their own beneath her bed linens. After a few months, and fielding far too many comments from his colleagues regarding his noticeable absences from the nightly entertainments, Milton realized he had to give up the widow in favor of his political career.

And so he did.

He purchased a gemstone-encrusted necklace from Rundell, Bridge & Rundell, paid a call on her in the middle of the day, and informed her he had to end their liaison.

Appearing a bit disheveled and clad only in a satin dressing gown, Edith gave him a brilliant smile until she guessed the reason for his visit. He explained their *affaire* was threatening his political career, offered her the black velvet box, and kissed the back of her hand as he gave her a bow.

Although Edith feigned disappointment—her lower lip extended into the pout of a spoiled woman told she couldn't have what she wanted—Milton had the distinct impression he had interrupted a tryst. "Don't keep your lover waiting too long, my dear," he whispered as he took his leave of her townhouse.

He would never forget the look of shock that appeared on her face just before he shut the door. *Didn't she realize that Lord Brougham's coach was parked directly in front of her townhouse?*

Milton shook his head of the annoying memory, made even more annoying by the thought of how much the necklace had cost.

That necklace would have looked far better around Adele's neck, he thought.

Now why didn't I remember that afternoon when Adele asked me who I might have married instead of her? He never would have proposed to Edith Harrington!

My, but how time allows one to forget the worst things in life.

How long would it take Adele to forget?

The thought of his wife had him glancing around the master bedchamber. He needed to see to a suit of clothing for the day, and he briefly wondered if Adele would help him with his cravat. Then he thought better of asking her when he remembered the threat of the vase.

She would probably strangle him with the cravat. Tie him up to the bedpost and leave him for the chambermaid to discover.

Poor chambermaid.

Hunger pangs—he never had made it to the kitchens in the middle of the night—as well as the chill in the air had him hurrying to dress himself. As for the cravat, he decided to skip it. And the topcoat, as well. Since he wasn't going anywhere—it wouldn't be any fun taking a sleigh ride by himself—he gave up on the waistcoat.

Dressed in only Nankeen breeches, boots, and a shirt made of fine lawn, Milton made his way to the breakfast parlor and prayed Adele wouldn't be bringing the vase with her.

Chapter 17

PREPARING TO PAY A CALL

*B*ack at *The Black Swan*

Her legs feeling a bit like jelly and her body still abuzz from what she and Alonyius had been doing last night and early this morning, Alice sighed as he worked to do up the buttons on her gown. "How long will you be, do you suppose?" she asked. He had just put voice to a plan to take a walk.

"I really don't know. I have a call to pay. A bit of business, you see. So it depends on how or if I am received. After that, I expect I'll be returning straight here." He paused a moment, gently turning her around with hands that gripped her shoulders. "You're welcome to join me, but it is a bit of a trek through town," he added with a hint of warning. "About a mile."

Truth be told, he couldn't decide if he really wanted her to know the real reason they were staying in Darlington another day. His master had insisted he pay a call on his family, and it seemed as if he had made sure of it by bribing their driver in the event the snow didn't force them to stay.

With Haversham and Higgins happily ensconced with their ladybirds, only Alice would be left with nothing to keep her occupied at *The Black Swan*. And with no idea the weather wasn't the only reason for their delay.

"Perhaps you could take a horse," Alice suggested. "Make the trip go a bit faster." Although she wanted to join the valet on his trek, she really didn't have the proper footwear to be walking in deep snow. Especially a mile. Two, considering there would be a return trip.

Alonyius grinned at her suggestion. "I haven't ridden a horse since I was at..." He almost said 'university', but thought better of it. He rather doubted she would believe he had attended Cambridge, although he had only done so for two years. By then, he knew he would be better suited to a life in service than working in the office at his father's mill. He sighed. "Well, it's been quite a number of years. Should I come upon a hackney, I shall take it."

This last seemed to appease the lady's maid, and she gave him a wan smile. She wasn't quite sure how she should send him off. A kiss, or a hug? A handshake seemed far too impersonal given what they had been doing only an hour ago.

It was Alonyius who kissed her then, a sweet kiss in that it was brief, but one he followed with a peck on her nose. "I've left some coins on the desk so that you might have a luncheon brought up," he murmured. "Or there is a public house just a few doors down from here. Far better than the one downstairs. Just promise me you'll be careful."

Heartened by his concern, Alice nodded. "I will." She gave him a quick kiss before he gave her a bow, placed his short top hat on his head, and took his leave of the room.

He seemed to take all the heat with him as well.

Glancing about the room, Alice realized she couldn't spend the entire day waiting for the valet to return. She would go mad with boredom. Regretting not having joined Alonyius, she wondered if she might discover which direction he took and catch up to him. Fresh air would do her some good. If she couldn't find Alonyius, she would simply enjoy luncheon at the public house he mentioned.

Hurrying to her valise, she rummaged around in search of another pair of stockings and her only pair of half-boots. Within minutes, she had pulled on her redingote and had a woolen scarf wrapped about head. Helping herself to the collection of coins on the desk as well as the key, she took her leave of the room and descended the stairs to the public room below.

Haversham greeted her as she passed through the room, a tankard held up in salute. Pausing at his table, she gave a nod to the tavern maid who sat next to the driver. "Good morning, Mr. Haversham. I trust you're enjoying our unexpected stop," she said.

The driver gave a snort. "Can't say it was all that unexpected," he replied with a grunt. "Seein' as how Banks needed to pay a call and all."

Alice frowned, straightening at the odd comment. "You knew about the call?" she asked, a bit sheepish with her query.

"Oh, yeah. It's partly why we're stuck here."

"Partly?" Alice repeated, noting how the tavern maid seemed to glare at her.

"Well, we could ha' left this afternoon, seein' as how the mail coach just came from the north, but we wouldn't be gettin' to Hexham before dark. Better we go in the morning."

Alice nodded. "I see." She didn't, really, but what else could she say? "And where might Mr. Banks have gone on his call?" she asked, trying not to sound too curious. "I hope he didn't have to walk too far."

Haversham angled his head first to one side and then the other. "Mill House isn't so far. A mile maybe?"

"Mill House?"

"Yeah. The big mansion. Belongs to the bloke who owns the local textile mill."

Nodding, Alice gave a quick curtsy. "I do hope he makes it just fine in this weather," she said before turning to take her leave.

Mill House? What on earth would the valet be doing paying a call on a mansion in Darlington?

She inhaled sharply.

Was he under consideration for a position there? He had

mentioned something about being familiar with the area. *I grew up near here,* he had said last night, his comment whispered whilst he held her after that first time he had made love to her. Perhaps he had asked that they stay so he could interview for a position.

He hadn't said a word about leaving London, though. About leaving the earl. He had been the aristocrat's valet for one-and-twenty years!

A bit panicked, Alice emerged from the smoked-filled public room of the coaching inn and looked about in both directions. There was no sign of Alonyius, but she marveled at the number of people who hurried about as she inhaled the cold, crisp air. When she spotted an older woman coming out of a butcher's shop, she hurried up to her. "Pardon me, but could you point me in the direction of Mill House?"

The woman gave her a quick look up and down, as if she was assessing the value of her clothing. A gnarled finger pointed east. "Only mansion at the end of that lane," she murmured before she turned as if to go on her way. "But haven't heard they're looking for any housemaids," she warned.

Alice glanced down at what she wore, wondering what had given away her profession. Her redingote almost covered her carriage gown, but the worn hem of the out-of-date gown was clearly on display.

"Valet, is what I heard," the woman said as she turned around again and leaned in a bit. "Seein' as how the owner's grown a bit round about the belly. Probably can't reach his buttons to do them up hisself." This last had the woman giving a guffaw before she headed off with her purchases.

Left dumbfounded, Alice stared at the retreating back of the old woman.

Valet?

That could only mean one thing, she realized. Alonyius *was* applying for a position. Given his record of having been a valet to an earl for so many years, how could he not be hired?

Then she remembered Haversham's comment. The owner of Mill House owned a textile mill. He was a man who had apparently grown quite large around the middle. Of course he would hire someone of Mr. Banks' experience!

Determined to reach Alonyius before he made his way into the Mill House mansion, she quickened her steps in the direction the old woman had indicated.

At least fifteen minutes passed as she struggled to keep her feet beneath her in the snow and ice. The dark red brick structure, at least three stories tall and quite wide, was indeed the only house at the end of a long lane flanked by a series of live oaks. A small stone fountain topped with a Greek statue stood in the middle of the circle drive. Thin Italian poplars decorated the front of the Georgian building, and fashion-able arched windows flanked the double doors and graced the entire first story of the building. Smaller windows lined up with their first-story counterparts along the second story. The white painted portico above and the carvings on either side of the doors provided little in the way of protection from the elements.

But what had Alice sighing in disappointment were the boot prints in the snow.

They led all the way to the front doors.

Alonyius had already made it into the mansion.

By way of the front door, it seemed.

This is odd, Alice thought.

Glancing to the left and then to the right, Alice looked in vain for a way to get to the back of the house. Given the snow, there didn't seem to be an obvious path to a servants' entrance.

Slowing her steps, Alice wondered what to do. She couldn't exactly knock on the door. What would she say when the butler answered? *I'm here for the man who is inter-viewing for a position. Oh, and might you have one for me, too?*

On the verge of tears and feeling ever so much the fool,

she made her way to a stone bench at the side of the half-circle drive. Pushing the snow off the seat with the tail of her scarf wrapped around one chilled hand, she settled onto the cold stone and decided she would simply wait for Alonyius to complete his interview. It couldn't take that long, she reasoned as she rewrapped her scarf around her head and face and her arms around the front of her body.

As for what she might tell the man when he emerged from the house? Well, she would think of something.

Please don't accept the position wouldn't work, but something else might.

Chapter 18

A COUNTESS LEARNS SOME HISTORY FROM A HOUSEKEEPER

*B*ack at *Torrington House*
Adele took a steadying breath, her sobs finally having turned to a few hiccups now and again. Her mind a jumble—she wanted to apologize to her husband at the same time she wanted to throttle him—she busied herself with dressing in the only carriage gown she could manage without his help. It meant wearing only stays instead of her usual corset, but it wasn't as if anyone would see her.

The butler? The housekeeper? A housemaid or a footman? There were so few servants on staff at Torrington Park, she thought she might go an entire day without seeing someone. Or perhaps they were all hiding, afraid to meet the new mistress of Torrington Park.

A door down the hall slammed shut and a rather loud curse sounded by way of the dressing room door. Adele stilled herself. *Milton?* she wondered, rather frightened. Why, the word was so loud, she was sure the neighbors had heard it.

That is, if there *were* any neighbors.

She had no idea how far away the nearest people lived in this part of Northumberland.

The thought had her considering whom she might know.

Dr. Darius Jones lived somewhere nearby. He was an

archaeologist, she remembered. The brother of the Duke of Westhaven, Dr. Jones spent his days studying Hadrian's Wall and the artifacts left behind by the Roman soldiers who used to occupy this part of England. She briefly wondered if Dr. Jones might be planning a trip to London in the next day or so. Perhaps she could join him in his coach.

She shook the thought from her head, realizing she didn't even know the man well enough to request a ride. Besides, given the deep snow that blanketed most of England, she rather doubted the man could even get all the way to London. Then she'd be stuck in a coaching inn for who-knew-how-long waiting for a mail coach or some other means to get back to London.

Which had her wondering once again as to the fate of her maid and Milton's valet. She found she missed Simpkins, if only because she wanted the woman's company. Even a complaining Simpkins would provide better company than having no company.

About to depart for the breakfast parlor, Adele paused.

Would Milton be there?

The very last person she wanted to see at the moment was him. Perhaps if she rang the bell, a maid might come. If she could order breakfast to be brought up, she could eat in the bedchamber.

She glanced about, not pleased with the prospect of spending the entire day in the mistress suite. She had already read every book she had brought with her, and there were no other diversions available in this room.

What would she do all day?

Sighing, she glanced about. What's the worst that could happen should she take breakfast in the parlor?

Her husband might make an appearance.

On his knees and groveling, she hoped.

He had some explaining to do. Some promises to make.

Allowing a sigh, she wondered if she would allow him the time to do so.

Every moment Adele thought she could abide his presence was followed by the thought of Edith Harrington, and she decided she simply couldn't.

Not yet. The wounds caused by his words were far too fresh.

Taking a deep breath, she carefully opened the door and peeked around the door jamb. No one seemed to be about, so she slipped from the bedchamber and made her way toward the main stairs. She almost made it, but the housekeeper appeared from around the corner and gave her a deep curtsy.

Adele gave the older woman a nod and said, "Good morning," before continuing on her way.

"Good morning, my lady," Mrs. Miller replied with a brilliant smile. "May I be allowed to say how happy we are to have you here for the holiday?" she added, her head tipped to one side.

Pausing in her descent, Adele turned and gave the woman a wan smile. "How kind of you," she managed. She had half a mind to ask the woman if Milton had ever entertained any of his widows at the former hunting lodge, but thought better of it.

Could she abide any more news of her husband's former lovers?

But suddenly emboldened, she climbed back up the top two stairs and asked, "Pray tell, what other women has his lordship brought here to Torrington Park in the past?"

The housekeeper's brows furrowed as she considered the question. "There haven't been any other women here, my lady," she answered with a shake of her head. "Well, exceptin' for the late countess, God rest her soul, and his lordship's cousin's wife, of course. But the Grandbys only visit here a few times a year," she added quickly. "When he brings the scotch to age in the cellar."

Adele blinked. "Not a one?" she queried. She knew about the scotch, of course. Milton practically bragged about how good his cousin was at running the earldom's distillery somewhere outside of Hexham. Her own brother did the same out of one of the Devonville estates, although it was located just south of the border with Scotland.

Mrs. Miller shook her head. "Torrington Park was a hunting lodge for many years, my lady. No women allowed, is my understanding. It wasn't until his lordship inherited that this property was made suitable for living year 'round, and then only because his mother insisted she have a place to sleep when she came up for Christmastime, if you catch my meaning."

Considering the older woman's words, Adele gave her a nod. "Thank you. You've been most informative," she managed before turning to head down the stairs. She couldn't help but think the housekeeper's words were rehearsed. As if Mrs. Miller had been coached to answer a particular way so as not to raise suspicion among any of the women who were in residence at some point throughout the year.

"I do hope the earl didn't catch a chill," the housekeeper commented as she tucked her chatelaine into a rather large pocket in her day gown.

Adele paused in her descent and turned her head. "A chill?" she repeated.

"A few minutes ago. Why, the man had locked himself out of his bedchamber, and he wasn't wearing a stitch of clothing, my lady," Mrs. Miller remarked, her eyes round. "Had to let him into his bedchamber, I did."

A combination of spite and jealousy had Adele regarding the housekeeper with suspicion for a fraction of a second. She finally allowed a grin. "I do hope you weren't too terribly traumatized by the ordeal."

Mrs. Miller blinked before she matched the grin with one of her own. "I've been the housekeeper here since back when it was a hunting lodge, milady. 'Taint nothing that can do that to me."

It was Adele's turn to blink. The woman was older, but her comment suggested Torrington Park's conversion from an enclave for the Grandby men to an estate home had been rather recent. "How long ago was that, pray tell?"

The housekeeper seemed to consider the question for a moment. "Back in ninety, I think it was. The last countess, God rest her soul, couldn't abide the late earl's choice in decor. She had the first floor completely redone to suit her tastes. After that first Christmas she stayed here."

Performing a bit of math in her head, Adele realized the redecoration had to have happened just after Milton inherited the earldom. As for the ground floor, given the number of animal heads and antlers mounted on the walls in the great hall, the dowager countess obviously hadn't touched it. Now Adele wondered if Milton insisted on keeping the hunting lodge aesthetic. She wasn't about to ask any more of the housekeeper, though. The woman no doubt had a good deal to do given the number of rooms in the place.

"Thank you again. Do have a good day," Adele murmured before she continued on her way down the stairs.

Now that she knew Milton was in the master suite—he hadn't passed her and the housekeeper—she figured it was safe to go to the breakfast parlor. As to what she would do after breakfast, she had no idea. But there were at least a dozen rooms in which she could do it.

And there was a library.

Chapter 19

THE PRODIGAL SON
RETURNS

*M*eanwhile, at Mill House in Darlington
Shedding his cape coat and leather gloves in the vestibule of Mill House, Alonyius called out a greeting. When no butler had appeared at his knock, he had let himself in. If the ancient servant was the same man who had served Mill House the last time he was in residence, Alonyius was quite sure the man was deaf and a bit slow.

"Hullo," he called out again as he moved to the bottom of the stairs.

"Who's there?"

His mother, clad in a day gown of deep red Merino, her gray hair braided and wrapped into a coronet atop her head, suddenly appeared at the top of the stairs and angled her head. "Alonyius! You came!" she cried out in delight.

Grinning broadly, Alonyius took the central stairs two at a time to meet her at the top. "Mum, you look positively radiant," he said before giving her a kiss on the cheek.

"And you look as if you walked all the way from the mail coach," she scolded, one of her tiny hands moving to brush away some of the snowflakes from his hair.

"*The Black Swan*, yes," he replied with a roll of his eyes. "After four days in a coach, I needed the exercise."

The hand moved to take his. "You mean being tumbled

three ways to Thursday wasn't enough exercise?" she countered, a gleam in her eye.

Alonyius blinked. "Mother!" he scolded, suddenly wondering if she had spies at *The Black Swan*.

"Well, it certainly looks like you were. I don't think I've ever seen so much color in your cheeks."

The valet rolled his eyes. "That would be because I've been out in the *cold*," he countered with a nod, still rather shocked at her earlier comment.

"I do hope it wasn't with Mildred," she said with a good deal of worry.

Alonyius blinked again. "Mildred?" he repeated.

"She's one of the tavern maids at *The Black Swan*. Give you the clap, she will," she warned with a raised finger.

Not particularly sure he wanted to know how his mother knew such a thing, Alonyius sighed. "Then our coach driver will have that honor," he stated in a lowered voice, realizing that with a simple wave of her crooked finger, she was about to take him on a tour of the first floor of the house. He knew she had been busy finishing the rooms along the north wing. They had never been furnished when his father first had the house built in 1768. While Alonyius was in residence, the family had always lived in the rooms in the south wing.

He dutifully followed her from room to room, commenting on her choice of colors and on the furnishings. Despite her humble beginnings, he realized his mother had good taste. Expensive taste. Which could only mean the mill was still profitable.

"So, what do you think? Could you see yourself living here again, darling?" Mrs. Banks asked in a voice filled with pleading.

Alonyius couldn't help the bit of uncertainty he felt at her query. "If I must," he finally agreed, rather stunned by how she simply assumed he would be moving back to Mill House. Although he had been a bit concerned about what might have happened to the house in the year since he had last visited, Alonyius found it in the same condition or, in some cases, in even better shape. That meant that either the servants were doing their jobs better or there were more of them.

Truth be told, he was rather surprised at how elegant everything seemed, the furnishings looking as if they had come straight from Chippendale's studios, the carpets from Axminster, the draperies from...

"I had your brother weave the draperies especially for each room," she said proudly, as if she could overhear his thoughts. "Except for the sheers. Those are from Austria, of course."

Of course, he considered, not exactly familiar with where certain fabrics were sourced these days. He had been too long out of the family business to know such details, and he had no desire to learn unless it was absolutely necessary.

"Come to my parlor for some tea. We'll get you warmed up right quick. How long do you have before you must be on your way again?"

Alonyius gave the question some thought before saying, "A couple of hours, I should think." He didn't want to leave Alice alone too long at the coaching inn. She probably had finished any sewing she had brought with her, and even if she used the coins he had left her to buy a luncheon at the public house he had mentioned, there were only a few shops within walking distance in which she could spend her afternoon.

"Good. You can join us for luncheon," Mrs. Banks said as she led him to a large chair in the parlor.

"Your letter said Thel wasn't doing well," he said as his gaze took in the parlor, rather heartened to find the upholstery in good shape and a fire lit and crackling in the fireplace. A stack of split logs promised several days of warmth. Given the forest just beyond the backyard, there would be fuel for the Mill House fires for years to come. "Since I did not receive a notice of his passing, I have to assume he is recovering," he said with a good deal of hope as he waited for his mother to take a seat in her favorite settee.

She rang the bell on the side table and a maid appeared

within seconds at the door. "Tea, dear, and biscuits and cakes, too. My youngest son has come for a visit, so be sure to tell cook there will be three for luncheon."

The maid curtsied, a slight smile showing on her face. "Yes, ma'am." She disappeared as quickly as she had appeared.

Alonyius watched as the girl performed her curtsy and wondered how long she had been in service. "Seems young," he commented, one brow raised in question.

His mother leaned forward. "She is. I'm training her, though. She'll be a perfect lady's maid by the time one of you boys finally decides to take a wife."

Alonyius stiffened. "Thel is still unwed?" he countered. *Who the hell is supposed to take over Banks Textiles if Thel dies without issue?*

Well, the answer to that was him, of course, but he didn't want to be thinking about changing professions so late in life. He was four-and-forty! He tried not to relive the past few weeks as he worried he might have to be the one to take over the reins of the company. He had been mortified to discover his master had learned of Thelonius Banks' condition about the same time he had. His mother's letter had probably been on the same coach as the one Gregory Grandby rode in to get back to London!

Although he could learn the textile business again, it had been nearly a quarter of a century since Alonyius last stepped foot into the mill that produced some of the most beautiful woolens in all of England. His mother's Merino gown was a testament to their creations.

"Thel had an awful flu," his mother said as she clasped her hands together in her lap. "Why, he was sick for at least a fortnight, and then right in the middle of it, when he was at his worst, and I was sure he was going to leave us, Mr. Grandby arrived for a meeting," she explained with a wave of her tiny hand. "I'd had no idea he was coming, but if I had, I most assuredly would have sent him a letter to reschedule the appointment. I'm sure Mr. Grandby left here thinking his latest investment would fail."

Alonyius straightened, a bit alarmed at her words. "Latest investment?" *What has my brother been arranging with my master's cousin?*

"Why, yes. He helped your brother buy another loom. An *investment*, he called it. Makes the fabric in a larger width." She held out her arms as wide as they could go. "An entire blanket without any seams. Can you imagine?" she gushed, her hands clapping together when the maid appeared with a silver salver topped with pots and cups and saucers. "I'll do the pouring this time," she murmured, her comment directed to the maid. "But I'll teach you how to do it the next time."

"Yes, ma'am," the maid said as she dipped another curtsy. Alonyius could swear she blushed before she started to take her leave of the parlor, but then she suddenly turned around.

"What is it?" he asked when he realized his mother hadn't noticed the maid's delayed departure.

"Pardon, sir. I don't know that it's my place to say anything, but when I passed by the front window on my way up the stairs, I couldn't help but notice there are *two* sets of tracks in the snow leading up to the house. Sir," she added as an afterthought. "Should I be seeing to another guest? In another room, perhaps?"

Both Mrs. Banks and Alonyius stared at the maid before giving one another a glance.

Another guest?

Chapter 20

A MELANCHOLY EARL

L *ater that morning*
          Milton Grandby stared at his late breakfast and
          frowned. Although the cook had made his eggs the
way he usually liked them, they stared back at him like two
yellow suns in a cloudy sky. Next to them, the crisp rashers of
bacon promised flavors of salt and smoke while the toast
would taste of nuts and sweet butter.

If only he felt like eating.

He glanced over at the newly-ironed copy of the Hexham
news sheet. The date at the top was at least a week in the past
—he didn't even know what day it was today—and he found
he didn't care.

He mentally cursed Edith Harrington. Then he
proceeded to curse every Harrington he knew, including
Stanley, Earl of Mayfield, and his other sisters, Caroline,
Helen, and Elizabeth. He decided not to curse Julia Harrington, the earl's only daughter. She was one of Milton's
goddaughters, after all, and couldn't have known what her
Aunt Edith was busy doing over ten years ago.

What she was probably doing last night.

The woman was a Merry Widow, after all. And there
were any number of men looking to keep her that way. All
vying for her attention in bed in the hopes they would be the

one to convince her it was time to take a husband and vow to only bed him.

Except, why would she?

She had a fortune. She had no reason to abide Society's strictures. No reason to commit herself to just one lover when there were so many willing to keep her bed warm.

Even if he had managed to get the woman to wed him, she would have kept a string of lovers on the side. She probably wouldn't even have hidden them from him. He would have been the laughing stock of Parliament had he actually gained her hand in marriage.

And for what?

A willing bed partner who was far too willing? Why, they would have had the most crowded marriage bed in all of England!

No. Far better for him to have loved her and left her when he did. Time had proven she would have kept her string of lovers. Time had proven she would never make a suitable Countess of Torrington.

Not when he had the perfect countess.

Adele.

Milton sighed.

"Would you like coffee, my lord?"

Raising his head from where it hung on his chest, Milton regarded the footman who held a silver pot above his cup. "I suppose," he finally answered. He watched as the dark liquid filled the cup, curls of steam swirling about above the edge. He recognized the cup and his plate as part of the pieces his mother had purchased for when she stayed at Torrington Park.

It's positively barbaric you don't have good china here, she had said that first Christmas she stayed at Torrington Park. Within a month, a crate of Coalport China's finest was delivered in the back of a dray cart. The servants who unpacked the dishes filled the cupboards in the butler's pantry with the settings, probably snickering at the sight of the pattern whilst they did so.

Blue Cairo Bird.

Well, it was appropriate for a hunting lodge, he considered, rather hoping Adele had been served her breakfast on the china.

"Did the countess come down for breakfast this morning?" he asked before the footman had taken his leave of the breakfast parlor.

"She did, my lord, although she took her coffee in the library." The man gave a bow and disappeared.

The library.

Well, he should have known Adele would be in the room with the books. He hadn't paid a visit there for... well, since they had met there for coffee and walnuts before dinner the night before. When she straddled him whilst he sat in the divan, and he had his way with her.

Or had she had her way with him?

It was a wonder she was there! He thought she would loathe the library after what they had done in the room.

Perhaps if he allowed her to spend most of the day there, she would read a few books and forget their awful morning. Forget and meet him in his bedchamber where they could kiss and make love until the wee hours of the morning.

Or perhaps she would read some story about philandering husbands and believe he was one.

Curse Edith Harrington. Curse all the Harringtons! He thought, just then remembering to exclude Julia. She was nearly of an age to be married, but she wasn't yet, so she was innocent in all this. As far as he knew, Julia hadn't been taking lessons from Aunt Edith.

He could only hope.

He dropped his head to his chest and sighed.

"Would you like another serving of eggs, my lord? Or some more bacon, perhaps?"

Jolted from his reverie, Milton stared at his plate, stunned to find he had cleaned it. He dared a glance around, expecting to find a dog or other creature who might have helped himself to the breakfast. A sudden burp reminded him that he had eaten it all despite his rather melancholy mood.

"I have had quite enough," he replied as he regarded the unfamiliar footman. "Have we met?"

The footman shook his head. "Gabriel, my lord."

"Good to meet you," Milton managed. He dared a glance inside his cup and realized that he had emptied it, too. "I do believe I'll have more coffee, though," he added.

"Very good, my lord."

Within moments, his cup was refilled and his plate was taken from the table. Not sure what else to do, he drained his coffee, donned his greatcoat, and made his way to the stables.

There were horses who would probably appreciate his attention.

Chapter 21

A MANOR HOME RECEIVES
ANOTHER GUEST

*B*ack at Mill House
Alonyius frowned, the maid's words about there being another guest rather odd. He was about to tell her there wasn't another guest because he was sure his tracks were the first and only in the fresh snow. But curiosity had him standing. He moved to the parlor window.

Overlooking the Greek statue and fountain in the circle drive and positioned in the middle of the long manor house, the window gave the perfect vantage for the lane leading up to the house. He realized immediately the maid spoke the truth, for there was another set of footprints in the snow, the steps closer together and smaller of foot.

He angled his gaze, even pressing his face against the cold glass in an attempt to make out where the steps led. One set followed the drive along the front of the house but circled around. He was so intent in studying the wing of the manor house closest to the carriage house, he was unaware of his mother as she stepped up to the window and gazed out in the other direction.

"Why, there is someone else out there," she murmured. "There on the bench," she pointed. She suddenly pulled back her gnarled finger as if she just then remembered pointing was rude. "Why, the snow makes her look like a statue."

Alonyius followed her gaze and frowned. For a moment, he thought the shape looked like an old woman, what with the way her scarf-clad head and shoulders seemed hunched over. Then he let out a gasp when he realized he recognized that scarf.

He had seen it every day for the past four days.

"Oh, dear God. It's Alice," he murmured as he hurried from the window and out the parlor. "Get some blankets," he yelled as he descended the stairs. *What the hell is Alice doing here?* Had she followed him? *Not possible*, he thought, remembering no one had been behind him as he made his way down the lane.

He didn't bother with his coat but sailed out the front door to a blast of cold air that nearly took his breath away.

Almost slipping on the icy drive, he slowed his steps and managed to make it to Alice without falling. "Alice," he said with some urgency. He could see her eyes were closed, and when she didn't respond, he pushed away the scarf and placed his hands on either side of her face. He winced when he saw her lips were nearly blue. Gathering her into his arms, he stutter-stepped his way back to the house, heartened to find another servant holding the door open.

"We need a foot warmer. And blankets," he said as he continued to carry Alice through the vestibule.

"You can put her up here in the Blue Room, dear," his mother called down to him as she waved from the top of the stairs. "This way. Regan is seeing to some more tea."

He hurried up the stairs, his worry increasing when Alice didn't respond. She felt light in his arms, and he was reminded of how comfortable he had been with her covering half of his body only a couple of hours ago.

His mother led him along the long hall and into one of the guest bedchambers, the mahogany furnishings smelling of lemon polish and fresh-cut wood.

Alonyius paused in the doorway, realizing this bedchamber was next door to the one he had used when he lived at Mill House. If he remembered correctly, there was a connecting door between them.

He was about to chide his mother—had she chosen this bedchamber deliberately?—but thought better of it when Alice finally moved in his arms.

"Do you like it? I just had it redone last year. No one has even stayed here," Mrs. Banks went on as if the situation was no more serious than an unexpected visitor.

"Alice," Alonyius whispered as he settled her half-sitting onto the bed. When only a slight moan could be heard above the chattering of her teeth, he began unwinding the frozen scarf from around her head. Meanwhile, his mother regarded him with an odd expression before suddenly stepping forward to undo the buttons down the front of the redingote.

"So, she is the reason you look as if you've been tumbled three ways to Thursday," she remarked with a wan smile.

"Mother!" Alonyius scolded again, glancing around to be sure none of the servants were about. He had to hope Alice hadn't overheard the comment.

"You needn't deny it, dear," she went on, her expression changing before she sighed and said, "Like father, like son."

Alonyius helped his mother remove the redingote, but he paused as he considered her words. "It's true. She is a lady's maid," he murmured as he rested the front of Alice's chilled body against him. He was about to undo the buttons he had done up only the hour before but realized he really shouldn't undress the maid with his mother standing there. Instead, he leaned down and pulled off her half-boots.

The citrus scent from her soap wafted past his nostrils, reminding him of how he had washed her hair the night before. Of how she smelled when he had made love to her. Of how she had looked that morning, her sleep-tousled hair curling around her face and her skin glowing. But worry quickly replaced his reverie when Alice didn't seem to be responding. She was shivering though. He was sure her teeth were still chattering. And he wanted nothing more than to simply hold her until all of his warmth seeped into her body.

Where was the foot warmer?

"For whom is she a maid?" Mrs. Banks asked in a whisper. She moved to pull down the velvet counterpane and the bed linens. Heartened to see there were blankets atop the linens, Alonyius lifted Alice onto the bed and quickly covered her. The scent of citrus once again wafted past his nostrils.

Giving his head a shake, Alonyius realized he hadn't introduced his mother to the woman he had been holding as if she were as delicate as bone china. "For my master's wife, Lady Torrington," he replied. "Her name is Alice Simpkins. She's been employed by her ladyship for nearly twenty years," he added, knowing his mother would appreciate hearing of her loyalty. He didn't add that he had no idea how she knew where he was, or why she had come. Why she had come and simply taken a seat on a cold, stone bench.

Had something happened back at The Black Swan?

Why hadn't she knocked on the door? Certainly his footprints in the snow showed that he had come in that way.

"She smells heavenly," Mrs. Banks said as she sniffed the air. "Why, she smells just like you do. Did you share a bath, perhaps?"

Alonyius didn't miss the sound of hope in her voice. He shook his head. "Only the bathwater," he replied in a whisper.

"Oh, well, you'll have to give bathing together a try. Your father proposed to me after our second bath together—"

"Mother!" Never once in his life had he wondered why his father had decided to marry a lady's maid. Now he would wonder for the rest of his life how they had ended up in a bathtub together.

"We had already made love several times by then," she whispered, her manner most sober as she ignored his expression of shock. "Why, I think I was expecting your brother when your father finally showed up at her ladyship's door and told her he had come for me. Lady Torrington was ever so gracious, though—"

"*Lady Torrington?*" Alonyius repeated as he swung around to regard his mother, his brows furrowing in confusion. For a brief moment, he thought she might have lost her faculties and become a candidate for Bedlam.

"Why, yes. Your master's mother. I had been her lady's maid since her come-out, you see, and she had just married Torrington. Your master's father. That's when your father decided he wanted me to be mistress of Mill House. Can you imagine?"

He really couldn't at that moment, but he was spared from having to respond when a footman appeared at the door. The servant carried a foot warmer wrapped in a bath linen and held it out as if he didn't know quite what to do with it.

"I'll take that," Alonyius said as he hefted the large water bottle from the servant. His mother lifted the bed covers at the end of the bed, and he settled it in place. Before pulling the covers back over the top of it, he carefully moved Alice's stockinged feet so they rested next to it. At least she had pulled on an extra pair of stockings, he noticed.

With nothing more to do but wait, he found he had to sit down. He did so on the edge of the bed, one hand covering Alice's where it lie hidden beneath the counterpane.

Returning his attention to his mother, he realized he had never been told how his parents knew each other. "How, pray tell, did you two even meet?" He was struggling with trying not to imagine his mother in a bathtub with his father.

"Why, at the drapers, of course," she replied in a huff, as if her son should have known. "Marcus had just delivered the most spectacular bolt of deep red Merino to Howell's..." She held out the skirt of the gown she wore to emphasize her point. "And Lady Torrington saw it and demanded she be sold the entire bolt. It took an entire bolt to make a gown back in those days," she added with an arched eyebrow.

"The whole nine yards?" Alonyius countered. *My, how*

fashion has changed. He was fairly sure there were at least two gowns in every bolt these days. Maybe three.

"Indeed. So, your father gave me the bolt and stared at me for the longest time. Like he'd been struck by lightning."

Alonyius wondered if his mother was playing some poor joke on him. "As in a *bolt* of lightning?" he whispered. He couldn't help but grin at his mother's tale. Daring a glance down at Alice, he was heartened to see her eyelids fluttering open and her expression indicating she was following every word of his mother's story.

Poor thing.

His mother tittered before her attention went to Alice. "There you are, dear. Why, I was just telling my son that I thought he looked as if he'd been—"

"Mother!"

"—Struck by lightning, and here you are."

Alice allowed a wan smile. "Hullo," she managed, the word sounding rather hoarse. Her eyes suddenly widened as she inhaled sharply and moved to sit up. Alonyius placed a hand at her shoulder and gently pushed her back down.

"I think it's too soon to sit up just yet," he whispered.

Wondering where she was, Alice gave him a nod before she taking a moment to review the scene around her. The bed on which she lay was rather comfortable, and the furnishings she could see from her vantage had her thinking she was in an aristocrat's home. She suddenly remembered why she had come—Alonyius was there to see about a position—and realized just why everything seemed so elegant. So why was the woman referring to Alonyius as if he was her son?

And how would she explain the reason for her visit?

"I wish to apologize, milady. I—"

"Oh, nonsense, darling," Mrs. Banks said with a wave of a hand. "I had to meet you. And you didn't think my son had enough sense to bring you with him, of course, so I appreciate you doing it for him." She screwed up her face a bit. "Or something like that. Let's get you some tea, shall we?"

As if on cue, Regan entered the bedchamber with a small tea set. Alonyius moved out of the way, his gaze directed at Alice as he watched the color return to her cheeks.

Due to embarrassment, no doubt.

"Oh, he wanted to bring me, I think," Alice murmured in the valet's defense. "He offered, you see, but thought it would be too cold for me to walk this far. I don't have the proper boots." The walk hadn't been so terribly bad. It had been the waiting on the cold stone bench for him to come out of the manor house that sapped what little strength she had left. She hadn't eaten anything before making her way to Mill House. Then she had passed out from hunger and the cold before he found her.

The old woman angled her head to one side, her confusion apparent. "Then why did you decide to come by yourself, dear?"

Alice gave Alonyius a beseeching look before turning her attention back to the old woman. "I thought he was here about a position. That he was to be interviewed for the valet's position. To be hired by the man of the house, and leave Lord Torrington's service," she explained with a shake of her head. "I found I couldn't abide the thought, but by the time I arrived, it was already too late." She turned her attention back to Alonyius, realizing she must sound like a lovesick schoolgirl. If only she could take back those last words, even if they did have Mrs. Banks beaming in delight.

Alonyius stared at Alice for a long time, stunned by her words. That she would brave the cold and snow and risk her very life because she thought he was leaving the Earl of Torrington's employ had him realizing two things.

Make that three.

Despite her reputation at Worthington House, she was merely a passionate woman whose frustration at an impossible situation had finally boiled over in the form of complaints. He was pretty sure he knew what she had been doing and what was causing her poor disposition. The change of scenery and the company on this trip had her behaving in what he realized was probably her normal manner.

She obviously cared for him. Perhaps she even felt affection for him. Why else would she balk at the thought of him taking a position in a different household? One that was hundreds of miles from London?

His immediate reaction to seeing her nearly frozen on the stone bench had been carried out without thought. Panic had him realizing he had to get her into the house. Warm her up. Keep her safe.

Would he have reacted the same for any other woman? For there was a moment when he couldn't bear the thought of losing her. Certainly that must mean he felt something for her. Something that wasn't just lust.

"Why, I do believe my son owes you an explanation," Mrs. Banks said in a huff. "He wasn't here about a position at all. At least, I don't think he was." She turned her gaze on Alonyius. "Although your brother *is* in need of a valet," she said *sotto voce*, suddenly wondering how the lady's maid knew of the position. Alonyius certainly didn't seem to know.

Rolling his eyes, Alonyius gave his head a shake. "Only if my brother was on his death bed, I suppose, and I had to take over running the mill." He hadn't realized until just then that he needn't worry about taking over Banks Textiles, at least not yet. His brother was apparently on the mend and back at the mill.

Mrs. Banks angled her head. "So, you weren't considering the valet's position? Your brother's been looking for one," she repeated.

Alonyius shook his head. "No, Mum."

"Well, at least I know you'll come home when you're needed," his mother said brightly. "You two will stay for luncheon," she insisted suddenly. "Something tells me you haven't eaten, and all those tumb—"

"Mother!"

"—Lightning strikes and such probably have you both on the verge of fainting."

Having already drained a cup of tea and well aware she needed to eat something, Alice could only agree. As for the lightning strikes, she had no idea what the woman was talking about. She hadn't seen any lightning during her walk to the house. "Until the coach leaves for Northumberland in the morning, I have no place I need to be."

Alonyius nodded. "It is the same for me," he agreed, pausing before he added, "But I should probably spend a bit of time with my brother." He wondered if Thelonius was truly recovered enough to be back in his office at Banks Textiles. "I suppose he's at the mill now?"

His mother opened a tiny locket that dangled from her chatelaine and aimed it toward the light from the window. Alice realized she was looking at a pocket watch. "If he's keeping track of time, he'll be home in a half-hour. If he waits until he's hungry, he will have been home a few minutes ago." She gave a giggle, apparently amused by her own joke. "In the meantime, let's get you settled in your bedchamber, darling," she said as she turned her attention on Alonyius.

He frowned. "I wasn't planning on staying the night," he replied.

Lifting her chin in a show of defiance, his mother shook her head. "Of course, you weren't. But you will. And I won't abide any arguments from either one of you to the contrary," she added as she included Alice in her edict. "Besides, the beds here have got to be better than any at *The Black Swan*."

Goodness, but with what they'd been doing in one of those beds, Alice hardly noticed if it was comfortable or not. "But, I... I have no clothes with me," she argued.

The older woman's tiny hands flitted about. "Oh, I'm sure we can find you something to wear, dear heart. If not a gown, then we'll simply wrap you in our finest wool. We're in possession of a textile mill, you must know."

Well, I know that now.

What Alice still didn't understand is why Alonyius worked in service in London when his family owned Banks

Textiles. She dared a glance at the valet, rather liking his look of amusement. His mother was quite a charming woman.

The maid reappeared at the bedchamber door, giving a curtsy when Mrs. Banks acknowledged her. "Luncheon is served, ma'am."

Allowing a sigh, the old woman said, "Well, I think we'll just have to start without your brother," she said as she stood up. Alonyius was quick to stand and offer his arm.

As if on cue, a slight commotion sounded from the ground floor. "That will be him now," Mrs. Banks said with a grin. She turned to Alice. "Are you feeling well enough to come down to the dining room, my dear?"

Alice nodded. "I think so, ma'am."

Mrs. Banks turned and gave her son a quelling glance, as if she expected he should already be seeing to their guest. He was already helping Alice off of the bed. He knelt and slipped her half-boots back onto her feet, tying the laces before sliding a hand surreptitiously up the back of her calf. He told himself he was merely ensuring she was no longer chilled, but he thrilled at the sudden start she gave in response.

When he was sure Alice could walk on her own, he offered his other arm, and the three made their way to the top of the stairs.

A man who looked as if he could be Alonyius' twin brother appeared from the vestibule, his top hat held in one hand as a butler saw to removing his great coat. "Al?" he called out, a grin splitting his face. "I expected you three days ago."

Alice dared a glance at Alonyius and then back at the man who was obviously Thelonius Banks. A bit on the portly side, the man displayed blondish-gray hair trimmed quite short and wore a suit of clothes that had been beautifully tailored.

"I don't know why you would," Alonyius replied. At the bottom of the stairs, he left the ladies and held out a hand, as if expecting to shake his brother's. "I am at the mercy of my employer when it comes to these visits, and we only left London Tuesday last."

Thelonius ignored the hand and wrapped a beefy arm around his brother's back. "I see you've finally taken a wife. Now you'll have Mum expecting me to be courting. I'm always saying I haven't got time for it, though," the man said as he let go his hold on his brother and moved to stand in front of Alice.

She inhaled as if to counter his claim, but he was quick to lift her cold hand and brush a kiss over her knuckles. "How do you do? I am Thelonius. My, but you have a cold hand there. But you know what the French say? *Mains froides, coeur chaud.*"

Alice nodded as she took back her hand. "Oh, they're not usually this cold," she murmured, balling her hand into a fist at her side as she felt a blush color her face. "Miss Alice Simpkins," she added, dropping a curtsy. "Lady's maid to the Countess of Torrington. It's very good to meet you, sir."

Thelonius dared a glance at his mother, who seemed to beam in delight as she angled her head, her attention on her younger son. Meanwhile, Alonyius looked as if he wished a chasm would open up in the floor and swallow him whole.

"Like father, like son, eh?" Thelonius said as an impish grin revealed a dimple. "You've obviously made my mother very happy, even if you're not betrothed to him," he said in a hoarse whisper. He straightened. "The mill is officially closed for the holiday. I have sent everyone home with a pheasant and a sixpence and told them not to return until the twenty-seventh."

Alice's eyes widened. Such a generous employer! She always had the day after Christmas off, of course, but never so many days before!

"What my brother really means is that the looms will be cleaned and oiled on the morrow, so there won't be much work for the others to do," Alonyius explained as he once again offered his arm to Alice. "And it's not fair that the lace-makers have to work if those making the fabrics do not."

His brother had already stepped up to offer his arm to his mother, and the four made their way to the dining room.

Her head swimming in wonder at the strange manor in which she found herself, Alice dared a glance up at Alonyius. He seemed so at home, so at ease. But she supposed if he had grown up here—she still wasn't sure if he had ever called Mill House his home—he would be comfortable. Indeed, to see how he carried himself, how he wore his clothes, the cut of his hair, the shine on his boots, she thought him to the manor born.

And yet he looked no different from when he was at Worthington House. Why hadn't she noticed his bearing before?

As for the manor itself, Alice was only beginning to take in the vast great hall and the rich detail of the place. Every bit as elegant as Worthington House in both furnishings and art, Mill House differed in that it was rather wide and three stories in height, while Worthington House was thin and deep and four stories tall. Here, the dark paneled walls of the hallway were adorned with paintings all the way to the end, where carved doors led to a library and what she thought might be a salon. Her attempt at making out the signature on a painting was cut short when they were suddenly in the elegant dining room.

Never having been served a formal meal in a home's dining room, Alice realized she was in for a treat. A servant would be waiting on her. Alonyius pulled out a chair for her and then moved to the opposite side of the table. Meanwhile, his brother seated their mother at one end before he took the carver at the other end. Within minutes, the meal was served by several footmen and a maid, and Alice simply ate and listened as the members of the Banks family seemed to carry on several topics of conversation at once. When a question was directed her way, she answered quickly, but didn't ask anything in return. Fascinated by how the brothers interacted, she didn't want her presence to change their entertaining banter. Their discussions ranged from sheep to mechanical devices to fibers to laborers and all about the struggles of importing wool.

By the time the dessert was served, Alonyius and his brother were talking about the mill and the happenings in town, all while their mother beamed with happiness.

"I take it this does not happen very often," Alice said in a quiet voice meant only for Mrs. Banks' hearing.

"Only once a year, my dear, but they pick up right where they last left off. Why, they might actually finish everything they need to say to one another if Alonyius spends the night."

Was there a chance the valet wouldn't spend the night at Mill House? Alice supposed a carriage might take them back to *The Black Swan* if Alonyius insisted, but she had come to believe that wouldn't happen until the morning.

No matter where they spent the night, she hoped they might have a moment alone before they had to leave Mill House.

She had so many questions!

Chapter 22

A COUNTESS ENCOUNTERS A CHAMBERMAID

*L*ater that afternoon

Had she had any idea Edith Harrington Pendleton, Countess of Pendleton, would have been her husband's second choice for a wife and countess, Adele would never have married Milton Torrington.

At least, that's what she was telling herself as she finished another chapter in the awful book she was reading.

The Treasure of a Pirate.

Where was Lord Sommers when you needed a piffle of a book? she wondered, nearly tossing the leather-bound volume against the wall. That someone had thought this particular dreck worthy of a binding was a testament to their lack of taste. Their lack of understanding of what true love was truly about. Their lack of...

Experience.

She sighed and glanced at the Rococo clock on the fireplace mantle. Had she really just read an entire novel in two hours?

What would she do for the rest of the day?

She glanced out the room's only window, heartened to see the sun still shining despite the clouds that had probably shrouded the area for weeks.

Perhaps she would venture out of doors for a quick walk

around the house. Maybe pay a visit to the stables. The horses could probably use some company. *Have they even been exercised this week?* she wondered.

Making her way to her bedchamber, she was glad the trunk that had been loaded onto their traveling coach had been the one containing her carriage gowns. Rummaging through it, she found one made of wool and shook it out. Almost tempted to pull it on over the one she already wore, she instead wriggled her way out of her gown and changed into the wool one. About the time she realized she needed help with the buttons, there was a knock at the door.

She stilled herself. Had Milton seen her come in? Or...

The door suddenly opened, and a chambermaid appeared. The girl gave a start. "Oh, I apologize, my lady," she squeaked, just about to pull the door closed.

"Don't go," Adele replied. "I am in need of assistance with the buttons. Can you help?"

The chambermaid gave a curtsy and moved to do up the buttons. "Yes, my lady."

Adele realized she might get some answers about Torrington Park from the girl. "How long have you worked here," she asked, her tone rather conversational.

"Just five years, my lady. This is my favorite time of the year to work here, though, seeing as how it's almost Christmas."

"Oh?" the countess replied. "Pray tell, what's so different?"

The girl finished up the buttons. "Why, the hanging of the greens, of course. In just two days. It will be so much better with you here. It's always been just the earl and his valet, you see, and the men aren't as good about seeing to making the day *festive*. Oh, they'll bring in the greens and maybe help hang them up, but they don't bother with the ribbons or the fripperies. You will be there, I hope," she added, her enthusiasm suddenly waning.

Turning around to regard the servant, Adele gave a nod. "Of course, I will," she replied, rather interested to hear that it was only Milton and his valet. The butler had suggested others might be joining them. Others being...?

"Tell me, do you know if there are any others expected to arrive for the holiday?" She must seem like a very poor hostess if she didn't even know who had been invited to share in their Christmas.

Giving her head a shake, the chambermaid replied. "Sometimes the earl's cousin comes with the scotch, but seeing how the weather's been so bad, I rather doubt he'll make the trip."

Adele frowned. "Tell me, what is it we need to decorate this place?" she asked of the maid.

The girl gave a slight shrug. "The pine cuttings, of course. Some wire to make the wreaths. Ribbons for the big bows, and ribbon for the bows for the tree—"

"Is there some ribbon here we can use?" Adele interrupted. She wondered if a trip to Hexham would be required.

"There's red velvet fabric in the storage room, and Cook saw to some red ribbon when she was last in town. She managed to get some marchpane, too, seeing as how she wanted to make a special luncheon to serve everyone whilst we do the decorating. She makes the most beautiful fruits with it, all dipped in sugar and..." He eyes suddenly widened. "Exceptin' that was supposed to be a surprise, my lady. Do you suppose you might forget I mentioned it?" she asked in a pleading voice.

Adele blinked, realizing the girl referred to marzipan. The thought that a cook in such a remote area of England would know how to fashion the festive fruits from almond paste was welcome news. "Of course. All forgotten," she assured the maid. "Now, from where does the tree come?"

The chambermaid blinked. "I don't know, my lady. The footmen usually see to that."

"And the wire?"

Shaking her head, the girl finally said, "The stables, maybe? Mr. Haversham saw to it last year, seein' as how he was sweet on Watson, and she told him he had to help make wreaths. He did, of course, seein' as how he wanted to keep Watson happy since he and Watson like to..." She stopped talking, her face suddenly taking on a reddish cast.

Adele was forced to suppress a grin when she realized exactly what the girl was about to say. "Then I do hope Mr. Haversham arrives in the next day or so," she replied. "He's driving the servants' coach, which has apparently been stuck in Darlington."

Nodding, the chambermaid seemed ever so relieved. "I'm so glad to hear it. Seein' as how Watson gets a bit cranky when she goes too long without a tum—" The girl suddenly stopped talking again, her eyes rolling up in embarrassment.

Knowing exactly what the chambermaid was about to say, Adele was suddenly reminded of her lady's maid. Simpkins hadn't made mention of having a lover in a long time. She hadn't asked permission to spend the night elsewhere—at least, not since Adele had wed.

Is that why she's been so disagreeable? Adele wondered.

Before she could give it another thought, the chambermaid curtsied again. "Mrs. Miller will be wondering as to my whereabouts, seeing as how I was just supposed to collect the chamber pot, my lady."

Adele gave the girl a nod. "Thank you for letting me know about the hanging of the greens. We'll see if we can't make the great hall the grandest it's ever been," she said. Grabbing a winter coat, she headed out of the bedchamber and made her way down the stairs.

Somewhere outside, there were trees that were going to have to be trimmed. And some wire, perhaps in the stables, to make those trimmings into magnificent wreaths.

Pulling on her coat without the help of the butler, she helped herself to her muff and made her way outside.

Chapter 23

AN ENCOUNTER IN THE STABLES

A few minutes later at Torrington Park

The soft neighs of Friesians as well as the odor of manure greeted Milton as he made his way into the stables of Torrington Park. Necessary for the planting and harvesting of the crops grown in the nearby fields, the large beasts were rarely out of the stables when winter covered the rolling hills of Northumberland. He had spent the past half-hour regarding the terrain around the hunting lodge, wondering if the harvest would be better than this past year's. Northumberland hadn't faired as poorly as some lands to the south, but he knew the people here wouldn't survive another year if the cold continued.

A snort and a bit of stomping had him stopping at the stable of the largest horse.

"Good to see you, too," he said, pulling open the huge wooden door imprisoning the beast. The hinges made a sound of protest as he did so, a reminder of the cold. Having grabbed a brush from the wall of tools just inside the entrance to the stables, Milton gave the huge horse a pat on his withers and began brushing him. The quiet, even strokes allowed him the time to think, although he would have preferred the numbness found at the bottom of a bottle of scotch just then and had half a thought to simply return to the lodge and lock himself in the study.

There were too many weapons on the wall in there, though. If Adele found him, she might use one of the lances to impale him.

Probably after she used the mace to throttle him.

He gave an involuntary shudder at what else she might do with the weapons of war that could be found in the ancient study.

"Haven't seen you in a year," he murmured quietly. His comment was answered with a short snort, a puff of white rising from the Friesian's nostrils. "A good deal has happened since then. I married the love of my life," he murmured as he gave the Friesian a long stroke across his back. "I cannot tell you how different life is with a wife."

The horse suddenly lifted his head, as if he agreed with the earl.

"Best decision I ever made," Milton said as he continued to brush the beast. "I could have married any one of a dozen women, but I didn't," he continued, as if the horse could understand his every word. "I waited until I had the opportunity to marry the one woman I knew was perfect for me."

A whinny had him pausing in his ministrations. The Friesian had side-stepped a bit in the stall and turned his head, as if he found it necessary to regard the earl with both eyes.

"Don't argue with me," Milton ordered with a shake of his head. "I knew I would marry her back when she was still in the schoolroom," he stated in no uncertain terms. "She was my best friend's sister. Always knew I would marry her."

The horse bobbed his head again, stepping so he faced the earl before he gave his head a shake.

Milton frowned. "I am not lying," he insisted, his hands going to his hips. "I even told her brother I would marry her," he insisted. "How was I to know some upstart would ask for her hand? That she would agree to marry him?" he continued, as if the horse could understand every word he was saying.

Perhaps he could.

His head was shaking as if in disgust.

"Well, I know that *now*," Milton replied, continuing with the even brushing of the beast's thick hide. "So then I had to wait until the the cur finally died."

The horse let out a rather loud whinny.

"I did not kill him," the earl insisted. "I rather wish I had. And I did not know about Weston until it was almost too late," he added, almost as an afterthought. As long as he was admitting his feelings for his countess to the beast, he figured he had better make it clear he was completely unaware there were others interested in the woman.

Money did that, though. Inherited fortunes were magnets for men who needed blunt. Who had debts.

Weston had been one of those men.

"Thank the gods Lady Ellsworth eavesdrops on her husband's conversations," he stated with a sigh. "Told my love that Weston was after her fortune to pay his gambling debts." He paused in his story as he continued brushing the horse. "Which meant I could finally make my move."

Turning its head sideways, the horse actually seemed to be listening to his words.

"Och, so now you believe me, you dumb beasty," he accused, his voice bitter. Milton continued brushing the horse, his breathing suddenly uneven as he considered how his stupid words of earlier that morning may have marked the end of his marriage. "I love her, dammit. Have since before I went off to university. And then I go and make some stupid comment about that damned Edith Harrington—the *trollop!*—and now I wonder if I will ever see my love again," he bellowed in despair.

The Friesian snorted and neighed in response, a hoof digging into the straw at its feet so when it lifted the leg, the straw sailed backward and sent a waft of dust sailing through the stall. The other horses, similarly disturbed, began voicing their protests and stomping their hooves.

Milton stared at the Friesian, wondering what had the beast so upset. Surely it didn't understand his situation.

Did it?

A movement behind him had him turning to find Adele regarding him with tear-filled eyes.

"Adele? What's wrong?" he asked in alarm as he dropped the brush and moved to take her into his arms.

She seemed to melt against him, a sob causing her entire body to shake as he wrapped his arms around her shoulders. "Nothing," she whispered with a slight shake of her head. "Nothing at all."

The earl continued to hold his wife, just then wondering how long she had been standing there in the stables.

Had she overheard his entire conversation with the Friesian? *She must think I'm a candidate for Bedlam!*

"I love you," he said quietly, his lips next to her ear. "I always have." *I was such a damned fool.*

"I know," she whimpered, her arms tightening their hold on him. "I know that now."

Neighing loudly, the Friesian stomped and bobbed his head.

"Day after tomorrow. Christmas Eve. A sleigh ride. I promise," Milton said to the horse before turning his attention back to his wife. "You will join me, I hope?"

Adele nodded. "I will," she said in a whisper. "But before that, we have to see to cutting some pine boughs. From the trees around the lodge."

The earl regarded her for a moment. "Have you been speaking with Mrs. Miller?" he wondered in a whisper.

She shook her head. "A chambermaid, actually. I've just learned all about your hanging of the greens."

Pulling her hard against his body, Milton held her for several moments. "We don't have to do it if you don't want to," he whispered.

"Of course we do," she countered. "I want to. Anything

to make that great hall a bit more festive for Christmas Day. Make those trophy heads a bit less noticeable."

Grinning, Milton allowed a nod. "If you'd like, I can see to their complete removal," he offered. He hadn't been responsible for any of them, and didn't much care whether they were left hanging or were hidden in the cellars.

Adele shook her head. "No need," she replied with a watery grin. "We'll simply work them into the decor."

The earl nodded. He stilled himself a moment and furrowed his brows. "I wouldn't have married her," he stated suddenly.

Allowing a sigh, Adele rested her head against his shoulder, a sob interrupting another sigh. "I know. Just as I wouldn't have married Weston," she countered.

Milton gave a nod, just then realizing how raw he still felt at learning about her lovers. Especially her former brother-in-law. "I'm still a bit annoyed about Stephen Worthington," he claimed, his voice quite at odds with his words.

Stiffening in his arms, Adele pulled away and regarded him for a moment. "You needn't be. I never would have married him, either."

Milton was about to say something about the man, but decided against it. Better that he accept the way things had worked out rather than regret that he hadn't married her all those years ago. Back when he had a chance to be her one and only husband.

Besides, they had the rest of their lives to make up for lost time.

Chapter 24

A MOMENT ALONE, A NIGHT TOGETHER

Several hours after dinner

Pulling on a borrowed night rail and marveling at the quality of the fabric, Alice allowed a sigh. What an odd day! What a delightful hostess! What a beautiful home!

After luncheon, the men had disappeared into the study, presumably to discuss the family business. Meanwhile, Mrs. Banks had taken her on a tour of the home, obviously proud of the manor house her husband had built with the profits from his textile mill. Although she didn't talk much about her late husband, Mrs. Banks seemed ever so curious about her son's life at Worthington House.

And then she had asked the question for which she seemed the most interested in learning the answer.

When did the lightning strike?

By then, Alice understood what the woman was asking. She was sure Alonyius wouldn't have said anything about having bedded her, but it was apparent his mother assumed they were lovers.

As for a lightning strike, Alice couldn't decide if there had been a moment that had her realizing she had feelings for the valet. *It was more like a slow... sizzle*, she had finally answered, remembering the sound of bacon as it cooked in the kitchen and how that sound grew louder the longer it was in the pan.

She was well aware of how her face must have colored up just then. *We have known each other for seven months, and yet we never gave each other a second glance. Until this trip, I believed he was completely ambivalent about me. Or that he disliked me because I have displayed such a sour countenance these past few months.*

And Mrs. Banks had sighed in that way that made it apparent she rather hoped her son might have found a mate.

Not having had a chance to speak with him in private, Alice realized she would probably have to wait until they were in the coach on the morrow to discuss anything with him. She was sure he thought her a fool for following him.

What could she tell him that wouldn't make her sound as if she had some sort of crush on him?

Perhaps he already knows.

Would it be awkward to sit across from one another in the coach? To remember their moments of intimacy and wonder if they might continue?

Settling onto the bed—at some point, it had been remade and the counterpane and blankets turned down— Alice was studying the fine linens between her thumb and forefinger when she suddenly realized she wasn't alone.

Turning to her right, she found Alonyius regarding her from an open door. Wearing a dressing robe in dark wool, he looked as if he could have been the master of the house.

He could have been, she remembered then, if what his mother had told her was true. *He still one day might be.* The sound of hope in his mother's voice had been unmistakable.

"Hullo," she murmured, moving toward him. His arms were around her in an instant, her body pulled against his in a hug that nearly robbed her breath.

"May I join you?" he whispered, his nose buried in her hair. He smelled of port and pipe tobacco and wool, a heady combination.

A sense of relief settled over Alice. At least matters wouldn't be awkward between them for now. "I'd like that," she replied. She glanced at the door behind him. "I'm guessing that's your bedchamber through there?"

Alonyius nodded as he closed the door.

"Then I suppose your mother will, as well," she added with a grin and an arched eyebrow.

Alonyius sighed, his head bending so his forehead rested on hers. "I must apologize for her—"

"Please, don't," she whispered, giving her head a slight shake. "She's a delightful woman and only wants you to be happy."

Straightening, he seemed to consider the comment a moment. "And here I thought she just wanted grandchildren," he murmured. He lifted her into his arms and placed her on the bed. Doffing his robe, he settled onto the bed and pulled the linens and blankets over them both. Once he had her pulled partly atop his body and had one arm wrapped around her shoulder, he allowed a sigh. "I do hope she didn't scandalize you too much."

Realizing he wasn't going to make love to her—perhaps he thought it inappropriate in his mother's house—Alice wondered if he would answer her questions. "She did not. I found her completely charming. She's a lovely woman." Pausing a moment, she added, "Until she mentioned it, I never would have guessed she had been a lady's maid."

Alonyius sighed, wondering if his mother had told her of her time in service, or if Alice had merely overhead his mother talking when they were attempting to revive her after finding her nearly frozen. "It's the reason she can pass so well as a middle-class matron," he whispered. "Until today, I didn't know she had been Lady Torrington's maid, though."

"But you knew she had been a lady's maid?" Alice half-asked.

"Oh, yes. She was quite proud of her years in service. Daughter of a maid and a footman, she was, although I think there was a merchant or two in her lineage," he remarked.

Alice considered his words a moment. "Why did you go into service?"

"You mean, why did I become a valet when I could have stayed here in Darlington and helped run a textile mill?" he countered, one eyebrow arching up to better display his sarcasm. There wasn't a hint of humor in the response, but his next words had Alice raising her head from his chest. "Because if I hadn't, I would be living here at Mill House, and I would be running a textile mill."

"You didn't want to be involved in the family business?"

Alonyius sighed. "Not if I could help it. Life in the city called, you see, and my mother's profession seemed an honorable way to make a living. I already knew how to sew —she taught me because she claimed she wasn't going to be the one to fix my clothes. And I had no intention of becoming a tailor." He made the statement with a hint of humor, but he suddenly frowned. "And now I'm just realizing why it may have been so easy for me to land the position with the Earl of Torrington in the first place," he murmured in awe.

Alice regarded him with furrowed brows before she understood what he meant. "Because she had been his *wife's* lady's maid?" she guessed. "But that was a long time ago."

The valet nodded. "They are a loyal family, though. Besides, when I went to work for his lordship's father, the man was already well past his prime. The valet he employed —the one that had been with him since his university days— had died. I suppose his lordship wasn't about to hire someone his own age but rather one he could pass along to his heir. He only lived two years after he hired me," he added in explanation.

Allowing a wan smile, Alice nodded her understanding. "But didn't your current master have his own valet?"

"A poor excuse for one, it seems. His lordship kept me on after his father's passing, apparently because I can sew, and the other valet could not. And possibly because I had come to London already knowing of the best tailors."

Alice gave him a grin and then settled her head back onto his chest. "Did you ever regret your decision?"

There was a long pause before he responded, which had Alice thinking perhaps he had fallen asleep. "Twice. On the occasion of my father's passing. The letter saying he was ill did not reach me in time for me to make arrangements to see him, but his lordship was quite accommodating. Allowed me the use of a coach and driver to return here for the funeral."

Alice was stunned by this bit of information. Although she hadn't been impressed when she learned her employer was to marry the Earl of Torrington, and he had not risen in her estimation after the wedding, she found her opinion of Milton Torrington improving the more she learned of the man whilst on this trip. "And the other time?" she prompted.

Alonyius sighed, his chest rising and falling beneath her cheek. "When he married."

Alice lifted her head and regarded him in surprise. Despite the darkness, the dim glow from the fireplace allowed her to see him well enough to note his serious expression. "Because he was no longer a carefree bachelor? I heard he was quite promiscuous."

"Not like you might be thinking," he argued. "His dalliances were not brief. He was always monogamous for the duration of his *affaires*, usually for an entire Season, and they were always with unattached ladies. Usually widows," he explained in his lordship's defense. "As far as I know, he never stepped foot in a brothel. Well, at least not after the occasion of his sixteenth birthday."

Alice continued to gaze at Alonyius, rather stunned to learn her ladyship may have married a more honorable man than she had thought. "Do you find Lady Torrington difficult?"

Alonyius shook his head. "Not in the least. She is a rather gracious lady. But I know his lordship waited a long time to finally marry her, probably too long."

"But, he couldn't. She was—"

"He should have married her before Mr. Worthington made his intentions known," he interrupted.

"But that would have meant he intended to marry her..."

She paused as she suddenly sucked in a breath. "Are you saying—?"

"He probably felt affection for Lady Torrington when she was still in the schoolroom," he whispered.

Alice regarded the valet for a long time, stunned at hearing his claim. "Yet, you claim to regret having been his valet when he married."

"Only because his decision to marry meant his move to Worthington House."

"You don't like it at Worthington House?"

Alonyius sighed again. "I did not at first. Remember, those of us who moved from his lordship's townhouse to Worthington House were seen as... usurpers. Invaders, almost. As if we had been at war and were the victors claiming the spoils. Ours was not a warm welcome."

Remembering quite well how the servants at Worthington House had reacted to learning the earl would be moving in, Alice was secretly glad the valet couldn't see her blush of embarrassment. "I was one of those servants," she admitted quietly. Having been one of the only upper servants in the house, she found the addition of another forced a change in household, not the least of which was where she sat during meals.

"You were," he agreed with another sigh. Perhaps he had avoided the lady's maid at every turn because of those first few weeks. Now he wondered if they would have become lovers sooner if they hadn't experienced such a rocky start.

"The household staff lived in fear of being sacked those first few weeks. We had so little warning. He proposed, and they were married so quickly—"

"It was the same in our household," he argued gently. "There were only two positions assured of remaining the same."

Alice's eyes widened when she realized to which two positions he referred. "Ours," she murmured in understanding.

"And yet, I clearly remember the spectre of uncertainty, and the fear of change, and how powerless we all felt."

"As do I," she murmured, reaching up to kiss the corner of his mouth. "And now? Do you still have regrets?"

The valet seemed to hug her closer to his body. "Only that we must be up at dawn to make our way back to *The Black Swan*," he said with a hint of humor. He kissed her then, a simple kiss, but one that left her feeling reassured. Within moments, she was sound asleep.

Alonyius was awake far longer, however, wondering if he had made a mistake in bedding the lady's maid. No matter what happened going forward, things would always be different between them. He had to hope they wouldn't be awkward around one another.

Lightning had struck, it seemed. But he didn't want to be burned alive.

Chapter 25

A MAID ISN'T MISSED
ONE BIT

eanwhile, back at Torrington Park
"Your butler said something about expecting more people to join us for Christmas," Adele said as she pulled aside the counterpane so Milton could join her in bed.

The earl gave a grunt as he doffed his robe onto the counterpane and settled into the mattress. One of his arms snaked behind Adele's shoulders to pull her close. She suddenly let out a yelp and scrambled to get away from his chilled body.

"You're freezing!" she complained, gingerly returning to his side when she caught his look of chagrin.

"I apologize, my sweeting. My valet would normally have a fire going in the master suite, but since he's not here—"

"You should have a word with your butler in the morning," Adele said with a sigh. Despite assurances that she was the mistress of Torrington Park, she still didn't feel comfortable ordering the maids to see to duties they usually didn't perform, and the butler really was her husband's servant.

Although she expected to miss her lady's maid again this day, she found she had not—other than that moment just before the chambermaid appeared. With Milton preferring her hair down and his enthusiasm at helping her undress, she found preparing for bed rather easy. Attempts at pulling on a night rail were met with protests, however.

Why bother, my sweeting? I'm only going to strip it off of you, Milton complained the night before. And so she would quickly climb into bed wearing only the necklace she had worn to dinner.

Getting ready for the day—and for dinner—proved far more difficult.

Milton wasn't nearly as willing to help her dress, even if they planned to go out of doors. Still, with a bit of cajoling and scolding, he would eventually tie her corset and do the buttons on the back of her gown. She might have allowed him to help with her stockings, too, but she discovered he was too easily distracted by her bare ankles and the soft skin of her thighs. She was soon left boneless and breathless as he had his way with her—before breakfast, no less!

Preparing for dinner could be just as distracting—and arousing. She might actually make it out of her bedchamber fully dressed and simply coiffed, but getting into the dining room that way could be a challenge. Last night, she had appeared in the library at Worthington House, dressed and ready for coffee and walnuts when Milton announced he had to have her. Thank the gods there was a divan the perfect length over which she could straddle him. Left giggling at his antics, Adele found she couldn't be too terribly upset with her husband. The man's desire for her seemed almost insatiable! Far better he tumble her than one of the servants, a situation she learned from the Torrington Park housekeeper had apparently never happened during his tenure as earl. As for the time before he inherited the earldom, the housekeeper couldn't—or wouldn't—say.

Adele found she rather liked the arrangement she had with Milton playing lady's maid, though. She actually looked forward to the playfulness of mornings, despite the chill in the air or the gray gloom beyond the window. And if Simpkins were here, the lady's maid would only complain about the cold. The lack of servants. The condition of the servants' quarters. The ancient kitchens. And anything else she found not to her liking.

At some point in the past few weeks, Adele had come to realize the woman needed to be reassigned.

She would have fired Simpkins outright, but after the night in the dining room when Milton had announced no servants would be let go, she realized she couldn't. What kind of message would it send to the other servants? Why, the staff would think her positively evil.

"There won't be anyone else joining us for Christmas," Milton murmured.

Adele blinked, her reverie interrupted by her husband's odd response. "Because of the weather?"

Milton shook his head in the pillow. "I didn't invite anyone else."

Angling her head in her own pillow, Adele remembered their discussion the month before. "Why ever not?"

Pulling her closer to his body, as much to warm himself as to simply hold her, he sighed. "I admit it. I am selfish. I don't wish to share you with anyone."

Rather alarmed at the odd comment, Adele raised herself onto an elbow. "Share me?" A random thought that perhaps his male relatives expected to avail themselves of her body had her wincing. And that thought had her eyes widening in horror.

"Not like *that!*" Milton countered, his own alarm at her reaction apparent. His manner quickly turned to humor, a chuckle bubbling up to bring a huge grin to his face. Before long, the two were laughing until tears dripped from Adele's eyes.

"Now, now, there's no need to cry," Milton whispered, leaning over to kiss her wet cheek.

"I wish to fire Simpkins."

Milton blinked and pulled away to regard her with an arched brow. "Oh?" was his first reply. He stared at her for another moment before allowing a nod. "I wasn't aware you were unhappy with her services. Your hair always looks as if she's spent hours pinning it up," he remarked. "She must, because it takes me far too long to get all the pins out," he added with a frown. After a moment, he sighed. "She's been with you a long time."

Adele shook her head in the pillow, one hand going up to wipe the tears from her other cheek. She sniffled. "Her services are perfectly acceptable," she countered. "It's just the manner in which they're rendered I can no longer abide, I suppose."

Settling back down into the bed, Milton allowed a sigh. "Has she done something... untoward?"

Adele shook her head in her own pillow. "No. She's just become... rather unpleasant. She complains about anything and everything. I used to enjoy the time she spent pinning up my hair and taking it down at night, but now I find I dread it."

"And I've gone and made it impossible for you to let her go," the earl muttered, remembering the comment he had made in the dining room the month before. It was apparent the footman had shared his edict about how none of the servants in Worthington House would be fired. As a result, the maids seemed especially solicitous whilst performing their duties, and the footmen seemed to jump to attention whenever he entered a room. And the kitchen staff... well, he hadn't really noticed a change down there, he supposed. They would be the last to go if there had to be firings, and they seemed to know it.

"I just realized tonight that I really don't miss her," Adele whispered. "In fact, I'm a bit relieved she's not here." She paused a moment, turning her head toward him. "But now all I can think about is how your valet must be having the worst time of his life back in Darlington, or wherever they have ended up. Having to spend time in her company, I mean." She regarded Milton for a moment, her brows furrowing when she paid witness to another huge grin develop on his face. "What is it?" she asked, once again lifting herself onto an elbow. "Pray tell, what do you find so amusing?"

A look of guilt crossed Milton's face before he chuckled. "Do not fash yourself over my valet, my sweeting. Knowing Banks, he's probably in the middle of a tumble with your lady's maid right this very moment."

Adele sat up straight on the bed, the sudden movement causing the counterpane and linens to leave her naked husband almost completely uncovered. "Simpkins? In bed with *Banks?*" she wailed, her eyes round with shock.

Milton slowly sat up, clearing his throat as he retrieved some of the bed linens and re-covered his torso. He wrapped an arm around his wife's back, pulling her over as he lowered himself back down to the bed. Adele was forced to follow him down. "Now, now. Banks has a way with women," he whispered softly. "I'm quite sure he knows how to turn the crankiest crone into a rather happy hen," he murmured before giving her a kiss. He moved their bodies so Adele was beneath his. "Why, if he hasn't done it already, he will have a maid named 'Merry' living up to her namesake in no time at all," he added in a whisper. He continued kissing her, his lips trailing down her jaw, her throat, her collarbones as Adele struggled to catch her breath. He disappeared beneath the linens to crawl down the front of her body, leaving soft kisses in his wake.

"Are you implying Simpkins merely needs a... a good tumble?" Adele whispered hoarsely, suddenly finding it hard to concentrate on the matter at hand when her husband was doing everything in his power to see to it that she couldn't.

He reappeared from beneath the covers and gave a nod. "I am. Simpkins is sure to have a happy Christmas." He disappeared again, and Adele gave a cry of surprise when his hands slid beneath the globes of her bottom. Her knees suddenly lifted and fell apart as his questing tongue saw to flicking her suddenly engorged womanhood.

"As will I," Adele replied, her breaths becoming labored as his tongue and lips did their worst.

Or best.

Could anything be more pleasurable? More intense? More... *more?*

When she finally begged for him to stop, Milton re-emerged from under the covers, hurriedly crawling back up her body. His mouth settled onto one of her breasts as he buried his rock-hard cock into her wet and welcoming haven. Her hips immediately lifted, her knees gripping the sides of his body.

His movements, controlled and slow at first, soon turned more frantic, his thrusts faster and deeper, his hunger for her breasts and nipples leaving tiny marks in the tender skin. Spurred on by her soft mewling, he lifted his torso higher and watched in wonder at how her breasts bobbed in time with his trusts. When he lowered his mouth to hers, he reveled in how her nipples grazed his chest, parting the crisp, gray curls and eliciting gasps of delight and quiet mewling from Adele.

At one time, he thought this kind of intercourse far too coarse to employ on an English miss—that it might only be appropriate with a paid mistress—and partly because he preferred it this way, he hadn't pursued a wife. The series of widows he had squired about during the past ten Seasons had changed his mind on the matter, though, a few assuring him his spirited lovemaking was just as welcome as the more reserved efforts he saved for mornings.

Discovering Adele was amenable no matter the mode of intercourse merely confirmed that he should marry her—few aristocrats could claim willing wives when it came to the bedchamber. The two suited one another no matter the topic of conversation, and he rather enjoyed ribbing her on occasion. She rarely took his teasing seriously. That she was so pleasant to be with outside of a bed only reinforced his decision to ask for her hand. And the fact that she already owned her own palatial townhouse in Mayfair meant there was no need for him to arrange a larger London residence.

What more inducement did he need?

Nearly ready to allow his release, he completed the kiss and dared a gaze into Adele's eyes. He found her watching him with heavy-lidded eyes and a half-smile. He was vaguely aware of how her hands gripped his hips, of how her long fingers slid over his buttocks. He would not last long if she moved just one of those fingers to the back of his manhood, or if she reached a bit further and touched his sac.

As if she could read his mind, he was suddenly aware of her reaching to stroke him, to hold his sac and press it against her quim at the very moment he thrust into her one last time.

Her chest lifted from the bed at that moment, her mewling turning to a cry. His own growl filled the cold quiet of the bedchamber as his body stiffened, and he finally collapsed atop Adele. "You minx," he murmured before falling into a light sleep.

*S*everal minutes later, when Adele's breathing had returned to normal and she had the covers up and over both of their intertwined bodies, she allowed a long sigh. Moments like this allowed her to review the day, repeat phrases she had heard in her head to analyze them, relive the highlights, and wince at the disappointments.

Other than her earlier despair over the possibility he might have had feelings for Edith, Adele could think of nothing else that had happened on this trip to disappoint her. Nothing particularly annoying. Scary, perhaps, when she recalled the night they had spent at the *Angel Inn*—she was quite sure they shared their room with a ghost—but she wasn't about to mention the incident to Milton.

Despite the weather and the inconvenience of not having a maid or a valet, the two of them had enjoyed the day prior. Sleeping in later than usual, having breakfast in bed, and finally venturing out to the stables were merely preludes to what she hoped would be perfect days for the remainder of their stay.

If we made Torrington Park our regular home, would it always be like this? she wondered.

Well, life up here in Northumberland would become rather lonely, she decided. There wouldn't be ladies calling on her the days of the week when she wasn't calling on them. No balls or soirées to attend. No theatre or other evening entertainments to mark the time.

She sighed. Had her life really become just a series of *ton* events? A series of visits to Mayfair parlors and Hyde Park? A series of dinner parties and *musicales* and...

There had to be something more to life, she reasoned. Not that she didn't enjoy the life she had been born into, of course. But...

Adele sighed again, the movement of her chest bringing Milton out of his stupor to lift his head to regard her for a moment by the light of the dying fire. "Dammit, my love, but you are an excellent lay," he whispered before settling down so his head rested on the pillow next to hers.

Adele couldn't help the giggle that escaped just then, causing the bed to vibrate and her one uncovered breast—the other was buried beneath her husband's chest—to jiggle.

"I'll be sure to inform my brother," she teased in a whisper.

"Minx," he accused as one of his hands moved to cover her breast. "I'm crushing you, aren't I?"

"Not at all," she whispered, her hands moving to his back so that she could trail her fingers over the bumps in his spine. These days, they weren't so evident beneath his flesh, but she always delighted in how he reacted as her fingers barely skimmed them.

"I could spend the entire night just like this," he warned.

Adele thrilled at the comment. How many wives of aristocrats could claim their husbands spent the entire night in their beds? "Then please do."

Milton suddenly lifted his head, one of his bent arms supporting his head as he did so. He glanced about, rather surprised to discover she already had them covered by the bed linens and the counterpane. He returned his attention to her, just then realizing they were still joined together. Although it was entirely too soon to consider making love to her again, he thrilled at the thought that he could by merely remaining tucked inside her. "Your legs must be—"

"Already comfortably settled," she whispered with an arched eyebrow. Indeed, she would provide a rather loud complaint should he decide to remove his body from where it currently rested.

"Minx," he accused again.

"And don't you forget it," she replied as she used a hand to pull his head back down to her shoulder.

Milton whispered, "I love you," and drifted off to sleep, his only thoughts on heirs and spares and the earldom.

He needed an heir, and he rather hoped he had fathered one on this night.

Chapter 26

A FINAL MORNING IN
DARLINGTON

*J*ust *before dawn on Monday, December 23, 1816*
Alonyius was aware of a slight movement just
before soft lips kissed his cheek. For a moment,
he thought perhaps his mother had come into his
bedchamber and was trying to wake him.

She'll find my bed empty, he thought with a bit of amusement. Of course, she would find the situation just as amusing, the wicked woman. He was sure his mother knew
exactly what she was doing when she had him bring Alice to
this bedchamber.

Since his mother wasn't the one kissing him on the
cheek, there was only one other who would dare do such a
thing.

Alice.

He grinned and turned his head in her direction. "I
rather like waking up like this," he murmured, moving to
wrap an arm around her shoulders to pull her closer.

"I almost didn't wake up. The bed is so comfortable." *You
are so comfortable.* "But it's just after four o'clock. We really
must be getting back to the coaching inn," she whispered.
"Haversham told me we'll be leaving at dawn."

The reminder had Alonyius opening his eyes and
glancing down the front of his body. Even covered with bed

linens and quilts, his cockstand was quite evident as it tented the counterpane.

Alice followed his line of sight and giggled. "At least part of you is awake." She suddenly sobered and then crawled atop him, spreading her legs so her knees were on either side of his hips. With the nightrail bunched up around her hips and the covers still over most of her body, she created a rather warm tent of her own.

Well aware of what she intended to do, especially when her quim suddenly pressed against the hardened length of his manhood, Alonyius lifted himself onto his elbows. "You cannot make a sound," his whispered in warning.

He could only imagine his mother walking in on them.

Pausing in her slight movements, she nodded her understanding. Then she arched her back and lifted her torso until his manhood impaled her. The hitch in her breath—and in his—was barely audible as he filled her to near bursting. Before she moved again, she crossed her arms over her head and jerked the nightrail from her body.

Alonyius watched from below, his eyes widening in the dim light. Her lithe body was suddenly on display. Her mass of long hair swayed as she shook it out when the night rail cleared her head. After she tossed the garment behind her, Alonyius pushed himself up on his elbows again, his tongue flicking out to touch her breasts and nipples.

Gasping at the unexpected assault, Alice realized his move had left her almost unable to lift and lower herself. But then his hands moved to cup the globes of her bottom. Forced to grasp him about the shoulders, she allowed him to take over the movements. His mouth was suddenly open on one of her breasts, his tongue doing wicked things to her nipple as he lifted her so his manhood nearly escaped her body. The pressure from his hands suddenly slackened, and she dropped back down, his manhood filling her once again. He repeated the movements all the while feasting on each of her breasts and nipples, silencing whatever sounds he might have allowed as he moved closer to his release.

Alice bit the inside of her mouth in an attempt to keep silent as his rhythmical movements increased in speed and intensity. The tension that he built within her crested when his thumbs suddenly moved to where their bodies were joined, pressing and rubbing against her swollen womanhood until she shattered. The cry she might have emitted was swallowed when she dropped her head and his mouth suddenly covered hers. Not a second later, his entire body stiffened, spasmed, and seized, his hands once again moving to her bottom to hold her tight against him. When he finally took a breath, inhaling as if he'd been under water for too long, he allowed his head to fall against her chest.

Alice moved one of her hands to the back of his head and held him there for several minutes. *If only we could stay like this. Just like this. Never move. Never leave this bed.*

If only.

But they did have to move. Alonyius suddenly dropped back onto his pillow, his breathing labored as one of his hands covered a breast and the other pulled her down.

"I find myself hoping that whatever possessed you to do that will do so again," he whispered, giving her a kiss on her shoulder.

Alice grinned and settled her head next to his on the pillow. She kissed his cheek again. "I'm quite sure it can be arranged." She allowed a deep sigh and then slowly lifted her body from his, wincing when his manhood finally sprang free. At his moan of disappointment, she almost returned to the bed. But she knew if she did, she might never leave it.

She had half a mind to ask Mrs. Banks if there might be a maid's position available at the house, just so she could enjoy the comforts found in the Blue Room.

Alonyius wouldn't be there, though, she remembered. At least, not if he continued his employment under Lord Torrington.

Pulling on her corset, she was about to attempt to do the ties by herself when Alonyius was suddenly behind her. "Allow me," he whispered. When he was finished, he turned her around in his arms and kissed her on the lips one last time. "We'll have several hours in the coach today," he hinted in a hoarse whisper.

"I'm looking forward to it."

She wasn't, really, for riding in the coach meant cold feet. But if they rode on the same side, in the direction of travel, she knew she would feel warm just from his presence.

Thelonius Banks' coach was already parked in front of Mill House when Alonyius and Alice finished dressing. Alice had made up the bed in an effort to hide their carnal activity while Alonyius made a mess of his in an effort to make it appear as if he had actually slept in it. Folding the borrowed nightrail—she had actually worn it the entire night —Alice left it on the end of the made up bed.

With his shaving kit and valise back at the coaching inn, Alonyius could do nothing more than pull on his clothes. Not having more than the coins, a comb, and a small sewing kit in her small reticule, Alice could only pin up her hair into a simple bun.

"I'm going to give my regards to my mother," Alonyius whispered before he moved down the hallway in the opposite direction from the wing in which they had stayed. Alice waited for him at the top of the stairs, startled when the maid from yesterday—Regan, if she remembered correctly— appeared at the base of the stairs.

"Good morning, ma'am. Breakfast is served in the parlor."

Breakfast? Alice dared a glance down the hall, stunned to find Alonyius already on his way back in her direction.

"She's not in her bedchamber," he said in a worried voice.

Alice sighed, a grin forming. "Because she's in the breakfast parlor, it seems."

The two descended the stairs and found the matriarch of Mill House drinking a cup of tea.

"There you are!" Mrs. Banks said brightly. "You cannot go without first having something to eat."

Although Alice was sure she couldn't eat this early—she never did at Worthington House—the coddled eggs and rasher of bacon placed in front of her by a footman, followed by a plate of toast and a cup of tea, soon had her changing her mind.

"You've probably already worked up an appetite by now," Mrs. Banks said, directing her comment to her son.

Alonyius felt the blush of embarrassment color his throat and silently thanked the gods his cravat was covering it. "I'm quite sure I don't know what you mean," he responded lightly. "I slept rather soundly last night."

The older woman merely grinned and turned to Alice to give her a wink.

Alice blinked. "As did I. The bed was ever so comfortable. I must thank you again for your hospitality." She quickly sipped her tea. Was their carnal act of earlier that morning so obvious? Or was Mrs. Banks merely hoping her son had found a lover?

"Well, my dear, you are *always* welcome here. You'll be even more welcome if you bring my son along, of course," the old woman replied with a titter.

"I shall do my best," Alice responded, not sure what else to say.

A few minutes later, they climbed into the Banks coach. Alice had barely gotten settled into the squabs when it came to a halt and Alonyius reached over to open the door. "We're here," he said as he stepped out and turned to help her down.

"Already?" Alice couldn't believe how quick the ride was compared to how long it had taken her to walk from the coaching inn to Mill House the day before. But she couldn't give it another thought when she spotted the Torrington coach. The horses were nearly hitched up.

"Come. We still have to pack," he reminded her. They hurried into *The Black Swan* and nearly walked into Higgins.

"You're going the wrong way," the groom said in surprise, his gaze darting between the two.

"I left something behind," Alice said in the hopes he wouldn't guess they hadn't stayed there the night before. "I have to go back to the room."

"Och, damn women," Higgins said *sotto voce* as Alonyius passed him.

The valet merely nodded and made his way through the public room and up the stairs. Although he had hoped to shave, he realized he didn't have the time. Perhaps he could do so at another stage stop along the way. They had at least one, probably two before they arrived at Torrington Park.

Alice gathered the few things in the room that weren't already in her valise and waited while Alonyius did the same. A quick glance at the fireplace showed the tub had been removed, although her ball of soap was still on the hearth. She stuffed it into her valise, the scent of citrus reminding her all over again what it had been like to have her hair washed by a man's hands. She was still ruminating on the thought when she realized Alonyius was next to her.

"A pleasant thought?" he queried.

Grinning, Alice nodded and pulled out the ball of soap. "Very," she replied.

Giving her a quick kiss, Alonyius straightened and led them out of the room and out of the coaching inn. A few minutes later, they were seated in the traveling coach, facing the direction of travel with a foot warmer already in place on the floor.

Alice was quite sure she never felt so warm in all her life.

Chapter 27

THE SERVANTS ARRIVE

ive hours later

Ensconced in the library and enjoying a rather titillating tale of a knight and his maiden, Adele didn't hear the ruckus created by the arrival of a coach at Torrington Park. Even if she had, she would have done her best to ignore it in favor of learning exactly how a knight in battle armor was capable of engaging in sexual intercourse with so much metal covering his body. Certainly his manhood would have been as protected as his chest, she thought before remembering there was a suit of armor in the hallway of the first floor. She made a mental note to study it the moment before her husband appeared in the doorway.

"The servants' coach just arrived," he announced. From the tone of his voice, Adele couldn't decide if he was pleased by the news or not. Although they had managed with dressing one another—indeed, she had delighted in it, if for no other reason than her husband had to learn how to do the opposite of what he usually did—Adele lacked suitable clothing and went about with her long hair undressed. She had a feeling she looked much like the maiden in the book she was reading, if not a bit older.

Adele set aside the book and gave him a grin. "I'll finally

have some appropriate attire," she replied as she stood up and moved to join him.

He gave her a kiss on the corner of her mouth and took one of her hands in his. "The weather has turned rather fine. If you're up for it, we can have a couple of footmen join us to trim those trees you mentioned and gather some greenery. Cut down a tree. Prepare this place for Christmas."

Stunned by his suggestion, Adele seemed lost in thought for a moment before she gave him a brilliant smile. "Why, that sounds like a perfect way to spend the afternoon. I'll even have appropriate clothing once the trunks are delivered to my bedchamber.

"And I'll finally have a place to put all those boxes," he said with a hint of mischief.

Adele frowned. "Where are they now?"

Milton straightened and shook his head. "I'm not telling. No peeking allowed until Christmas morning."

Rolling her eyes, Adele was about to assure him she had no intention of touching the packages when the butler appeared behind her husband.

"Yes, Trasker?"

"Your trunks are being delivered to the mistress suite, and your lady's maid and the valet have been shown to their quarters." He paused a moment. "Shall I have Simpkins meet you in the mistress suite, my lady?"

Adele allowed a sigh. Her reprieve from her lady's maid was over, she realized. "Before you do, can you tell me how you found her countenance?"

The butler blinked. "Why, Simpkins seemed in very good spirits, my lady. She also voiced concern about the laundry and said she would see to it right away as she didn't wish you to be inconvenienced any longer."

It was Adele's turn to blink. "Did she?"

A bit relieved to hear that the lady's maid was in a good mood, Milton made mental note to corner his valet and congratulate the man on a job well done. Perhaps they could get in a game of billiards whilst Adele dressed for an afternoon of gathering evergreen boughs and choosing a tree.

"Have Simpkins meet her ladyship in the mistress suite," Milton ordered. He turned to Adele. "In the meantime, I shall have a word with Banks. Learn what happened on the trip and get an accounting of the expenses and all that before we head out." He turned to the butler. "Have a couple of footmen ready to help with cutting and gathering the greens. Her ladyship noticed several of the evergreen trees around here could use a good trimming."

"Of course, my lord," Trasker replied. He gave a bow and hurried off as Milton turned to find Adele lost in thought.

"What is it?" he asked.

Adele gave him a grin. "Curiosity has me wondering what happened to have my lady's maid in good spirits," she murmured.

Pretending ignorance, Milton gave her a kiss. "I look forward to hearing a report," he said as he offered his arm. He escorted her up the stairs to her bedchamber and then went to his own, closing the door before heading to the door to the dressing room that connected the two suites. He was about to go into the dressing room, but realized Adele's maid was busy hanging up gowns and arranging footwear.

Cupping an ear to the door, he struggled to overhear any of their conversation and finally gave up.

He would have to learn what he needed to know from Banks.

*A*lice gave her mistress a curtsy and a brilliant smile as Adele entered the mistress suite. "Good afternoon, my lady," she said.

"And to you," Adele replied, rather surprised to find most of the trunks already emptied of their contents and a pile of laundry collected into a bed linen. "I know I must look positively medieval with my hair like this ..."

"It's rather fetching," Alice replied with a grin. "But I can do it up for you if you'd like."

Noting the laundry, Adele lifted a brow. "I suppose you already know there's no laundress here at Torrington Park," she said with a sigh.

"Mr. Trasker informed me. I was about to see to it, but it can wait if you'd like me to help you change your gown or do your hair," she offered, her manner still rather pleasant.

Adele angled her head. "I think just a change of gowns, for now. We're going out to gather the greens to decorate the great hall tomorrow," she replied. "I'll have you do my hair when I change for dinner later."

"Yes, milady. Would you like your hunter green riding habit? Or the blue one?"

Still rather stunned at her maid's happy demeanor as well as her choice of what to wear when gathering pine boughs, Adele realized there probably wasn't really an appropriate gown for such an exercise, and if there was, she didn't have it. "The hunter green, I should think. And while you see to it, perhaps you can tell me what happened these past few days. You've probably had an awful ordeal," she added as she turned to allow Alice to undo the fastenings of her gown.

Alice couldn't help the flush of color her face suddenly displayed, and was rather relieved her ladyship was facing away from her. "It wasn't so awful, milady. Although *The George* was closed for the season, there were some rooms available at *The Black Swan*. Mr. Banks saw to the arrangements."

"He seems a rather capable man," Adele replied, stepping out of her gown.

"Oh, he is, milady." *And rather skilled in areas other than his duties as a valet.* She had to suppress the urge to say more —a frisson passed through her body at the very thought of him—even though she desperately wished to talk about it. For the entire trip from Darlington, she had thought to keep their liaison a secret from everyone. Now she was near to bursting with wanting to tell someone.

As she held out the riding habit, Alice realized her

mistress was staring at her, her head held at an angle. "You're blushing," the countess accused. "In fact, you look as if you've been tumbled three ways to Thursday." The words were said in a light-hearted manner, and a grin turned into a smile as Adele regarded her with an upraised brow. "Do I have the right of it? Oh, do tell. There's no one around here with whom to share any gossip," she urged.

Alice blinked. And blinked again when she realized there was no hiding it. "Something like that," she finally admitted.

Adele stepped into the riding habit and said, "Well?"

Finally allowing a smile—she could barely contain her happiness—Alice recounted a bit of what had happened during her stay in Darlington. "He washed my hair," she said suddenly. At the look of stunned surprise on her ladyship's face, she added, "We had to share a room as there were only two left at the inn."

"He didn't stay with the drivers?"

Clearing her throat, Alice wondered how much to tell about what she suspected the drivers were busy doing in their room. "I don't believe there would have been enough... space," she hedged.

It was Adele's turn to blush. "Oh, of course. Mr. Haversham seems to make friends at every stage stop," she agreed, one of her brows left arched in query.

"Indeed. He was quite popular in Darlington. At least for a couple of the tavern maids," Alice admitted sheepishly. "As was Mr. Higgins, although I can't say as how I ever saw him until a few minutes before we took our leave," she added, her brows furrowing in wonder. She suddenly burst into a fit of giggles, which had Adele grinning ear to ear.

"Mr. Banks could pass as a gentleman," Adele commented, wanting to learn more about her husband's valet. "Why is that, do you suppose?" Most servants who worked in Mayfair could probably change their speech to make them sound as if they were to the manor born, but she had always been struck by how Banks carried himself. His coats and breeches were as fine as anything her husband wore, his cravats made of silk and his jewel-toned waistcoats elegant but conservative. She didn't think she had ever seen him wear livery.

Rather stunned by the insight, Alice nodded as she finished doing up the buttons on the front of the riding habit. "He is the 'spare heir' to a rather prosperous woolen mill, milady. The fabric used in this coat was made there, in fact."

Furrowing her brows, Adele stepped back and glanced down at the Merino wool habit. Trimmed in black with jet buttons, it had been her choice for riding during the fashionable hour for the past couple of years. "Then why, pray tell, is he working in *service?*" she asked in a lowered voice.

Alice moved the vanity chair so Adele could sit down as she retrieved a pair of black boots. "His mother was Lady Torrington's lady's maid," she stated, not sure how else to answer just then. Although Alonyius had explained the honor of working in service, it wasn't until that moment that Alice understood his meaning. "She instilled in him the importance of—"

"Torrington's mother?" Adele interrupted. She nearly fell onto the vanity chair. "*My* Torrington's mother?"

Nodding, Alice knelt to remove Adele's slippers and put on the boots. "Just for a few years. Until the man that was to be her husband met her at a draper's shop..."

"And insisted she marry him when she told him she needed the whole bolt of wool for Lady Torrington's winter gown," Adele finished, her attention directed on something in her mind's eye.

"Why, yes." Alice finished lacing up one of the boots. She dared a glance up at Adele. "How did you know?"

Shaking her head as if to clear it, Adele allowed a wan smile. "My mother told me that story. I should have liked to meet that maid. Or at least have been there that day in the draper's shop."

"She's a wonderful woman. Rather batty, really. But ever so humble and—"

"You *know* her?"

Alice nodded. "I met her day 'fore yesterday. I was actually a guest at Mill House last night. I stayed in a beautiful blue bedchamber." *With Alonyius at my side*, she was tempted to add. "I even had breakfast with Mrs. Banks this morning, well before dawn. She was a most gracious hostess. A very doting mother—Mr. Banks' older brother lives there, you see. And she's training a new maid." Alice continued to nod as tears filled her eyes.

Adele leaned over and lifted Alice's chin in one of her hands. "Why the tears?"

Swallowing, Alice took a quick breath. "I think I'm in love with Mr. Banks."

It was Adele's turn to blink. "Well, I suppose this means he did more than wash your hair?" she half-asked in a hoarse whisper, amusement evident in her voice.

"Oh, yes. He has kept me quite warm despite the chill," she admitted before allowing a watery grin. "He's a very... attentive lover," she added as color once again suffused her face.

"Well," Adele said as she stood up and shook out her skirts. "For your sake, I hope his mother has instilled in him the importance of honor," she whispered, the serious comment at odds with her expression. "You could be with child." Despite the hint of warning, the words sounded almost hopeful.

Rising to her feet, Alice rolled her eyes. "I rather think I'm too old to consider that possibility," she said with a grin, gathering up the bed linen with the laundry. "If there's nothing else, I'll see to the laundry now." She gave a curtsy and made her way out of the bedchamber.

Although Alice's comment about being too old was said with only her situation in mind, she had no idea how it affected her mistress, for Adele held her slight grin until her lady's maid was out of the bedchamber.

When Alice was halfway down the hall, Adele allowed the tears to fall.

Chapter 28

A CONVERSATION WITH A VALET

Meanwhile, in the billiards room
As the early afternoon light flooded in through the west window, Milton allowed a sigh. Not yet two o'clock in the afternoon, the coming sunset would be a combination of brilliant oranges and pinks. The colors would hang in the sky even after twilight took over, a few stars winking into existence well before dinner was served.

The clear sky portended a cold night, and Milton considered how lucky he was to have settled the spat with Adele the day before. They had never fought before, never raised their voices to one another. He felt awful for having left her so angry. So bereft. All because she was jealous of a woman for whom he had no feelings. Probably never had, other than the bit of contempt he had felt the last day he had paid a call on Lady Pendleton.

Well, it served him right for having carried on with so many women before he could finally marry Adele. Now that she was assured he wouldn't be seeing any of those other women—most not even in a social sense—she had allowed him to hold her and wipe the tears from her cheeks with his handkerchief. This afternoon, they would see to the pine boughs for the hanging of the greens, and tomorrow, after the great hall was decorated, they would go on a sleigh ride. All would be well at Torrington Park.

Realizing he wasn't alone, Milton turned to find his valet regarding him from just inside the open door. "Come in!" he called out, waving a hand to indicate that Alonyius was welcome in the billiards room. "'Bout time you made it. I take it the trunks were too heavy for the servants' coach?" he added with an arched brow.

Banks nodded. "Indeed. Poor Haversham only managed to get a few miles from Darlington before we were forced to turn back. *The Black Swan* provided accommodations and meals, of course, so we have been living in relative comfort for the past couple of days, my lord."

Milton eyed his valet a moment, quite sure Banks looked as if he had more color in his skin. A lighter air about him. Why, the man looked... happy. "You got laid," he accused with a teasing grin. "Who was she? The tavern wench? Or the kitchen maid at *The Black Swan?*"

Banks clamped his mouth shut and made sure he displayed an impassive expression. "Neither, my lord." He didn't offer more, but realized he should have at least attempted to change the subject when his master's eyes suddenly widened.

"Simpkins!" Milton spread his arms wide and grinned in delight. He sobered and angled his head to one side. "I do hope you weren't too inconvenienced. It was rather sporting of you to do it. When we discussed it before we left, I truly didn't think you would be able to bed the ol' biddy."

Banks winced at the earl's words, not sure how to make it clear he wasn't inconvenienced in the least. Nor was bedding the lady's maid the awful chore Lord Torrington seemed to think it was. Truth be told, he had developed feelings for Alice Simpkins, but he dared not admit that to the earl just then. Not when the man was behaving as if Banks had fallen on his sword.

He had in a way, but not in the way the earl thought he

had. If Alice continued to allow his attentions, he would be falling on it for the rest of his life.

"My lord, it wasn't an inconvenience, I assure you," he managed finally. "Simpkins is a lonely woman who merely craved the attentions of a man. Not having engaged in... a carnal *affaire* for some time," he continued, lowering his voice a bit. "I was happy to do your bidding." He winced again at how his words must have sounded. Why, his comment was no better than those made by the ladybirds who practiced their profession on the London Bridge or in the brothels in Covent Garden.

"She's happy now, though," Milton replied, his voice filled with hope.

"I believe so." Banks blinked and gave his head a shake. "Yes, she is happy." *And I intend to keep her that way*, he nearly added.

"You must be famished," the earl suddenly stated. "When was the last time you had a decent meal?"

The valet allowed a sigh of relief at the change of subject. "We ate this morning at my brother's house," he said with a nod. "I presume the drivers ate at *The Black Swan*." He extracted the purse the earl had given him upon their departure from London. There were still some coins in the velvet pouch. "I don't know if there's enough for the trip back to town, but I think we did rather well, my lord." He held the pouch out to his master.

Milton shook his head. "Keep it. Consider it compensation for what you had to do," he said in a jovial manner.

Feeling as if he'd been punched in the gut, Banks frowned and shook his head. "No, my lord. I don't require any compensation in that regard." He paused, finding it difficult to rein in his sudden anger at his master.

The earl regarded his valet for a moment, remembering just then that Banks had never lacked for funds. Money wasn't an inducement, probably given he had funds from another source than his meager servants' pay. "Well, then perhaps you can win some by beating me in a game of billiards," he suggested, holding out a cue for the valet.

Alonyius allowed an expression of interest, but shook his head. "I appreciate the invitation, my lord, but I have duties to see to. Perhaps later?" he managed. He didn't wait for a response but gave a bow. "Excuse me, my lord." He turned on his heel and took his leave of the billiards room.

Frowning at his valet's abrupt departure—he had hoped they could get in a game of billiards before he met Adele to gather some pine boughs—Milton wondered why the man had reacted so. He replayed Banks' comments in his mind and was left wondering two things.

Make that three.

Had Banks actually *enjoyed* his time with Simpkins?

Or had the poor man suffered so badly he was considering ending his employment?

What had happened with respect to his family's textile business? Was Banks upset because he was expected to resign his position, take his leave of London, and move to Darlington? Or had the valet learned he was no longer in line to inherit the textile mill?

Milton Grandby vowed to learn exactly what had happened in Darlington. And he knew the perfect woman to ask.

Chapter 29

IT'S BEGINNING TO FEEL…

J ust beyond the front doors of Torrington Park
Although Adele expected to be blasted by cold air when she stepped out the front doors of Torrington Park, she was surprised to discover a sunny sky and little in the way of wind. "I thought you said it was always windy here," she admonished her husband when he stepped alongside her.

"It is. We're on the opposite side from where it's coming from," he replied, jerking a thumb over his shoulder. "Shall we?"

Milton offered his arm, and she placed a hand on it. "Just where are these pine trees you wish to butcher?" he wondered as he glanced around. There wasn't a tree line anywhere close by.

"Why, the first one is right here," she said as she turned to her right.

That's when Milton realized they wouldn't be venturing far from the castle-cum-hunting lodge. A series of pine trees, spaced several yards apart, lined the entire perimeter of the building. Armed with a hand saw, one footman moved ahead and stood waiting for instructions while another carrying a pruning shears joined him. Another could be seen in the distance on his way from the stables. He was pushing an empty wheelbarrow.

"They've obviously done this before," Adele murmured.

"Indeed, although I think it's been a few years." He motioned toward the ornamental trees visible from their vantage. Several were in need of trimming. "Would you like to do the honors? I'm not sure what it is you'd like in the way of wreaths and such."

Adele's eyes widened. "I've never done this before," she replied.

Milton frowned. "Who made the wreaths for Worthington House? I remember seeing them last year on the front door and above the fireplace," he argued.

Rolling her eyes, Adele leaned closer to her husband and whispered, "I bought them already made up. I do every year. I get them from a nursery in Chiswick," she added when she saw the look of surprise on her husband's face. "All I do is add the ribbon."

The earl gave a nod. "So then we shall learn this together. Devlin," he called out.

The footman carrying the hand saw replied, "Yes, your lordship?"

"What do you recommend?"

He listened and watched as the man noted several branches in need of cutting.

"And perhaps that one there?" Adele asked as she pointed to an arched branch that seemed a bit out of place.

"Yes, my lady," Devlin replied.

"Make it so," Milton ordered.

Between the two footmen, several pine boughs came free of the tree. Adele was happy to gather the branches as they started to fall, her arms laden until the wheelbarrow was close enough to take them. They moved onto the next tree and did the same, Milton taking a turn at the saw until a bough fell to the ground. By the sixth tree, the wheelbarrow was full.

"Is that enough for the wreath for the front door, do you suppose?" Milton wondered.

Adele giggled. "It's probably enough for three doors."

The footman bearing the pruning shears gave a shake of his head. "Beggin' the ladyship's pardon, but you'll need at least this much for just one good wreath," he said.

Adele straightened. "Where are the wreaths usually... created?" she asked.

"The main hall, milady. On the big table. The dowager countess used to make them with several maids and a footman or two."

Nodding her understanding, Adele directed the footman with the wheelbarrow to take the load to the main hall.

"Milady?" he replied, his brows furrowed in what looked like worry.

Adele angled her head. "What is it?"

The footman seemed a bit uncertain.

"Haven't you heard it's bad luck to take the greenery into the house before Christmas Eve?"

Adele blinked and then gave her head a quick shake. "Of course, it is. Just..." She wondered what to say next.

"Just make a pile outside the front doors, and one of the other footmen can see to getting it all moved into the great hall in the morning," Milton finished for her. He turned in her direction and added, "This is all a bit new for my countess, since Christmas isn't celebrated all that much back in the capital."

Giving him a nod of thanks, Adele realized she was a bit out of her element. "Hurry back. It seems we have more trees to trim," she said with quelling glance in her husband's direction. She was ever so glad her lady's maid had arrived. It seemed she would be in charge of wreath-making on the morrow.

For more than an hour, the team of five moved along the perimeter of Torrington Place. Although the wind was blowing a bit on the west side of the structure, Adele found it tolerable, and she told her husband so when they had completed their twentieth tree.

"If we weren't working so damned hard, you would

notice, trust me," he countered as he sawed a particularly large branch from the bottom of a misshapen pine. "A few years ago, it was far colder than it is today," he added, referring to the Christmas of 1813.

"It's a bit more enjoyable than I expected," Adele replied, thinking of all the creations they could make from what they had cut. Besides round wreaths for the doors and a few large walls, she was imagining sprays for the tops of fireplaces in several rooms, including their bedchambers. Why, the scent of pine would be a welcome addition to the rooms of Torrington Park. She could only hope there was enough wire and ribbon to dress them properly.

When the last tree had been trimmed and the wheelbarrow had been filled and emptied six times, the group reached the other side of the front doors. A mountain of pine boughs greeted them.

"Well, my lady, it seems as if you've become a first-class pruner," Milton teased as one of the footmen wheeled the cart to the front of Torrington Park. He couldn't remember the last time the pines had undergone such a trimming.

"I never thought to learn so much about pine trees," she countered, rather glad she'd had the opportunity to spend the afternoon outside. At no time had she felt chilled or otherwise uncomfortable in the cold, and yet white clouds had billowed about their heads with every breath and with every word spoken.

"Me neither," Milton agreed.

"I think we shall be making wreaths all day tomorrow," she said in awe, rather alarmed at all the greenery. "I do hope you have rolls of ribbon."

Her husband ignored the comment about ribbon, but made a note to ask Mrs. Miller where his mother might have kept the wide, red fabric she used to make her bows. "And we'll be going for a sleigh ride, of course," Milton reminded her. "A tradition during the holiday. Haversham will hitch up one of the draft horses, and we shall go on a ride. 'Bout time you learned what what it means to be a countess up here," he added with an arched brow. "See all your lands."

Adele allowed a grin. Having only ever ridden on a sled, she found she was looking forward to a ride in a horse-drawn sleigh.

About time, indeed.

Chapter 30

A CONVERSATION IS OVERHEARD

A couple of hours earlier

Alice squeezed her eyes shut at overhearing the earl's words. She hadn't meant to eavesdrop on the conversation between Alonyius and his master, but she couldn't help but slow her steps when she heard Lord Torrington's ebullient greeting. The man had been so happy to see his valet, she had to allow a grin.

And then her name had been spoken.

From there, the conversation seemed to have focussed on her, and what the valet apparently had agreed to do before they had even left London.

How could I have been such a fool? she wondered for the tenth time. Alonyius Banks hadn't paid attendance on her because he was interested in her in *that* way, or because he had developed a tendré for her, or because he felt the least bit of affection for her.

He had bedded her because his master had paid him to!

The humiliation was almost too much. Tears threatened even before she could make her way to the laundry room. The cook had left three pails of hot water, and she had half a mind to simply dunk her head into one and drown herself.

Instead, she went about washing the clothes, her bouts of sorrow interspersed with anger, the means and speed by which she rubbed the clothes on the washboard. Her sobs, so intense and so loud, robbed her of breath. Attempting to fish a hanky from her pocket only reminded her there wasn't one. Instead, she allowed the tears to drip into the wash water, each disappearing in the slight bubbles from the lye.

She had been so preoccupied with Alonyius that morning, she hadn't performed her normal rituals whilst dressing. He had been the one to see to buttoning her gown, to putting on her stockings, to slipping on her half-boots and placing her redingote on her shoulders before they made their way downstairs. And then there had been the delightful breakfast with his mother before they departed in his family's coach for the ride back to *The Black Swan.*

They had packed quickly, knowing Haversham would be expecting them in the traveling coach once the horses were finished being hitched up. The little bit of bread and cheese his mother had forced them to take along had been shared whilst Haversham directed the horses in a fevered attempt to reach Torrington Park before one in the afternoon.

Finding her mistress in a rather happy mood had only accentuated her own. Lady Torrington had even remarked on her countenance. *Why, you look as if you've been tumbled three ways to Thursday,* her ladyship had said when Alice was dressing her earlier.

Sure her face displayed the blush of a school girl, Alice had simply nodded her head. *What a fool I was to tell her everything,* she realized.

But it had felt so good to grin again! She couldn't remember a moment in the past few months when she had felt amusement or humor or any reason to smile whilst in the company of her mistress.

And then Lady Torrington's face had changed to one of understanding. Of realization.

Why the tears?

The question had been so simple, and yet when delivered in a voice that made them sound so sympathetic, Alice had nearly cried tears of joy.

I think I am in love with Mr. Banks, she had managed, deciding just then she really shouldn't have admitted such personal details to Lady Torrington.

Especially when her ladyship seemed so concerned she might be with child. Which was ridiculous.

Wasn't it?

Except it really wasn't, now that she thought about it. A wet hand went to her belly as a jolt of fear gripped her. She could lose her position!

Or not.

Lady Torrington wouldn't let her go. Besides, Lord Torrington had decreed no one would lose their positions.

She returned her attention to the last of the laundry, rinsing the items and wringing them out as she wondered about her ladyship's earlier attentions.

Lady Torrington had been her only employer for nearly twenty years. The fact that she showed any interest in her personal life at all was a wonder given how most servants were treated in the homes of aristocrats. But now that she had been at Torrington Park for a couple of hours, Alice realized Lady Torrington was probably just lonely. There weren't very many people living in the former hunting lodge-cum-castle, and certainly no others of her class. If there were neighbors, they certainly weren't close by. Why, she probably had no one else with whom to talk.

Lady Torrington had listened to her recitation of what had happened the day the servants had been forced to turn back due to the deepening snow, of the next day at *The Black Swan,* and the need for Alice to take a room with the earl's valet. About how he had washed her hair. Her night at Mill House, although she hadn't admitted to sharing her bed there. She didn't mind admitting she wished the snow had continued to fall, though.

Now, she wished she had frozen to death that day they attempted to leave *The Black Swan.*

Alonyius Banks had only showered her with his attentions because his master had requested he do so. And Lord

Torrington had felt so sorry for his valet, he had offered him payment, as if the man was some sort of paid consort.

A male prostitute.

New tears streamed down her cheeks, the salty liquid dripping into the rinse water. She took a deep breath and willed herself to finish the laundry. Simply get it hung up on the lines that were strung about the room. She thought about hanging herself on one of them, but realized they weren't high enough and probably not strong enough to do the job properly.

When she completed her task, she wiped her cheeks on the sleeve of her gown and made her way back to her quarters.

At least, that's what she thought she was doing. Before long, she realized she was lost, and to make matters worse, she hadn't seen another soul since the cook had directed her to the laundry room.

Exhausted, tears once again pouring from her eyes, she simply entered the next room she could find, shut the door, and sank into the nearest divan.

Chapter 31

A REVERIE INTERRUPTED

A couple of hours later
Alice would have continued to weep but for the sudden light that appeared from the hallway. She was sure she had shut the door, which could only mean someone had entered the room.

Glancing around, she wondered in what room she had taken refuge. The light revealed a floral pattern on the adjacent chair, and for a moment Alice thought she must be in either the parlor or a lady's salon. That is, until she spotted a collection of weapons along one wall. Although she knew some parlors made for suitable war zones among ladies who found fault with one another, their weapons were usually words, not spears and lances. The thought of Lady Pettigrew impaled on one of them brought a moment of amusement to her otherwise sullen mood.

The presence of weapons meant this must be a man's room. A study, perhaps.

"Simpkins? Is that you?"

The unmistakeable voice of Adele Torrington had Alice straightening on the divan in which she had settled. She glanced about the room, still not certain where she was in this strange excuse for a castle.

"It is, my lady," she managed between sobs. She quickly stood, turned, and gave a curtsy.

Adele regarded her lady's maid for a moment, the light from the hallway sconces illuminating the maid's face enough to show she had been crying.

And for a long time.

Her eyes were red-rimmed and quite bright in the bit of light that illuminated the study.

"Whatever in the world is *wrong?*" Adele asked as she hurried to join Alice. She stood before her, one hand going to a hip. The scent of pine boughs wafted about her, a testament to what she had been doing for the past couple of hours. Given the lack of light from the window, Alice realized darkness had descended on the hunting lodge.

"Nothing, my lady," Alice replied, her head shaking with her words.

Adele gave her a quelling glance. "If you think for one moment I'm going to believe you, please know that you are, and always have been, a terrible liar."

Alice inhaled sharply, not aware her mistress held such a poor opinion of her ability to tell untruths. But then, how many had she ever told? "Truly?" she whispered.

Resisting the urge to affirm her maid's query, Adele gave her another quelling glance. "I have never heard you cry so loudly," she accused. "What has it been? Nearly nineteen years?"

Attempting to concentrate on her mistress' words, Alice considered the time she had been in service to Adele Slater. "Twenty," she finally admitted.

"You sounded as if you were about to *die*," Adele accused.

"Yes," Alice agreed. Death would be welcome right about now. It would have been welcome four hours ago, back when she heard the words that made her realize all of Alonyius Banks' attentions had been at the behest of his master. She turned to regard her mistress. "Do you suppose you could do the honors? Put me out of my misery?" she whispered with a nod toward what looked like a spear that was mounted above the fireplace.

Sighing loudly, Adele shook her head. "Not on your life," she replied with a huff.

Well, that was the point, wasn't it?

"Not until you tell me what has you acting as the largest watering pot in all of England. *Faith!* I could hear your sobs all the way down to my bedchamber. I thought the place might be haunted!" The countess took a seat on the divan, frowning a bit when she realized how deep she sank into the ancient cushions. The stuffing would need to be redone on this piece, she thought, mentally adding it to her list of changes for the hunting lodge.

Alice's eyes widened. *Yes, that was it.* She could die, become a ghost, and haunt Alonyius Banks until the day he died! It would be just like a plot in one of her ladyship's Gothic novels, the books she read when she probably should have been doing embroidery. Alice was about to put voice to the thought when she realized Lady Torrington would have none of it.

"A few hours ago, you were the happiest woman in all of England," Adele accused. "You said you thought you might be in love."

Angling her head to one side, Alice finally turned slightly to regard her mistress. "I was," she agreed, her face screwing into concern when she just then realized how the divan's cushion didn't seem to hold up. She had half a thought they might sink to the floor at any moment.

"What the hell happened?"

Blinking at her mistress' use of a curse, Alice straightened on the divan as best she could. She considered how to respond. She considered lying, but thought better of it.

Apparently she was the worst liar in all of England.

"I didn't mean to eavesdrop, milady, but I was on my way to launder the clothes when I overheard his lordship speaking with his valet." She paused, not quite sure what to say next.

"Go on," Adele encouraged, suddenly realizing her

husband's conversation may have been the source of her lady's maid's consternation. And all the tears. *Faith!* She didn't think it possible for a woman of Simpkins' age to cry so much! Although, if she gave it a bit more thought, she would have to admit the woman was only a bit older than she was, and she could certainly act as a watering pot on occasion.

She had just the day before, in fact.

"I heard my name, you see, otherwise I wouldn't have paused. But it seems Mr. Banks only showed me attention because Lord Torrington asked him to do so," Alice whispered, tears once again spilling from the corners of her eyes. "Paid him, too. He must have known I was unhappy and thought I was in need of a tumb..." She stopped, realizing what she was about to say.

And just why it was that Lord Torrington knew she was unhappy in the first place.

Because her mistress had told him.

Had Lady Torrington asked her husband to arrange a liaison with his valet? To provide a tumble in an attempt to lighten her mood and make her more pleasant?

Alice turned her attention onto Adele, her eyes widening in alarm. "Did you...?"

Having allowed her thoughts to come to the same conclusion as her maid, Adele shook her head. Several times. "I said *nothing*," she claimed. And then she remembered the brief—very brief—conversation she'd had with him that night when Milton had told her about his plans to travel to Northumberland. "Or rather, very little," she whispered as her attention seemed to settle onto a wood carving of a deer on the nearest table. "I did mention I found your countenance rather disturbing of late." At Simpkins' gasp, she added, "Well, you have been rather difficult these past few months. You complain all the time—"

"I have been unhappy, I admit," Alice agreed.

"You've been derelict in some of your duties... "

"Because I was trying to see to the new scullery maid's

duties." The answer came out in a whisper interrupted by a sob. She repeated the words in an attempt to be understood.

Adele stilled herself. She frowned. "*Wot?*"

Alice allowed another sigh, this one free of sobs. "She doesn't yet know all her duties. She's so young. A bit slow, too," she added with a finger waving in a circle next to her head. "I started my years in service in the kitchens, you see, so I know what's required to keep the cook happy. I've been trying to perform some of her duties in an attempt to help. But it's not doing any good, and I've become impatient and angry and... rather *bitter*," she admitted in a whisper surrounded by several sobs. "She just doesn't *learn*."

Rolling her eyes, Adele made a mental note to take up the issue with the housekeeper. She'd had no idea the new scullery maid wasn't up to snuff. But then she remembered her husband's edict that no servant would lose their position, and she sighed. "I don't suppose there might be a different task she is better suited to do?" Adele asked, her voice full of doubt.

Sniffling, Alice nodded. "She would make an adequate household maid, my lady. The kitchens are just beyond her ken."

"Why didn't you tell me any of this when the poor girl was first hired?" Adele wondered in a whisper.

Alice considered the question and allowed a sigh. "Because the earl was right. I have been... unhappy. I missed having a man in my life. I am nearly forty, and I have no hope of a husband. No hope of having children. I am alone..."

Adele's arms were around her shoulders, pulling her hard against the side of her body. "Nonsense," she murmured. "I'm nearly your age. Younger than Queen Charlotte, and she's still giving birth to babies."

Sniffling again, Alice nodded. "Except I rather doubt his lordship's valet will be marrying me just because his lordship asks it of him," she countered with a sob.

Nor would she agree to such a union. The very last thing

she wanted was a man who bedded her only because his master required it of him.

True, Adele thought for a moment, rather wishing she had never told her husband of her frustration with Simpkins. Why, she hadn't even brought up the issue with the maid first. She might have discovered the problem with the scullery maid before they took their leave of Worthington House and made arrangements for Libby to be repurposed somewhere else.

Another thought had her frown changing to a look of contemplation.

What if Alonyius Banks did feel some affection for her maid? Men were usually terrible actors, especially for longer than an hour or two at a time. They could be compelled to do things against their will—money was always a suitable motive, as was revenge, or a dare—but after a time, they returned to their usual demeanor. She'd had enough men in her life to know first hand, after all.

Mr. Banks didn't strike her as a man who would do something against his training. Against his upbringing. He was the son of a lady's maid, after all. A woman who had defied convention and married the owner of a woolen mill because he said he fell in love with her at first sight. All because he had shown up at the Torrington townhouse in London and announced to Lady Torrington that he was taking the maid with him to marry her.

What lady's maid wouldn't jump at the chance at a life in the middle class?

Except, as Adele remembered the story, the lady's maid hadn't immediately agreed to the union. She had instead made several requests of Marcus Banks, not the least of which was a period of courting and assurances she could run the man's household as she saw fit.

Apparently, Marcus Banks accommodated her wishes.

"Is there a chance Mr. Banks wasn't acting on the earl's suggestion?"

Alice sniffled. "The words were quite clear, my lady."

Disappointed, Adele tried a different tactic. "What does your heart tell you?" she asked in a quiet voice. "Although there are men who can act well—I've seen a few on the stage at the Royal Theatre—I find that most men cannot. They wear their hearts on their sleeves, and they are obvious in their affections."

Alice considered her mistress' words and finally nodded. "I appreciate your attempt to console me, my lady, but I do not believe Mr. Banks holds any true affection for me," she whispered. The last of her words were nearly lost in the sob she tried hard to suppress.

Really—Mr. Banks wasn't worth her tears, nor another moment of her time. So why was she so upset? She had duties to perform. Laundry to fold and put away. A lady to dress in... she dared a glance at the clock over the fireplace... only an hour.

Taking a deep breath, she turned to Adele and asked, "So, what gown would you like to wear for dinner this evening, milady?"

Managing to keep from blushing—she had worn no gown at all for the past few dinners—Adele gave the question some thought. All the clothes Alice had packed for the trip were now in her dressing room. "The blue sapphire silk, I should think," she replied after a time. "With the diamonds." She didn't smile as she suggested the gown, though. There was a certain earl with whom she needed to have a rather pointed conversation, and she wanted to be fully clothed and look the part of his countess when she did so.

Besides, after all this time of thinking her maid an old maid, she finally understood just why Alice Simpkins was bitter.

And she found she couldn't blame the maid one bit.

Chapter 32

SOMEONE IS MISSING FROM THE SERVANTS' SUPPER

A few minutes later

Although three trestles usually provided enough space to feed the household staff of Torrington Park, the afternoon arrival of four servants from Worthington House required another one be set up in the dining area off the kitchens. Banks was assisting one of the footmen with the trestle when a blast of cold air had them directing their attention to the kitchen's only exterior door.

Haversham appeared in the opening, hat in hand. He looked a bit lost.

He had managed to unhitch the horses from the traveling coach and see to getting them settled into their stalls, but there was no sign of a groom or stableboy to show him where he would be staying. Giving the short, round cook a nod, he said, "Smells mighty good in here, Mrs. Watson." Indeed, the scent of fresh-baked bread mingled with roast beef and several vegetables had his stomach growling in anticipation.

The apple-cheeked woman regarded the driver a moment, obviously recognizing him from his prior visits to the hunting lodge. A pleasant expression appeared before her nose suddenly wrinkled. "It did before you arrived, Mr. Haversham. You, sir, are in need of a bath."

Taken aback by the cook's claim, Haversham frowned.

"That bad, huh?" he asked as he took an experimental sniff of his forearm. "If I take a bath, do you suppose—?"

"It's *Miss* Watson, but Watson will do," she interrupted, not about to allow the man to proposition her in the presence of the two kitchen maids who had been hired since the man's last visit. She pretended not to know the man. "You must be Haversham. Mighty tall, you are." She turned and lifted a mug from a counter, thrusting it in his direction. "Chocolate was hot a while ago. Thought you'd be in well before now," she stated, one eyebrow arching up as if to indicate he should have come straight to the kitchens before seeing to the horses. "I got some pots of hot water on the stove for your bath." She indicated several stock pots on the large stove while she stirred what looked like soup in another. "Figured at least one of ye from London would need a bath."

She whirled about and led him to a small room just off the kitchen. A metal tub was set up, ready for water and a bather. "Linens are there are on the shelf. Hope you have some clean clothes. Or at least some that don't smell so bad," she added with an animated wave of her hand in front of her face. She hurried back to the soup. "Mary can see to your laundry," she added as she pointed to a young girl who was adding coal to the stove. "Please tell me you have some that don't smell of horse."

Haversham was about to admit that he didn't—he only had two shirts to his name.

Mary waved in the groom's direction, giving him a quick curtsy, but she hurried off to another task before he could acknowledge her.

"A bit slow, but she's catchin' on," the cook murmured. "Mrs. Miller—if you remember, she's the housekeeper—has a room all ready for you on the second floor."

The driver gave a shake of his head. "Second floor? Of the house?" he asked in disbelief. He usually had to stay in a room above the stables

"Of course, in the house. You're not a beast," she countered impatiently. Her expression suddenly changed, though, and she regarded the driver with a very different gaze. One that suggested she regarded him in an entirely different light. "Or *are* you?"

Blinking at the question, Haversham's face suddenly reddened. "I'm not, but... I suppose I could be," he stuttered, not sure if she was propositioning him or teasing him. Just the moment before, she had acted as if she didn't remember what they had been doing the last time he was at Torrington Park.

The cook rolled her eyes. "Go on now. Servants' tea is served at six."

Haversham blinked again, rather amazed at how the chubby cook could move about the kitchen so quickly, all the while keeping up an almost one-sided conversation and tending to her soup.

He caught sight of Banks as the valet assisted in setting up the trestle and moved in that direction.

"You heard the cook," Banks said before Haversham could say anything. He did lean in a bit, though, and whispered, "Sounds like you still have another willing bedmate." The tavern wenches at *The Black Swan* had obviously kept the large man occupied whilst they were stranded there.

Pausing in his approach, the groom gave him a quelling glance. "I spend the past few hours freezing to get you here, and this is the greeting I get?" he complained, although his words were followed with a grin.

"Your expertise in driving is much appreciated, Mr. Haversham," Banks replied with a nod. "It's merely the odor about you that is not."

With that, Haversham pulled on his gloves and helped himself to two of the pots of water on the stove. Once in the bathing room, he decided to simply keep his clothes on whilst bathing.

He had no clean clothes to change into, after all.

. . .

hen the chimes of the butler's clock indicated it was six o'clock, several servants rushed to fill the trestles as Mary set steaming bowls and platters in the middle of each. Banks held back a moment, deciding to wait until Simpkins made an appearance. He hadn't seen her since they departed the coach earlier that afternoon, and as they were two of only five upper servants in the household, he hoped they might sit across from one another.

"Do join us, Mr. Banks," Watson said as she waved him to one of the seats at the third trestle.

Banks dared a glance back to the kitchen entrance, and when it was apparent no one else from the household staff would be joining them, he reluctantly took a seat.

"Something wrong, Mr. Banks?" Mrs. Miller asked as she passed him a plate of sliced beef. He took it and gave a shake of his head.

"I was just waiting for Simpkins, is all."

"You'll be waiting all night then," the housekeeper replied as she piled several sliced carrots onto her plate.

Besides being shocked at the number of available vegetables displayed on the trestles—they were sometimes rationed during dinners at Worthington House—Banks blinked at her comment. "Has something happened?" he wondered, realizing he had to be careful in how he put voice to his concern.

"Says she's not feeling well and won't be joining us, is all," Mrs. Miller commented. "Poor thing's insides are probably all jumbled up after all that traveling," she added lightly.

The valet considered the words, tamping down the worry he felt just then. After having spent the last two nights in bed with the lady's maid and having enjoyed their conversations as well as their quiet time in the traveling coach, he was wondering how he might manage to continue their tryst at Torrington Park.

His reverie was interrupted by a question from one of the footmen curious about the news from London. For the next half-hour, he, Haversham and Higgins took turns answering queries while the staff members ate. When most stood up to see to the set up and serving for the formal dinner for the earl and countess, Banks conferred with the cook.

"Might I be allowed to take a tray up to Simpkins' room? In the event she's feeling better?" he asked in a whisper.

Involved in removing the leftover food from the trestles, Watson gave him a sidelong glance. "Promise you're not just keeping it for a midnight snack for yourself?" she half-asked in a teasing voice. "'Cuz around here, you can just come down directly and help yourself," she added when she noticed his look of confusion.

"I promise, it's not for me," he assured her with a shake of his head. "If I wasn't so stuffed, I might consider your offer, though," he added, hoping she hadn't taken offense at his refusal.

Without a word, the cook removed a tea tray from a cupboard where it looked as if there were dozens. She dished up several foods onto a plate, added some utensils and presented the tray to him. "Wait a moment, and I'll get some soup," she said as she hurried off. A moment later, the tray held more food than any one of them had eaten that evening, including Haversham. "Hope she's feeling better," she murmured before turning her attention to the foods for the formal dinner.

"I do, too," Banks replied as he regarded the generous helpings. He made his way to the nearest staircase and found he looked forward to surprising the lady's maid.

With any luck, he'd be allowed to surprise her in other ways later that night.

Chapter 33

A DINNER IS DELIVERED

A few minutes later

Fairly sure he knew which room Alice Simpkins had been assigned to, Banks made his way down the corridor along which most of the servants had their rooms. Given the poor state of what had passed for servants quarters back when the lodge was first built, those rooms in a different wing had been abandoned long ago in favor of what might have been guest bedchambers along the east wall of the lodge. Although the rooms were generous in size, the single fireplace in each meant that most of the furniture was positioned at the end closest to the warmth. Banks had thought there was enough space remaining to host a small soirée in the room to which he had been assigned.

Aware he would need to report to Lord Torrington's bedchamber by half-past seven, he figured he had at least thirty minutes to spend with Alice.

Tapping the back of his knuckles against the door, he listened intently.

"Yes?" The muffled voice was an indication of just how thick the doors were, a bit of assurance they wouldn't be heard should he spend the night in her room instead of his.

Banks balanced the tray on one arm while he opened the door with the other. Peeking around the edge, his gaze went to the window. Leaning a shoulder against the tapestry-covered stone wall, Alice stared out the uneven glass, her attention on something apparently far away. Banks thought she looked ten years younger, what with her hair wound up into a different bun and her new bangs swept off to one side.

"The housekeeper said you wouldn't be down for tea, so I brought it to you," Alonyius said in a quiet voice as he stepped in and pushed the heavy door shut behind him.

Startled out of her reverie, Alice stared at him before blinking a few times. "Tea?" she repeated.

The valet set the tray on the room's only table and hurried in her direction, intending to take her into his arms. When she suddenly gave a start away from him, her back pressed against an ancient tapestry, he noticed her reddened eyes. "What's wrong, Alice? When you didn't come down for tea, I got worried... "

"Get out," Alice whispered, the words urgent. "How dare you?"

Banks blinked and paused in his approach, his expression turning to one of hurt. He supposed she was rather shocked to find him in her bedchamber. "I dare because I care about you," he countered, rather stunned by her curt words. "When you didn't come down for tea, I got worried."

When he was about to move closer, she held out a staying hand. "How much did he pay you to say *that?*" she hissed.

Recoiling as if he'd been punched in the gut, Alonyius shook his head. "What... what are you talking about?"

Alice rolled her eyes. "You needn't deny it, Mr. Banks. I know everything. Now take your leave, or I shall... I shall scream," she warned, her fingers curling into fists at her sides.

Shaking his head, Banks continued to regard her with a look of confusion. "Alice. What has happened? I beg you, tell me how it is I have fallen out of your good graces..." And in such short order. He had last seen her only six hours earlier! And every inch of her six hours before that!

One of her arms lifted and she pointed to the door. "I relieve you of your... *obligation*, Mr. Banks. I do hope you profited greatly from your... *sacrifice*," she whispered, the clipped words indicating her annoyance. And her hurt.

Still not sure of her meaning—*sacrifice?*—Alonyius realized he had better take his leave. Should she begin to scream, why, the entire household would learn of their *affaire*, and then he would be forced to ask for her hand in marriage.

He was nearly to the door when he suddenly paused. Although he hadn't considered proposing to Alice, it wasn't out of the question.

Was it?

He found he rather enjoyed her company. He certainly enjoyed their time in bed together. Why, once he had determined how to coax her sensual side out of hiding, the woman was a wonderful lover. Generous, too. His cock nearly hardened at the thought of how she had climbed atop him, of how she had impaled herself on his tumescence and brought him to completion only that morning. After their quiet conversation the night before, he found it difficult to think of anything else.

Anyone else.

Who would have thought a man of his age would be so capable? Well, besides the earl, of course. Alonyius was well aware his master was a master when it came to the activities performed in a bedchamber.

And some other locations.

But after that first awkward night, Alice seemed to welcome his advances—even initiated this morning's encounter when he thought it would be selfish to do so. The past two days had been so remarkable, he had hoped they could simply continue their liaison, perhaps agree to some sort of permanent relationship.

Which had him wondering if she would ever find herself with child.

Could she have children?

The thought caused a twinge somewhere deep in his chest. Given his occupation, he had never thought to marry. To father children. Meanwhile, he watched as other servants took spouses, some not even in the same households. One of the maids in Worthington House was due to give birth next month, her husband a footman in a neighboring home. Another footman had just married a servant at Norwick House.

He and Alice were of an age when children were probably out of the question, but a marriage would provide them with companionship. A bedmate. A friend for life.

He straightened, his reverie interrupted when Alice suddenly stomped her foot.

"Out!" she exclaimed, her hoarse whisper loud enough to be heard by anyone in the room.

"I do not know why it is you think I have... *profited* from our time together, but I admit to feeling richer for it. I am very sorry that you do not." With that, Alonyius took his leave of Alice's quarters and made his way to the earl's suite.

*T*ears of anger and hurt once again streaming down her face, Alice fell into the nearest chair and stared at the closed door. *How dare he show his face here?* Did he think his ruse hadn't been discovered? How long did he believe he could continue to bed her before she would learn of his arrangement with the earl?

Well, he knew she wouldn't be helping him line his pockets any longer. As for her demeanor, well, she would just have to feign happiness—nay, *contentment*—whenever she was in the company of her mistress. Or anyone else, for that matter. Let the servants wonder what had her displaying a new expression. A new attitude.

Hunger had her attention turning to the tray the valet had brought with him. She leaned over and lifted the cover from a plate laden with beef and vegetables. Lifting the cover from another plate, she blinked at the sight of a bowl of soup, a curl of steam escaping from its surface. Swallowing a sob, she had half a mind to take the entire tray back to the kitchens without eating any of it. But to do so would be a waste, especially given how valuable vegetables had become given the poor harvest this year.

Helping herself to the utensils—the man had apparently thought of everything but something to drink—Alice tucked into the meal. She finished every last bite before drying her tears and hurrying off to the mistress suite.

Chapter 34

GETTING DRESSED FOR DINNER AND READY FOR REDRESS

$\mathcal{A}$t exactly fifteen minutes past seven o'clock, Adele allowed a sigh and dared a glance at her bedchamber door. Now that Simpkins had arrived at Torrington Park, she expected the lady's maid to resume her duties—broken heart or not. Although Simpkins was still in the study when she had taken her leave, she was quite sure the maid wasn't about to impale herself on one of the weapons on display. In fact, the woman seemed almost right as rain.

As if on cue, a knock sounded through the thick wooden door.

Giving a start, Adele glanced at the clock again and called out, "Come!"

Simpkins entered and gave a quick curtsy. "Good evening, milady," she said, sounding ever so happy as she hurried to the dressing room and pulled out the sapphire silk gown and a pair of silver slippers.

Adele blinked, stunned at how different her maid appeared. She had changed into newly-pressed livery, and although it was still evident Simpkins had been crying earlier that day, her countenance suggested she had recovered from her broken heart.

Completely.

"I see you managed to get the wrinkles out," Adele

commented as she turned to face Simpkins so she could unbutton the riding habit.

Alice stared at her mistress for a moment, thinking she had referred to her face just then. She gave a quick shake of her head when she realized the countess meant the dinner gown. "Just needed a hot iron, milady." Torrington Park might have been a hunting lodge at one time, but now it boasted at least a few of the accoutrements of a household located in London.

Angling her head to one side, Adele regarded her maid for a moment. "Did you have tea with the rest of the staff this evening?" she wondered. Despite having been at Torrington Park for several days, Adele still didn't have a feel for how the servants got on in their positions. Mrs. Miller certainly seemed as if she was all business, but the countess wondered if the housekeeper had merely been putting on a show for her sake when she came across the woman yesterday morning.

"I did not milady," Simpkins replied as she held the silk gown open for Adele to step into. "A tray was brought up to my room, though, so I did have some supper." She dared not admit just how much she ate, but it was far more than usual.

Had Banks thought her a glutton when he prepared the tray? Or had someone else dished up the food?

"That was rather kind of whomever delivered it," Adele murmured as she turned to allow her maid to do up the fastenings at the back.

Simpkins didn't reply, just then remembering the look of hurt on Alonyius Banks' face when she ordered him out of her room. Had he been acting? Earlier, her mistress had suggested that unless they were great actors of the stage, most men couldn't act.

Well, Banks certainly could.

She had to wonder just how gullible he thought her to be. His parting words suddenly echoed in her ears. *I do not know why it is you think I have profited from our time together, but I admit to feeling richer for it.* Her fingers suddenly slowed their movements.

"What is it? Is something wrong with the gown?" Adele wondered as she turned slightly.

Simpkins blinked and resumed buttoning the gown. "Not at all, my lady," she murmured. "Just had to remove an Irish pennant is all." When she had finished, she moved to put the diamonds onto Adele's ears when the countess suddenly gave a huff and Simpkins turned around to find her mistress giving her a look of impatience. "What is it, my lady? Did you... did you wish to wear different earbobs this evening?"

Adele regarded her lady's maid for a moment before allowing a sigh. "Not at all," she said with a wave of her hand. "Did something else happen? With Mr. Banks?"

Her eyes widening—why would Lady Torrington ask such a question?—Simpkins finally gave a nod. "He... he was the one who delivered the tray to my quarters, milady."

Adele's eyes widened, her first thought to say something rude about the valet. But then she thought better of it when she remembered he probably knew nothing about having been discovered. "I take it you didn't throw it on the man."

Simpkins gasped. "No, milady," she said with a shake of her head. "'Twould have been a waste of rather good food."

Resisting the urge to grin at her lady's maid's reaction, Adele leaned forward. "But you... spoke with him."

Allowing a sigh, Simpkins nodded. "I did. I told him to get out. And when he didn't, I threatened to scream."

When the lady's maid didn't continue, Adele gave her an expectant look. "*Then* did you at least throw the tray at him? Without the food?"

Simpkins blinked. "No, milady. When I accused him of profiting from our time together, he said something about being richer for having spent time in my company. And then he took his leave." She leaned forward and attached the earbobs onto Adele's ears. Stepping back, she gave them each a quick glance to ensure they were even.

Frowning, Adele seemed deep in thought for a moment before she finally looked up to find the servant regarding her with a look of concern. "I never for a moment thought Lord Torrington capable of paying a servant to... to bed another," the countess whispered. "But it seems he has done so." She shook her head, obviously troubled. "I do hope that at least the valet provided you with a... a night to remember," she struggled to get out.

A blush rising to cover her entire throat and face, Simpkins merely nodded. She couldn't help the memory of what that servant had done to her. Of how he had held her. Of how he had kissed her. Of how his caresses had set off shivers of delight beneath her skin. Of how he had pleasured her until she could take no more, and then had finally allowed his own.

Of his assurances that her breasts were a perfect size...

"Milady, might I ask if you've ever heard a man say, 'more than a mouthful is waste'? With regard to... a woman's bosom, I mean?" Simpkins struggled to ask, her face still rather red.

A slow smile spread over Adele's own face before she leaned toward her maid and said, "I've heard the expression, of course, but had any man ever said it to *me*, they would have found themselves tossed out of my bedchamber on their ear." She arched an eyebrow at the end of her comment and thrust her chest out as if to reinforce her claim.

Simpkins gave a nod, realizing just then that her well-endowed mistress had far more than a mouthful when it came to breasts. If a man believed what Alonyius Banks said, then he probably wouldn't be attracted to such a well-endowed woman.

Adele's eyes suddenly widened. "Did Banks say that to you?"

The blush continued to suffuse her face. "He did," Simpkins whispered, her head nodding. "He even said it as if he meant it, but..."

"Perhaps he did," Adele said with a shrug, no longer

wondering at the sudden sadness that had settled over her maid. She turned suddenly and angled her head. "Get some rest, Simpkins. I won't need you again for the rest of the night."

A rather loud and unusual sound had both Adele and her lady's maid jumping just then. "What was that?" Simpkins asked as she hurried to the door.

"The dinner gong," Adele said with a roll of her eyes as she rose from her chair and joined Simpkins at the door. "Torrington's father brought back a mounted gong with him from a trip to the Orient," she added as she took her leave of the mistress suite.

And depending on his answers this evening, I might just have to hit Milton on the head with the mallet.

Chapter 35

A COUNTESS CONFRONTS
HER HUSBAND

A few minutes later
"Did you order your valet to bed my maid?"

Milton blinked. He straightened and turned to regard his wife just as he was about to pull out a chair for her. This was their first formal dinner since arriving at Torrington Park.

And the first dinner they would share at a table since settling their first spat.

He blinked again.

"*Order* is a rather... strong word," he finally replied, his expression giving away his guilt better than his comment.

She gave a rather loud sigh. "Milton! What were you *thinking?*" Adele's question was asked in a hoarse whisper in the hopes it wouldn't be overheard by the rather tall footman who probably hovered outside the dining room.

The earl leaned forward and matched her whisper. "Did it work?"

It was Adele's turn to blink. She also rolled her eyes before she suddenly stepped away from the chair he had pulled out for her. She wasn't about to have this conversation over the length of the dining room table.

Stunned by her sudden departure from her end of the table and in his direction, Milton prepared himself as if he expected to be slapped.

Or punched.

Or both.

Adele had done neither in the past, but he was quite sure she was capable of bodily harm just then. Why, her eyes blazed with anger far more than did the diamonds that decorated her ears and her throat. *Good thing she isn't carrying the mallet for the dinner gong,* he thought as he watched her hands curl into fists.

"But I thought Simpkins looked... *happy,*" he whispered as Adele approached him, her displeasure even more apparent up close.

"She *was* until she overheard your conversation with Banks," Adele said as her fisted hands went to her hips. "This afternoon," she clarified, just in case he tried to claim he hadn't had such a conversation with his valet.

The move not only made her appear every bit the countess she was, it also put her décolletage on its very best display. Milton couldn't help that his eyes darted in that direction. He had always had an appreciation for his wife's rather generous charms—whoever said 'more than a mouthful was a waste' was obviously daft—and he couldn't help the effect that such a sight had on his nether region. For a moment, he forgot what his wife had just said.

"Don't you *dare!*" Adele hissed as her hands covered her bosom.

His attention back on her face, the earl realized he had better think of something quick. It had taken an entire day to get back in her good graces over what had been said the morning before, and he never wanted to spend a day like that ever again. "I didn't know what else to do," he finally admitted.

Adele frowned, her hands dropping to her sides. "What made you think you had to *do* anything at all?"

Milton allowed a sigh and dared a glance in the direction of the door before he answered. "You said Simpkins was complaining. That you wished to let her go. After what I said in the dining room at Worthington House last month—loud enough for the footman to hear—I couldn't exactly let you fire her. So I thought perhaps her countenance might be improved... "

"Improved?" Adele repeated in disbelief.

Giving a one-shouldered shrug, Milton nodded. "She merely required a good tumble, and I could think of no better... *tumbler* than my valet."

Well, he could, but he wasn't about to offer *himself* to the lady's maid.

Adele blinked as she gave her head a quick shake. "You *bounder!*" she accused. She was about to inquire just how it was her husband knew his valet was a good tumbler, but thought better of it. This wasn't about Banks.

Well, not entirely, anyway.

Milton nodded. "I used to be. Which is how I knew it would work. And it seemed it did work until your maid eavesdropped on our conversation," he added, as he just then realized what Adele had said earlier. He puffed out his chest just a bit. "So, she was happy with Banks'... *attentions* then?" he dared, hoping to assuage Adele just a bit. At least she didn't look as if she might put him into an early grave.

Or leave him with a blackened eye.

Or a split lip.

Or both.

Allowing an audible sigh that seemed to rid her of her anger as well as most of her breath, Adele sank into the nearest chair at the table. "She was... in *love* with Mr. Banks, I think," she whispered. "I've never seen her so radiant. Why, she hasn't put voice to a single complaint since our arrival, even though she's had to unload all my trunks and even do the laundry," she explained in a quiet voice. Lifting her face to regard her husband with another sigh, she asked. "How much blunt did you offer him to do it?"

Milton shook his head. "I didn't," he replied before he settled into the carver. He allowed a long sigh and shook his head. "My sweeting, it's not like it is for a woman," he said in a hoarse whisper. "The compensation *is* the tumble for a man, you see. The pleasure he gets out of it."

Adele gave him a quelling glance. "Was it... *unpleasant* for him do you suppose?" Knowing how Banks comported himself when at Worthington House—all business and never a hint of impropriety or even emotion, for that matter—Adele realized she wouldn't know if the man was happy or sad or in pain or even sick.

Frowning, Milton considered how Banks had responded to his gentle jibes. The valet had certainly seemed uncomfortable with his questions, and he hadn't said an unkind word about Simpkins. Indeed, he had mostly seemed tongue-tied. "If it was unpleasant for the man, he certainly didn't put voice to it," he murmured, still deep in thought. "Not that he would, of course." Banks was all about doing his duty. Always had been.

Sons of maids tended to be like that.

Had the man thought it his duty to bed the lady's maid once I suggested it? he wondered, a sense of guilt making him wonder what he might have to do to make everything right again.

Devlin, the footman, appeared with the first course. When he noted where Adele was seated, he seemed unsure of what to do. Her dinner service was still at the other end of the table.

"I'll be eating here this evening," Adele piped up, indicating the space at the table in front of her. "And every other night, as well," she added with an arched brow.

Acknowledging her with a bow and a, "Verra good, milady," the footman set about moving her place setting before he poured wine and placed the soup bowls in front of them. As soon as he was out of the room, Adele turned her attention back to Milton. "It's sure to be awkward between them." She didn't even want to consider what it might be like for them in the traveling coach when they had to head back to London!

Was Simpkins capable of bodily harm? For a moment, Adele felt rather sorry for Banks, for she rather doubted the man would defend himself against the lady's maid. Even though Simpkins seemed only sad now, Adele knew how anger usually followed the sadness in a broken relationship.

She knew because she had experienced it first-hand.

Still considering his rather one-sided conversation with Banks in the billiards room, Milton was left wondering just how awkward it would be. "They're our age, sweeting. Surely they're both mature enough to work out a suitable schedule where they don't have to *see* one another," he replied with a shake of his head. At Adele's look of shock, he added, "We did. Or rather, *you* did. I didn't see you once all day yesterday."

"That's because I made sure I wasn't in the study or the billiards room," Adele countered with an arched brow. It wasn't difficult to hide when she knew which rooms were the favorites of her husband. She felt a bit of guilt when she noted his momentary look of hurt.

"I'll speak with Banks tonight. Before I come to your bedchamber," Milton amended, hoping he would still be allowed to share her bed. After yesterday's fiasco, he had no intention of attempting to sleep by himself again. "See if I can't gauge what really might have happened." He helped himself to a spoonful of soup. "Did she... cry?" he asked in a hesitant whisper.

Turning to her meal, Adele gave a nod. "She was a veritable watering pot, and not a hanky in sight."

Milton's expression of disgust was almost comical. "I promise I shall never intentionally make you cry," he said suddenly. "I find a crying woman most vexing. No matter what I say, it's wrong, and if I don't saying anything at all, it's wrong."

Well, at least he has the gist of it, Adele thought, deciding his comment needed no response.

They continued to eat in relative silence for the rest of the meal, Adele's thoughts on her maid and Milton's on how he planned to surprise his wife in the morning.

And satisfy her later that evening. He did not want to imagine her wielding the gong's mallet in his direction.

Chapter 36

AN EARL WONDERS WHAT HE
DID WRONG

*L*ater that night

Milton regarded his reflection in the ancient cheval mirror. At least he had placated Adele enough that she wouldn't rebuff his advances this evening. But how the woman had come to believe he had paid his valet to bed her lady's maid was beyond his ken.

When a quick knock at the door was followed by his valet appearing around the edge of it, Milton waved him in. He watched the man's reflection as the valet moved to join him at the mirror, looking for any signs that he was upset or saddened by what had happened that afternoon. As usual, his passive expression gave away nothing.

"Normally, it wouldn't be any of my business what you do on your own time, Banks, but I believe there's been a misunderstanding."

Straightening, his face a study in confusion, Banks regarded his employer for a moment before allowing a nod. "I am of the same opinion, my lord," he finally replied.

The earl angled his head. "Seems I may have given you the wrong... *instructions* regarding Miss Simpkins," he murmured. "I never meant for you to have to do something you didn't wish to," he added, his manner rather awkward.

"But I haven't, I assure you, sir," Banks replied in the same low voice.

Milton frowned and regarded his valet a moment. "I was under the impression you spent time in her company."

"I did," Banks acknowledged. "I have. Several days in the traveling coach."

Continuing to frown, the earl considered the simple responses. "What about the nights?" A bushy, arched eyebrow accompanied the question.

Tempted to inform his employer it was none of his business, Banks finally allowed a sigh. Had Simpkins informed her ladyship of what had happened between them? Were they both in danger of losing their positions over it? Or was this about something else entirely?

"Part of the reason I was able to return your purse with so many coins still in it is because *The Black Swan* could only spare two rooms for our party," he said carefully. "And I did not share one with Haversham and Higgins." This last was said with an arched eyebrow that mirrored his master's.

Rocking back on his heels, Milton Grandby regarded his valet with an expression that suggested he was a bit confused. "Which implies you shared the room with Simpkins," he stated.

"I did," Banks admitted with a curt nod. When the earl continued to arch his bushy eyebrows, as if he was waiting for the valet to say more, Banks sighed. "Contrary to my initial opinion of Miss Simpkins, I found her completely agreeable. Rather pleasant, in fact. Indeed, I was glad to be in her company," he claimed.

When his master's eyebrows continued their upward journey to his hairline, as if he was waiting for a confession, Banks sighed again. "She was a most willing lover," he finally whispered.

It was the earl's turn to sigh. "Then she must have developed a tendré for you. My countess was not happy with me at dinner tonight."

Banks' eyes widened before he displayed an expression of confusion. "I am aware Miss Simpkins is... unhappy with me, but I cannot sort why that might be. She seems to believe I somehow *profited* from my time with her. And not in any manner other than a monetary way," he added, his brows furrowing in another attempt to figure out why she had come to that conclusion.

"She overheard our conversation in the billiards room," Milton admitted with a shake of his head. "Since I don't remember you saying very much, she must have heard me make a rather crude remark to that effect," he admitted, his voice kept low in the event his wife was listening to their conversation on the other side of the dressing room door.

"Oh," was all Banks could manage just then. He closed his eyes, remembering the earlier comments the Earl of Torrington had made and fully understanding why it was the lady's maid would assume the worst. "Oh."

"I apologize," Milton said quietly. "It was wrong of me to assume you wouldn't find Simpkins... beddable." He suddenly frowned. "Was she... beddable?" he asked suddenly.

Despite his position, Banks managed a rather quelling glance. "Very, my lord," he responded, his words clipped as he ignored the earl's apology. Given Torrington's opinion of the lady's maid, he rather doubted the man would believe anything else he told him about Alice Simpkins, though, and so he merely stood waiting for the earl's next question.

But the earl didn't ask one. Instead, his brows furrowed and he sank onto his bed, his shoulders slumping. "I owe the lady's maid an apology as well," he murmured sadly. He dared a glance at this valet. "She's not been happy this past year, and..."

"For good reason," Banks replied, his hands going behind his back to clasp together. Another moment at his sides, and he might have been tempted to punch his master in the jaw.

Torrington frowned. "Enlighten me."

Banks considered the order for a moment before he said,

"She has taken on the impossible task of seeing to it the scullery maid is able to keep her position despite her inability to perform the duties required of the position."

Blinking, the earl regarded his valet for a moment. "Whatever do you mean?"

"She's up well before dawn, down in the kitchens, preparing it the way Cook expects it to be when she starts her day. Libby cannot... she does not have the..." He paused, not sure how to explain that the girl couldn't grasp how to do the various duties expected of her.

"Capacity," Torrington finished for him.

"Exactly," Banks agreed with a sigh.

"And my recent comment about not letting go of any servants ensures she is able to keep her position despite not being able to perform it," he finished, understanding the problem somewhat. "But why would Simpkins think it necessary to do the girl's duties?"

Sighing, Banks wondered if he was betraying the maid's trust in him by telling his master about Libby. "I do not believe it's my place to say why, my lord."

Milton stood up, the sudden move forcing Banks to take a step back. "Then I shall discover the reason for myself," he announced, after which he promptly took his leave of the master suite.

Left in his master's quarters wondering what was left for him to do, Alonyius had two thoughts.

Make that three.

He was a bit worried for Alice's reputation. If Milton Grandby was on his way to the maid's quarters, he could only hope the other servants didn't come to the wrong conclusion as to why he might do so.

Alonyius could only imagine how much trouble the man might find himself in should the Countess of Torrington believe he was having an *affaire* with her lady's maid.

Serves him right, the valet thought with a sigh.

His uncharitable thought was replaced by another. *Poor*

Alice. Despite what she believed he had done, he still felt affection for her. Affection he was sure would never again be requited.

And then another finally cemented itself in his brain, and he realized what he had to do.

Chapter 37

AN EARL EATS CROW

few minutes later, in the servants' wing

Learning in which room Alice Simpkins had been assigned should have been easy. Simply ask the housekeeper, or the butler, or any of the staff of Torrington Park.

Normally, Milton would have done such a thing, but with it being well after nine o'clock at night, it seemed far too inappropriate. What would the other servants think to discover him in search of his wife's lady's maid? Why, they might think he was carrying on an *affaire* with her! And although she was a rather handsome woman—she had probably been pretty when she was younger—the very last thing he wanted was any kind of scandal involving another woman. Not after the day he had experienced yesterday.

"Good evening, Lord Torrington," Mrs. Miller said. "Are you looking for someone in particular?" she asked when Milton turned and gave a quick nod. Her curtsy was a barely-there dip.

"Tomorrow is the hanging of the greens, and I've a surprise in mind for my countess. But I need her lady's maid to help me pull it off. By chance, would you know which room is hers?"

The housekeeper's expression suggested she might believe his story. "Why, the second door on the left. I made sure she has an eastern vantage," Mrs. Miller replied with a grin.

"How kind of you," Milton replied. "Is everything in place for the... wreath-making?" he asked then. After all the work they had done to create enough pine boughs to decorate every room in the lodge, he didn't want the branches to end up rotting outside the great hall.

There was a pause as she considered his query. "I know nothing about it," she replied with widened eyes. There was actually a hint of fear there, as if the idea of making wreaths was a complete unknown for the woman.

Finally, Milton thought in delight. He had managed to discombobulate the housekeeper. "We'll need the wire and ribbon fabric the late dowager countess used when she was here making wreaths and what-not," he said. "You do remember, do you not?"

Mrs. Miller nodded. "Of course, my lord," she said with another nod. "I'll see to it right away." She gave a curtsy and hurried off, leaving Milton to allow a sigh of relief before he turned and regarded the second door on the left.

Lifting his hand, he hesitated before finally rapping his knuckles against the thick wood. There was a chance the lady's maid wouldn't answer. A chance she would slam the door in his face. A chance she wasn't even in...

"Good evening, my lord," Simpkins said as she opened the door a bit wider. "You wished to speak with me about the surprise?"

Milton blinked. Had she heard everything he said to the housekeeper? He had always thought the doors too thick to hear anything said in the halls. "Indeed." He was about to suggest they go to a parlor when she stepped aside.

Giving a glance down the hall, Milton decided it was safe enough. He hurried in but stopped and made sure his back was to the adjacent wall. He gave a bow to her curtsy and then scanned the room. Although no one else was there, it appeared she could have hosted a small soirée given the amount of open space in the back.

"Are all the servants' quarters this large?" he asked in awe.

Simpkins sighed. "I'm sure I wouldn't know, milord."

The earl ducked his head. "Of course not. How could you?" He sighed again.

"Are you here to fire me, milord?"

Milton blinked. "No. No one is being sacked," he replied with a shake of his head. "Now, if I could sack myself, I would. I always thought my cousin, Gregory, should have been the earl. But since I was born a few months ahead of him..." He allowed the sentence to trail off.

Alice frowned. "But your father was the earl," she countered, quite sure he had come to the title by being the oldest heir.

"True," he acknowledged. "I suppose there was no hope for me," he added. He sighed again. "Have you ever eaten crow?"

It was Alice's turn to blink. "Twice that I can recall. My mother made it when there was nothing else available to feed us."

Closing his eyes when he realized she had taken him literally, Milton waited a moment.

"Oh. You meant the other kind, I suppose," Alice offered before she frowned. "Once, then. When I accused another servant of having lifted a necklace from her ladyship." At the earl's sudden interest, she added, "It was merely misplaced. Not of my doing, I assure you. But I felt awful, and I apologized immediately, milord." She wasn't about to add that the servant had left the employ of her ladyship and gone on to become the head housekeeper for another estate.

"I have many times. I hope this is my last. I made a grave error in... judgement."

"My lord?" Alice couldn't believe what she was hearing. Whatever could the earl have done that he needed to apologize to her?

"I knew of your recent bout with... unhappiness. My countess mentioned it over dinner last month. Before we embarked on this trip, I thought to improve matters by seeing to your... happiness. I happen to employ a rather dutiful valet whom I thought could see to those ends."

Feeling a bit light-headed—Alice could hardly believe the earl's words—she tried to control her breathing. "You do, yes," she agreed.

"I mentioned it to him, and then realized how ludicrous it sounded—as if I was expecting him to fall on his sword..." He paused and rolled his eyes. "To make someone he did not know or particularly care for, happy again. I told him to forget what I'd said, but it seems he could not. Or did not."

Alice stared at the earl. "May I ask how you much you offered for him to... make me happy, milord?"

Frowning, Milton shook his head. "I didn't offer money," he replied quickly. "Well, I did tell him to keep the leftover coins from the trip here, but I do that every year as a sort of payment for him finding us the best coaching inns. But it wouldn't have done any good if I had offered any blunt."

Inhaling sharply at this bit of information, Alice stepped back a bit. "Pardon?" She was sure there was compensation offered to bed her. *Why else would...?*

"Mr. Banks is not like most men when it comes to money," the earl went on. "I'm not sure if you're aware, but he is an heir to a rather prosperous textile mill, and will be an equal owner of a manor house in Darlington upon the death of his mother."

Alice nodded. "I am aware, milord," she replied, her heart suddenly racing.

"If Mr. Banks showed you any kind of interest—carnal or otherwise—he did so of his own volition. And since I've been informed my overheard words to him caused a broken heart or two, I find I must apologize," he said, his voice kept low in the event it could be heard outside the door. He didn't want the entire staff knowing about what had happened earlier that day. "I don't expect you to forgive me, but I do hope you won't hold my words against *him*."

Her eyes suddenly bright with tears, Alice struggled to catch her breath. She remembered Alonyius' reply to her earlier accusations that evening. Of how he had profited by simply knowing her.

"Oh, my lord," she said as she considered what she must do. What she had to do. "Now *I* am the one that needs to eat crow."

His eyes darting to the side, Milton wondered what she meant. "And to whom do you owe an apology?"

"Him," she said simply. Her small hands wrung together at her waist. "This cannot wait until morning. I cannot let him spend the night thinking I despise him. I said the most awful things to him."

The earl bobbed his head about, deciding he agreed with her. 'Never go to bed sorry' was as important as 'never go to bed angry'. "I expect he's still in my quarters. When he's finished, I'll make sure he... pays a call?" He wasn't exactly sure that was the best solution, but what else was there?

A bit of hope for her future once again burning inside, Alice nodded. "I would appreciate that. And if he doesn't come, then I suppose I will have my answer." Try as she might, she couldn't keep her lower lip from trembling.

The earl gave her a quick nod, turned, and opened the door.

Adele stood on the other side, her look of annoyance and the way her brows suddenly furrowed a rather unwelcome sight just then.

Chapter 38

APOLOGIES ABOUND

One second later

"Lady Torrington!" Milton said with as much enthusiasm as he could muster. He turned and said, "Thank you, Miss Simpkins," with a nod before shutting the door. A few servants poked their heads out of their rooms, but quickly retreated into their quarters and shut their doors when they realized they might be seen by the earl paying witness to his late evening visit to another servants' quarters.

Adele glared at him, but held her tongue, waiting for him to explain himself.

"It's not what it looks like," he whispered.

"I know that," she replied in a hoarse whisper. "But did you really have to take fifteen minutes to apologize? I thought you would be back in your bedchamber by now."

Milton gave a shrug. "It takes a while to eat crow," he countered, his voice kept low. "Anyway, you knew I was going to apologize to her. Why...?" He stopped when he realized she held a folded note in her hand. "What's this?" He took the note from her, although she didn't give it up easily.

"I think it's a letter of resignation," she whispered. "From Mr. Banks."

The earl had the note unfolded and was reading the beautifully rendered script even as Adele said the words he never thought to read.

> *Recent changes in my family's situation require my immediate presence in Darlington. I do not expect I will be relieved of these obligations; therefore, I must tender my resignation immediately. Yours in service, Alonyius Banks.*

"Bullocks," Milton breathed. "When did he give this to you?"

Adele shook her head. "He didn't. I found it on your bed when I went to find you. You were supposed to help me..." She glanced about to be sure no one else was in the hall. "Undress me," she finished in a whisper.

Milton nodded. "As much as I want to do that, and believe me, I do, I really should discover Banks' whereabouts."

His countess nodded her understanding. "Don't be up too late, dear. We have wreaths to make in the morning," she reminded him, giving him a quick kiss on the corner of his mouth. She hurried off, leaving the earl in the middle of the hall.

Well, he can't have gone far, Milton thought as he considered the options. It wasn't as if the man could walk to Darlington.

He would require transportation. He would need a horse.

Intending to send a footman to the stables to look for the valet, Milton turned around to find Mrs. Miller regarding him from where she stood a few feet away.

How does she do that? Milton wondered.

"May I be of help, my lord?" she asked brightly. She was still fully dressed in her regular drab day gown, her chatelaine hanging from one pocket.

"Which room was Banks assigned to?"

Her eyes widening, the housekeeper gave a nod in the direction she faced. She walked with the earl to the end of the hall. "This one," Mrs. Miller said as she stood back, apparently expecting the earl to kick open the door.

He gave her a nod and knocked on it instead. "Mr. Banks?" he called out, trying to keep his voice down lest he wake any more servants. When there was no answer after another moment, he opted to try the knob and found the door opened easily.

Although there was evidence someone had been in the room, there was no sign of Mr. Banks.

Milton cursed.

*A*t the other end of the hall, Alonyius Banks halted in his haste to get to his quarters. Having left the note for his master to find later that night, he had then made his way to the stables to see about borrowing a horse. Although he didn't relish the thought of traveling at night, the weather had improved, and he had a linen filled with a substantial meal, thanks to the leftovers from his lord and ladyship's dinner. Besides, he found he simply couldn't face another day at Torrington Park given what had happened on this one.

To have begun the day with a woman in his arms—a woman he now realized he loved—and then to have been falsely accused of taking payment for his attentions toward her was simply untenable.

The Earl of Torrington had made mistakes during his tenure, as would anyone in his position. Yet, at every turn, he had apologized for them. Done what he could to make things right. In this case of what had to be a simple misunderstanding, he bore some of the responsibility.

Nay, he bore all of it.

It was the earl's words that Alice had overheard from the billiards room. His words that had her believing the valet had been paid to bed her. To improve her countenance.

But his own lack of a suitable rejoinder to the earl's comments hadn't helped, to be sure. *I could have made my position more clear. Insisted I wasn't inconvenienced. I could have told him I planned...*

Damn.

At this point, Alonyius was quite sure there was no making this right. What could his master do, after all?

What can I do?

Alice Simpkins was convinced he was no better than a... than a prostitute!

He needed to do something quick, though, for there were two people going into his quarters this very moment. When they discovered he wasn't there, they would be stepping out and possibly directing their search elsewhere. They might come this way.

They will come this way, he suddenly realized. There was no exit from that end of the hall!

Alonyius did the only thing he could. He ducked into the nearest room he could and quietly closed the door, his back pressed against it so he could listen. Listen and wait until they left the hall so he could grab his valise from his room and take his leave.

Which meant he was entirely unprepared for the soft body that collided with his, for the small hands that cupped his cheeks, and the lips that took purchase on his for a kiss he wasn't expecting.

The scent of citrus enveloped him, reminding him of his favorite bath. Of the delectable body that had been in that water. Of that body when it was beneath him.

His body responded before he could, his manhood remembering quite well what this body had done to him earlier that very morning.

Just this morning? Christ, but this had been a long day!

When the lips left his, they spoke in soft, hurried words. "I'm so sorry. I'm so, so sorry." And then they kissed him again, only to pull away before he could respond. "Oh, Alonyius, can you ever forgive me?" And then they resumed the kiss that he was still trying to return.

His hands finally went to her sides, gripping her waist in

an attempt to push her away. But one of her hands went to the back of his head, pulling it down to meet hers. The ticklish sensation of her fingers spearing his hair sent a shiver through his entire body, and then he simply gave up trying to fend off her advances.

When she finished the soft kiss, she allowed a wan smile. "The earl was here a few minutes ago. He came, and he... he *ate crow*. He explained *everything*," she whispered frantically. "I'm so sorry I misunderstood. I should have known you wouldn't do anything unless it was of your own volition." She suddenly glanced down his front and regarded him with a look of worry. "Why are you wearing your coat?"

The question jolted Alonyius out of his stupor, but he simply stared at Alice for several moments. "I... I was about to leave for Darlington," he stuttered, suddenly wondering why the hell he would attempt to do such a thing after nine o'clock on a winter night. On a horse.

Am I daft?

He closed his eyes in a effort to steady himself. *Yes, but only because I am lovesick,* he considered. Never having experienced such a heady feeling, he was unprepared for how it affected him. One moment, he was as happy as he had been in his entire life. A moment later, he wished he were dead.

At this moment, he was somewhere in-between. Confused and relieved, tired and a bit bruised, he realized how odd his words must sound to the woman whose warmth was melting his hardened heart.

Alice stared at him, giving up part of her hold on him to step back. "But, why?" Her eyes suddenly widened. "Did something happen at Mill House? Is your mother—?"

"Not that I'm aware of," he managed with a shake of his head. He glanced down to find her wearing a night rail and nothing more. Her bare feet poked out from beneath the hem, her toes crunching up after a moment.

"I changed into it as soon as the earl left. I was praying you would... you would come and spend the night with me again," she murmured, her body falling against the front of his. She knew she should have at least pulled on a dressing gown when he stepped into her room, but she'd been so glad to see him—so shocked he had appeared only moments after the earl's departure—she couldn't help her immediate reaction.

Had he been just outside the door when the earl paid his call?

Alonyius closed his eyes as he moved his hands to the sides of her shoulders. He rubbed her arms a bit, as if he had to be sure she was real. "I'm not sure what to say," he whispered, finally wrapping his arms around her shoulders. He held her then. Held her and kissed her hair.

"Then come to bed."

The invitation was rather welcome just then. He was so tired—physically exhausted and emotionally drained—he merely nodded. From the muted conversation taking place at the other end of the hall, he knew the housekeeper and the earl were still nearby. "They're looking for me."

"The earl is. He wishes to apologize," Alice said as she undid the buttons of his great coat. She pulled the front open and helped to slide it from his shoulders.

"I tendered my resignation."

Alice paused in pulling the coat from his body, but she turned and draped it over the room's only chair. "He won't accept it," she stated with a shake of her head. "He values you too much to allow you to leave.'" She moved to stand in front of him and then slowly undid the knot in his cravat. He didn't help as she unwound it from around his neck, careful not to crush it any more than it already was. Undoing the buttons of his topcoat and then his waistcoat, she dared a glance up at him.

He was watching her, his expression not giving away his thoughts on anything.

"Can you ever forgive me, do you think? I should have known you wouldn't take pay for bedding me," she whispered. "I don't know why the earl's words bothered me so." She gripped his shirt, her small fists catching folds of the lawn fabric and jerking them from his breeches so he could pull it from his body. Instead of folding it as she knew he usually did, he tossed it toward the chair.

"I forgive you," he whispered as he gathered her into his arms.

"I love you," she said, her words almost lost in how her face was buried into his neck, her flat breasts pressed into his bare chest.

"What did you say?"

Alice pulled away a bit. "I love you. I love you." The second time was said much louder, so loud it could probably be heard out in the hall. Heard by anyone who might be passing by at just that moment.

Especially by the earl.

"Banks? Are you in there?" The unmistakeable voice of the Earl of Torrington sounded through the wooden door.

"I am, my lord," Alonyius replied, turning his head so his voice was directed along the wall.

"I do not accept your resignation."

Grinning, Alice whispered, "I told you."

Alonyius sighed. "Understood, my lord."

There was an awkward pause before the earl's voice sounded again. "See you in the morning then. Nine..." There was a bit of shuffling and a slight pause before Torrington continued. "Ten o'clock, but no later. Tomorrow is the hanging of the greens. That goes for both of you," he added.

"Very good, my lord."

The sounds from the hallway faded away, a few of the doors down the hall shut once again, and Alonyius sighed. The servants would no doubt enjoy a bit of gossip on the morrow. "If I don't get into a bed this moment, I shall fall down."

Alice led him to the bed and then stood before him.

However would he have made it to Darlington? Why the man looked as weary as she felt, although his appearance had buoyed her spirits enough to make her smile. "Would you like me to fetch your valise?"

He shook his head. "No. Well, maybe." He closed his eyes and allowed a grin. "It's behind the bed in my quarters."

Feeling ever so sorry for the valet, Alice pulled on a dressing gown, took a torch from the sconce on the wall, and made her way to his room. When she returned with his valise, she found him completely undressed and crawling under the covers.

A moment later, she joined him.

"Thank you, my love," he murmured, pulling her close. "I shall reward you in the morning."

They were soon both asleep.

Meanwhile, out at the stables

"Where do you suppose he is?" Haversham wondered as Higgins joined him at the stable's main door.

"Dunno. Do you think he got caught?"

Haversham shook his head. "He's a clever fellow. He wouldn't get caught."

"Prob'ly burying her as we speak."

"Yeah, that's prob'ly it." Haversham allowed a sigh. "Could hardly believe it when they both got out of the coach this afternoon. I was sure he did her in about ten miles out."

"Me, too, what with the way the coach was jerking about," Higgins agreed.

The two stood in silence for some time, their breaths coming out in white puffs.

"Well, I'll be taking the earl and his countess for a ride in the sleigh tomorrow afternoon," Haversham commented.

"Gonna help with the wreaths?" Higgins asked, his hands shoved into his pockets as he continued to watch for the valet's return. "Heard the guv'nor cut down a bunch of trees."

Haversham gave the groom a quelling glance. "Thought I might. Never done it 'afore."

"I heard wire is involved, so I thought I best help."

"Who told you that?" Haversham asked.

Higgins gave a slight shrug. "The cook."

The driver straightened and glared at the groom. "Watson?"

"Yeah. Watson," Higgins agreed, his gaze traveling up to find the driver glaring at him. "What?"

"You... spending any time with her?"

Shaking his head, Higgins replied, "Just eating her food."

Haversham seemed to relax a bit. "Well, seeing as how I've been up since 'afore dawn, I'm gonna get to bed."

"Seein' as how I was up 'afore you, I think I will as well," Higgins countered. "What do we do with the horse?"

Haversham sighed. "How likely is it Banks is gonna leave 'afore dawn?"

"Prob'ly take until then just to dig a hole."

"Ground's so frozen, it'll take longer than that," the driver said with a huff. He turned around and led the horse back to a stall. A moment later, he joined the groom and the two walked back to the house.

Heading down the hall to the servants' quarters, they gave each other questioning glances until they both stood outside the same door.

"This isn't your room," Haversham said.

"'Taint yours neither," Higgins replied.

The heavy wooden door opened to reveal the apple-cheeked cook. Dressed in a night rail, her orange hair hidden by a voluminous mob cap, Watson gave the two a quelling glance. "What took you so long?" She grabbed one of their hands in each of hers and pulled them both into her room. Daring a quick peek around the edge of the opening to be sure no one saw her visitors arrive, she quietly shut the door.

She might have been a bit late in getting to the kitchens the following morning.

Chapter 39

IT'S BEGINNING TO SMELL A LOT...

he following morning, Tuesday, December 24
A rather happy woman on this fine Christmas Eve day, Watson suddenly frowned as she prepared breakfast for the Torrington Park servants. Having cracked a dozen eggs into a large cast iron fry pan, her nose suddenly lifted into the air. Abandoning her station at the stove, the eggs slowly becoming opaque as the whites cooked, she directed one of the maids to take over. "Turn these in a minute or two," she ordered before she continued to follow the strange odor. "And get the ham slices in a pan." Just before she took her leave of the kitchens, she gave a glance back at her domain. "What is that smell?" she wondered out loud, her nose lifting into the air.

"Happy Christmas, Miss Watson. That odor you smell is pine. The great hall is filled with pine boughs," the other kitchen maid said with a grin as her arms spread wide. "Devlin said they spent more than two hours gathering them yesterday." Although she claimed she wasn't sweet on the tallest footman in the household, the kitchen maid certainly spent a good deal of her time in the man's company—when she wasn't in the kitchens.

The cook angled her head to one side, remembering this wouldn't be a normal day in Torrington Park. Besides having to see to feeding the usual servants, there were four additional servants as well as the earl and countess. The hanging of the greens would commence whenever the footmen had the tables set up in the great hall. Instead of serving a luncheon or a tea later in the day, she would serve the equivalent of an indoor picnic. Later, she would make a light dinner for everyone in the household, and then, if the new countess allowed it, there would be the servants' ball later that night.

Just the day before, the earl had informed her things would be a bit backwards this year. *I wish to start the season with a ball,* he had said when he found her in the kitchen. *Not hold off until Twelfth Night.*

She remembered frowning, thinking she already had too much to do on Christmas Eve as it was! With servants to feed as well as the earl and his countess, how was she supposed to create all the nibbles for the ball?

His next words had her grinning though. *I've seen to it we have all the sweets and bubbles we need for such an occasion. I brought them with me from London.*

So happy was she to hear she had been absolved of baking biscuits and cakes for a ball, Watson had been tempted to kiss the man. But seeing as how he was married now, she merely thanked him and said she would see to the rest.

As for bubbles, she wasn't quite sure what the man meant. Were the servants expected to take baths, too?

For the past ten years of Twelfth Night balls, it had just been the earl and the butler and the footmen dancing with the female servants. This year, the countess would be part of the festivities, and Watson hoped Lady Torrington would deign to dance with the male servants.

In the meantime, wreath-making required a different sort of service. Tea and coffee. Foods easily eaten with fingers. Cakes. A high tea, of sorts, she had decided. Grinning broadly, she hurried off to the pantry to gather what she could to make meat pasties and scones.

. . .

"*D*o you smell that?" Milton asked as he inhaled. He experimentally sniffed his fingers, rather stunned to discover they still smelled of pine.

"Indeed," Adele murmured, her nose buried into his neck. "Bay Rum, is it not?"

Milton blinked. "I was thinking pine," he replied, just then realizing why she responded as she did. He buried his nose in her hair. "And citrus," he added in a whisper. "Happy Christmas."

Adele sighed. "Is it?" she wondered, referring more to the date than to whether it was happy or not. As of dinner the night before, she had no idea how her lady's maid would respond to such a greeting. She almost wondered if she still had a lady's maid.

Would Simpkins have recovered from her heartbreak?

Rather doubtful. Although the woman had put on a good show whilst helping dress her for dinner, Adele knew she was still rather raw from learning Mr. Banks' attentions may not have been true. She hadn't required the woman's services after that, Milton assuring her it was better he see to her needs than to ring for Simpkins.

And so she hadn't.

Milton had been almost mum on the topic of his valet, merely saying he was still in residence and would remain so until Milton saw fit to die. *Then he can go to Darlington*, he had added in a huff.

Which had her wondering something.

"What happened last night?"

Milton blinked. "You don't remember?" he asked with a good deal of disappointment in his voice. "I thought the neighbors were going to pay a call to find out what all the screaming was about," he added when he saw her look of consternation. When Adele blinked at him, he lifted himself onto one elbow and gave her a quelling glance. "You begged. You pleaded. You screamed, 'yes,' at the top of your lungs, and then you whimpered a bit," he claimed before he finally allowed a grin. "It was absolutely the best night of my life." He sobered suddenly. "You're quite sure you don't remember?"

Adele allowed a broad smile, one hand moving to his chest to give one of his nipples a quick flick. "Of course, I remember *that*," she replied in a whisper. "You were ever so attentive," she added before giving him a kiss. When she pulled away, she said, "I was wondering about my lady's maid, is all."

Inhaling slowly, Milton allowed a wan smile to develop. "Time will tell, my sweeting, but I do believe your Simpkins is an even more content woman this morning," he murmured.

"So, you did apologize? Just before I found you in her quarters?" she chided. She couldn't imagine what the servants must have said over their breakfast that morning, but she was sure there would be rumors her husband was having an *affaire* with her lady's maid.

He nodded. "And begged forgiveness. Which she accepted after a time."

"Was he there?"

"He, who?"

Adele gave her husband a quelling glance. "Your valet, of course."

"Well, not when I was there," he replied with a shake of his head. "I explained everything to him when he came to my bedchamber last night. That was before I went to speak with Simpkins, but when I returned, he was gone." Although such behavior by most servants wouldn't have been tolerated, Milton didn't expect to see the man until ten o'clock that morning. He glanced over at the clock on the mantle, rather happy to see he had another hour or so before they would be interrupted.

"Is he angry with you, do you suppose?" Adele wondered. At her husband's furrowed brow, she added, "I would be furious. Why, I would certainly be tempted to tender my resignation and move to Darlington to live in Mill House and have servants wait on me instead of having to wait on an earl who has ruined my chances at love with a lady's maid," she added in a rush, a good deal of spite in her voice.

Her husband sighed before suddenly covering her lips with his, one of his hands smoothing over and around a breast as he moved his body atop hers. When he finally pulled away, just enough so his lips still touched hers, he said, "I love you. I love you even when you're angry with me." He kissed her again, and continued to do so until she whimpered and all the anger seemed to flow from her body. And then he buried himself in her, relieved when she seemed to welcome him, more relieved when her knees lifted to press against his thighs, and even more relieved when she met his every thrust with one of her own.

"He's not angry, I promise you," he whispered between thrusts.

"Oh?" Came her breathless reply.

"I'm about to see to making it right," he managed.

"Indeed?"

"Larger quarters."

"Huh?"

"Time off."

A quick gasp was her only response.

"A proper wedding."

Adele clenched on his manhood, rather stunned at hearing the simple words.

Milton held still, his body on the verge of giving in to his release. "A wedding trip."

Her hands suddenly gripping his buttocks, she pulled him hard against her quim, and a moment later, her chest lifted from the bed, and she allowed a happy sigh. "Happy Christmas."

"You minx," he accused, just before he seemed to shatter into a billion tiny pieces of intense pleasure.

"Don't you forget it," Adele whispered with a happy sigh.

Chapter 40

IT'S BEGINNING TO LOOK A
LOT...

In the great hall
At eight o'clock in the morning, two footmen carried a long table into the great hall. Piled high with pine boughs, the room's original trestle was the source of the scent that permeated most of the lodge this morning. A wheelbarrow, overflowing with even more branches, had been rolled into a corner.

"Where did you find that one?" Devlin asked as he nodded toward a trestle similar to the one hidden beneath the greenery. That trestle had probably been in place for over three-hundred years, he considered.

"Back there." Gabriel nodded toward a row of tapestries that hung beneath the animal heads. "Behind the rugs. There's another one, too, so we'll have enough seating for dinner tomorrow night, too."

Devlin was about to inform him the rugs were called 'tapestries' when two maids arrived with their arms full of red fabric. "Where shall we sit?"

Gabriel was quick to pull out a bench for the maids. "Why, right here, miladies," he said as he waved them over to the second trestle. "You'll want to wear some old gloves, though. Keep the sap off your fingers," he added as he pointed to several pairs of leather gloves that had been piled next to the pine boughs. Although a few looked as if they had been worn by the gardeners, others were obviously old gloves worn by prior generations of Torrington ladies.

Several cutting tools and rounds of wire were scattered about. "Haversham said he would see to cutting the wire for you. Oh, and don't forget to make a kissing bough, if you would. We didn't have one last year."

The two maids exchanged knowing glances, as if they had deliberately overlooked northern England's replacement for mistletoe. The one they had made two years ago had been made of an evergreen bough, flowers fashioned from paper, apples, and fabric dolls representing Mary, Joseph and Jesus. A footman had seen to hanging it above the door that led to the kitchens and then insisted he be kissed every time a maid had to make her way through the door.

Hence, no kissing bough last year.

Trasker entered and set about building up the fire. Despite the size of the massive fireplace, it was barely able to provide enough heat to keep the room comfortable for anyone near the front doors. Once everyone in the lodge gathered in the great hall, the room would grow warm and feel cozier as the decorations were created and hung.

By the time the footmen had the last table in place, a kitchen maid had joined the other maids. Haversham, looking a bit bleary-eyed, limped into the great hall and started work on cutting the wire.

Two more footmen, followed by Trasker, made their way in carrying chairs. Having dressed the countess and styled her hair for the day, Alice arrived and looked a bit sheepish as she wondered what to do. Another maid waved her over to join in making small ribbon bows. Alice couldn't help noticing the look of surprise Haversham directed her way, almost as if he didn't expect to see her communing with the other servants of Torrington Park. Well, just because they didn't make wreaths for Worthington House didn't mean she didn't have an appreciation for how they did Christmas in the country! She set to work learning how to make the bows and ignored the driver.

*H*aving sent her rather joyous lady's maid to join the others working on the greens for Christmas, Adele made her way through the dressing room. Her relief at seeing Simpkins so content that morning had only added to her own happiness. She and Milton had enjoyed a rather spirited round of lovemaking earlier that morning, after which he had presented her with a lovely necklace. The pendant, a jeweled version of a holly leaf, was strung on a gold chain. He had it around her neck and fastened even before she got out of bed.

I'll wear it today, she had said. *With my red Merino wool gown.*

Not particularly familiar with the various fabrics from which his wife's gowns were made, Milton merely nodded and offered a comment about it being appropriate for the occasion.

Now Adele wondered just how important the occasion of the hanging of the greens was in this household.

Before she reached the door into the master suite, she realized Banks was still seeing to her husband. Hearing his voice, she paused. She didn't intend to eavesdrop. She didn't intend to overhear her husband's words.

But she couldn't help but listen.

"I want nothing more than to keep her happy, you see. Sometimes that means I will say and do things that are quite... stupid. Idiotic, really."

"I am well aware of your affection for Lady Torrington, my lord."

"I'm not finished. I'm trying to beg your forgiveness here. It was foolish of me to suggest you bed her maid, and worse that I brought it up again yesterday. I should have known you couldn't be compelled to do such a thing if it didn't suit you."

There was a moment of silence. Perhaps her husband's words had the valet fainting.

Had he ever apologized to the valet before?

Adele waited for the tell-tale sound of a *thud* that would indicate Banks had hit the Axminster carpet, but instead she heard only silence for a time.

Perhaps the man had taken his leave of the bedchamber.

What if he had left in a huff? She couldn't blame the upper servant if he had, but if he had taken his leave—if he did leave the earl's service—she would lose her lady's maid, she was sure. Simpkins would follow Banks wherever he went.

She almost moved to open the door, but Banks' finally spoke.

"Although I experienced the longest day of my life yesterday, I appreciate having lived it. I now understand what you mean when you speak so highly of your countess, and I also know how easy it can be for simple words to be misunderstood." There was a pause as he inhaled. "But you should know that I had every intention of leaving your employ last night—"

"I read your note of resignation."

"—And the only reason I did not take my leave of Torrington Park was because..."

The words suddenly ceased, and Adele held her breath in anticipation of hearing the rest. The silence lingered. She nearly cried out in exasperation before her husband spoke after another quiet moment.

"Vexing creatures, are they not?"

"Very, my lord."

"But well worth the trouble they cause."

This last had Adele straightening, her annoyance apparent in how her brows furrowed. She almost—almost—flung open the door, but thought better of it.

Milton would know she had overheard his words.

"Might I have your permission to spend time in her company whilst you're on your sleigh ride this afternoon?"

Adele gave a start. It was Christmas Eve. Milton had promised to take her on a sleigh ride once the great hall was decorated.

"You don't need my permission."

"Very good, my lord."

Sensing it was safe to enter, Adele gave a quick knock on the dressing room door and entered the master suite. Banks was still buttoning the earl's topcoat when she said, "Happy Christmas."

Banks immediately stepped back and bowed while Milton held out a hand in an invitation for her to join him. "How does it look down there?" he asked.

Adele dared a glance at his nether region, her brows furrowing. She couldn't exactly say anything in front of his valet!

"In the great hall," Milton clarified, his eyes crinkling in delight when he realized his unintended entendré.

Her eyes widening with understanding, Adele gave a shake of her head. "Why, I haven't been down there yet. I sent Simpkins a few minutes ago." She watched for some kind of reaction from the valet, but he was as stone-faced as a statue. "I was hoping to go in with you," she murmured.

"I won't be long," Milton replied. "But I do think you should go in first. See what the maids are up to. This place may lack the appropriate number of servants, but at least the maids here are a creative sort."

Adele nodded. "If you think so. But what about breakfast?"

The earl shook his head. "Watson does things a bit different for the hanging of the greens," he said. "Serves tea and coffee and some nibbles we can eat whilst we do the work," he explained with a grin. "It's a sort of soirée but with pine boughs," he added.

Turning her attention to the valet, she asked, "Is that true?"

Banks stared at her a moment, his attention on her gown. It seemed as if he was about to say something, but thought better of it. He finally gave a nod. "His lordship has described it perfectly, my lady. And no one will go hungry." He didn't add that the servants had already been served a small breakfast earlier that morning, mostly because he and Simpkins had elected to miss it in favor of spending more time in her bed. A not very comfortable bed, but he had hardly noticed.

Adele nodded her understanding, wondering why he had stared at her with such an odd expression. After a moment, she said, "I wish to thank you, Mr. Banks."

The valet's eyes widened. "My lady?"

The countess allowed a brilliant smile. "You have brought such joy to my lady's maid. I have known her for nearly twenty years, and I have never known her to be so happy. She is a different woman, and it's all because of you."

Banks visibly swallowed as his face took on a reddish cast. "You're welcome, my lady," he said with a nod. After a moment, he said, "If there's nothing more, my lord, I should probably join those in the great hall."

"Go on," Milton said as a waved a hand toward the door. "We'll be down shortly."

Alonyius gave a bow and took his leave of the master suite, the countess' words repeating in his mind. Had anyone else made such a declaration, he might have been tempted to end his liaison with Alice Simpkins simply because he didn't want the responsibility for someone else's happiness. But now that Alice had made her feelings for him quite clear—her apologies the night before followed by what he had woken up to find her doing to him that morning—he found he didn't mind so very much.

He wanted to be the reason she was happy.

Damn, but where had that thought come from? he wondered. After the hellish afternoon he had experienced yesterday, did he truly want the possibility of another emotional upheaval should the woman misunderstand something he said? Something he did?

During those hours of reliving her accusations and her

anger, Alonyius realized he had never felt more lonely in all his life.

Which was worse? The possibility of Alice being angry with him again? Or the loneliness he realized he might experience for the rest of his life?

He was on the verge of comparing the two when he entered the great hall and nearly stopped short. Nearly every servant at Torrington Park was busy doing something. His gaze immediately found and stopped on Alice, her beatific smile directed on one of the maids with whom she sat and tied a red ribbon into a perfect bow.

The red ribbon reminded him of the red gown Lady Torrington wore, and he wondered if the countess was aware of where the fabric had been manufactured. If her modiste even knew of its origin in Darlington. The shade was one his mother insisted his father make every year, despite what fashion might dictate the mill create.

When acquiring the wool from Spain became too difficult—the Napoleonic Wars had devastated the Merino sheep herds there—his brother had found a new source in Portugal. Seeing Lady Torrington wear it so regally had him experiencing a bit of pride he hadn't allowed himself to feel in many years. He wasn't responsible for its creation, of course, but his family's business had made its fortunes on the Merino wool. And that red was his mother's favorite.

To get a closer look at her creations, Alonyius strolled over to the table where Alice was working. Struck by the sudden need to simply touch her, to make her aware he was there, he grazed a fingertip along her shoulder. From the way her body suddenly shivered, he knew a skitter of pleasure had danced up her spine. Leaning over a bit as he feigned interest in what the maids were doing, he murmured, "Happy Christmas, ladies." Then he glanced around the open room and frowned. He suddenly moved to join Devlin and asked, "Where's the tree?"

The tall footman blinked. "Oh, my," the man replied,

looking as if something rather important had been forgotten. "We never cut one down. Nor did we get the Yule log."

Within minutes, a crew was dispatched to see about finding an appropriate tree, and Alonyius set out with them, giving Alice a quick glance as he took his leave.

Unable to hide her smile, Alice continued to work on ribbons as the maids chatted.

*O*nce his valet had taken his leave of the master suite, Milton turned to his wife and gave her a quick kiss. "My gift is perfect with that dress," he said as he reached for the pendant, lifting it with two fingers.

"Your valet certainly seemed to think so. Why, did you see how he stared at me?"

Milton angled his head and finally allowed a grin. "He was actually admiring your gown." He reached out and fingered the wool. "The fabric of your gown," he clarified. "Red Merino wool is the specialty of Banks Textiles."

Adele's eyes widened. "Do you suppose this is the fabric that had Mr. Banks falling in love with your mother's lady's maid?" she wondered in awe.

Milton angled his head before allowing a shrug. "I have absolutely no idea," he replied in a whisper. "But I do know that if you don't take your leave of my bedchamber this very minute, I shall be divesting you of that gown and having my way with you in my bed."

Adele blinked, almost tempted to let him. But her absence in the great hall would be noted—if it hadn't been already. "Do hold that thought until later tonight, won't you?" she said as she kissed the corner of his mouth.

A rather odd sound erupted from her husband's throat as she took her leave of the master bedchamber, making sure she gave his nether region one more glance before she disappeared.

Faith! If the two of them continued as they had been doing, she was sure she would be with child soon—if she wasn't already. They still hadn't discussed his need for an heir, but she was determined to give him one despite her age. Eight-and-thirty wasn't truly *old*, but it was certainly past the time she should be starting a family.

As she descended the stairs, Adele wondered at the muted conversations just ahead. And then she was suddenly in the great hall. Adele could almost ignore the phalanx of animal heads that decorated the perimeter of the room. The great hall was a beehive of activity.

Her gaze took in the clusters of servants either seated at trestles or bent over tables as they created the wreaths and sprays that would be used to decorate the great hall and the other rooms in Torrington Park.

Delighted with how much had been accomplished without her direction—she wasn't sure how much she would have been able to provide—Adele simply took a seat and watched for a time. The men wrapped and bent the wire while the women saw to the decorations. Lengths of red fabric were made into massive bows that were then tied onto the wreaths or sprays with yarn. When the largest was complete, a footman climbed a ladder and saw to mounting it above the fireplace. Two others were nailed to the front doors.

At noon, the earl finally joined the fray. The scullery maid appeared with trays of small pasties and scones, and she was followed by the other kitchen maid who carried a large tea service. Behind them, a footman wheeled in a cart with plates and cups. Watson appeared carrying a platter on which a color collection of fruits was arranged. On closer inspection, Adele realized they weren't fruits at all, but decorations made of march pane. Before long, the group quieted as they ate and drank, and it was then Milton took the opportunity to make his announcement.

"Some of you may recall a time when this household celebrated Twelfth Night," he began as the quiet conversations ceased. At the mention of 'Twelfth Night', a sudden pall seemed to settle over the group.

Alice glanced about, wondering at the other servants' reactions. In Worthington House, the night of January fifth merely meant the opportunity for the servants to throw a soirée of their own in the small ballroom. Although her mistress employed a quartet for the evening and saw to several bottles of champagne, the rest of the staff was responsible for seeing to the evening's festivities. The servants wore their Sunday best, the kitchen staff saw to the foods and a punch, and everyone—upper and lower servants alike—enjoyed an evening of dancing and merriment.

"We haven't done it here at Torrington Park in over ten years, and this year will be no different."

Adele's eyes widened when she heard the sudden collective sigh of relief from those seated around her, almost as if their memories of Twelfth Nights were unpleasant. Apparently the January fifth ritual hadn't been popular with these servants, she realized.

"I paid witness to my countess' approach to Twelfth Night last year," Milton went on, giving a nod to a maid who saw to leaving a cup of tea near where he had been sitting. "Music was provided by musicians she hired for the occasion, everyone danced and made merry, and she provided the champagne." This last caused a murmur among several of the maids, and one even tittered before being shushed. "Since she spent the evening in my company in—"

"Torrington!" Adele admonished, her face taking on the unmistakeable blush of embarrassment.

"—in *Church*," the earl continued, not missing a beat, "the Worthington House servants put on a ball. They dressed as they liked, and they enjoyed an evening of merriment." He cleared his throat and continued. "Instead of Twelfth Night, I am proposing we celebrate *tonight* with a ball. "Then, two days from now—the day after Christmas—will be a day for you to do as you wish. You may visit your families, or go shopping in Hexham, or spend the day in quiet contemplation. You will not be expected to work the entire day or night."

Murmurs of approval followed his description as several servants tried to gauge each other's reaction to this bit of news.

When Alice noticed how Haversham glanced over at Watson and got a wink for his trouble, Alice realized she knew exactly what those two might do in 'quiet contemplation'.

And they might not be so quiet about it.

Why Mr. Higgins displayed such an odd expression was beyond her ken.

"If you're all in agreement, then I shall see to the music and the champagne for tonight," Milton concluded. "Shall we say, seven o'clock this evening?"

A chorus of positive responses had him nodding. "Then continue with the hanging of the greens, and we shall see to making this hall an appropriate setting for a ball."

With that, the earl sat down next to his countess and sipped his tea.

"They love you," Adele said in a hoarse whisper.

"They do." He gave her a sideways glance. "It's not just because of the champagne, though. I know several can't stand the stuff."

Adele allowed a grin. She hadn't liked the stuff much the first few times she had tried it, either. Now, it never seemed as if one glass was enough. "How many bottles did you bring?"

"There's a case in my bedchamber."

"Milton!" she countered. "How—?

"The crate was in our coach. I half-expected to hear one of the bottles explode during our travels, but I think they were nearly frozen. The cold must have helped settle the bubbles."

Adele grinned as she considered his words and then suddenly sobered. "Where are you going to find musicians on such short notice?"

He allowed an arched brow. "Hexham is not that far away, my sweeting. Mr. Banks made the arrangements for a well-reviewed quintet before we left London. Westhaven's brother, Darius, is an archaeologist there, and he made the recommendation."

Her eyes widening at this bit of news, Adele realized her husband had been planning for the servant's ball for some time. "And if they hadn't agreed to your plan?"

Milton furrowed his brows, almost as if he hadn't considered the possibility. "Then I suppose we would have had our own *musicale* in the parlor this evening."

Adele leaned over and kissed him on the temple, not a bit concerned about who might pay witness to her act of public affection.

When she noticed her lady's maid suppressing a grin, she straightened. "I don't suppose you know a bishop in possession of a special license?" she half-asked, remembering how luminescent Simpkins had appeared when she reported for duty at ten o'clock that morning. Adele was sure she had never seen a happier woman in all of her life. Such a contrast to how she had looked when Adele found her in the study yesterday afternoon. "Who could be compelled to perform a wedding ceremony in the next few days? Who wouldn't mind that music might play following the ceremony?" she continued, one eyebrow arching with her queries. Some bishops were far too strict with their wedding rules, she thought. Circumstances sometimes required a bit of leeway.

Frowning, the earl gave a shake of his head. "Oh, so now you're in agreement with my plans to legitimize our valet and lady's maid," he teased.

"Something like that," she replied. "Are we being ridiculous?"

Her husband regarded her for a moment, rather pleased she wasn't such a stickler when it came to rules. "No," he finally answered. "This is Northumberland, though. We might just as well send them over the border. No reading of the banns required in Scotland."

Giving him a quelling glance, Adele sipped her tea and wondered if—or when—there might be an announcement of an engagement. If the two upper servants did marry, perhaps they would do so in Darlington. Mr. Banks' family was there. If what Simpkins had said was true about Mrs. Banks, the old woman would be thrilled to see one of her sons marry.

A sudden thought had her frowning.

She might be without Simpkins' services for a week or more.

Her reverie was interrupted by a ruckus at the front doors. The thick wood planks had both been opened wide, allowing a chilly draft to flow into the lodge. A chorus of complaints sounded before several footmen appeared in the opening. Dragging a rather tall evergreen tree into the hall, the footmen put on a show of near-exhaustion as they pulled their burden. Behind them, two footmen were carrying the tree's trunk. As soon as several footman rolled what appeared to be a large log into the hall, the doors closed.

Adele watched in wonder as one servant pulled a rather large wooden contraption from behind one of the tapestries. The square frame on the bottom supported a number of angled boards that didn't quite meet in the middle. "What—?"

"Just watch," Milton interrupted, a grin splitting his face. "They've done this before. Many times."

"Why is there a *tree?*" Adele asked, rather startled an entire tree had been dragged indoors.

"It's a tradition. Mum's family was from Germany. They always had a tree for Christmas, so we've always had a tree at Torrington Park."

Returning her attention to the footmen, she watched as several joined forces to lift the tree—it had to be at least ten feet tall!—and position it so its trunk was centered over the support structure. Devlin, the tallest of the footmen, lifted the center of the tree as the others guided the trunk into the slot, angling it up and lowering the base of the trunk in steps until the tree was standing upright. Since the lower branches nearly hid the support structure, the tree suddenly appeared to stand on its own.

The maids cheered and clapped, one of them rushing off to pull aside another of the tapestries to reveal a wooden crate. Two footmen pulled the crate from its hiding place and removed the top.

Amazed at the tree, Adele breathed, "I want one of those for Worthington House."

Milton chuckled. "A nearby carpenter built it for my mother many years ago," he said. "She insisted on a tree that was nearly as tall as this hall, but there was no easy way to keep it standing."

Adele's eyes widened. "How did they even get it in here?"

"As I recall, a horse was involved," he replied with an arched brow.

Horrified at the thought of a horse in the great hall, Adele's attention was suddenly directed to the animal heads mounted near the top of every wall in the room. Well, she supposed a horse was no worse than the deer and elk—or even the bears—that looked down on her. "What's in the crate?" she asked, her attention directed to where two maids were bent over the wooden box.

"Why, the best part, my sweeting."

Her curiosity too great to simply sit and watch, Adele joined the maids to peer into the crate. Her gasp of surprise had the two maids regarding her nervously. "We usually set it up on the fireplace mantle, milady."

Adele dared a glance at the giant fireplace, its mantle bare of decoration. At least a huge wreath hung well above it on the wall.

"Then we shall put it there again," she said as she reached down and pulled a porcelain shepherd from the straw packing. Glancing at the bottom, she realized it had been imported from Italy. One of the maids pulled out a sheep while the other lifted a kneeling Mary from its resting place.

"Is there a stable?" Adele asked, thinking they should set it in place before adding all the other figurines.

"There is not, milady."

Adele glanced over at the table where the scraps and

trimmings from the pine boughs had been collected. "Let's see if one of these gentlemen can be compelled to build one," she murmured. She held onto the shepherd as if it was the most important part of a nativity scene and hurried off to where her husband's valet stood with the footmen. A ladder had been erected next to the tree, and one of the servants was near the top putting the small bows on the ends of the branches.

"Do you do any carpentry, Mr. Banks?"

The valet acknowledged her with a slight bow and allowed a grin. "I have been known to wield a hammer on occasion, but I do so poorly," he replied with a shake of his head. "What is it you require?"

"A stable," Adele replied. She held up the figurine. At Alonyius' look of confusion, she gave her head a shake and added, "For the nativity scene," she clarified, turning toward the fireplace. The maids had managed to get most of the pieces into place, the figurines clustered in the middle of the mantle. "It doesn't have to be perfect. In fact, it probably shouldn't be."

Nodding his understanding, Banks said, "I'll see what can be done, my lady." He gave the countess a bow and headed off to where Haversham had taken a seat.

"Do you suppose it would be possible to use that wire to hold together these bare branches?" Alonyius asked as he pulled several together to form what would be the back wall of the stable. He arranged the various lengths so the tallest was in the middle and the shortest pieces were on the ends.

"I suppose I could," the driver replied at the same time Alonyius foraged for more branches appropriate for two side walls. "What is it I'm to make?"

"A stable," Alonyius replied, giving a nod toward the mantle.

Haversham stared at the collection of porcelain figures for a long time before he finally turned his attention back to Alonyius. "'Taint never seen anything like that 'afore," he murmured.

Although he had never seen a nativity scene made of such large figures, Alonyius had grown up in a household with a smaller set. The pieces at Mill House were made of ceramic and painted in muted colors. "It's much grander than the one I have seen," he agreed, deciding not to admit his family had displayed one every Christmas he could remember.

Haversham nodded, his face suddenly screwing up into a grimace. "Changed your mind about killing her, huh?"

Blinking, Alonyius angled his body so he faced the driver. "I'm quite sure I don't know what you mean," he answered, a bit of alarm coloring his voice.

"Simpkins. Me and Higgins thought you had finally offed her last night. That's why you needed the horse. Am I right? So you could make your escape 'afore she was missed."

Alonyius rolled his eyes, stunned by the driver's words. That both Haversham and Higgins had believed such a thing had him wondering why the two thought him capable of such a horrible act. "Why ever would I wish to kill Miss Simpkins?" he countered in a hoarse whisper. "I'm considering making her my w...." He caught himself before he could complete the word, stunned at what he was about to say. He was also oblivious to Haversham's reaction. The man's eyebrows lifted so high, they nearly became part of his hairline. "Making her my dance partner for the first dance this evening," Alonyius managed to say instead.

Haversham blinked. "I know it was a rough ride gettin' up here, Banks, but I done think your brains may have become a bit scrambled," he claimed.

It was Alonyius' turn to blink. "I have my faculties about me, I assure you," he countered in a low voice verging on the hint of menace. "Miss Simpkins is an excellent servant and not to be referred to in such an unkind manner," he added, daring the driver to say anything more on the matter.

"I'll see to the stable," Haversham stated with a quick nod. He turned his attention to the sticks of wood Alonyius had arranged on the table.

Alonyius nodded and stepped away. He inhaled sharply,

as if he'd been holding his breath. *What the hell? Where had that thought about making Alice his wife come from?* He couldn't believe what he had almost said! What he had almost given away with the simple words!

Daring a glance at Alice, he was heartened to see her suddenly glance in his direction, as if she knew he was watching her. He allowed a slight grin and gave a nod.

What else could he do just then?

Chapter 41

AN AFTERNOON OF WONDER

Later that afternoon
Early afternoon sunlight streamed into Alice's quarters, a rare occurrence considering the recent weather. Having just seen to dressing Lady Torrington for her sleigh ride with the earl, she hurried to the window in the hopes of watching some of the ride. She studied the landscape, amazed at how far she could see from the second story now that the fog had cleared and the sun had made an appearance.

Beyond the stables below, where the tracks of the horse-drawn sleigh led from the carriage house to the stables, a row of trees marched across the white expanse. She wondered if they acted as the earldom's property line, or if they were merely meant to provide protection from the wind. The shape of the rolling hills beyond the trees was made less evident by the layer of snow that covered them, but she could imagine how green they might appear when spring finally replaced winter.

If spring ever came to England.

The country could not afford another year of no summer. Word had come from the United States that parts of their lands had been hit just as hard by the cold and snow. Those seeking a better life in Europe—respite from the cold and rain—found similar circumstances in the northern countries. The thought of widespread famine had her worrying what might happen next year. Lord Torrington was a wise man, though. She had to hope he had a solution for his earldom, perhaps like the one the Earl of Gisborn had employed by building more greenhouses on his lands in Oxfordshire.

There is certainly enough land here in Northumberland for greenhouses, she thought as she turned her attention back to the stables. Haversham had hitched up a huge draft horse to the sleigh and was driving it around to the front doors of the lodge. Lord and Lady Torrington were going for a ride, and it would be a couple of hours or more before her services would be required again.

Alonyius Banks was in the same position with respect to his master. He knocked on the lady's maid's door in the hopes of spending a few stolen moments in her company.

"You came," she said after she opened the thick wooden door. She found him glancing to his left and right.

"May I come in?" he asked in a whisper.

Grinning, Alice stepped aside and said, "Of course."

"I figure we have at least two hours," he said as he hurried into the room, turned and gathered her into his arms. "Do you have any duties you need to complete before they return?"

She shook her head, rather intrigued by his behavior. "I finished the repairs on her ladyship's gowns this morning. Before the hanging of the greens," Alice murmured as she allowed him to hold her in a comforting embrace. "And her laundry just after we arrived yesterday," she added.

"I may have to prevail upon you to do his lordship's, as I have no idea how to do laundry," Alonyius whispered.

Alice lifted her head and gave him a quelling glance. "I'm sure Mrs. Miller can see to it," she replied, grinning when his hold on her tightened. She thrilled at how his hands smoothed up and down her back as he held her, their warmth seeping into her spine.

Alonyius suddenly stilled his movements. "I apologize. I

have thought of nothing but you since last night, and although I truly wish to tumble you every which way but..." He actually considering mentioning something about 'Thursday' but thought better of it. "Every which way possible, I wonder if I might simply... hold you... for a time." His expression gave away his torment. The events of the day before had left them both a bit raw. A bit exhausted. A bit tentative with one another.

Alice blinked, only slightly surprised by his request. "I'd like that," she agreed with a nod, glancing about in an effort to determine just where they might sit. Besides the bed, the room's only other pieces of furniture were a dresser, a chair, and a small table. She glanced back at the bed. "Take off your coat and shoes, and... lie down," she suggested as she leaned over to remove her slippers.

"Allow me," Alonyius said as he knelt before her.

Alice inhaled sharply as he lifted one of her ankles with a firm hand and removed the black leather slipper with the other. She held up the skirts of her livery as he did the same with her other foot, gasping again when his hand lingered a bit too long and a finger trailed along the line of her ankle. He lowered his face to her foot and kissed the top of it. "Have any others done this?" he asked as he dared a glance up at Alice.

Alice blinked. Was he joking? "No," she said as she gave her head a shake. "If you're not careful, I shall require it of you whenever you are in my company, though," she warned with a teasing grin.

Standing up, Alonyius smiled. "And I shall be happy to do your bidding," he whispered as he doffed his top coat.

Her breath caught, and Alice swallowed. What a life they might have should the two of them continue this *affaire!* Before she could respond, his lips were on hers, suckling and supping and leaving her weak in the knees. When he finally pulled away, he bent and lifted her into his arms. Turning slightly, he lowered her onto the bed and then climbed onto it, pulling her body next to his. As she had done when they shared a bed at *The Black Swan*, Alice nestled her head into the small of his shoulder and moved a leg to settle betwixt his. "Are you comfortable?" he asked in a quiet voice.

"Hmm," Alice replied, sliding a hand over his chest. "I could fall asleep like this," she whispered, remembering the night at *The Black Swan*, when first exhaustion and then intimacy had her falling asleep in his arms. The thought of what he had done at the coaching inn had her lifting her head to regard him. "If Lord Torrington didn't compel you to... to tumble me, then what made you...?" She allowed the question to trail off in frustration before she finally tried a different approach. "Why did you suggest we share a room at *The Black Swan*?" she struggled to get out. His insistence that they take a room together—despite the fact that he could have shared a room with the driver and groom—had her nearly scandalized until he finally explained himself that first night. Assured her he only had her safety in mind. Safety and comfort.

Warmth.

Now, she wondered if his motivation was something entirely different.

Alonyius gave a huff and turned his head slightly. "Besides necessity? There were only two rooms available, and I could not abide sharing a room with two men who only had sexual intercourse on their minds."

"Yes. Besides necessity," she pressed.

Alonyius sighed. "Something you did in the coach earlier that day," he murmured. "And every day since we left Worthington Park."

"What?" Alice asked, giving a start that had his arm moving to hold her down.

"You smiled."

Blinking a few times, Alice again lifted her head from his shoulder and regarded him for a moment. "Whatever do you mean?"

"We were talking about... I don't even remember," he said with a slight shake of his head. "But you looked out the window and this smile—this beautiful, radiant smile—appeared on your face, and I realized I had never seen you before."

Alice frowned. "But—"

"I hadn't, actually. Not like you were in the coach. I've only ever seen you at the servants' table during supper, or walking in the halls at Worthington House. You were always so... dour. So serious. As if you thought your duties disagreeable."

"They are not," she said with a shake of her head.

"I know that now," he countered, giving her a peck on her forehead. He regarded her for a moment. "You're rather gorgeous when you smile," he murmured. "Which is just one of the reasons I changed my poor opinion of you."

Alice swallowed, some of his words hurting far more than if he had simply ignored her in the coach. "Just my smile?" she responded in a quiet voice.

Alonyius tightened his hold on her and allowed a chuckle. "The farther we got from London, the lighter your countenance. As if you had escaped some evil monster under whose shadow you had been forced to live."

Considering his words, Alice had never thought of her employment at Worthington House as some kind of evil monster. Perhaps the circumstances could be thought of in that regard, though. She had paid witness to an untenable situation and had taken on a responsibility that left her feeling wrung out. Unappreciated. All because she didn't want the scullery maid to suffer as she had back when she held the position in a different household.

"It's true. I have not been happy of late at Worthington House," she admitted. "I used to be quite happy, though. But then Lady Worthington remarried, and some of the staff changed, and..." She stopped when Alonyius suddenly lifted himself onto an elbow, forcing Alice to roll onto her back. He stared down at her.

"Were you unhappy your mistress found a new husband?" he asked as he stared down at her.

Alice's eyes widened, realizing how her words must have sounded to the earl's valet. He was one of the new staff members who had invaded Worthington House, after all.

"Not at all," she said with a shake of her head. The white pillow covering beneath gave her the appearance of an angel with a puffy halo about her head. "But other things changed."

"Such as...?" he prompted.

His gaze was intense, and Alice knew she had to tell the truth. He would know otherwise. She sighed. "Lord Torrington is not nearly as strict as Mr. Worthington was with Bernard, so some of the footmen aren't as keen about finishing their duties in a timely manner. The household maids spend far too much time cleaning rooms and don't always see to the coal for the fireplaces. Although Mr. Bernard wouldn't normally allow such laxity, I believe he has joined their ranks. Because he knows there won't be any reprimand from Lord Torrington. It's almost as if the earl thinks his countess should be in charge of the butler." This last was said as if it were a scandal, but the butler was supposed to report to the man of the house—not the lady.

Frowning, Alonyius considered her words and finally allowed a nod. "I understand your frustration," he stated as he settled back onto the bed. "But you must remember that Bernard had to report to Lady Torrington for over a year before she remarried. There wasn't a man of the house to which he could direct his queries." At her nod of understanding, he gave a sigh. "Having said that, I must ask that you adjust your expectations of the household."

Alice frowned. "Adjust?" she repeated in confusion.

"You must, or you shall forever be disappointed by the lessened decorum of the household." His arm moved beneath her shoulders, and he pulled her back atop him. "By now, you have probably noticed that Lord Torrington is not a man who lives by most of Society's rules. He doesn't even abide being addressed by his proper title. That's why everyone calls him 'Grandby' instead of 'Torrington'," he explained gently.

"I always wondered about that," Alice admitted. "Almost as if he doesn't want to be the earl."

"He doesn't, although he's perfectly suited to the job. Why, I don't recall him missing more than two or three sessions of Parliament since he inherited. You see, he thinks his cousin, Gregory, would make a better earl, and Mr. Grandby already has a half-dozen heirs," Alonyius added, almost as if he agreed with the earl.

Alice furrowed her brows. "Doesn't he expect Lady Torrington to provide an heir?" Her ladyship wasn't so very old, and given how many times Alice had discovered the earl in the mistress suite, she figured they must enjoy the marriage bed.

Alonyius blinked and gave the question some thought. "I cannot say for certain, but I will admit the man gave me his stash of French letters upon the event of his wedding," he said with an arched brow. Not that they had done him much good. Although he had used three or four while he bedded a neighboring maid a few months ago, he hadn't had an occasion since then that required their use. He realized just then he probably should have packed a few for this trip. He had just never imagined he would be bedding Alice Simpkins— or anyone else, for that matter—and so he had left them behind at Worthington House. "I would expect he intends to get a child on your mistress." *What better time than now?* Away from London, the earl and countess were free to spend as much time in each other's company—in each other's bed —as they wanted.

"She will make a wonderful mother," Alice murmured. "More attentive than most, I should think."

"Lord Torrington will be the attentive one," Alonyius countered. "And he'll spoil his children rotten, I tell you," he added with a grin. "Especially a daughter." He sobered when he caught Alice gazing at him. "Wot?"

"You adore the man," she accused gently.

Furrowing his brows, the valet finally gave a nod. "Despite my early opinion of the man—and what transpired over the course of our trip here—he is the best master I could hope for," he said in a hoarse whisper. "My plan is to continue in my position until the day he either dies, or I do."

Alice blinked. *My plan.* So perhaps that meant he had no intention of moving back to Darlington to run his family's textile mill. But then, plans had a way of changing.

"So you won't move back to Darlington?"

Alonyius stilled himself, realizing he hadn't told her about the time he had shared with his brother whilst his mother kept her entertained with stories.

About what he and Thelonius had discussed.

"I have made an arrangement with my brother, and he should have already explained it to our mother," he whispered. "Thel is committed to finding a wife and to getting a child on her in the next year. Despite his off-the-cuff comment about not having time to court, he does have a lady in mind," he added with an arched brow. "He has been secretly courting her, only because he feared our mother might smother her before she'd had a chance to learn of Mum's... idiosyncrasies."

"Your mother will be so pleased," Alice murmured.

"As am I."

"And I rather enjoy those... idiosyncrasies," she added with a grin.

Alonyius kissed on the top of her head, glad to know she didn't think of his mother as a candidate for Bedlam. "His heir will be raised to learn the business and to run it when Thel can longer do so. In the meantime, I am to remain in my position and will only return to Darlington to run the business if something should happen to Thel before his heir is ready to assume control of the business."

Such a simple plan, and yet his words had Alice wincing. She realized she didn't have a plan in place for herself. She merely lived each day, not considering the past or the future. "I rather imagine you shall outlive his lordship and enjoy a rather generous pension," she murmured.

Alonyius chuckled, pulling her closer and giving her a

kiss on the lips. When he pulled away, he sighed. "I will admit to another reason for having changed my poor opinion of you," he murmured, his arm relaxing behind her shoulders so that her head once again settled into the small of his shoulder. He felt her body tense beneath his hold, though, knowing she was bracing herself for whatever was to come.

"Another?" she repeated, her eyes widening in wonder.

The valet nodded and took one of her hands in his. "I know what you've been doing at Worthington House. In the mornings, before anyone else is up and about and in the kitchens."

Alice inhaled sharply. How had Alonyius discovered her morning ritual? She was sure her clandestine trips to the kitchens had gone unnoticed by anyone in the household.

In an effort to help the helpless scullery maid, she would finish whatever Libby hadn't completed the night before as well as prepare the kitchen exactly as the cook expected it when she arrived to make the servants' breakfast at half-past six. "How do you know?" she whispered, her eyes widening in alarm.

Alonyius leaned over and bussed her on the side of the head. "I'm usually awake at five, so I hear the latch on your door when you sneak out. One morning, out of curiosity, I followed you, thinking perhaps you were either there to purloin something from the pantry—"

"Never!" she interrupted in dismay.

"—Or you were having a clandestine meeting with a servant from another household—"

"I suppose that could be a possibility," she hedged, although she followed the comment with a teasing grin.

"—But imagine my surprise as I watched you don an apron and do the work of our hapless scullery maid," he said before giving her a gentle kiss on her temple.

Alice inhaled sharply, rather shocked someone had discovered her secret. And Alonyius of all people. "Do you think others in the household realize Libby may never learn the duties of her job?"

"I do," he replied with a nod. "If they don't already know."

Alice allowed a look of disappointment. "You won't tell anyone?" she half-asked, inwardly wincing when she remembered she had already divulged her secret to Lady Torrington.

"I admit I have already made Lord Torrington aware of the situation. Just last night, in fact," he murmured. Alice nodded her understanding when he promised, "But I shall tell no one else." He paused to kiss her forehead, as if he was sealing his promise with the simple gesture. "You see, my younger sister started her service as a scullery maid," he explained in a quiet voice. At Alice's expression of surprise— at no point had Mrs. Banks mentioned having a daughter— he added, "She traveled with me to London when I was hired by the late earl, and then she refused to return home. She liked the city too much to go back."

"Did she marry someone?"

Alonyius gave a snort. "I rather *wish* some poor sod had taken a shine to her and married her."

"Why ever do you say it like that?" Alice wondered.

Alonyius gave a slight shrug. "She made for a very poor scullery maid, which you and I both know is a rather sad state of affairs." The scullery maid held the entry-level position within most households. If a servant couldn't make it as a scullery maid, it was doubtful they would be elevated to a better position or be hired in a different household.

"Did she lose her position?" Alice asked in alarm. Despite the hours they had spent in conversation, she didn't even know Alonyius had a sister. "Which house?"

He shook his head. "You cannot tell a soul," he warned.

Alice frowned, wondering in whose household his sister might have worked. "I won't," she assured him.

"*The Elegant Courtesan*," he whispered, his eyebrows arching up to indicate she probably shouldn't have asked. "Despite working in an upscale brothel, Eva prevailed because someone there saw to it she learned what had to be done each day," he explained before he turned his attention back to Alice.

"She must have prevailed somewhere else," Alice whispered. "*The Elegant Courtesan* has been closed for... " She allowed the sentence to trail off as she tried to sort how many years it had been since the Earl of Norwick had married. It was rumored his current wife, Clarinda Ann Brotherton, had only accepted his proposal because her father had made arrangements for her to marry the earl. As a condition of his marriage to her, David Fitzwilliam had been forced to sell off his gambling hell and close the exclusive brothel. "At least three or four years now."

"Indeed," Alonyius replied with a smirk. "My sister is now Lady Norwick's housekeeper."

Her mouth dropping open in astonishment, Alice regarded the valet in disbelief. "Barbara Banks is your *sister?*" she whispered in disbelief, and then she rolled her eyes when she wondered how she hadn't sorted it for herself. Clarinda, Countess of Norwick, was a good friend of Lady Torrington's. The two hosted one another for tea several times a week. "I would not have thought it possible," she started to say and then stopped.

"What is it?" Alonyius prompted. He thought she referred to his sister having worked at a brothel and how unlikely it would be to be hired in an earl's household. But given his sister had been in service to that same earl—or his business, rather—it made sense that he would see to it his loyal employees had positions when *The Elegant Courtesan* was closed.

"It's how I started in service," Alice said with a sigh. "As a scullery maid. At Fitzsimmons Manor. For Lord Chamberlain. Long before he married, of course," she added with a wave of her hand.

"But you were probably the very best scullery maid at Fitzsimmons Manor," Alonyius said with a grin, thinking Alice would have been fastidious in her chores.

"I was the worst!" she countered with wide eyes before

she suddenly sobered and sighed. "But one of the other kitchen maids took pity on me, and..." Alice stopped, inhaling sharply at the thought of how she was trying to do the same for Libby.

She wasn't really doing the girl any favors by doing the work for her, though. She should have been teaching the girl how to accomplish the tasks on her own. "I've been doing this all wrong," she murmured, her eyes lifting to meet his gaze.

Alonyius kissed her then, a gentle kiss that had her eyes closing. Her breath held as his lips slid over hers until they suddenly locked in place.

He had rarely kissed other women—the act was far too intimate to enjoy with a casual lover—so he found it interesting he felt compelled to kiss Alice so frequently. Perhaps it was because her lips swelled a bit with each kiss. They took on a glossy shine and were tinted a darker red after his attentions. Or perhaps it was because Alice always seemed so surprised by them. She was certainly willing, her tongue tangling with his when given the chance, her soft moans as encouraging as how she pressed her body against his.

When Alonyius finally ended the kiss and pulled away, he touched his forehead to hers.

"What was that for?" she whispered, well aware her cheeks were as flushed as her lips were red from his unexpected kiss.

"We've been gone from Worthington House for... eight days," he said simply. "If Libby is to make it as a servant at Worthington House, she has had eight days to prove herself. Since we may not return for another..." He paused as he considered how much longer they might stay at Torrington Park and quickly did the math in his head. "Fifteen days or more, we will not learn of her fate until the middle of January," he added carefully.

Alice nodded her understanding. "And since Lord Torrington has decreed that no one will lose their positions—"

"—Then she will still be a servant at Worthington House," Alonyius finished for her.

Grinning, Alice leaned against his side and sighed. "He is a good employer, isn't he?" she whispered.

"The very best," Alonyius agreed. He kissed her again, and continued to do so until the sounds of jingling bells had them both turning their attention toward the window.

"They've returned," Alice whispered.

Sighing, the valet gave her one last kiss and lifted himself from the bed. "I best get to the vestibule. As should you," he murmured. He reached for her slippers and made quick work of sliding them back onto her feet. Once he donned his top coat, straightening it on his shoulders with a shrug, he gave her a quick bow and took his leave of her quarters.

Alice sighed and finally stood up from the bed, straightening her livery before following the valet at a respectable distance. Once they were both in the vestibule, they stood side by side as they waited for their employers to come in from the cold.

Chapter 42

THEN COMES A QUESTION

*D*usted with snow, their cheeks red from the cold, the Earl and Countess of Torrington spilled into the vestibule of Torrington Park in a fit laughter. Stomping the snow from their boots, the two sobered as they regarded their servants with mischievous grins.

"We shall have to do that again on the morrow," Milton said as he turned to allow Banks to remove his cape coat.

"It was positively invigorating," Adele gushed as Alice helped to remove her mantle. The lady's maid draped it over an arm as she held the snowy fur muff and a scarf that appeared as if it had been dragged through the white stuff.

"Haversham has a better idea of the lay of the land now," the earl stated. "So we shouldn't find ourselves in such deep snow."

"I thought I'd be stuck in that drift for good when we tipped over," Adele countered. Although her words suggested they'd had an accident, the manner in which she spoke them was rather lighthearted.

"Tipped over?" Alice repeated in alarm. Her gaze darted from Lady Torrington to the earl and back again. No wonder the two looked as if they had rolled in the snow. They probably had!

"Oh, we're fine," Adele assured her with a wave of her

gloved hand. "Poor Mr. Haversham took the worst of it. I'll never forget the look of that horse when he turned his head around to look at us, though. I could swear he was grinning," she said, *sotto voce.*

"That's because he was," Milton replied with a smirk. He gave his valet a nod. "He's a Friesian with a sense of humor. Did the same thing two years ago. Cantered right up to the edge of that hill and then suddenly turned so we'd tip sideways," he said as the blade of his hand moved through the air to illustrate how the sleigh ended up on its side.

"You could have been injured, sir," Alonyius said with a frown.

"Unlikely. Drowned in snow is more the case," Milton replied, one of his eyebrows arching up. He suddenly shivered.

"Mrs. Miller is seeing to tea," Alice stated. "Where would you like it, milady?"

"The warmest room in the house," Adele replied as she made her way into the grand hall. On any other day, she would have given an involuntary shudder at entering the massive room, but not on this day. A fire burned in the giant stone fireplace at one end, the tree in one corner was dressed in red ribbons and candles, and the greenery of the season hung above the nativity scene on the mantle. The new stable, appropriately rustic, looked as if it had always been part of the set. Even a star, carved from wood, had been mounted on the highest point of its pine needle thatched roof.

She wouldn't have noticed the animal heads mounted on wood plaques at the tops of the walls except that several had swags of greenery strung over their antlers and horns.

Sighing, she was reminded of how she giggled like a schoolgirl at Milton's amusing tales as they made their way to Hexham in the sleigh. She couldn't remember a time she had felt so unencumbered by the strictures of the *ton.*

"Parlor, then," Alice said with a nod, referring to where tea would be served. "Would you like to change out of your boots, milady?"

The countess shook her head. "Not yet. Perhaps after tea."

Alice bobbed a curtsy and hurried off with the outerwear.

Still in the vestibule, Alonyius dared a glance in her direction before turning his attention back to his master. "Will there be anything else, my lord?" he asked.

Milton shook his head, but gave a nod in the direction of the retreating lady's maid. He had noticed her bee-stung lips and realized what might account for them. Adele's had the same appearance after a spirited round of kissing. "She seems... happy," he murmured, his voice kept low.

Alonyius couldn't help the flush that colored his neck. "I believe she is, my lord," he replied, well aware that the countess had overheard the earl's comment.

"So... everything is sorted between the two of you?"

The valet nodded. "It is, my lord," he acknowledged. He cleared his throat. "Would you have any objections if I was to ... consider... taking a wife?"

A slow smile developing on his face, Milton shook his head. "I would not," he stated. "And I rather doubt her lady-ship would mind, either." He turned and regarded Adele for a moment, just to ensure she shared his opinion.

She gave a shake of her head, but said, "As long as the wedding trip isn't overly long, I suppose." Although she had been without her lady's maid's services for a few days, she found she rather enjoyed having Simpkins style her hair and help her to dress. The maid was far more efficient than Milton given he merely wanted to undress her all the time.

And he was absolutely no help when it came to styling her hair.

Adele suddenly inhaled sharply and added, "As long as it's Miss Simpkins we're discussing," she amended quickly.

Alonyius allowed a grin. "It is my lady," he admitted, a bit sheepish. "I merely lack a ring and a marriage license. I can see to both when we're back in London."

Milton angled his head to one side. "If you're up for a Christmastime wedding, I believe we can see to both."

Frowning, Alonyius wondered what the earl could mean. "If it's possible, then I suppose I would be amenable," he hedged. "Though I still have to propose."

Screwing up his face in annoyance, Milton replied, "Well, of course you'll be amenable. And so will she. I'll pay for the license and give you a ring if that's what it takes."

Adele allowed a sound of surprise but was soon smiling broadly. "A Christmastime wedding!" she cooed.

Alonyius stared at his master for a moment, suddenly realizing just how guilty the man must still feel over what had happened with Alice. "Very well, my lord," he finally replied.

He only hoped the ring would be gold and not a ring of paper from a cheroot.

As it turned out, the Earl of Torrington's idea of a ring was far grander than a cheroot band. Grander even than a simple gold band. For when he and the valet went up to the master suite, Milton regarded the collection of brightly colored boxes still littering his bed and plucked a small one from the pile. He gave it to the valet and said. "May I suggest a Christmas day proposal?"

Alonyius regarded his master for a moment before returning his attention to the box he held. "Was this intended for the countess, my lord? I really shouldn't accept it if—"

"It's not one of Stedman and Vardon's finest", the earl stated with a shake of his head. "I only bought it because I thought to have a bauble or two handy in the event something important might happen. And it seems it has."

His brows furrowing, Alonyius started to give the box back to the earl, but Milton's staying hand stopped it.

"I had hoped my countess would have news for me whilst on this visit," Milton said in a quiet voice. "But it's become apparent she's not yet been blessed with a child." He arched an eyebrow. "Until a few weeks ago, I didn't much care if we had children or not, but now..." He allowed the sentence to trail off, as if he couldn't put voice to whatever had changed his mind.

At first, Alonyius held his tongue, remembering all too well the number of times the earl had insisted his cousin Gregory would make the better earl. If his master died without issue, Gregory Grandby would become the Earl of Torrington.

He opened the small box and peered inside, stunned to see a diamond mounted on a gold band. Not a particularly large stone, it was the perfect size for the width of the band. He imagined how the ring would look on one of Alice's small fingers, imagined the look on her face when he gave it to her.

Imagined the words she might say.

Although he might have been able to purchase the jewel with the monies he had saved over the years, he certainly wouldn't have much left.

Not that money really mattered, he supposed. Not after what he had learned during the afternoon he had spent with his brother.

Alonyius closed the box and returned his attention to the earl. Curiosity suddenly got the best of him. "May I inquire as to what happened to change your mind, my lord? I ask only because..." He stopped, blinking because he wasn't quite sure why it was suddenly so important to know.

Is this what happened to a man who waited too long to take a wife? Who waited too long to consider heirs and spares? The earl was well past the age to consider starting a nursery. The countess would be forty in a couple of years. And yet it seemed as if they were both regretting their impending mortality.

Milton regarded his valet a moment before he provided a most unexpected response. "I think my countess wants a child," he whispered, as if he feared Adele might be listening outside the door. "She's become *insatiable*, I tell you! If I don't get a child on her soon, I won't be able to *walk*."

Alonyius blinked. And blinked again. Prepared to feel

sorry for his master, his eyes suddenly widened in amused surprise at the earl's response. He could barely suppress the chuckle that nearly erupted from his throat.

That is, until he remembered he and the earl were nearly the same age.

Before this trip, Alonyius had never given any consideration to the idea of taking a wife. Of having children. And yet the earl seemed to think it was still possible. For him, it was almost a necessity.

Alonyius finally nodded. "Perhaps we'll have a blizzard, and there will be nothing to do except bed your wife, my lord," he offered in a lighthearted manner.

Milton's eyes widened. "Then I really will be lame," he replied, the crinkles around his eyes deepening before he suddenly allowed a chuckle. "Happy, though, to be sure."

Giving his master a nod, Alonyius thanked him again for the generous gift of the ring and excused himself from the master suite.

He had a proposal to prepare.

Chapter 43

FESTIVITIES OF THE SEASON

*L*ater that day

As Alice hung up her ladyship's carriage gown and matching redingote, she wondered at that evening's entertainments. She thought it rather odd that the earl would have the servants celebrating on the night of Christmas Eve rather than the evening of January fifth. But then she realized it was unlikely any servants would wish to make their way to Hexham or wherever the nearest church might be located tomorrow morning. During that day's hanging of the greens, several maids mentioned they hadn't been out-of-doors for days given the cold weather and snow. Perhaps the early ball was a means of providing exercise. A chance at a bit of revelry.

Alice wondered what she could wear to such a fête. Although she had one gown she considered her Sunday best, it wasn't really appropriate for a ball. Alonyius would look dashing in whatever he wore, she thought, his clothes fitting as if they had been custom-made for him.

She blinked, realizing they probably were.

Having walked all the halls of all three stories of Torrington Park, she had finally found the chapel. The small room in one corner of the lodge was as tall as two stories, its arched ceiling held up by what appeared to be curved beams. Light from its two stained glass windows gave the room a golden glow, the color repeated in the vestments on the altar and in the gilt decorating the pews. She wondered if the staff would use it for a Christmas morning service.

Adele appeared in the doorway. "I'm so glad to have found you," she said as she hurried into the bedchamber.

Alice gave a look of alarm. "What is it, milady?" she asked as she dipped a curtsy.

"We need to find an appropriate gown for you to wear to the ball tonight," the countess replied, already halfway to the dressing room. "And one for me, I suppose. I've been told I should expect to dance with every footman in the household."

"Milady?" Alice's eyes were wide as she watched her mistress breeze into the dressing room and begin a search through the gowns that hung on the pegs.

"It's important, Simpkins. I want you to look your very best this evening."

Alice blinked, not sure how to respond. She was further dumbstruck when Adele appeared in the dressing room doorway holding her very best turquoise and sarcenet ball-gown. "But, I cannot wear such an expensive gown, milady! What if...? What if something should spill on it, or if one of the footmen steps on the hem and tears it?"

Giving her maid a shrug, Adele said, "You'll clean it or fix it as you always do. Let's see if this fits you."

Touching the sarcenet as if it were made of gold leaf, Alice gave Adele a worried glance. "Milady, I would be sick if I couldn't repair it."

"Nonsense. I've worn it twice in London and don't expect I'll do so again—"

"Which is why we packed it for this trip, milady. So you could wear it for the Twelfth Night ball," Alice argued, just then realizing she was putting voice to a protest. Why, her words almost sounded like a complaint. "But I would love to wear it. Truly."

The countess gave her a brilliant smile. "That's the spirit." She moved to stand behind Alice and undid the buttons down the back of her livery.

"What would you like to wear, milady? The green satin is rather festive," Alice suggested.

"I thought of that, but I don't wish to draw any attention from the tree or the other greenery. Everyone did such beautiful work today. I cannot believe how that great hall has been transformed. Why, when the candles are lit, we won't even notice those gruesome animal heads."

Alice grinned, turning around so she could address her mistress. "So the red satin?" Her eyes suddenly widened. "Or the gold silk?" she offered, realizing she had only packed three gowns suitable for a ball, and only those that seemed best suited for Christmastide. The only reason she had packed the turquoise and sarcenet gown was because her ladyship had requested she do so.

Adele held the turquoise gown over Alice's head as the maid shed her livery. In another moment, the rich fabric had settled over her shoulders and fallen around her to reveal a near-perfect fit. Near-perfect because the bodice was rather loose. "I can pin it tighter," she claimed as she pinched the sides between her thumbs and forefingers.

The countess blinked as she regarded her maid. "You look positively gorgeous," she claimed, gripping the maid's shoulders and turning her so her image was reflected in the cheval mirror. "And biddable, too."

Alice couldn't help her gasp of surprise. She had never tried on the elegant gown. Never given a thought to what she might look like in such a confection. She hadn't dared.

And then she realized what the countess had said.

Biddable.

The maid stared at Adele, about to ask what the woman meant when Adele was suddenly searching through a valise.

"Which are the paste and which are the real jewels?" the countess asked, pulling out the boxes from the bottom of the valise.

"The ones at the very bottom are the real ones, milady," Alice said. "The box beneath the fake bottom."

The countess opened both boxes and contemplated the riot of jewels before her. "You shall wear gold, of course. And..." She glanced at her maid, apparently deciding what kind of jewel would look best with the gown.

"The topaz, milady?" Alice offered, realizing she would have to do her hair in a style that would allow the earbobs to show to their best effect. Before she knew quite what was happening, Adele had threaded the earbobs through her piercings and was already going back for the matching necklace.

"I don't know that I want to outshine the other maids, milady," she said as Adele secured the gold and jewel necklace around her neck.

"On this night, it is a necessity," Adele countered, as if she knew something Alice didn't know. She gave a sigh as she regarded her lady's maid. "Can you do something less severe with your hair? I rather like what you've done with the front, dear, but..." She stopped and allowed a sigh.

Alice smiled. "I can, milady. But in the meantime, what will you wear? The red or the gold?"

Pretending to ponder, Adele was tempted to simply wear what she had on—she'd had Alice help her change back into the red Merino wool gown she had worn that morning—because it seemed appropriate for the season and because of how Mr. Banks had stared at her. But she reconsidered when she remembered she was trying to impress her husband. Seduce him, really, but impressions were so important. "The gold," she murmured. "With the gold and ruby earbobs and this necklace," she said as she fingered the holly pendant that hung just below the hollow of her throat.

"You'll be resplendent, milady," Alice said as she moved to the dressing room and gathered the gold silk gown in her arms. She passed by the cheval mirror, nearly pausing when she didn't recognize her own reflection.

"As are you," Adele murmured, giving her lady's maid an arched brow coupled with a grin. She turned to allow her maid to undo the fastenings of the red wool gown. "Torrington said the fabric of my gown is from Banks Textiles," she added in a conversational tone.

Alice slowed her movements. "It's Mrs. Banks favorite color in this wool," she replied. "She was wearing a similar gown when I visited Mill House."

The countess considered her lady's maid's comment for a moment. "How did you find Mrs. Banks?" she asked as she stepped into the gold gown, wincing when she realized Alice had to kneel down in order to hold open the silk. The turquoise silk and gold sarcenet billowed out in a cloud around her maid as she did so.

"She's a very amenable woman," Alice said as she lifted the gold gown and helped Adele thread her arms into the long sleeves. She started to do up the few fastenings in the back. "I never would have guessed she was a lady's maid before her marriage to Mr. Banks. To the valet's father," she quickly amended. "Although she is ever so humble. And rather... batty." She didn't add that the woman was still hoping one or both of her sons would bless her with a grandchild she could spoil rotten.

Adele let out a titter. "I know of her story, of course," she admitted. "Which is why I'll allow you to marry your Mr. Banks." The words were out of her mouth before she realized the valet probably hadn't yet proposed.

"Milady?" Alice took a step back, rather stunned at the comment.

Turning around to regard her maid, Adele rolled her eyes. "Should Mr. Banks propose, of course," she added with an arched brow. She allowed a sigh, as if she realized her gaffe. "If he doesn't propose after seeing you in that gown, then you shall be better off without him," she announced, moving to take a seat at the vanity.

Alice pretended ambivalence as she removed several pins

from her ladyship's hair and worked to create a slightly more elaborate styling from the way she had done it earlier that day. There wasn't another maid in Park Lane who could style hair as well as she could. She wondered then if it was the reason the countess continued to employ her despite her sour countenance these past few months.

"Could you see yourself married to the man?" Adele asked, watching in the looking glass as Alice repinned several locks of her hair into a chain of curls atop her head.

"I have not allowed myself such a luxury, milady," Alice replied. "After my rather unfortunate misunderstanding yesterday, I cannot imagine Mr. Banks would tolerate me for anything other than an occasional tum..." She stopped, stunned she was about to admit she would carry on an *affaire* with the valet and not expect an offer of marriage in return.

Adele regarded her maid's reflection in the mirror. "Even if what you say is true, perhaps Mr. Banks is in want of a wife for just such a purpose."

Blinking, Alice continued her work on Adele's coiffure. "Would that be an acceptable reason to wed, do you suppose?" she asked. "Merely for the purpose of sharing a bed?"

Adele nearly rolled her eyes again. "My dear, I do believe most men marry for that reason and only that reason," she countered.

Given how enjoyable their times in bed together had been, Alice had to think the same could be said for some women.

Including me.

"I shall consider your words should Mr. Banks put voice to a proposal," she allowed, hoping her ladyship hadn't placed any bets on the matter.

But why would Alonyius propose when he knew damn well she would bed him without such a formal arrangement?

Such a permanent arrangement?

Determined not to allow the thought to lessen her enjoyment of the evening, Alice completed her mistress' hair styling and watched as the countess made her way through the dressing room and into her husband's bedchamber.

Then she set about doing her own hair.

When she was done, she was quite sure she could have passed for any older woman of the *ton*.

Chapter 44

A BEAU FOR A BALL

A few minutes later

Several servants had already gathered in the great hall, all of them dressed in their Sunday best and similarly coiffed for the Christmas Eve event. Those who had been in service to the Torrington earldom for more than a year or two knew what to expect on this night—an enjoyable evening of dancing and merriment, of games and gifts, of randy footmen and reluctant maids.

And a rather insatiable cook who seemed to have her sights set on the grooms from Worthington House. More than one footman was relieved to be relieved of that particular duty.

A quintet of musicians had set up in the only corner not already occupied by the tree or a door or the stairs to the first story. Having seen to appropriate chairs for the group, Trasker waited a moment before hurrying off to the fireplace. Two footmen had rolled the Yule log to just in front of the massive opening where a bright fire already crackled. Later that evening, after everyone who considered it good luck to sit on the log before it was burned had a chance to do so, the tree trunk would be rolled into the fireplace.

He glanced around before taking an experimental seat on the massive log, just to be sure it didn't roll too easily. He didn't want a housemaid to be accidentally unseated while taking her turn.

Although custom claimed a log of this size would burn until Epiphany, the butler expected more wood would be required after only a few days. He'd done this before. Many times.

As the musicians tuned their instruments, Alonyius Banks made his way into the hall and to the only man in the group who was standing. He bowed and introduced himself to the familiar man—the quintet had performed for last year's Twelfth Night ball—and said, "Thank you again for agreeing to such an unusual request." He held out a pile of coins as payment for their services.

The viola player gave a nod. "Got nothin' else to do on such a cold night," he replied. "Seein' as how three of us are widowers and the other two haven't yet taken a wife."

Alonyius frowned, just then giving the other musicians a glance. Indeed, three were older gentlemen while the other two looked as if they were barely out of school. "I doubt we'll keep you too late," he said with a nod. "But I'm sure we can find you rooms should you wish to spend the night."

The group seemed amenable to the arrangement. "When would you like us to start the dancing music?"

Knowing his master was ready to come down at any moment, Alonyius said, "When Lord Torrington makes an appearance, I should think. A country dance, perhaps. Long-ways, to start, of course. Something... festive."

"Anyone here allowed to waltz?" asked the man with a French horn.

Alonyius allowed a grin. "I shouldn't think there would be any complaints if you played at least two," he replied, his gaze going back to the main entrance from the stairs. A few more servants had joined the growing crowd, such as it was, although the woman for whom he was waiting hadn't yet made an appearance. Neither had her mistress, though.

Probably still doing the countess' hair, he thought, his anxiousness growing with every minute. *I've never been this nervous*, he thought with a bit of annoyance. This was simply a servants' ball. Nothing more. Just because he might decide to bestow a ring on one of Alice Simpkins' fingers shouldn't have him so discombobulated.

Why, he might change his mind and decide to propose at another time. A different place.

Coward, he chided himself, his thumb and forefinger gripping the gold band through the fabric of his waistcoat. He had slid the ring into a pocket and wanted to ensure he hadn't lost it.

Glancing about the great hall, he wondered just where he might give her the ring. Or perhaps he would save it for later. Although they hadn't discussed in which room they would be spending the night, he rather doubted they would go to his. Ever since Alice had gone after his valise the night before last, he hadn't stepped foot in the quarters assigned to him.

As for how he might broach the subject of marriage, he had an idea for how he would ensure her cooperation. He would simply tell her his plan for them and then not give her an option to accept or reject it.

We shall marry, he thought to say, and then realized it didn't seem right to simply state the fact. But he couldn't—he wouldn't—allow her a moment to think on the subject. He didn't want her taking a week or a month or more making a decision he was quite sure she would make in his favor.

Would she turn him down if given the chance?

The thought had him frowning. She had never been married. She might prefer her bit of independence. Might prefer their arrangement remain exactly as it was.

Although they hadn't really spoken of a formal arrangement. An *affaire*.

Or an informal one, for that matter. He had simply seen to joining her in whatever bed she was in.

A brief thought that perhaps she would prefer to sleep alone was quickly dismissed. She wanted him in bed with her, he was sure. At least for the warmth.

I have become nothing better than a blanket.

Shaking the thought from his head—he was an excellent bedmate—he thought to ask Alice her opinion of the matter. How he would broach such a subject might prove a challenge. When would he ask such a question? Certainly not on a night when he simply held her body against his. Better he do it on one of those nights when he was sure he had satisfied her carnal needs.

Such as this night. He had every intention of bedding her. Every intention of leaving her boneless and breathless. Of leaving her with no doubt with whom she would be spending the rest of her life.

His quiet confidence faltered a bit as he surveyed the great hall. Some of his nervousness had to do with Lady Torrington. This was her first Christmastide at Torrington Park—her first Christmas Eve—and he found he wanted her to enjoy it. Wanted her to be impressed with what the servants had accomplished since she and the earl had disappeared after their sleigh ride that afternoon.

Wanted her to return for every Christmastide hence.

That last thought had him frowning, realizing his wish was rather selfish. If the Torringtons returned to the hunting lodge, he would have the opportunity to visit Mill House again. His lordship would insist on it.

"Your face will freeze like that if you're not careful, Mr. Banks."

Alonyius gave his head a shake, stunned to find Mrs. Watson regarding him. He almost didn't recognize the cook. She looked most elegant wearing a green velvet panniered gown—even if it was of a style from the last century, and her ever-present mob cap had been replaced with a rather jaunty red ribbon. "I rather doubt that, Mrs. Watson. Happy Christmas, by the way."

"You could have warned me we'd be doing this tonight instead of a fortnight from now," she scolded.

"Believe me when I say I would have if I had *known*," the valet replied defensively. "Still, from my brief visit to your kitchens a few moments ago, you appear to have outdone yourself with the refreshments. Indeed, everyone has done a remarkable job of it."

The woman beamed. "Because I didn't have to bake biscuits! I take it you helped in that regard?"

Alonyius straightened, remembering the rather odd request he'd had from the earl the month before. *Procure six dozen Dutch biscuits and be sure they're packed in tins. Oh, and have Cook make some Christmas cakes as well.* At the time, he could only guess what the earl intended to do with the sweets.

"I merely followed the earl's orders," he replied, his hands clasping together behind his back.

"When did you marry the lady's maid?"

Taking a careful breath—his first reaction was to gasp—Alonyius wondered at the cook's query. Not *when will you marry the lady's maid?*

Did all the servants at Torrington Park think they were married?

"You needn't deny it," Watson went on, a quick shake of her head threatening to dislodge the mountain of red and gray curls mounted atop her head. "I just wanted you to know it's why I haven't expected you to pay a call on me in my quarters, is all," she said in a hoarse whisper, one eye winking. Her attention was suddenly on someone else— Haversham appeared on the stairs—and she hurried off, leaving the valet a bit discombobulated.

Alonyius had never paid a visit to the cook's bedchamber in the past, nor did he have any plans to do so.

Suddenly rather glad Haversham had taken up with the cook, Alonyius took a deep breath and regarded the great hall.

All the trestles had been pushed to the tapestried walls and were dressed in red linen tablecloths. The kissing bough, hastily finished once the small dolls had been located in one of the storage rooms, had been hung just inside the front doors. Although no one was expected to come through those doors now that the musicians were in residence, Alonyius knew that particular location would become more popular as the evening progressed.

He intended to have a certain woman under the ball of greenery at least once before taking her upstairs.

Several maids, already dressed for the evening's entertainments, appeared from the kitchens. Their arms were laden with large salvers of sweetmeats, sugared plums, and cakes. On one silver tray, Dutch biscuits had been arranged in decorative spirals.

Having seen to the purchase of most of that evening's refreshments, Alonyius was relieved to see they still appeared edible.

Following the maids, a footman carried a pail filled with snow and several bottles of champagne. Another maid, dressed in a velvet gown of deep red with a matching turban, appeared with a cart of stemmed glasses. The trestles were soon filled with the evening's refreshments.

"Anything we may have forgotten?" Trasker asked as he joined the valet. Although he looked much like he did during the day, the portly butler had replaced his cravat with a black equivalent.

My senses, Alonyius nearly answered. "If so, I couldn't begin to guess. Devlin did a fine job locating that Yule log," he commented.

"Yes. Let's hope we can get it into the fireplace when it's time," the butler replied, remembering how many servants it had taken to get the thing into the hall. "What are they waiting for?" he asked as he motioned towards the musicians. The quiet strains of tuning instruments hadn't yet segued to music.

"The earl. As soon as Lord Torrington appears on the stairs, they know to start."

Trasker nodded and a second later gave a start when the music suddenly began. "La Belle Assemblée March", a short piece, had most of the servants hurrying to take their positions for the country dance to follow. Alonyius turned to see the Torringtons descend the stairs and watched as they joined the two lines of servants facing one another. He was rather stunned at the simple gold gown her ladyship wore and wondered if she had been concerned about outshining the maids. This was the servants' ball, after all.

She still outshines them, he thought, seeing as how the countess wore gold and jewels. Her hair looked as if Alice had spent hours dressing it.

She probably did, which is why she isn't here, Alonyius thought with a bit of annoyance. His attention was on the dancers when the Scottish tune, "Earl Breadalbain's Reel", had them moving. Just as the music changed to "Revenge," Alonyius dared another glance in the direction of the stairs, and he sucked in a breath.

Alice stood on one of the steps in the middle of the staircase, her startled gaze and growing smile taking in the dancers and the change in the room since she had last been there. He stared at her, wondering if the prince in the story of a late gentleman's daughter-turned-maid felt as he did just then. When the cinder girl appeared at the top of the stairs wearing a gown of blue and slippers of glass.

Thunderstruck.

Mum would say it was lightning, he thought, a slight grin forming just as Alice finally looked in his direction. Her gaze locked on him for a moment—that is, until he suddenly moved. He disappeared for a moment in the midst of the longways dancers, and then was suddenly several steps below her.

Alice managed a curtsy before making her way down to where Alonyius waited for her. He bowed and offered his arm, so she placed her gloved hand on it. "Happy Christmas," she said in a breathy voice.

"And to you, my lady," Alonyius replied, his gaze taking in the jewels at her neck and ears. Despite her status as a lady's maid, she looked as if she could have been a countess.

Blinking—only because he was staring at her—Alice was tempted to wave a gloved hand in front of his face. But she rather liked seeing him appear so... beholden.

So awestruck.

Mrs. Banks would say it was lightning, she thought with a grin. When she could finally look away—the valet did finally regain his wits—it was to discover how much the great hall had changed since that afternoon's sleigh ride. My, but she hadn't remembered Worthington House ever appearing as festive as the great hall did just then—even for Lady Torrington's annual *musicale*. Besides the candles that lit the tree and those suspended in the rustic chandelier, the room glowed with the light from several candelabras. *A hundred candles,* she thought as Alonyius led her to the end of the line of maids who had formed up for the next dance.

Despite having worked with several of the maids earlier that day to tie the bows that now decorated the tree, she barely recognized them. They had spent a good deal of time on their hair and wore gowns they had probably sewn themselves.

Not sure what to do at first, she simply watched as the dancers farther down the line joined in the middle and worked their way through the tunnel created by the couples who held their hands above them. She followed suit and was soon enjoying the dance, her glittering gown swaying about her ankles.

Just as she was sure she knew what to do next, the dance ended and the music changed to "Crookie Den". The Scottish reel had the servants quickly forming into three circles of six, and laughter ensued as some of the footmen couldn't quite keep up.

Breathless at the end, Alice stepped away from the other maids and fanned herself with a gloved hand. Several servants moved to the refreshment tables, but before she could do so, Alonyius was suddenly there offering her a glass of champagne.

"You are allowed, I hope," he said with a mischievous grin.

Her eyes widening at his query, she was about to admonish him when she realized he was having a bit of fun. She was tempted to down the entire glass in a single gulp—the dance had been exhilarating. "I am," she replied with a grin. She allowed her gaze to take in his clothing. Although he always appeared impeccably dressed, there was something different tonight. It wasn't until she spotted the butler that she realized the two upper servants wore black cravats.

"It was rather generous of Lady Torrington to allow you the use of her jewels this evening. The necklace was a gift from the earl on the occasion of her birthday last year."

Alice shook her head. "Oh, these are not real. They're paste," she insisted, her expression suddenly changing when she noticed the valet giving a slight shake of his head, as if he knew better. Then she remembered she hadn't been the one to remove them from the jewel box. Her ladyship had done that.

"We'll be careful with them of course," he murmured, imagining how she would look wearing them and nothing else. "Will you honor me with both of the waltzes this evening?"

Alice gave the valet a nod before her expression suddenly changed. "I'm not sure I know how to dance a waltz, Mr. Banks," she replied, her voice coming out a bit breathy.

The valet gave a shrug. "Then I shall teach you," he countered. "Your gown and those jewels require you show them to their best advantage."

Sure a blush colored her face just then—she had finally managed to get her breathing under control—Alice said, "Lady Torrington insisted I wear it."

"It's gorgeous," Alonyius whispered, not trusting his voice just then. "They're playing a sauteuse. The music isn't the right timing for a waltz, but I can at least teach you the steps," he offered.

Even before she could agree, the valet had her heading in the direction of the front doors. There, the light from the candles didn't quite reach. When they were well away from the dancers performing the small leaping steps of the sauteuse, Alonyius reached for one of her hands and placed it in his. "Put your other on my shoulder."

Alice's eyes widened. "So close?"

"No. You will stay there, and I shall stay here, and when we move..." He pushed her so she had to take a step back. "We will keep this same distance between us." He waved the hand that had been placed at her waist to indicate the open area between them. He stepped forward again using his other foot, the hand moving back to her waist to indicate how she needed to move.

"This is rather scandalous," she murmured as he moved her again, his steps taken in half the time of the music being played just then.

"It's meant to be," Alonyius whispered. "But with the waltzing music, it goes a bit faster." He moved them so their steps took them in an arc.

"You're awfully close," Alice breathed moving her hand from his shoulder to wave about in the area between them.

"A deliberate maneuver, I assure you," he murmured, his eyes nearly black in the shadows.

At the moment her brows furrowed, he suddenly stopped and bent to kiss her.

Had they been alone—had they been anywhere but in the great hall—she might have allowed the intimacy. But not now. They were at the servants' ball where anyone could see them! She was about to push him away when her gaze took in where they were standing.

Under the kissing bough.

"You bounder!" she accused when he finally lifted his lips from hers. She dared a glance at the other servants, aware that some had taken notice of exactly where they were. And of what they had been doing.

A few of the maids tittered while one of the footmen called a form of congratulations to the valet for being the first to gain a kiss beneath the kissing bough. The music had stopped at some point, as if the musicians wished to pay witness to whatever was going on near the front doors.

"I did not mean to embarrass you," Alonyius said as he moved them out from under the mass of greenery and paper bows. "There are those here who think we are..."

At the precise moment Alonyius thought to inform Alice of his plans for her—for them—the Earl of Torrington cleared his throat and Trasker proceeded to quiet the small crowd so their master could speak.

Once Milton had their attention, he motioned for Adele to join him at the front of the assembly. "Happy Christmas! I do believe my countess and I have managed to dance with just about everyone here, so we'll be taking our leave shortly so you can enjoy yourselves without fear of censure."

A murmur of approval passed through the assembled servants before he continued. "For those who were not present at Torrington Park when we first arrived, I'd like to introduce my countess. I have known Lady Torrington since she was in leading strings—"

"Milton!" she admonished him.

"Because she was my best friend's sister. Always wanted to marry her, but I had to wait until she was available."

Amusement sounded from those in attendance. "Tonight, she will help me distribute the boxes I would usually give you the day after Christmas."

This bit of news had the murmurings changing to gasps of surprise. Even Alonyius had to suppress his shock, his attention completely on the earl as Alice stepped aside to put more space between them.

"I can't keep them a secret any longer, and since they've been covering my bed since I arrived, and since I'd like to sleep in my own bed—"

"Milton!" Adele whispered in shock.

"It's a far larger bed, my sweeting," he countered, his rejoinder resulting in a round of laughter. "I should like to give them away tonight."

Several applauded and everyone seemed excited by the news.

From under the tree, the earl pulled out several boxes.

Decorated with brightly colored ribbon, bows and a pasteboard tag on which a name was written, the boxes were those the earl had brought in his own coach. He called off a name as he held each one up before giving it to Adele. She took it to the person who stepped forward and gave them the box as well as a "thank you" for their service.

When he called for Mrs. Miller and Trasker, the two servants stepped forward. He presented them each with rather large boxes, his grin broad as he teased the two. "My countess would say the best gifts come in small packages, but I do hope you'll agree these are good, too." He turned his attention to the small crowd. "Spyglasses," he said in a hoarse whisper, his comment met with guffaws.

His claim was countered when Mrs. Miller pulled an ivory brush and comb set from her box, her eyes wide with her delight. Trasker refused to open his, claiming he would do so when he was in his quarters. A round of hisses resulted, but the staid servant held his ground.

The last two boxes were for Alice and Alonyius, the upper servants hesitant as they moved to the front of the group to accept them.

"We'll not be requiring your services until the morning," Adele whispered as she gave them each the smallest of all the boxes that had been under the tree.

Not too surprised by her words, Alice dipped a curtsy. "Yes, milady. Ten o'clock?"

Adele nodded.

When everyone had a box—including the musicians— the earl bade them a happy Christmas and goodnight. Offering his arm to Adele, the two bowed and curtsied to the staff and made their way up the stairs.

"Why aren't they staying?" Alice asked in a whisper.

"The earl never does. This is the servants' ball, after all," Alonyius replied as he motioned for the musicians to continue playing. A moment later, "L'Hipparchia", a piece appropriate for a quadrille, had several groups of four forming into square sets.

Glancing about, Alice noticed a few of the maids opening their boxes, their eyes widening in delight. She watched as one maid pulled an orange from her pastebox box followed by several coins. Another shrieked when she discovered a length of wide satin ribbon as well as the coins. "Do they all get money?" she asked, *sotto voce.*

Alonyius nodded. "They do. And all the same amount, from the scullery maid to Mr. Trasker," he explained. "The other gifts are a bit of a guess for him, but he always seems to guess right given the reactions I have seen thus far," he added, his brow furrowing when he regarded the box he held.

"What did we get?"

The valet allowed a shrug before he grinned. "I have absolutely no idea."

"Certainly not an orange," Alice murmured. Her pasteboard box was too small.

"Nor an apple," he countered, realizing his box was too small for even plums or peaches.

"Candied nuts?" Alice offered as a guess. She rather enjoyed pecans after they had been drizzled with caramelized sugar, but the earl wouldn't have known that about her. Neither would her mistress.

Alonyius shook his box, but when no sound—not even that of loose coins—was made from the movement, he gave his own head a shake. "I have no idea," he said, a bit confused. He was sure his master would bestow him with the same sort of gifts the footmen had received.

The two regarded their boxes for a long time before Alice finally plucked the end of the ribbon that untied the elaborate bow. Pulling the two parts of the small box apart, she stared inside for a moment before she dared a glance up at Alonyius. He was reading a paper that had been folded several times to fit in his box, his expression rather curious.

"What is it?" Alice moved to pull out the folded paper from her box, but one of Alonyius' hands suddenly closed around her gloved hand.

"Not yet," he said with a shake of his head. "Tomorrow. Wait until tomorrow, won't you?"

Tempted to ignore his words, Alice regarded the folded note before she dared a glance up. Although Alonyius' expression was still unreadable, she finally nodded and slid the two parts of the box together. Gathering up the ribbons, she retied the bow as best she could. "Is it... bad news?" she asked then, a sense of dread settling in her stomach.

"No," he replied in a whisper. "It's the very best, actually." He dipped his head a moment before allowing a sigh. He reassembled his box and slid it into a pocket, and he did the same with Alice's at the same moment the strains of the "Slow Waltz" started. "Will you honor me with this dance?"

Alice nodded. "This will be our third," she whispered, her eyes suddenly wide. But Alonyius already had her hand in his and another at her waist.

"You won't be dancing with anyone else this evening," he said then. At the same moment, he stepped forward, his strong lead forcing Alice to do his bidding. She was about to argue with him about the dancing, but thought it might come out sounding like a complaint and thought better of it.

Besides, the dancing required her complete attention. By the time they had completed a revolution around the room, she found she loved dancing the waltz. She loved being guided by strong hands while resting a gloved hand on a broad shoulder. Loved the simple one-two-three timing and the way her gown flowed in a circle around her feet. Loved how the other couples moved in the same repeating circles and yet were completely disconnected from them. She loved the music.

What she found she didn't love so much was that no matter where they were in the dance, there was that space between the two of them.

Perhaps it was fortuitous, then, that when the music ended, they were left beneath the kissing bough. Alice closed that space in an instant, her body pressed against the front of

Alonyius as she stood on her tiptoes and kissed him quite thoroughly.

When Alice finally pulled away—she was completely unaware of those who watched them, of those who averted their eyes at the shameless display of affection—Alonyius simply stared at her for the longest time.

"Marry me," she said in a whisper, her gaze suggesting she might simply be rehearsing the words in her mind. Now that they were out, though, she wasn't about to take them back. Not when the man had kissed her so thoroughly so many times. Not when he had made love to her with such fervor and then with such tenderness. Not when his gaze seemed to pin her in place, as it was doing this instant, as if he intended to take possession of her.

No, she wasn't about to take back what amounted to a demand.

Alonyius blinked, his brows furrowing at the same time his mouth formed a grin. *She didn't exactly ask*, he realized as he dropped his forehead to her hair. "I will," he agreed, his lips moving to hers for a quick kiss. Quick, because the excited murmurs and giggles from the other servants had increased in volume despite the Scottish reel the musicians were playing.

"What are they doing?"

Alonyius dared a glance at the assembly and realized everyone was taking a turn at sitting on the Yule log.

"Not that we're in need of any, but I suppose we should take a seat for good luck," he murmured.

Unfamiliar with the custom of sitting on the Yule log before it was pushed into the fireplace, Alice nodded and allowed him to escort her to where a few of the staff members waited in a line in front of the huge log.

Trasker regarded them with an arched brow. "I wasn't aware you two were married," he said with what could only be described as a stern expression.

Alice was about to deny the man's assumption, but Alonyius squeezed her hand ever so gently before lifting it to his lips. "I can understand why you wondered," Alonyius remarked, pulling the ring from his pocket. "Seeing as how my sweeting hasn't been wearing her ring," he added as he moved to pull the long glove from Alice's hand so he could slide the gold band onto one of her fingers. The diamond glittered in the light from the fire, and Alice stared at it with as much awe as the butler was displaying.

"Why, that must have set you back a bit," Trasker murmured, almost immediately regretting his words. He straightened, his manner suddenly more serious. "Whatever you do, don't allow Mrs. Miller to see that." He reached into his own pocket and pulled out a simple gold band. "Or she'll never agree to marry me."

Alice and Alonyius exchanged glances of surprise—at no point had there been any hint that the butler and housekeeper were considering marriage.

"I shall keep this hidden whilst we're here at Torrington Park," Alice replied, daring another glance up at Alonyius, realizing he must have intended to give it to her sometime that evening.

Probably when he proposed.

She didn't have a chance to consider that thought before it was their turn to sit on the Yule log.

Glad for the linen that covered part of the bark—Alice was sure the sarcenet would snag if it touched the tree— she allowed Alonyius to help her as she lowered herself to the log. A moment later, he was next to her, and a round of applause followed before they were back to standing so the next servant could take a seat.

"Is this a waltz?" Alice asked as she became aware of the music.

Grinning, Alonyius nodded. "Would you do me the honor of dancing with me?"

Alice matched his grin. "I will."

Chapter 45

MORNINGS ARE BEST FOR WICKEDNESS

January 1, 1817

The sensation of fingernails gently parting his hair had Alonyius slowly awakening. A tickle skittered beneath his scalp, which set off a shiver through his entire body. Warm breath washed over his face before soft lips pressed onto his forehead. He couldn't help the grin he displayed as those same lips moved to his temple, to beneath his ear, to the side of his neck. But he didn't open his eyes until the musical sound of Alice's giggle—a giggle!—broke the pre-dawn silence.

He had no idea how the earl had managed to procure a marriage license on his behalf. The only thing he could reason was that the Torringtons had paid a visit to someone important in Hexham the day of their sleigh ride. But the folded paper in his small gift box was his ticket to a wedding without the need for the reading of the banns.

We could have taken a trip over the border, he thought with a hint of amusement. Saved the earl the cost of the license and the vicar who performed the private ceremony the day before in the chapel of Torrington Park. Private because all the other servants had come to believe the two were already married.

Because Alice's box was stuffed into one of his pockets,

she didn't learn what was in it until Christmas morning. The twenty-pound bank note was accompanied by a note from the earl suggesting she use part of it as her dowry and the rest for the bride clothes she would require when she and her husband paid a call at Mill House.

You are excused from service for two weeks for your wedding trip, but no more than that. My countess despairs at my poor attempt at styling her hair.

Alonyius slid a hand down her side and over the flare of her hips, the bare flesh warm beneath his hand. Although he didn't want to move, his manhood certainly did. "You wicked woman," he murmured as he suddenly flipped her onto her back and settled himself atop her.

Alice let out a sound of startlement before giggling again. "Good morning, husband," she whispered as she lifted her legs to wrap them around his lower torso.

"It seems it is," he replied as he slowly entered her, giving her an arched eyebrow when he realized just how ready she was for his hardened manhood. "How long have you been awake?"

Sighing when he was fully pushed into her, Alice slid her hands up his sides and to his shoulders. "Not long," she whispered as she lifted her chest so the tips of her nipples grazed his crisp, graying curls. A tooth caught her lower lip, denting the plump flesh as if she had to suppress a cry of delight.

The move had Alonyius lowering his eyes to the flat pads of her breasts. He lifted himself a bit so her nipples were no longer touching him. Her mewl of disappointment was quickly replaced with a more pleasant sound as his lips took purchase on one of those nipples. Gently kissing it before laving the blade of his tongue across its tip, he thrilled at his wife's reaction. With her head thrown back into the pillows and her torso lifted from the bed in a display of wanton lust, she might have been the most sought after courtesan in all of London. Instead, she was simply a woman with whom he had spent hours getting to know whilst traveling in a coach during one of the worst winters on record. Who would have ever believed a lady's maid could capture his attention—and his heart—in such short order?

Short order? Christ! I've known this woman for as long as the earl has been married, he reminded himself.

When he was suddenly aware of fingers spearing his short cropped hair, he moved his attentions to the other nipple. He would have spent more time worrying the tender bud with his lips and teeth, but his manhood demanded surcease, as did Alice, it seemed. Her mewling and gentle pleas, not to mention how she clenched his erection, as if to coax the seed from his manhood, were all the encouragement he needed. His first few thrusts were slow, meant to tease and please.

When Alice's palms moved to grip his buttocks, he increased the pace and plunged into her harder and harder. The feel of her undulations around his manhood set off his release, a spasm of pleasure gripping his body as hard as her hold on him. He swallowed her cry of pleasure with a kiss, one he couldn't sustain when he was forced to take a breath. Gasping, he attempted to lift his body from hers. Lacking the strength, though, he slumped onto her, his head coming to rest next to her neck. Between gasps for air, he kissed her cheek before murmuring, "I may be too old for this."

He felt Alice's giggle burble up through her body before the musical sound erupted. Despite his momentary inability to move, a grin appeared on his face. "I know I have said it already, but your are a wicked woman," he accused gently.

Alice slowly turned her head to regard him, her nose nearly colliding with his. "Ah, but I am a happy, wicked woman," she countered, giving him a kiss on the nose. "Thanks to you. Happy New Year, by the way."

Alonyius sighed. Happy, indeed.

Chapter 46

SNOW IS BEST FOR THE REST

*M*arch 1817

Milton Grandby, Earl of Torrington, entered White's at precisely seven o'clock, a footman quickly seeing to his greatcoat. His arrival each night was so precisely timed, other gentlemen set their chronometers based on when he stepped into the men's club. One of the club's butlers was even spied resetting a mantle clock above a fireplace a moment after the earl took his usual seat.

Milton's visits usually lasted a mere forty-five minutes so that he might arrive home at exactly eight o'clock for dinner with his wife. Despite the short amount of time, he was afforded an opportunity to enjoy a pre-dinner drink. He spent the time conferring with other members of the peerage, taking a peek at the betting books, and listening to the day's gossip. Ensconced in his favorite overstuffed chair, he sipped a brandy as he surreptitiously listened to the conversation of some gentlemen at a card table. Although Milton wasn't a gossip monger, he still rather enjoyed hearing it whenever he had the chance.

"I have rather momentous news to share this evening," a viscount was announcing proudly as he finished shuffling a new deck of cards.

"Did your horse finally win a race?" a baron asked, his

elevated eyebrow suggesting his comment was made in jest. The viscount frowned. He dealt the cards as if he'd been doing it since he was in leading strings.

The explorer, Harold, Lord Everly, leaned in to pick up his cards. "Now, now. Don't be making fun of his bay. That nag came in second last week," the earl scolded. The adventurer had been in London only a fortnight, his most recent trip having been to the southernmost tip of Africa in search of strange fish. His avocation—the study of natural sciences —had him traveling around the globe more often than he was home in London.

Everly took a look at his cards and was about to scold the viscount for his bad deal when he decided he might be able to bluff his way through this hand.

"Thank you, Everly," the viscount acknowledged with a nod. "No, gentleman, my wife has seen to it I will be a father. Probably before Parliament reconvenes in the fall," he stated proudly. He picked up his own cards, giving them a quick glance before looking up to accept congratulations from around the table.

"My wife will be relieved to hear of it," a knight commented, his attention on his cards. "Only last week, she claimed your wife looked as if she was eating a few too many cakes at tea."

Milton had to stifle a chuckle at the comment lest he be discovered listening. Just last week, he'd made a similar comment to Adele, although he was careful to add that he rather liked her with a bit more meat on her bones. She'd been far too thin when they married.

The viscount gave the knight a nod. "Well, she is, at that, but she is eating for two now," he commented, his proud grin never leaving his face, even as he was forced to fold.

"She'll be in good company," the baron commented as he considered his hand and the growing pile of chips in the center of the table. "Seems there will be a crop of heirs born this fall."

Lord Everly looked up from his hand, deciding he might

not be able to bluff his way through this hand after all. "That would be due to that nasty snowstorm we had last December, just after Christmas," he stated with some authority.

The viscount made a sound that could best be described as a snort. "As I understand these matters, Everly, *snow* had nothing to do with it."

The other three gentlemen guffawed in response. "Oh, yes it does. What else are you going to do when you're trapped in your country estate for three straight days?" the baron asked, making a rude gesture with his hands.

"And your wife complains of boredom and the cold?" the knight added rhetorically, his eyebrows waggling suggestively.

"I daresay, I remember wishing I was married during that long week," the baron murmured as he pretended to study his cards.

In the middle to taking a sip of brandy, Milton stilled his movements.

We were in Torrington Park. There was that snowstorm just after Christmas Day.

He held the brandy on his tongue for a very long time, finally swallowing when the alcohol threatened to burn a hole in his mouth. He remembered that snowstorm quite clearly. Remembered where he was during the second and third days of it. Remembered where Adele had been—usually under him, although there had been those rather delightful times when she was on top of him—and he suddenly realized why it was she looked as if she'd been eating a few too many cakes at tea.

Lord Everly piped up and said, "Be prepared to bed your wife more frequently. Her appetite for your favors will be insatiable. At least, it is for most of the females of our species when they are breeding." A hearty round of laughter erupted from the table as the viscount's back was slapped and pounded.

Milton's heart pounded in his chest. His pulse pounded in his head. *How did Everly know such things?* The earl wasn't married. *But he's a naturalist,* he reminded himself.

Milton's breaths came a bit too quickly. He stared at his brandy as if he didn't recognize it. *I'm going to be a father.* The words, barely formed in his mind, repeated themselves with a bit more certainty.

Downing the rest of his brandy as if he'd spent a week in the desert, he quickly made his way to his coach, his early exit from the club causing one of the butlers to pick up and study a mantle clock to ensure it still worked. The groom on the back of his coach, Higgins, did a double-take. "My lord?" he managed to get out as he moved to open the door and set down the steps.

"Stedman and Vardon in Bond Street, and make it fast," Milton ordered, stepping into his coach. He was barely seated when the coach lurched forward to make its way up St. James Street. He took the opportunity to breathe, feeling rather proud that he had enough sense to stop at a jewelers to secure a rather expensive bauble before heading home for dinner. *I'm going to be a father*, he thought again. For a man of his age—he was past forty—to marry a widow—who, as near as he could tell was in her late thirties—to discover he was going to be a father, was, well, it wasn't exactly a *miracle*, he knew. Lord Seward had fathered his fourth son when he was in his seventies, and although some claimed he'd had a bit of help in that regard (there had been rumors he'd been cuckolded by his wife), the boy was the spitting image of him.

Poor child.

But for Milton to think of himself as a father was ... almost unthinkable. He was the godfather to the sons and daughters of the *ton*, not a *father*.

Adele, bless her heart.

Why hadn't she said anything? Was she afraid he didn't want a child? She must have known he needed an heir. Was she waiting for the right time to tell him? Perhaps she intended to tell him tonight during dinner. She'd said something about arranging for his favorite meal to be served that evening.

Or did she even know she was expecting?

That last thought had him pausing suddenly. There was something different, he was sure now. It wasn't just that she had put on a few pounds. She was ... more beautiful, to be sure, her smile more radiant. And she was certainly more willing to be bedded. Christ, she'd been in his bed as much as he'd been in hers this past month or so!

What had Everly said?

Be prepared to bed your wife more frequently. Her appetite for your favors will be insatiable.

He was still ruminating on insatiable appetites when the coach came to a stop in front of the goldsmith's shop. He was out of the coach before the footman could even move to get the door open, hurrying into the shop at Number 36.

Scanning one of the display cases, he wondered what would be appropriate. He'd never bought jewelry for an expectant wife before. Necklace? Bracelet? Ear bobs? Brooch? All of the above? And with what gemstone?

"May I be of assistance, my lord?" Mr. Stedman wondered, stepping up to the counter where Milton's attention was directed at a collection of necklaces displayed on black velvet.

When the earl looked up, a panicked expression on his face, one of Stedman's eyebrows lifted. "Have you forgotten a special occasion, perhaps?" he asked, *sotto voce*. The jeweler noted the man's nervousness. "Or, is there one about to occur?"

"Yes," Milton replied with a quick nod of his head. Not knowing if Stedman could be trusted to keep a secret, Milton was trying to decide how to broach the subject of an appropriate gift.

"Does it involve your... *wife?*" Stedman ventured. He had to be careful—too many men of the *ton* purchased baubles for their mistresses—usually of better quality than the ones they purchased for their wives.

"Yes."

Stedman nodded, pulling a tray of necklaces from

another drawer. "Does she look better in blue or red?" he asked then, showing him a display of sapphire and ruby necklaces featuring his signature gold filigree chains and settings. He pulled out another tray, this one showing two rather ornate diamond necklaces. "Or white?"

Milton pondered the questions, thinking she looked her very best when she was wearing nothing at all.

Was there any reason he had to *choose* a color? Why not all of them?

"I'll take one of each," he announced, pointing in turn at one of each that he supposed would look especially lovely on his naked, expectant wife.

Mr. Stedman's eyebrows lifted so they nearly joined his hairline. "Very good, my lord," he answered with a nod, secretly wondering what momentous occasion could induce a gentleman to purchase *three* necklaces for his wife. Had the earl been caught with another woman? "Should I have them... delivered?"

His own brows furrowing, as if they had to even out Stedman's still mighty high brows, Milton shook his head. "Heavens, no. I wish to give them to her tonight."

"*All* of them, my lord?" the jeweler replied, obviously astonished by the earl's proclamation.

"Yes. Of course. After dinner. Or maybe one during dinner, and one during dessert, and the other one after dinner." He checked his Breguet. "Which is scheduled to start in fifteen minutes," he said in a voice filled with enough warning that Mr. Stedman was motivated to move the selected necklaces into black velvet-lined boxes with great speed.

"Thank you," the earl stated as he collected the three necklace boxes and headed for the door. "Wish me luck."

Rather happy to have made such a large sale, and to such an esteemed gentleman as the Earl of Torrington, the jeweler stared at the door to his shop for a long time after the earl had departed. "I might have wished him luck if he had actually *paid* for his purchases," Stedman grumbled to the now empty shop. He took out a large sheet of parchment and prepared to complete a bill of sale to have sent to Worthington House.

*F*ifteen minutes later Adele Torrington descended the central stairs in Worthington House, her shoulders pulled back and her head held as high as she dared. Glancing down, she was a bit dismayed to discover she couldn't see the next step down. At least her lack of vision wasn't due to her swelling abdomen, which wasn't really that swollen.

Yet.

Her ample bosom was the culprit. Apparently Banks— she was still struggling to think of her lady's maid having the same name as her husband's valet—had tugged on her corset strings a bit more than usual. The swells of her breasts were mounded well above the neckline of her low-cut gown. The deep sapphire blue silk brought out the violet of her eyes and contrasted beautifully with her golden blonde hair, its streaks of gray indicating just the barest hint of her age. Her hair was caught up in an elegant coiffure featuring a series of curls across the front and a chignon in the back. Tiny sapphire ear bobs hung from her ears, bouncing against her neck as she took each step.

At the sound of the front door opening, she paused, hoping her husband had finally returned from White's. He was late tonight—not especially so, but enough so that the flutterbies in Adele's stomach had more time to fly about. After her walk with Clarinda, Countess of Norwick, earlier that morning, she had decided tonight was the night she would tell Milton her news.

She still hadn't quite sorted *how* she would tell him, but she would.

Maybe during the soup course.

No, that wouldn't do. If he was too stunned or upset at the news, he might leave the dining room and order the rest of his dinner be taken to his apartment.

Perhaps during the fish course. Her stomach roiled at the thought of fish, and she remembered her instructions to the cook that no fish be served that evening.

Dessert, she decided. She would tell him over dessert.

Holding her pose on the steps, Adele waited patiently as she heard the butler welcome the earl. She heard her husband ask about dinner. She imagined Milton removing his great coat, imagined him giving Bernard his top hat and cane. She imagined him looking slightly tousled and ever so confident and calm and collected ...

She blinked as she realized she was suddenly staring down at him. Milton had come from the vestibule—no, he had *shot* out of the vestibule, as if from a cannon, his eyes wild, his hair even more so, his hands filled with small black boxes. He had been running, and when he was halfway to the dining room, he had attempted to stop, his Hessians sliding on the marble floors and leaving black streaks in their wake until he could turn around and retrace his steps. Then he had finally come to a dead stop at the bottom of the stairs.

"Hallo," he managed to say as he stared up at her, his mouth hanging wide open, his arms dropped to his sides, the flat boxes barely held by his long, tapered fingers. When he closed his mouth, his cheeks puffed out a bit, and then he opened his mouth again, as if he couldn't believe what he was seeing. Adele had to stifle a giggle when she was reminded of one of Lord Everly's tropical fish.

"Good evening, Milton," she answered, resuming her regal descent down the stairs. When she reached the last one, she curtsied.

Moving all the boxes he held to the crook of one arm, Milton bowed and brought her hand to his lips, kissing the knuckles. "Are you... are you going somewhere?" he wondered, his voice very quiet.

Adele arched an elegant eyebrow. "I am." She motioned toward the dining room. "Would you care to join me?"

Milton swallowed, his gaze taking her in from the tips of her satin slippers to the top of her curls, pausing briefly on her décolletage.

Adele found herself wondering if he had misinterpreted her invitation and intended to join her *there* by planting his face between her breasts.

"I would, my lady," he replied, his casual and confident demeanor having just then returned. He held out his available arm and Adele placed a hand on it, giving him a tentative smile as they followed his black streak marks to the dining room.

"I bought you a gift," Milton stated as he indicated the boxes barely held in the crook of his arm.

Adele angled her head, intrigued by the way he said the words. "*A* gift?" she repeated, giving the slim boxes a pointed glance. She knew from experience what they contained. "Is assembly required?"

Milton placed the slim boxes on the table between where they would be sitting that evening. "A bit," he answered, his mischievous grin appearing. He lifted one of the boxes and peeked inside, quickly shutting it and setting it aside. "Wrong color," he murmured before lifting another box. He barely opened it and his eyebrows cocked. He glanced in her direction, shaking his head before closing that box. He set it atop the other one. Without looking inside, he gave the last box to her.

Drawing her long fingers along the top edges, Adele knew what hid inside boxes of this shape and size. She'd received enough gemstones during her time with Worthington to recognize a jeweler's velvet-covered pasteboard box. Gifts such as these were bestowed for a reason, though, and since there were no special occasions scheduled anytime soon... and there were *three* boxes... "Have you gone and done something *naughty?*" she asked then, a flush of color rising to her face. "Several times?"

Stunned at her question, and knowing her use of the word 'naughty' really did mean 'naughty,' as in, he'd been guilty of participating in some kind of bad behavior that involved Cyprians or courtesans, Milton's eyes widened. "No!" he claimed, his head shaking back and forth. "Well, only with you," he amended, looking ever so contrite. "The result of which is why I bought this...," he motioned toward the box, "... for you." One hand lifted to cover his eyes a moment when he realized he hadn't actually *bought* the necklaces—he'd managed to leave Stedman and Vardon without having *paid*, or at least arranging for the bill to be sent to him! It was a wonder a constable hadn't shown up at the front door.

At the sound of the front door being opened by the butler, Milton nearly panicked and then realized it was probably just the bill being delivered. Certainly Stedman would know to have the bill sent to him at home.

"What is it?" Adele asked, seeing the flash of distress cross his face.

"Well, open it," he replied, surprised she hadn't behaved like every other mistress he had ever employed by tearing the lid off the box before it was even out of his hands.

"I will. When you tell me *why*," Adele countered, rising up to regard him, her expression once more severe.

Milton blew air out from between his lips and shrugged. He remembered the discussion at the card table at White's. "Remember last Christmas? When we were snowed in at Torrington Park? And we spent all that time... being bad? And since then, you've continued to be rather bad? Insatiable, in fact." At Adele's suddenly arched eyebrow and startled expression, he hurried on. "Which I don't mind a bit. I rather adore it, really. I do," he was saying as his head bobbed up and down. "And now you look as if you've eaten a few too many tea cakes and..." His hand had suddenly moved to her belly, and he rested it there in a most protective manner. He let out a sigh.

"Milton!" Adele whispered. Her arms wrapped around his neck, one hand still clutching the box and her lips finding his to kiss him as thoroughly as she could.

When a housemaid suddenly entered from the butler's pantry, she gasped and quickly retreated from the room.

Milton stifled his chuckle and instead nuzzled Adele's neck with his nose and lips. "Did I get it right?" he asked then, suddenly wondering what he would do if he had misjudged the whole scenario.

"Oh, yes," Adele whispered, kissing his jaw and his neck. "I was going to tell you tonight. During the dessert course."

Taking a step back, Milton ran his gaze down the front of Adele again. "And I was going to give you that during the dessert course," he countered, his head nodding toward the black velvet box Adele still held. "But I rather doubt we'll make it to the dessert course, my love," he added. "Unless we take it up in my bedchamber," he suggested, an eyebrow waggling.

Adele smiled, her cheeks flushing pink. "You are incorrigible," she murmured. She held the box up between them. "Some assembly, hum?"

"I'll help you put it on," he offered as he took the box from her and opened it. The sapphires sparkled with blue-violet light, the gold glinting from the flames in the chandelier overhead.

"Oh, it's beautiful," Adele breathed, reaching out with a fingertip to gently nudge the necklace around the raised circle in the middle of the box. "I do hope it's a boy," she said then, her attention returning to him.

Milton shrugged. "I was thinking a girl, but if it's a boy, we can always be bad and have another," he suggested hopefully. *In for a penny, in for a pound.* Lifting the necklace from the velvet bed, he opened it around her neck and secured the clasp. He noticed Adele's attention on the other two boxes.

"Did you try to guess what color gown I would be wearing tonight?" she wondered, her fingers barely touching the gold filigree and sapphires that encircled her neck. She couldn't imagine what stones might be featured in the other necklaces.

"I didn't actually buy them to go with any particular

gown," Milton countered, his lips curling up as he regarded the sapphires, deciding they looked especially regal with the gown and ear bobs she was wearing at the moment. He tried to imagine her in just the necklace and ear bobs, and he found he rather liked that image even better. He glanced back at the table. "Now that I think on it, I was rather patriotic when I made my selections," he added, the mischief back in his eyes. "And a bit naughty, too," he added.

"Oh?" Adele replied, one eyebrow arching up. "Do tell."

Shrugging in that way he had of making himself seem cavalier and confident at the same time, Milton leaned closer and whispered in her ear.

Adele regarded her husband for several moments and angled her head to one side. "Indeed?" she commented. "Then what were you imagining me wearing...?" Her eyes suddenly widened. "Milton!" she admonished him.

"Oh, you can wear them with gowns, of course," the earl assured her quickly, hoping she hadn't just thought the very worst of him at that moment. "But, if you would be so accommodating, I would love to see these on you while you're... wearing nothing but my bed linens, so to speak. Perhaps later tonight?" he hinted hopefully.

Although her face kept its slightly flushed coloring, Adele gave him a teasing smile. "Milton Torrington, if I wasn't so hungry, I'd let you undress me and have your way with me right now. On this table," she whispered, leaning in to capture his lips with another kiss.

Milton's arms wrapped around her waist, pulling her hard against his body just as the maid reappeared with the soup course. Letting out a gasp, the servant immediately turned around and started to go back into the butler's pantry.

"Hold it right there," Milton ordered, pulling away from the kiss. He waved toward the maid. "We're ready for dinner. Truly." He placed Adele's hand on his arm and led her to a place to his right. "However, my lady will be eating here instead of way down there," he said, pulling the chair out from the table. A footman, who had apparently appeared from almost nowhere, hurried to reset the table so that Adele's serviette was in front of her before she'd even taken her seat. "And we'll be having the dessert course in my apartment," he added to the second footman who appeared with wine.

"Very good, my lord," the footman murmured as he poured the wine. Within seconds, the servants had disappeared and the two lovebirds were left enjoying their dinner.

They enjoyed the dessert far more.

ABOUT THE AUTHOR

A former technical writer and author of twenty-four historical romances, Linda Rae Sande enjoys researching the Regency era and ancient Greece.

A fan of action-adventure movies, she can frequently be found at the local cinema. Although she no longer has any tropical fish, she follows the San Jose Sharks and makes her home in Cody, Wyoming.

For more information:
www.lindaraesande.com
Sign up for Linda Rae's newsletter:
Regency Romance with a Twist
Follow Linda Rae's blog:
Regency Romance with a Twist